NEBULA AWARDS SHOWCASE 2018

ALSO AVAILABLE:

Nebula Awards Showcase 2017
    edited by Julie E. Czerneda

Nebula Awards Showcase 2016
    edited by Mercedes Lackey

Nebula Awards Showcase 2015
    edited by Greg Bear

Nebula Awards Showcase 2014
    edited by Kij Johnson

Nebula Awards Showcase 2013
    edited by Catherine Asaro

Nebula Awards Showcase 2012
    edited by James Patrick Kelly and John Kessel

NEBULA AWARDS SHOWCASE 2018

STORIES AND EXCERPTS BY

Alyssa Wong, Barbara Krasnoff, Sam J. Miller, Caroline M. Yoachim,
A. Merc Rustad, Brooke Bolander, Amal El-Mohtar, Fran Wilde,
Jason Sanford, Sarah Pinsker, Bonnie Jo Stufflebeam, William Ledbetter,
Seanan McGuire, Charlie Jane Anders, and David D. Levine.

THE YEAR'S BEST SCIENCE FICTION AND FANTASY

Selected by the Science Fiction and Fantasy Writers of America

EDITED BY
JANE YOLEN

an imprint of **Prometheus Books**
Amherst, NY

Published 2018 by Pyr®, an imprint of Prometheus Books

Cover illustration © Galen Dara
Cover design by Nicole Sommer-Lecht
Cover © Prometheus Books

Inquiries should be addressed to

Pyr
59 John Glenn Drive
Amherst, New York 14228
VOICE: 716–691–0133
FAX: 716–691–0137
WWW.PYRSF.COM

22 21 20 19 18   5 4 3 2 1

ISBN 978–1–63388–504–2 (paperback)
ISBN 978–1–63388–505–9 (ebook)
ISSN 2473–277X

Printed in the United States of America

For the members of SFWA who had the bad grace to elect me twice to be their president.

PERMISSIONS

CONTENTS

Nebula Award Nominees: Best Short Story

CONTENTS

Nebula Award Winner: Best Short Story

Nebula Award Nominees: Best Novelette

Nebula Award Winner: Best Novelette

Nebula Award Winner: Best Novella

Nebula Award Winner: Best Novel

CONTENTS

INTRODUCTION

This was an odd year for the Nebulas.

No, let me rephrase that because *every* year is an odd year for the Nebulas. Every year, some of the stories and books you and I voted for didn't win or the ones you or I hadn't been able to get into, even after multiple attempts, did. There was a challenge to a book's authenticity or provenance. Sad people wanted to win Nebulas through intimidation or stealth. The odds-on favorite movie did a nose dive. You get the picture.

Or someone you barely heard of was named the Grand Master.

(Raises hand.)

That's why it seemed to me to be an exceptionally odd year.

I was in my writing room supposedly—um—writing. The phone rang.

Oddly enough, it was neither a cold call nor a warning from the Hatfield, MA, police chief about scams targeted at the elderly. (My semi-official title these days.)

In fact, it was Cat Rambo who'd emailed me a day or two earlier to set up a phone date. For the uninitiated, Cat has been and will be SFWA's Glorious Leader for a while. As I had been for two years back in the late 1980s. Cat—as other presidents before her—was rigorous about sounding-out past presidents on SFWA matters, so I assumed it was one of *those* calls.

I said, "Hi, Cat, how can I help you?"

She said, "What would you say if I asked you to become our next Grand Master?"

I laughed. "Nice one. So what's the actual problem? What do you need to talk about?"

"No, actually, that's it," she said.

"Well, first of all, you'd have to poll the past presidents and I doubt you'd get an overwhelming vote."

"Already did and it's unanimous."

We both knew there was a bit of fudging there. I mean—I had a bunch of negatives. Most of my writing is *not* sf. (Let's consider that "most": There will be, by the time this book comes out, 365 other books of mine floating around, possibly even in outer space and off to that Mars colony that certain conspiracy theorists are saying has already begun!) Most of my books are about nature or history, or are fantasy or a combination of all three. Most are for young readers. And . . .

"Done deal," she said. "Can you come to the Nebs?"

For the first time in ages—you only have to ask my nearest and dearest and anyone I have ever been on a panel with—I was speechless.

I hung up. I did the happy dance. And then marveled at what an extremely odd year this was going to be.

I remembered when I was president of SFWA, my choice for Grand Master had been Isaac Asimov. No one could contest that. The only question the past presidents had was: "Why wasn't he a Grand Master before?"

My point exactly. I called him, left a message to call me back. He called back and I was out. The message he left on my machine was: "Tell Jane I called. My name is Isaac Asimov. A-S-I-M-O-V." The family had a good laugh about that one.

When I did finally connect with him, he was all Isaac A-S-I-M-O-V— funny, overcome, full of himself, and self-demeaning at the same time. His first question to me was, "Can I tell Clarke about it yet?" (Arthur C. Clarke, that is.) I understood—it was an old rivalry.

Months later at the Nebula Awards, because of a scheduling snafu that put the Nebs on the same weekend as Passover, we held a seder open to anyone— Jewish or not—who wanted to attend.

I sat next to Isaac.

During the (always interminably) long reading of the Haggadah and its history, Isaac took out a pen and began writing something on his paper napkin.

Of course I peeked.

Wouldn't you? It was Isaac A-S-I-M-O-V after all. And he was writing a limerick.

It began:

There once was a khan named Attila.
Of mercy had not a scintilla.
Da-da'-da-da-da'
Da-da'-da-da-da'
Da-da-dad-da-da-d-da-da magillah!

(Alas, I don't remember all of it.)

"Isaac," I whispered, that last line doesn't scan."

"Of course it does," he snapped.

I read it over again silently. Shook my head. "Isaac, that last line doesn't scan."

"Don't be silly," he said, dismissively.

"Isaac," I said, "you know more than I do about almost everything in the universe, but I know that last line doesn't scan."

He held up his hand and addressed the people at the seder with a booming voice. "Stop! I want you to listen to something. Jane says this last line doesn't scan." And of course he, being Isaac A-S-I-M-O-V and the newest Grand Master besides, we were all in awe to one degree or another, and we stopped the seder to listen.

He read the limerick out loud. Waited for applause. And the entire table full of writers, editors, readers said together, "Isaac, that last line doesn't scan!"

At which point he crumpled the napkin, poem and all, and shoved it into his pocket. Turned his back to me. Finished his meal in silence.

Though the next day, when he was officially awarded his Grand Mastership, he winked at me. So I suppose all was forgiven.

I don't think that particular limerick was ever published—though I may be wrong, and some fan will certainly let me know.

So, this has been an odd year for the Nebulas, but they are always odd in some way or another. I remember being at one where a fist fight between two very famous authors (both male) broke out. A hotel guard—very large with a hand gun strapped to his waist, jackboots, and a name tag that said (I am NOT making this up) LUCIOUS—broke up the fight.

But still we celebrated the winners. The results might not have been what you or I or everyone wanted or expected. But when really good stories—even great stories—go up against one another in the SFWA version of the O. K. Corral, there's going to be a winner and. . .

Well, not a loser any more. Just honor books. Now we have a time at the end of the Nebulas ceremony for the honor book winners' speeches to be read out loud. I even got to read a friend's honor acceptance speech for her because she had been scheduled somewhere else, and I gave it both the gravitas and the hype it deserved.

So though we always said it was an honor before, now it *truly* is an honor to be nominated. As someone who was nominated (and in the old terms "lost") a number of Nebulas, I would have loved to have given my intended speech instead of scrunching it in my pocket sadly, while dutifully applauding the winner. Yes, I admit it—I wrote out each speech just in case I won so I didn't babble a Sally Fields response.

Parenthetically, the two times I have won the Nebulas, I wasn't even at the con that year, and someone had to accept for me. Maybe I should consider doing that some more.

So here are some of my quick thoughts about what *did* win the 2016 Nebula, some of which you have ahead of you in this book.

First—because the award is closest to my heart—the winner of the Andre Norton award is an Andre Norton-type book with a kick! A book that harkens back to those old, worn-out paperback sf-fantasy novels but manages to haul them into the future, and pummels the prose into brilliant shape with a touch of steampunk as well: *Arabella of Mars* by David D. Levine, which should also be a winner for sweetest dedication ever.

Charlie Jane Anders's novel *All the Birds in the Sky* is a powerful blend of science fiction and fantasy plus lovely writing. The cast of characters are so well delineated that the novel can also serve as a writing lesson for those of you wanting to try that same doubled genre.

The Novella winner, *Every Heart a Doorway* by Seanan McGuire, is a lyrical, shimmering, surprising novella that brings us back to our childhood reading and forward into murder, magic, mayhem and deep-soul fantasy.

The Novelette winner, "The Long Fall Up" by William Ledbetter, is true science fiction with an emphasis on the science. Ledbetter, a thirty-year veteran of the aerospace industry is a strong writer, and he's not faking the science. The politics of birth and the place of women and pregnant women in space is a story that leaves a deep impression.

Amal El-Mohtar's winning short story is the crown jewel in the anthology. As a folklorist manqué, I love how she plays with elements from folk tales. Her story is "Seasons of Glass and Iron" (from *The Starlit Wood* anthology). It's a melding of several fairy tales. First, she has used the Norwegian "The Princess on the Glass Hill" to delineate one of the two main characters and problems. The second character seems to be from "East of the Sun & West of the Moon" combined with the Romanian story "The Sleeping Prince," and perhaps "The Black Bull of Norroway," all difficult and intriguing tales that I know and love. But Amal re-animates and re-imagines them through a feminist telescope, bringing the far-away and once upon a time into a newer, sharper focus.

Odd winners? You betcha, but in the best possible way.

—Jane Yolen

ABOUT THE SCIENCE FICTION AND FANTASY WRITERS OF AMERICA

The Science Fiction and Fantasy Writers of America, Inc., includes among its members many active writers of science fiction and fantasy. According to the bylaws of the organization, its purpose "shall be to promote the furtherance of the writing of science fiction, fantasy, and related genres as a profession." SFWA informs writers on professional matters, protects their interests, and helps them in dealings with agents, editors, anthologists, and producers of nonprint media. It also strives to encourage public interest in and appreciation of science fiction and fantasy.

Anyone may become an active member of SFWA after the acceptance of and payment for one professionally published novel, one professionally produced dramatic script, or three professionally published pieces of short fiction. Only science fiction, fantasy, horror, or other prose fiction of a related genre, in English, shall be considered as qualifying for active membership. Beginning writers who do not yet qualify for active membership but have published qualifying professional work may join as associate members; other classes of membership include affiliate members (editors, agents, reviewers, and anthologists), estate members (representatives of the estates of active members who have died), and institutional members (high schools, colleges, universities, libraries, broadcasters, film producers, futurist groups, and individuals associated with such an institution).

Readers are invited to visit the SFWA site at www.sfwa.org.

ABOUT THE NEBULA AWARDS

Shortly after the founding of SFWA in 1965, its first secretary-treasurer, Lloyd Biggle, Jr., proposed that the organization periodically select and publish the year's best stories. This notion evolved into the elaborate balloting process, an annual awards banquet, and a series of Nebula anthologies.

Throughout every calendar year, members of SFWA read and recommend novels and stories for the Nebula Awards. The editor of the *Nebula Awards Report* collects the recommendations and publishes them in the *SFWA Forum* and on the SFWA members' private web page. At the end of the year, the *NAR* editor tallies the endorsements, draws up a preliminary ballot containing ten or more recommendations, and sends it all to active SFWA members. Under the current rules, each work enjoys a one-year eligibility period from its date of publication in the United States. If a work fails to receive ten recommendations during the one-year interval, it is dropped from further Nebula consideration.

The *NAR* editor processes the results of the preliminary ballot and then compiles a final ballot listing the five most popular novels, novellas, novelettes, and short stories. For purposes of the award, a novel is determined to be 40,000 words or more; a novella is 17,500 to 39,999 words; a novelette is 7,500 to 17,499 words, and a short story is 7,499 words or fewer. Additionally, each year SFWA impanels a member jury, which is empowered to supplement the five nominees with a sixth choice in cases where it feels a worthy title was neglected by the membership at large. Thus, the appearance of more than five finalists in a category reflects two distinct processes: jury discretion and ties.

A complete set of Nebula rules can be found at nebulas.sfwa.org/about-the-nebulas/nebula-rules.

2016 NEBULA AWARDS BALLOT

NOVEL

Winner: *All the Birds in the Sky*, Charlie Jane Anders (Tor; Titan)
Nominees:
  Borderline, Mishell Baker (Saga)
  The Obelisk Gate, N.K. Jemisin (Orbit US; Orbit UK)
  Ninefox Gambit, Yoon Ha Lee (Solaris US; Solaris UK)
  Everfair, Nisi Shawl (Tor)

NOVELLA

Winner: *Every Heart a Doorway*, Seanan McGuire (Tor.com Publishing)
Nominees:
  Runtime, S.B. Divya (Tor.com Publishing)
  The Dream-Quest of Vellitt Boe, Kij Johnson (Tor.com Publishing)
  The Ballad of Black Tom, Victor LaValle (Tor.com Publishing)
  "The Liar," John P. Murphy (*F&SF* 3-4/16)
  A Taste of Honey, Kai Ashante Wilson (Tor.com Publishing)

NOVELETTE

Winner: "The Long Fall Up," William Ledbetter (*F&SF* 5-6/16)
Nominees:
  "Sooner or Later Everything Falls Into the Sea," Sarah Pinsker (*Lightspeed* 2/16)
  "The Orangery," Bonnie Jo Stufflebeam (*Beneath Ceaseless Skies*)
  "Blood Grains Speak Through Memories," Jason Sanford (*Beneath Ceaseless Skies* 3/17/16)
  The Jewel and Her Lapidary, Fran Wilde (Tor.com Publishing)
  "You'll Surely Drown Here If You Stay," Alyssa Wong (*Uncanny* 5-6/16)

SHORT STORY

Winner: "Seasons of Glass and Iron," Amal El-Mohtar (*The Starlit Wood*)
Nominees:
  "Our Talons Can Crush Galaxies," Brooke Bolander (*Uncanny* 11-12/16)
  "Sabbath Wine," Barbara Krasnoff (*Clockwork Phoenix 5*)
  "Things with Beards," Sam J. Miller (*Clarkesworld* 6/16)
  "This Is Not a Wardrobe Door," A. Merc Rustad (*Fireside Magazine* 1/16)
  "A Fist of Permutations in Lightning and Wildflowers," Alyssa Wong (*Tor.com* 3/2/16)
  "Welcome to the Medical Clinic at the Interplanetary Relay Station | Hours Since the Last Patient Death: 0," Caroline M. Yoachim (*Lightspeed* 3/16)

RAY BRADBURY AWARD FOR OUTSTANDING DRAMATIC PRESENTATION

Winner: *Arrival*, Screenplay by Eric Heisserer
Nominees:
  Doctor Strange, Screenplay by Scott Derrickson & C. Robert Cargill
  Kubo and the Two Strings, Screenplay by Mark Haimes & Chris Butler
  Rogue One: A Star Wars Story, Written by Chris Weitz & Tony Gilroy
  Westworld: "The Bicameral Mind," Written by Lisa Joy & Jonathan Nolan
  Zootopia, Screenplay by Jared Bush & Phil Johnston

ANDRE NORTON AWARD FOR YOUNG ADULT SCIENCE FICTION AND FANTASY

Winner: *Arabella of Mars*, David D. Levine (Tor)
Nominees:
  The Girl Who Drank the Moon, Kelly Barnhill (Algonquin Young Readers)
  The Star-Touched Queen, Roshani Chokshi (St. Martin's)
  The Lie Tree, Frances Hardinge (Macmillan UK; Abrams)
  Railhead, Philip Reeve (Oxford University Press; Switch)
  Rocks Fall, Everyone Dies, Lindsay Ribar (Kathy Dawson Books)
  The Evil Wizard Smallbone, Delia Sherman (Candlewick)

NEBULA AWARD NOMINEE
BEST SHORT STORY

A FIST OF PERMUTATIONS IN LIGHTNING AND WILDFLOWERS

ALYSSA WONG

Alyssa Wong lives in Chapel Hill, NC, and really, really likes crows. Her stories have won the Nebula Award for Best Short Story, the World Fantasy Award for Short Fiction, and the Locus Award for Best Novelette. She was a finalist for the 2016 John W. Campbell Award for Best New Writer, and her fiction has been shortlisted for the Hugo Award, the Bram Stoker Award, and the Shirley Jackson Award. Her work has been published in The Magazine of Fantasy & Science Fiction, Strange Horizons, Nightmare Magazine, Black Static, *and* Tor.com, *among others. Alyssa can be found on Twitter as @crashwong.*

There was nothing phoenix-like in my sister's immolation. Just the scent of charred skin, unbearable heat, the inharmonious sound of her last, grief-raw scream as she evaporated, leaving glass footprints seared into the desert sand.

If my parents were still alive—although they are, probably, in some iteration of the universe; maybe even this one—they would tell me that it wasn't my fault, that no one could have seen it coming. That she did this to herself. But that kind of blame doesn't suit me. Besides, they had always been exceptionally blind to matters regarding Melanie. They didn't even notice when the two of us would take to the sky together, Melanie blowing currents back and forth beneath our bodies, weaving thermals like daisy chains. We used to make sparks dance at the table, and our mom never said a word about it, except that it was rude to do things that other people couldn't in front of them, and also that we needed to learn to talk to people other than each other.

Melanie was better at everything than I was, the stormy bit and the talking bit both. She could split the horizon in two if she wanted, opening it at the seams as deftly as a tailor, and make the lightning curl catlike at her wrist and purr for her. She could do that with people too; Mel glowed, soft, luminescent. It was hard to look away from her, and so easy to disappear into her shadow.

But when things got too bad to ignore, the air in the house dark and crackling with ugly energy like the sky before a monsoon, she dug in and refused to leave. I was the one who abandoned our coast for another, promising I'd be back soon. And then I was the one who stayed away.

*   *   *

The day my sister ended the world, the sky opened up in rain for the first time in years, flooding the desert wash behind our house. The snakes drowned in their holes and the javelinas stampeded downstream, but the water overtook them, and the air filled with their screaming as they were swept away.

I'd tried to take a taxi home, but the roads disappeared in the flash flood, so I struggled out of the swamped cab and slogged the last two miles.

Melanie was outside, a small, dry figure in front of the ruined shell of our parents' house. She wore the only dress she had left—the rest our mother had burned when she'd found them. The rain bent around my sister in a bell shape, and electricity danced in her hands, growing bigger and bigger like a ravenous cat's cradle. Some time ago, lightning had shattered the cacti in the yard, splitting them in two and searing them bone-bare. Only their blackened skeletons were left, clawing upward out of the water like accusing fingers.

I know she felt me coming. Maybe it was a tremble in the dry ground beneath her feet, or a ripple of energy through the water that crashed around my waist. She glanced up, her eyes wide, bruised circles.

I remember that I yelled something at her. That time around, it could have been her name. It could have been a plea, begging her not to do what I could see was about to happen. Or maybe it was just "What the fuck do you think you're doing?"

The world hiccupped, warping violet, legs of electricity touching down around me, biting at my hair, singeing anything still alive beneath the water. I barely felt it.

"Why did you come back?" were the last words she said to me before she went up in flames, taking the rest of the universe with her.

* * *

It was simple, Melanie had once told me. "Here, Hannah. Pay attention, and I'll teach you how the future works."

She drew the picture for me in the air, a map of sparkling futures, constants, and variables; closed circuits of possibilities looped together, arcing from one timeline to another. I saw and understood; but more than that, for the first time, I saw her power as a single, mutable shape.

"That's beautiful," I said.

"Isn't it?" Melanie traced the air with her finger, tapping a single glowing point. "Look, that's us. And here's what could happen, depending on . . . well, depending on a lot of things."

Options chained like lightning strikes before my eyes, possibilities growing legs like sentient things. "If it's that easy, why don't you change it?" I blurted out. "Shape it to make it better for us, I mean."

Her eyes slid away from me. "It's not that easy to get it right," she said.

* * *

The day my sister ended the world, I was on a plane home for the first time in years. I'd managed to sleep most of the way, which was unusual, and I woke up as the plane was descending, a faint popping in my ears. It was sunset, and the flat, highway-veined city was just beginning to glimmer with electric light, civilization pulsing across the ground in arteries, in fractals.

But the beauty was lost on me. The clouds outside felt heavy, and my heart wouldn't stop drumming in my chest. Something was wrong, but I didn't know what.

I felt like I'd seen this before.

Time stuttered, and outside, it began to rain.

* * *

If I could knit you a crown of potential futures like the daisies you braided together for me when we were young, I would.

None of them would end with you burning to death at the edge of our property, beaten senseless in the wash behind the house by drunken college boys, slowly cut to pieces at home by parents who wanted you only in one shape, the one crafted in their image.

I would give you only the best things. The kindness you deserved, the body you wanted, a way out that didn't end with the horizon line ripped open, possibilities pouring out like loose stuffing, my world shrieking to a halt.

I would have fixed everything.

*   *   *

The day my sister—

No.

The day I ended the world, the very first time, my plane touched down early and I sprinted to catch a cab before the impending monsoon swept the city. This time around, I made it four miles from the house before a six-car pileup—tires slick, drivers panicked in the storm—stopped traffic entirely. It took everything in me not to shunt the water aside in front of everyone else, to stumble into neck-deep currents and anchor my feet to the asphalt below. It took forever to get home, and when I did, Melanie was not there.

An hour later, my sister's body floated up in the new river behind our house, covered in bruises, red plastic cups bumping at her bare feet, and lightning spiked white-hot through my chest, searing the ground of my heart into a desert. All I could see were cities burning, houses shelled, every regret and act of cowardice twisting through me into blinding rage.

And in that moment, perfect power was bright in front of me, a seam in space, in time, across myriad axes. I stretched out and grabbed it, and split the world in two. Its ribs reached out to me, and I reached back.

*   *   *

"You can't change this, Hannah," my sister's ghost said as I tore the sky apart, shredding the fabric of air, of cloud, of matter and possibility. The lightning danced for me now, bent and buckled for me the way it had only done for Melanie before.

I will, I will. I will fix this.

"You can't," my sister said. "It'll end the same way. Differently, but the same." "Why?" I screamed.

The world crashed, bowed like wet rice paper, spilled inward. Our parents' house a crater, the flame that was Melanie nowhere on the brightly lit grid of eventualities. No, no, no. Wrong again.

"I never meant to hurt you." Her ghost sighed as my hands blindly rearranged the components of reality. "I didn't mean for you to see it. This was never about you, Hannah. I wish you'd realize that."

*　*　*

The week before my sister ended the world, I didn't go home. I stayed in the theater and broke every plate, every mug in the green room, hurling the shards in the faces of every person who'd come to court me. I blinded my agent, I crippled my director, I hamstrung the rest of the actors with porcelain shrapnel. Gale-force winds whipped around me, a crushing power at my back, the storm building behind my pulsing temples, and I blew out into the city, heading downtown.

At Melanie's favorite bakery, where we'd ordered donuts as big as our heads the last time she'd come to visit, I ripped the boards out of the floor one by one, sending them flying through shattered windows. Icing splattered, electricity scorched wood and sugar alike; the scent of ozone was ripe and acrid in the air.

"Hannah," said my sister's reflection in the glass pieces on the floor. The gentle weight of her phantom hand on my shoulder burned, and time tugged at me again. "That's enough."

*　*　*

The blame circles back, hungry, and I recognize my own voice hissing from its mouth. *Your fault, Hannah. All your fault. You could have stopped this, but you were blinded by your own ambition, your own selfishness; you let the haze of the city—the toxic glamour and crystalline cold—seduce you away from the people you love.* And it was true. Even once in flight, the taste of glory lingered on my tongue the whole way home, sharp in the stale cabin air.

27

But Melanie and I had talked, we'd Skyped. Even if it had been through the computer screen, why hadn't I seen the storms at home crackling on the horizon, their dying sparks reflected in my sister's eyes?

*   *   *

"You're being selfish," my sister's latest iteration said as I whipped the storm into a dark frenzy over the barren mountains. I couldn't remember if the body in the wash this time was hers, or if that was a memory by now. "Hurting yourself over this is just a way of trying to get control over something that was never in your—"

Shut up. Shut

"—something that was never *yours* to control—"

up. Shut up.

The world ended with a bang, folding in on itself, the lines of the horizon collapsing like soaked origami. Our parents' house turned to glass, to fire, to energy sparking ripe and rich for the taking. I drained it, pulling it deep into myself until the house was empty, our parents gone. And then there was nothing but me and my sister, her imprint, her echo.

Melanie's ghost sighed. "I expected better of you," she said.

The void roared back to life, and tossed me out again.

*   *   *

So back to the city again, rewound further this time. Back, past the donut shop, windows never scorched, pastries never eaten. This time I didn't break anything. I went to auditions, cooked rice and fried eggs for dinner, and worked until my muscles screamed for me to stop, then worked more. For a week, I didn't speak unless I was using someone else's words.

The night before boarding the plane, I found myself whispering my secrets into the frigid night air, combing the space between skyscrapers with my tongue.

The city madness was getting to me.

I passed through the same airports like a shade, the route now familiar as the curve of my sleeping cheek in my weary palm.

I did everything right that time, and arrived home to find that the thunderstorm had demolished the airport, preventing anyone from landing.

*   *   *

The next time, I ended the world by myself, during a power outage. Life blinked out, softly, and screamed back into being.

The void spit the kitchen knife out at my feet, onto the floor of my Bushwick apartment, a taunt echoed in my perfect, intact wrists.

You selfish bitch.

The cycle remained unbroken. Gentle sparks kissed my hands in the dark, glinting off of the blade. My blood roared in my ears.

Again, then.

I reoriented the knife.

*   *   *

"Hannah. How many people are you going to destroy before you give up on me?"

*   *   *

Five times, five lines, lead and edges and crushed pills all yanked out of me, spit back further and further each time. I lined them up on my windowsill like the rejected possibilities they were, and let time spool itself out.

Not my fault, not my fault. I'd tried so hard, first to knit the cycle closed and then to slash it to pieces. But still the end danced away from me, the world bleeding into its next cycle.

"What the hell are you doing?" said my roommate for the fifth time, leaning against the doorframe as he did in every iteration. My sullen eyes saw his every possibility splayed out before me like a fall of cards: roommate disappearing into the bathroom to find his medications gone; roommate leaving for work and returning too late; roommate blackened and burned as the apartment went up in smoke; roommate helping me into bed and turning the light off before heading back into the kitchen to bundle up all of the knives.

"Thinking," I croaked. My hands itched with electricity, sparks I couldn't control dancing across my fingers.

"You and your weird sleight of hand shit." He sighed and tossed me my iPhone. "Your phone is ringing."

It took me a second to realize that the stupid anime song filtering out of the speakers was the one that Melanie liked, my ringtone for the home landline. But it wasn't her on the phone. It was my mother, who told me that Melanie had drowned in the pool in the backyard during a freak rainstorm, one that had ruptured from an empty sky. My heartbeat slowed, each second syrup-thick.

"But I thought I had more time," I whispered into the phone. It was true, I was supposed to have a few more days to think of things, to fix them—

"No one knows when God will take us home," said my mother. "He's in the Lord's hands. Always has been."

In my grief, I'd nearly forgotten about my sister, and in my absence, my apocalypse had shifted course without me.

* * *

The world ended anew with a shuddering sob, and I hit the ground running. This time, I touched down two weeks, two agonizing weeks, before I would board my plane, and the first thing I did was book an immediate red-eye home, hoping that if I got there early, I wouldn't be too late.

* * *

Wrong, wrong, wrong.

* * *

"What's life like in the city?" Melanie had asked me when she'd come to visit me, the spring before she died. I'd holed up in my dorm room to practice monologues for my senior showcase until my lungs burned, which probably meant I hadn't been breathing properly anyhow, and Melanie had demanded that we go outside. We'd gone downtown, where well-dressed students and decently-dressed visitors crawled the streets, looking for artisanal french fries. We'd settled in a donut shop about as big as Melanie's closet back home and were crunched up, knees to chests, on the inside windowsill.

She'd looked good, wearing the pale pink sweater I'd secretly sent her for her birthday, fingernails painted the way they never could be at home. But she'd also looked so tired, sallow almost, her face lined with the weight of our parents' words.

All the things that my friends expected me to say—*the city's great, it's exciting, I'm so lucky to live here, I love it*—flashed through my head. So did the things I'd never told anyone, that I couldn't tell anyone, because they wouldn't want to hear it. How the loneliness was crippling; how I'd been fired from three part-time jobs by now; how every day, on my way to class, I walked past the same madman in the tunnel moaning for Jesus, a mess of languages spilling from his bloody lips, past a banner ad that read: GET AWAY WITHOUT LEAVING NEW YORK.

"It's different," I'd said at last. *I don't know who I am without you*, I didn't say.

"I understand," Melanie had replied. I could tell that she did.

*   *   *

I have followed the path back, again and again, to that first stream of possibility. The events lined up so neatly that I could do them in my sleep, and sometimes did. They always led back to the desert monsoon, slogging through the water, my sister disappearing in a pillar of flame.

Why didn't you want me there to help you? I wanted to ask. *If you were this far gone, why didn't you ask me to come home?* I never got close enough to reach her through the wet-dust wind that snarled and roared around us, snatching my voice away.

*   *   *

There are timelines I don't think about.

There is a timeline where the power never touches me, where I make it home in time for the party at the neighbor's house, where a college boy's hands are around my throat, not my sister's, my legs kicking around his waist. Melanie scorches him to pieces, blackens him, shatters the boulders in the wash, and howls until her voice bleeds. Her tears fall into my eyes, sizzling and evaporating on contact, as the sky yawns above us, hungry, broken.

There are others, too, reaching back further along the daisy chain, when we were younger: slipping on ice, light cracking hard through my head; the agonizing sting of a scorpion on my arm, the stiffening of limbs, sudden tightness in my chest; Melanie in a dress for the first time, sobbing as our father screamed at her.

And forward, along the lines that branch out, fuzzing the borders of the future's shape: knives, dented, rejected by my gut; police sirens wailing, gunshots ringing into the crater where my city used to be, the scent of burnt sugar; a plane that never lands safely, erupting into flame on the runway.

I only remember these as faint echoes, like a story someone told me once but whose details I've forgotten. Did they happen? Yes. No. The chain frays, spreads out like roots, possibilities endless.

I'm sorry, I'm sorry, I'm sorry.

*　　*　　*

When Melanie and I were little, we'd lie on the carpet in the winter and warm our soggy feet by the radiator. This was when we still had a bad habit of jumping into snowbanks, exasperating our mom to no end. Melanie had just begun to learn how to melt shapes in the snow, the finest spark at the end of her index finger.

"I wonder why we can do these things," Melanie had said, closing her fist around the lightning glinting across her palm.

I grinned at her, reaching out to catch a bit of stray static dancing down her arm. "Dunno. Don't you think it's cool to be special? It's the one thing no one else can do but us."

She wagged a foot at the radiator. "It's kind of lonely, though."

"At least you have me."

"I guess so," she said. "That's better than nothing."

I tackled her to the ground and we spent the next ten minutes hitting each other with stuffed animals.

*　　*　　*

My sister always dies before the world ends.

The sky is marred with the scars of my efforts, and I am so, so tired. The storm hums in my veins, one more cycle in many. I can't count them anymore, numbers constantly in flux, ticking higher with each potential breath.

I wonder if this is what Melanie felt like every day of her life, so ripe with power, always at the precipice, always afraid to push in fear of making things worse.

This time around, I'm on the floor of my apartment, staring at my cell phone in my hand. My roommate is out and I've already missed my flight home. I let it pass, money evaporating into the void, meaningless.

Somewhere in the southwest, Melanie is walking out of the house, or is about to, her heart roaring with wildfire, lonely, alone. The sparks dance purple in her hands, lightning like veins through her arms.

You can't fix this. It was never yours to control.

But my hands fumble over the touch screen, thumbs sliding wet over her face on the contact screen. She's programmed in the same stupid anime ringtone I have on my phone, and it jingles inanely, all synthetic voices and pre-ordained sound.

I wait, mouth dry, my body shaking like the sky above the Mojave before it rains. Painted in brilliant, feverish strokes in my head, the daisy chain grows.

SABBATH WINE

BARBARA KRASNOFF

Barbara Krasnoff divides her time between writing short specula-tive fiction and working as a freelance writer for a number of tech publications.

She is a member of the NYC writers group Tabula Rasa, and her short fiction has appeared in a variety of publications, including Andromeda Spaceways Magazine, Space & Time Magazine, Electric Velocipede, Apex Magazine, Doorways, Sybil's Garage, Behind the Wainscot, Escape Velocity, Weird Tales, Descant, Lady Churchill's Rosebud Wristlet, Amazing Stories, *and the anthologies* Fat Girl in a Strange Land, Subversion: Science Fiction & Fantasy Tales of Challenging the Norm, Broken Time Blues: Fantastic Tales in the Roaring '20s, Crossed Genres Year Two, Descended from Dark-ness: Apex Magazine Vol. I, Clockwork Phoenix 2, Such a Pretty Face: Tales of Power & Abundance, *and* Memories and Visions: Women's Fantasy and Science Fiction.

Barbara is also the author of a nonfiction book for young adults, Robots: Reel to Real *(Arco Publishing, 1982).*

"My name's Malka Hirsch," the girl said. "I'm nine."

"I'm David Richards," the boy said. "I'm almost thirteen."

The two kids were sitting on the bottom step of a run-down brownstone at the edge of the Brooklyn neighborhood of Brownsville. It was late on a hot summer afternoon, and people were just starting to drift home from work, lingering on stoops and fire escapes to catch any hint of a breeze before going up to their stifling flats.

Malka and David had been sitting there companionably for a while, listening to a chorus of gospel singers practicing in the first-floor front apartment at the top of the stairs. Occasionally, the music paused as a male voice offered instructions and encouragement; it was during one of those pauses that the kids introduced themselves to each other.

Malka looked up at her new friend doubtfully. "You don't mind talking to me?" she asked. "Most big boys don't like talking to girls my age. My cousin Shlomo, he only wanted to talk to the older girl who lived down the street and who wore short skirts and a scarf around her neck."

"I don't mind," said David. "I like kids. And anyway, I'm dead, so I guess that makes a difference."

Above them, the enthusiastic chorus started again. As a soprano wailed a high lament, she shivered in delight. "I wish I could sing like that."

"It's called 'Ride Up in the Chariot,'" said David. "When I was little, my mama used to sing it when she washed the white folks' laundry. She told me my great-grandma sang it when she stole away from slavery."

"It's nice," Malka said. She had short, dark brown hair that just reached her shoulders and straight bangs that touched her eyebrows. She had pulled her rather dirty knees up and was resting her chin on them, her arms wrapped around her legs. "I've heard that one before, but I didn't know what it was called. They practice every Thursday, and I come here to listen."

"Why don't you go in?" asked David. He was just at that stage of adolescence where the body seemed to be growing too fast; his long legs stretched out in front of him while he leaned back on his elbows. He had a thin, cheerful face set off by bright, intelligent eyes and hair cropped so close to his skull that it looked almost painted on. "I'm sure they wouldn't mind, and you could hear better."

Malka grinned and pointed to the sign just above the front-door bell that read Cornerstone Baptist Church. "My papa would mind," she said. "He'd mind plenty. He'd think I was going to get converted or something."

"No wonder I never seen you before," said the boy. "I usually just come on Sundays. Other days, I . . ." He paused. "Well, I usually just come on Sundays."

The music continued against a background of voices from the people around them. A couple of floors above, a baby cried, and two men argued in sharp, dangerous tones; down on the ground, a gang of boys ran past, laughing, ignoring the two kids sitting outside the brownstone. A man sat on a cart laden with what looked like a family's possessions. Obviously in no hurry, he let the horse take its time as it proceeded down the cobblestone street.

The song ended, and a sudden clatter of chairs and conversation indicated that the rehearsal was over. The two kids stood and moved to a nearby streetlamp so they wouldn't get in the way of the congregation leaving the brownstone in twos and threes.

Malka looked at David. "Wait a minute," she said. "Did you say you were dead?"

"Uh-huh," he said. "Well, at least, that's what my daddy told me."

She frowned. "You ain't," she said and then, when he didn't say anything, "Really?"

He nodded affably. She reached out and poked him in the arm. "You ain't," she repeated. "If you were a ghost or something, I couldn't touch you." He shrugged and stared down at the street. Unwilling to lose her new friend, Malka quickly added, "It don't matter. If you wanna be dead, that's okay with me."

"I don't *want* to be dead," said David. "I don't even know if I really am. It's just what Daddy told me."

"Okay," Malka said.

She swung slowly around the pole, holding on with one hand, while David stood patiently, his hands in the pockets of his worn pants.

Something caught his attention and he grinned. "Bet I know what he's got under his coat," he said, and pointed at a tall man hurrying down the street, his jacket carefully covering a package.

"It's a bottle!" said Malka scornfully. "That's obvious."

"It's moonshine," said David, laughing.

"How do you know?" asked Malka, peering at the man.

"My daddy sells the stuff," said David. "Out of a candy store over on Dumont Street."

Malka was impressed. "Is he a gangster? I saw a movie about a gangster once."

David grinned again. "Naw," he said. "Just a low-rent bootlegger. If my mama ever heard about it, she'd come back here and make him stop in a hurry, you bet."

"My mama's dead," Malka said. "Where is yours?"

David shrugged. "Don't know," he said. "She left one day and never came back." He paused, then asked curiously, "You all don't go to church, right?"

"Nope."

"Well, what do you do?"

Malka smiled and tossed her hair back. "I'll show you," she said. "Would you like to come to a Sabbath dinner?"

*　　*　　*

Malka and her father lived in the top floor of a modern five-story apartment building about six blocks from the brownstone church. Somewhere between there and home, David had gone his own way, Malka didn't quite remember when. It didn't matter much, she decided. She had a plan, and she could tell David about it later.

She stood in the main room that acted as parlor, dining room, and kitchen. It was sparsely but comfortably furnished: besides a small wooden table that sat by the open window, there was a coal oven, a sink with cold running water, a cupboard over against one wall, and an overloaded bookcase against another. A faded flower-print rug covered the floor; it had obviously seen several tenants come and go.

Malka's father sat at the table reading a newspaper by the slowly waning light, his elbow on the windowsill, his head leaning on his hand. A small plate with the remains of his supper sat nearby. He hadn't shaved for a while; a short, dark beard covered his face.

"Papa," said Malka.

Her father winced as though something hurt him, but he didn't take his eyes from the book. "Yes, Malka?" he asked.

"Papa, today is Thursday, isn't it?"

He raised his head and looked at her. Perhaps it was the beard, or because he worked so hard at the furrier's where he spent his days curing animal pelts, but his face seemed more worn and sad than ever.

"Yes, daughter," he said quietly. "Today is Thursday."

She sat opposite him and folded her hands neatly in front of her. "Which means that tomorrow is Friday. And tomorrow night is the Sabbath."

He smiled. "Now, Malka, when was the last time you saw your papa in a synagogue, rocking and mumbling useless prayers with the old men? This isn't how I brought you up. You know I won't participate in any—"

"—bourgeois religious ceremonies," she finished with him. "Yes, I know. But I was thinking, Papa, that I would like to have a real Sabbath. The kind that you used to have with Mama. Just once. As . . ." Her face brightened. "As an educational experience."

Her father sighed and closed his book. "An educational experience, hah?" he asked. "I see. How about this: If you want, on Saturday, we can go to Prospect Park. We'll sit by the lake and feed the swans. Would you like that?"

"That would be nice," said Malka. "But it's not the same thing, is it?"

He shrugged. "No, Malka. You're right. It isn't."

Across the alley, a clothesline squeaked as somebody pulled on it, an infant cried, and somebody cursed in a loud combination of Russian and Yiddish.

"And what brought on this sudden religious fervor?" her father asked. "You're not going to start demanding I grow my beard to my knees and read nothing but holy books, are you?"

"Oh, Papa," Malka said, exasperated. "Nothing like that. I made friends with this boy today, named David. He's older than I am—over twelve—and his father also doesn't approve of religion, but his mama used to sing the same songs they sing in the church down the street. We listened to them today, and I thought maybe I could invite him here and show him what we do . . ." Her voice trailed off as she saw her father's face.

"You were at a church?" her father asked, a little tensely. "And you went in and listened?"

"No, of course not. We sat outside. It's the church on the first floor of that house on Remsen Avenue. The one where they sing all those wonderful songs."

"Ah!" her father said, enlightened, and shook his head. "Well, and I shouldn't be pigheaded about this. Your mama always said I could be very pigheaded about my political convictions. You are a separate individual, and deserve to make up your own mind."

"And it's really for educating David," said Malka eagerly.

Her father smiled. "Would that make you happy, Malka?" he asked. "To have a Sabbath dinner for you and your friend? Just this once?"

"Yes, just this once," she said, bouncing on her toes. "With everything that goes with it."

"Of course," her father said. "I did a little overtime this week. I can ask Sarah who works over at the delicatessen for a couple pieces chicken, a loaf of bread, and maybe some soup and noodles, and I know we have some candles put by."

"And you have Grandpa's old prayer book," she encouraged.

"Yes, I have that."

"So, all we need is the wine!" Malka said triumphantly.

Her father's face fell. "So, all we need is the wine." He thought for a moment, then nodded. "Moshe will know. He knows everybody in the neighborhood; if anyone has any wine to sell, he'll know about it."

"It's going to get dark soon," said Malka. "Is it too late to ask?"

Her father smiled and stood. "Not too late at all. He's probably in the park."

*   *   *

"So, Abe," Moshe said to Malka's father, frowning, "you are going to betray your ideals and kowtow to the religious authorities? You, who were nearly sent to Siberia for writing articles linking religion to the consistent poverty of the masses? You, who were carried bodily out of your father's synagogue for refusing to wear a hat at your brother's wedding?"

Abe had immediately spotted Moshe, an older, slightly overweight man with thinning hair, on the well-worn bench where he habitually spent each summer evening. But after trying to explain what he needed only to be interrupted by Moshe's irritable rant, Abe finally shrugged and walked a few steps away. Malka followed.

"There are some boys playing baseball over there," he told her. "Why don't you go enjoy the game and let me talk to Moshe by myself?"

"Okay, Papa," Malka said, and ran off. Abe watched her for a moment, and then looked around. The small city park was full of people driven out of their apartments by the heat. Kids ran through screaming, taking advantage of the fact that their mothers were still cleaning up after dinner and therefore not looking out for misbehavior. Occasionally, one of the men who occupied the benches near the small plot of brown grass would stand and yell, "Sammy! Stop fighting with that boy!" Then, content to have done his duty by his offspring, he would sit down, and the kids would proceed as though nothing had happened.

Abe walked back to the bench and sat next to his friend, who now sat disconsolately batting a newspaper against his knee. "Moshe, just listen for a minute—"

But before he could finish, Moshe handed him his newspaper, climbed onto the bench, and pointed an accusing finger at a thin man who had just lit a cigarette two benches over.

"You!" Moshe yelled. "Harry! I have a bone to pick with you! What the hell were you doing writing that drek about the Pennsylvania steel strike? How dare you use racialism to try to cover up the crimes of the AFL in subverting the strike?"

"They were scabs!" the little man yelled back, gesturing with his cigarette. "The fact that they were Negroes is not an excuse!"

"They were workers who were trying to feed their families in the face of overwhelming oppression!" Moshe called back. "If the AFL had any respect for the people they were trying to organize, they could have brought all the workers into the union, and the bosses wouldn't have been able to break the strike!"

"You ignore the social and cultural problems!" yelled Harry.

"You ignore the fact that you're a schmuck!" roared Moshe.

"Will you get down and act like a human being for a minute?" asked Abe, hitting his friend with the newspaper. "I have a problem!"

Moshe shrugged and climbed down. At the other bench, Harry made an obscene gesture and went back to dourly sucking on his cigarette.

"Okay, I'm down," said Moshe. "So, tell me, what's your problem?"

"Like I was saying," said Abe, "I'm going to have a Sabbath meal."

Moshe squinted at him. "Nu?" he asked. "You've got yourself a girlfriend finally?"

Abe shook his head irritably. "No, I don't have a girlfriend."

"Too bad," his friend said, crossing his legs and surveying the park around him. "You can only mourn so long, you know. A young man like you, he shouldn't be alone like some alter kocker like me."

Abe smiled despite himself. "No, I just . . ." He looked for a moment to where Malka stood with a boy just a little taller than her, both watching the baseball game. That must be her new friend, he thought, probably from the next neighborhood over. His clothes seemed a bit too small for his growing frame; Abe wondered whether he had parents and, if so, whether they couldn't afford to dress their child properly.

"It's just this once," he finally said. "A gift for a child."

"Okay," said Moshe. "So, what do you want from me? Absolution for abrogating your political ideals?"

"I want wine."

"Ah." Moshe turned and looked at Abe. "I see. You've got the prayer book, you've got the candles, you've got the challah. But the alcohol, that's another thing. You couldn't have come up with this idea last year, before the geniuses in Washington gave us the gift of Prohibition?"

"I want to do it right," said Abe. "No grape juice and nothing made in somebody's bathtub. And nothing illegal—I don't want to make the gangsters any richer than they are."

"Well . . ." Moshe shrugged. "If you're going to make this an ethical issue, then I can't help."

"Oh, come on," Abe said impatiently. "It's only been a few months since Prohibition went into effect. I'm sure somebody's got to have a few bottles of wine stashed away."

"I'm sure they do," Moshe said. "But they're not going to give them to you. And don't look at me," he added quickly. "What I got stashed away isn't what you drink at the Sabbath table."

"Hell." Abe stood and shook his head. "I made a promise. You got a cigarette?"

Moshe handed him one and then, as Abe lit a match, said, "Hey, why don't you go find a rabbi?"

Abe blew out some smoke. "I said I wanted to make one Sabbath meal. I didn't say I wanted to attend services."

Moshe laughed. "No, I mean for your wine. When Congress passed Prohibition, the rabbis and priests and other religious big shots, they put up a fuss, so now they get to buy a certain amount for their congregations. You want some booze? Go to a rabbi."

Abe stared at him. "You're joking, right?"

Moshe continued to grin. "Truth. I heard it from a Chassidic friend of mine. We get together, play a little chess, argue. He told me that he had to go with his reb to the authorities because the old man can't speak English, so they could sign the papers and prove he was a real rabbi. Now he's got the right to buy a few cases a year so the families can say the blessing on the Sabbath and get drunk on Passover."

Abe nodded, amused. "Figures." He thought for a moment. "There's a shul over on Livonia Avenue where my friend's son had his bar mitzvah. Maybe I should try there."

"If you've got a friend who goes there," Moshe suggested, "why not simply get the wine from him?"

Abe took a long drag on his cigarette and shook his head. "No, I don't want to get him in trouble with his rabbi. I'll go ask myself. Thanks, Moshe."

"Think nothing of it." Suddenly Moshe's eyes narrowed, and he jumped up onto the bench again, yelling to a man entering the park, "Joe, you capitalist sonovabitch! I saw that letter you wrote in the *Daily Forward* . . ."

Abe walked over to his daughter. "You heard?" he asked quietly. "We'll go over to the synagogue right now and see what the rabbi can do for us."

"Yes, Papa," Malka said, and added, "This is David. He's my new friend that I told you about. David, this is my father."

"How do you do, Mr. Hirsch?" asked David politely.

"How do you do, David?" replied Abe. "It's nice to meet you. I'm glad Malka has made a new friend."

"Mr. Hirsch," said David, "you don't have to go to that rabbi if you don't want to. I heard my father say that he and his business partners got some Jewish wine that he bought from a rabbi who didn't need it all, and I'm sure he could sell you a bottle."

Abe smiled. "Thank you, David. But as I told my friend, I'd rather not get involved in something illegal. You understand," he added, "I do not mean to insult your father."

"That's okay," David said. He turned and whispered to Malka, "You go ahead with your daddy. I'll go find mine; you come get me if you need me for anything. He's usually at the candy store on the corner of Dumont and Saratoga."

"Okay," Malka whispered back. "And if we do get wine, I'll come get you, and you can come to our Sabbath dinner."

Abe stared at the two children for a moment, then pulled the cigarette out of his mouth, tossed it away, and began walking. Malka waved at David and followed her father out of the park.

* * *

The synagogue was located in a small storefront; the large glass windows had been papered over for privacy. CONGREGATION ANSHE EMET was painted in careful Hebrew lettering on the front door. Evening services were obviously over; two elderly men were hobbling out of the store, arguing loudly in Yiddish. Abe waited until they had passed, took a deep breath, and walked in, followed by Malka.

The whitewashed room was taken up by several rows of folding chairs, some wooden bookcases at the back, and a large cabinet covered by a beautifully embroidered cloth. A powerfully built man with a long, white-streaked black beard was collecting books from some of the chairs.

While Malka went to the front to admire the embroidery, Abe walked over to the man. "Rabbi," he said tentatively.

The rabbi turned and straightened. He stared at Abe doubtfully. "Do I know you?"

"I was here for Jacob Bernstein's son Maxie's bar mitzvah two months ago," said Abe. "You probably don't remember me."

The rabbi examined him for a minute or two more, then nodded. "No, I do remember you. You sat in a corner with your arms folded and glowered like the Angel of Death when the boy sang his Torah portion."

Abe shrugged. "I promised his father I'd attend. I didn't promise I'd participate."

"So," said the rabbi, "you are one of those new radicals. The ones who are too smart to believe in the Almighty."

"I simply believe that we have to save ourselves rather than wait for the Almighty to do it for us," Abe rejoined.

"And so," said the rabbi, "since you obviously have no respect for the beliefs of your fathers, why are you here?"

Abe bit his lip, ready to turn and leave.

A small voice next to him asked, "Papa? Is it safe here?"

He looked down. Malka was standing next to him, looking troubled and a little frightened. "One moment," he said to the rabbi and walked to the door, which was open to let the little available air in.

"Of course it's safe, daughter," he said quietly. "Why wouldn't it be?"

"Well," she began, "it's just . . . there isn't a good place to hide. I thought synagogues had to have good hiding places."

His hand went out to touch her hair, to reassure her, but then stopped. "Malkele," he whispered, "you run outside and play. You let your papa take care of this. Don't worry about anything—it will all turn out fine."

Her face cleared, as though whatever evil thoughts had troubled her had completely disappeared. "Okay, Papa!" she said, and left.

Abe took a breath and went back into the room, where the rabbi was waiting. "This is the story," he said. "My little girl is . . . Well, she wants a Sabbath meal."

The rabbi cocked his head. "So, nu? Your child has more sense than you do. So have the Sabbath meal."

"For a Sabbath meal," said Abe. "I need wine." He paused and added. "I would be . . . grateful if you would help me with this."

"I see." The rabbi smiled ironically. "In other words, you want to make a party, maybe, for a few of your radical friends, and you thought, 'The rabbi is allowed to get wine for his congregation for the Sabbath and for the Holy Days, and if I tell him I want it for my little girl . . .'"

Abe took a step forward, furious.

"You have the gall to call me a liar?" he growled. "You religious fanatics are all alike. I come to you with a simple request, a little wine so that I can make a Friday night blessing for my little girl, and what do you do? You spit in my face!"

"You spit on your people and your religion," said the rabbi, his voice rising as well. "You come here because you can't get drunk legally anymore, so you think you'll maybe come and take advantage of the stupid, unworldly rabbi?" He also took a step forward, so that he was almost nose-to-nose with Abe. "You think I am some kind of idiot?"

Abe didn't retreat. "I know you get more wine than you need," he shouted. "I know how this goes. The authorities give you so much per person, so maybe you exaggerate the size of your congregation just a bit, hah? And sell the rest?"

The rabbi shrugged. "And what if I do?" he said. "Does this look like the shul of a rich bootlegger? I have greenhorns fresh off the boat who are trying to support large families, men who are trying to get their wives and children here, boys whose families can't afford to buy them a prayer book for their bar mitzvah. And you, the radical, somebody who makes speeches about the rights of poor people, you would criticize me for selling a few extra bottles of wine?"

"And so if you're willing to sell wine," yelled Abe, "why not sell it to me, a fellow Jew, rather than some goyishe bootlegger?"

There was a pause, and both men stared at each other, breathing hard. "Because he doesn't know any better," the rabbi finally said. "You should. Now get out of my shul."

Abe strode out, muttering, and headed down the block. After about five blocks, he had walked off his anger, and he slowed down, finally sitting heavily on the steps of a nearby stoop. "I'm sorry, Malka," he said. "Maybe I can go find the people that the rabbi sells to . . ."

"But David said his father could get us the wine," said Malka, sitting next to him. "David said that his father and his friends, they have a drugstore where they sell hooch to people who want it. Lots of hooch," she repeated the word, seeming pleased at its grown-up sound.

Abe grinned. "Malka, my sweet little girl," he said, "do you know what your mother would have done to me had she known that her baby was dealing in illegal alcohol? And by the way, I like your friend David. Very polite child."

"He's not a child," Malka objected. "He's almost thirteen!"

"Ah. Practically a man," said Abe, stroking his chin. "So. And his father, the bootlegger—he would sell to someone not of his race?"

"Well, of course," said Malka, a little unsure herself. The question hadn't occurred to her. "David said that they were looking for somebody to buy the kosher wine, and who else to sell it to but somebody who can really use it?"

*　　*　　*

Even from the outside, the candy store didn't look promising—or even open. The windows were pasted over with ads, some of which were peeling off; when Malka and her father looked through the glass, shading their eyes with one hand, it was too dark inside to see much.

"You stay out here," her father finally said. "This is not a place for little girls." He took a breath and pushed the door open. A tiny bell tinkled as he stepped through; Malka, too curious to obey, quietly went in after him and stood by the door, trying to make herself as small as possible.

The store looked as unfriendly inside as it did out. A long counter, which had obviously once been used to serve sodas and ice cream, ran along the right wall of the store; it was empty and streaked with dust, and the shelves behind it were bare except for a few glasses. At the back of the store, there was a display case in which a few cans and dry-looking cakes sat.

The rest of the small space was taken up by several round tables. Only one was occupied, and it was partially obscured by a haze of cigarette smoke. Malka squinted: Three men sat there, playing cards. One was short and fat, with the darkest skin Malka had ever seen; he scowled at the cards while a cigarette hung from the corner of his mouth. A second, much younger and slimmer, was carefully dressed in a brown suit with a red tie; he had a thin mustache, and his hair was slicked back so that it looked, Malka thought, like it was always wet.

The third man, she decided, must be David's father. He had David's long, thin face and slight build, but the humor that was always dancing in David's wide eyes had long ago disappeared from his. A long, pale scar ran from his left eye to the corner of his mouth, intensifying his look of a man who wasn't to be trifled with. As she watched, he reached into his pocket and pulled out a small flask. He took a pull and replaced it without taking his eyes off his cards.

Malka's father waited for a minute or two, and then cleared his throat.

None of the three looked up. "I think you're in the wrong store, white man," the fat man said.

Malka's father put his hands in his pockets. "I was told that I could purchase a bottle or two of wine here."

"You a Fed?" asked the man with slicked-back hair. "Only a Fed would be stupid enough to walk in here by himself."

"Ain't no Fed," the fat man said. "Listen to him. He's a Jew. Ain't no Fed Jews."

"There's Izzy Einstein," said the man with the hair. "He arrested three guys in Coney just yesterday. I read it in the paper."

"Too skinny to be Izzy Einstein," said the fat man. "Nah, he's just your everyday, ordinary white man who's looking for some cheap booze."

"I was told I could buy wine here," repeated Malka's father calmly, although Malka could see that his hands, which he kept in his pockets, were trembling. "I was told you had kosher wine."

The man with the scar stood and came over as the other two watched. Now Malka could see that his suit was worn and not as clean as it could be; he walked slowly, carefully, as though he knew he wasn't sober and didn't want to give it away. When he reached Malka's father, he stopped and waited. He didn't acknowledge the boy who followed him solicitously, as though ready to catch his father should he fall.

Malka grinned and waved. "Hi, David," she said, and then, aware that she might be calling attention to herself, whispered, "I didn't see you before."

David put his finger to his lips and shook his head. "So?" Malka's father asked. "You have wine for sale?"

"My landlord is a Jew," said David's father, challenging.

"So's mine. And I'll bet they're both sons of bitches."

There was a moment of silence. Malka held her breath. And then one corner of the man's mouth twitched. "Okay," he said. "Maybe we can do business." His two colleagues relaxed; the man with the hair swept up the cards and began shuffling them. "Where did you hear about me?"

"Your son David, here," said Malka's father. "He suggested I contact you."

"My son David told you," the man repeated, his eyes narrowing.

"Yes," Malka's father said, sounding puzzled. "Earlier today. Is there a problem?"

There was a pause, and then the man shook his head. "No, no problem. Yeah, I've got some of that kosher wine you were talking about. I can give you two bottles for three dollars each."

Malka's father took a breath. "That's expensive."

"Those are the prices." The man shrugged. "Hard to get specialized product these days."

David stood on his toes and whispered up at his father. The man didn't look down at the boy, but bit his lip, then said, "Okay. I can give you the two bottles for five dollars. And that's because you come with a—a family recommendation."

"Done," said Malka's father. He put out a hand. "Abe Hirsch."

David's father took his hand. "Sam Richards," he said. "You want to pick your merchandise up in the morning?"

Abe shook his head. "I've got to work early," he said. "Can I pick it up after work?"

"Done," Sam said.

Malka's father turned and walked toward the door, then turned back. "I apologize," he said, shaking his head. "I am an idiot. David, your son, has been invited to my house for dinner tomorrow night, and I have not asked his father's permission. And of course, you are also invited as well."

Sam stared at him. "You invited my son to your house for dinner?"

Abe shrugged.

"Hey, Sam," called the well-dressed man, "you can't go nowhere tomorrow night. We've got some business to take care of uptown at the Sugar Cane."

Sam ignored his friend and looked at Malka, who stood next to her father, scratching an itch on her leg and grinning at the success of her plan. "This your little girl?"

It was Abe's turn to stare. He looked down at Malka, who was nodding wildly, delighted at the idea of another guest at their Sabbath meal. He then looked back at Sam.

"Okay," said Sam. "What time?"

"Around five p.m.," Abe said, and gave the address.

"We don't have to be uptown until nine," Sam said to his friend. "Plenty of time."

He turned back to Malka's father. "Okay. I'll bring the wine with me. But you make sure you have the money. Just because you're feeding me—us—dinner don't mean the drinks come free."

"Of course," said Abe.

*   *   *

At five p.m. the next evening, everything was ready. The table had been pulled away from the window and decorated with a white tablecloth (from the same woman who'd sold Abe a boiled chicken and a carrot tsimmes), settings for four, two extra chairs (borrowed from the carpenter who lived across the hall), two candles, and, at Abe's place, his father's old prayer book.

Abe, wearing his good jacket despite the heat, and with a borrowed yarmulke perched on his head, surveyed the scene. "Well, Malka?" he asked. "How does that look?"

"It's perfect!" said Malka, running from one end of the room to the other to admire the table from different perspectives.

Almost on cue, somebody knocked on the door. "It's David!" Malka yelled. "David, just a minute!"

"I'm sure he heard you," said Abe, smiling. "The super in the basement probably heard you." He walked over and opened the door.

Sam stood there, a small suitcase in his hand. He had obviously made some efforts toward improving his personal appearance: he was freshly shaven, wore a clean shirt, and had a spit-polish on his shoes.

David dashed out from behind his father. "You see!" he told Malka. "Everything worked out. My daddy brought the wine like he said, and I made him dress up, because I said it was going to be religious, and Mama wouldn't have let him come to church all messed up. Right, Daddy?"

"You sure did, David," said Sam, smiling. "Even made me wash behind my ears." He then raised his eyes and looked hard at Abe, as if waiting to be challenged.

But Abe only nodded.

"Please sit down," he said. "Be comfortable. Malka, stop dancing around like that; you're making me dizzy."

Malka obediently stopped twirling, but she still bounced a bit in place. "David, guess what? There's a lady who lives across the alley from us who, when it's hot, walks around all day in a man's T-shirt and shorts. You can see her when she's in the kitchen. It's really funny. You want to come out on the fire escape and watch?"

David suddenly looked troubled and stared up at his father. "Is it okay, Daddy?" he asked. His lower lip trembled. "I don't want to get anyone mad at me."

Sam took a breath and, with an obvious effort, smiled at his son. "It's okay," he said. "I'll be right here, keeping an eye on you. Nothing bad will happen."

David's face brightened, and he turned to Malka. "Let's go," he said. The two children ran to the window and clambered noisily onto the fire escape.

Sam put the suitcase on one of the chairs, opened it, and took out two bottles of wine. "Here they are," he said. "Certified kosher, according to the man I got it from. You got the five bucks?"

Abe handed Sam five crumpled dollars. "Here you are," he said, "as promised. You want a drink before we start?"

Sam nodded.

Abe picked up one of the bottles, looked at it for a moment, and then shook his head, exasperated. "Look at me, the genius," he said. "I never thought about a corkscrew."

Sam shrugged, took a small pocketknife out of his pocket, cut off the top of the cork, and pushed the rest into the bottle with his thumb. Abe took the bottle and poured generous helpings for both of them.

They each took a drink and looked outside, where Malka and David sat on the edge of the fire escape, her legs dangling over the side, his legs folded. A dirty pigeon fluttered down onto the railing and stared at the children, obviously hoping for a stray crumb. When none came, it started to clean itself.

David pointed to a window. "No, that's not her," said Malka. "That's the man who lives next door to her. He has two dogs, and he's not supposed to have any pets, so he's always yelling at the dogs to stop barking, or he'll get kicked out." The children laughed. Startled, the bird flew away.

"So," said Abe.

"Yeah," said Sam.

"What happened?"

Sam took a breath, drained his glass, and poured another. "He had gone out to shoot rabbits," he said slowly. "I had just got home from the trenches. We were living with my wife's family in Alabama, and we were making plans to move up north to Chicago, where I could get work and David could get schooled better. He was sitting on the porch reading, and I got mad and told him not to be so lazy, get out there and shoot us some meat for dinner. When he wasn't home by supper, I figured he got himself lost—he was always going off exploring and forgetting about what he was supposed to do."

He looked off into the distance. "After dark, the preacher from my wife's church came by and said that there had been trouble. A white woman over in the next county had complained that somebody had looked in her window when she was undressed. A lynch mob went out, and David saw them, got scared and ran. He wasn't doing anything wrong, but he was a Negro boy with a gun, and they caught him and . . ."

He choked for a moment, then reached for his glass and swallowed the entire thing at a gulp. Wordlessly, Abe refilled it.

"My wife and her sister and the other women, they went and took him down and brought him home. He was . . . They had cut him and burned him and . . . My boy. My baby."

A single tear slowly made its way down Sam's cheek, tracing the path of the scar.

"My wife and I—we didn't get along so good after that. After a while I cut and run, came up here. And David, he came with me."

For a moment, they just sat.

"We lived in Odessa," said Abe, and, when Sam looked confused, added, "That's a city in the Ukraine, near Russia. I moved there with the baby after my wife died. It was 1905, and there was a lot of unrest. Strikes, riots, people being shot down in the streets. Many people were angry. And when people get angry, they blame the Jews."

He smiled sourly. "I and my friends, we were young and strong and rebellious. We were different from the generations before us. We weren't going to sit around like the old men and wait to be slaughtered. I sent Malka to the synagogue with other children. There were hiding places there; they would be safe. And I went to help defend our homes."

"At least you had that," Sam said bitterly.

Abe shook his head. "We were idiots. We had no idea how many there would be, how organized. Hundreds were hurt and killed, my neighbors, my friends. Somebody hit me, I don't know who or with what. I don't remember what happened after that. I . . ."

He paused. "I do remember screaming and shouting all around me, houses burning, but it didn't seem real, didn't seem possible. I ran to the synagogue. I was going to get Malka, and we would leave this madness, go to America where people were sane, and children were safe."

"Safe," repeated Sam softly. The two men looked at each other with tired recognition.

"But when I got there, they wouldn't let me in. The rabbi had hidden the children behind the bima, the place where the Torah was kept, but . . . They said I shouldn't see what had been done to her, that she had been . . . She was only nine years old." Abe's voice trailed away.

The children out on the fire escape had become bored with the neighbors. "Do you know how to play Rock, Paper, Scissors?" David asked. "Here, we have to face each other. Now there are three ways you can hold your hand . . ."

"Does she know?" asked Sam.

"No," said Abe. "And I don't have the heart to tell her."

"David knows," said Sam. "At least, I told him. I thought maybe if he knew, he'd be at rest. But I don't think he believed me. And—well, I'm sort of glad. Because it means . . ."

"He is still here. With you."

"Yes," Sam whispered.

The two men sat and drank while they watched their murdered children play in the fading sunlight.

THINGS WITH BEARDS

SAM J. MILLER

Sam J. Miller lives in New York City now, but grew up in a middle-of-nowhere town in upstate New York. He is the last in a long line of butchers. In no particular order, he has also been a film critic, a grocery bagger, a community organizer, a secretary, a painter's assistant and model, and the guitarist in a punk rock band. His debut novel The Art of Starving *was published by HarperCollins in 2017, followed by* The Breaks *from Ecco Press in 2018. His stories have been nominated for the Nebula, World Fantasy, and Theodore Sturgeon Awards, and have appeared in over a dozen "best-of" anthologies. He's a graduate of the Clarion Science Fiction & Fantasy Writers Workshop, and he's a winner of the Shirley Jackson Award. His husband of fifteen years is a nurse practitioner, and way smarter and handsomer than Sam is.*

MacReady has made it back to McDonald's. He holds his coffee with both hands, breathing in the heat of it, still not 100% sure he isn't actually asleep and dreaming in the snowdrifted rubble of McMurdo. The summer of 1983 is a mild one, but to MacReady it feels tropical, with 125th Street a bright beautiful sunlit oasis. He loosens the cord that ties his cowboy hat to his head. Here, he has no need of a disguise. People press past the glass, a surging crowd going into and out of the subway, rushing to catch the bus, doing deals, making out, cursing each other, and the suspicion he might be dreaming gets deeper. Spend enough time in the ice hell of Antarctica and your body starts to believe that frigid lifelessness is the true natural state of the universe. Which, when you think of the cold vastness of space, is probably correct.

"Heard you died, man," comes a sweet rough voice, and MacReady stands up to submit to the fierce hug that never fails to make him almost cry from how safe it makes him feel. But when he steps back to look Hugh in the eye, something is different. Something has changed. While he was away, Hugh became someone else.

"You don't look so hot yourself," he says, and they sit, and Hugh takes the coffee that has been waiting for him.

"Past few weeks I haven't felt well," Hugh says, which seems an understatement. Even after MacReady's many months in Antarctica, how could so many lines have sprung up in his friend's black skin? When had his hair and beard become so heavily peppered with salt? "It's nothing. It's going around."

Their hands clasp under the table.

"You're still fine as hell," MacReady whispers.

"You stop," Hugh said. "I know you had a piece down there."

MacReady remembers Childs, the mechanic's strong hands still greasy from the Ski-dozer, leaving prints on his back and hips. His teeth on the back of MacReady's neck.

"Course I did," MacReady says. "But that's over now."

"You still wearing that damn fool cowboy hat," Hugh says, scoldingly. "Had those stupid centerfolds hung up all over your room I bet."

MacReady releases his hands. "So? We all pretend to be what we need to be."

"Not true. Not everybody has the luxury of passing." One finger traces a circle on the black skin of his forearm.

They sip coffee. McDonald's coffee is not good but it is real. Honest.

Childs and him; him and Childs. He remembers almost nothing about the final days at McMurdo. He remembers taking the helicopter up, with a storm coming, something about a dog . . . and then nothing. Waking up on board a U.S. supply and survey ship, staring at two baffled crewmen. Shredded clothing all around them. A metal desk bent almost in half and pushed halfway across the room. Broken glass and burned paper and none of them had even the faintest memory of what had just happened. Later, reviewing case files, he learned how the supply run that came in springtime found the whole camp burned down, mostly everyone dead and blown to bizarre bits, except for two handsome corpses frozen untouched at the edge of camp; how the corpses were brought back, identified, the condolence letters sent home, the bodies, probably by accident, thawed . . . but that couldn't be real. That frozen corpse couldn't have been him.

"Your people still need me?" MacReady asks.

"More than ever. Cops been wilding out on folks left and right. Past six months, eight people got killed by police. Not a single officer indicted. You still up for it?"

"Course I am."

"Meeting in two weeks. Not afraid to mess with the Man? Because what we've got planned . . . they ain't gonna like it. And they're gonna hit back, hard."

MacReady nods. He smiles. He is home; he is needed. He is a rebel. "Let's go back to your place."

*   *   *

When MacReady is not MacReady, or when MacReady is simply not, he never remembers it after. The gaps in his memory are not mistakes, not accidents. The thing that wears his clothes, his body, his cowboy hat, it doesn't want him to know it is there. So the moment when the supply ship crewman walked in and found formerly-frozen MacReady sitting up—and watched MacReady's face split down the middle, saw a writhing nest of spaghetti tentacles explode in his direction, screamed as they enveloped him and swiftly started digesting—all of that is gone from MacReady's mind.

But when it is being MacReady, it *is* MacReady. Every opinion and memory and passion is intact.

*   *   *

"The fuck just happened?" Hugh asks, after, holding up a shredded sheet.

"That good, I guess," MacReady says, laughing, naked.

"I honestly have no memory of us tearing this place up like that."

"Me either."

There is no blood, no tissue of any kind. Not-MacReady sucks all that up. Absorbs it, transforms it. As it transformed the meat that used to be Hugh, as soon as they were alone in his room and it perceived no threat, knew it was safe to come out. The struggle was short. In nineteen minutes the transformation was complete, and MacReady and Hugh were themselves again, as far as they knew, and they fell into each other's arms, onto the ravaged bed, out of their clothes.

"What's that," MacReady says, two worried fingers tracing down Hugh's side. Purple blotches mar his lovely torso.

"Comes with this weird new pneumonia thing that's going around," he says. "This year's junky flu."

"But you're not a junky."

"I've fucked a couple, lately."

MacReady laughs. "You have a thing for lost causes."

"The cause I'm fighting for isn't lost," Hugh says, frowning.

"Course not. I didn't mean that—"

But Hugh has gone silent, vanishing into the ancient trauma MacReady has always known was there, and tried to ignore, ever since Hugh took him under his wing at the age of nineteen. Impossible to deny it, now, with their bare legs twined together, his skin corpse-pale beside Hugh's rich dark brown. How different their lives had been, by virtue of the bodies they wore. How wide the gulf that lay between them, that love was powerless to bridge.

*   *   *

So many of the men at McMurdo wore beards. Winter, he thought, at first—for keeping our faces warm in Antarctica's forever winter. But warmth at McMurdo was rarely an issue. Their warren of rectangular huts was kept at a balmy seventy-eight degrees. Massive stockpiles of gasoline specifically for that purpose. Aside from the occasional trip outside for research—and MacReady never had more than a hazy understanding of what, exactly, those scientists were sciencing down there, but they seemed to do precious little of it—the men of McMurdo stayed the hell inside.

So. Not warmth.

Beards were camouflage. A costume. Only Blair and Garry lacked one, both being too old to need to appear as anything other than what they were, and Childs, who never wanted to.

He shivered. Remembering. The tough-guy act, the cowboy he became in uncertain situations. Same way in juvie; in lock-up. Same way in Vietnam. Hard, mean, masculine. Hard drinking; woman hating. Queer? Psssh. He hid so many things, buried them deep, because if men knew what he really was, he'd be in danger. When they learned he wasn't one of them, they would want to destroy him.

They all had their reasons, for choosing McMurdo. For choosing a life where there were no women. Supper time MacReady would look from face to bearded face and wonder how many were like him, under the all-man exterior they projected, but too afraid, like him, to let their true self show.

Childs hadn't been afraid. And Childs had seen what he was.

MacReady shut his eyes against the McMurdo memories, bit his lip. Anything to keep from thinking about what went down, down there. Because how was it possible that he had absolutely no memory of any of it? Soviet attack, was the best theory he could come up with. Psychoactive gas leaked into the ventilation system by a double agent (Nauls, definitely), which caused catastrophic freak outs and homicidal arson rage, leaving only he and Childs unscathed, whereupon they promptly sat down in the snow to die . . . and this, of course, only made him more afraid, because if this insanity was the only narrative he could construct that made any sense at all, he whose imagination had never been his strong suit, then the real narrative was probably equally, differently, insane.

*   *   *

Not-MacReady has an exceptional knack for assessing external threats. It stays hidden when MacReady is alone, and when he is in a crowd, and even when he is alone but still potentially vulnerable. Once, past four in the morning, when a drunken MacReady had the 145th Street bus all to himself, alone with the small woman behind the wheel, Not-MacReady could easily have emerged. Claimed her. But it knew, somehow, gauging who-knew-what quirk of pheromones or optic nerve signals, the risk of exposure, the chance someone might see through the tinted windows, or the driver's foot, in the spasms of dying, slam down hard on the brake and bring the bus crashing into something.

If confronted, if threatened, it might risk emerging. But no one is there to confront it. No one suspects it is there. Not even MacReady, who has nothing but the barest, most irrational anxieties. Protean fragments; nightmare glitch glimpses and snatches of horrific sound. Feedback, bleedthrough from the thing that hides inside him.

*   *   *

"Fifth building burned down this week," said the Black man with the Spanish accent. MacReady sees his hands, sees how hard he's working to keep them from shaking. His anger is intoxicating. "Twenty families, out on the street. Cops don't care. They know it was the landlord. It's always the landlord. Insurance company might kick up a stink, but worst thing that happens is dude catches a civil suit. Pays a fine. That shit is terrorism, and they oughta give those motherfuckers the chair."

Everyone agrees. Eleven people in the circle; all of them Black except for MacReady and an older white lady. All of them men except for her, and a stout Black woman with an Afro of astonishing proportions.

"It's not terrorism when they do it to us," she said. "It's just the way things are supposed to be."

The meeting is over. Coffee is sipped; cigarettes are lit. No one is in a hurry to go back outside. An affinity group, mostly Black Panthers who somehow survived a couple decades of attempts by the FBI to exterminate every last one of them, but older folks too, trade unionists, commies, a minister who came up from the South back when it looked like the Movement was going to spread everywhere, change everything.

MacReady wonders how many of them are cops. Three, he guesses, though not because any of them make him suspicious. Just because he knows what they're up against, what staggering resources the government has invested in destroying this work over the past forty years. Infiltrators tended to be isolated, immersed in the lie they were living, reporting only to one person, whom they might never meet.

Hugh comes over, hands him two cookies.

"You sure this is such a good idea?" MacReady says. "They'll hit back hard, for this. Things will get a whole lot worse."

"Help us or don't," Hugh said, frowning. "That's your decision. But you don't set the agenda here. We know what we're up against, way better than you do. We know the consequences."

MacReady ate one cookie, and held the other up for inspection. Oreo knock-offs, though he'd never have guessed from the taste. The pattern was different, the seal on the chocolate exterior distinctly stamped.

"I understand if you're scared," Hugh says, gentler now.

"Shit yes I'm scared," MacReady says, and laughs. "Anybody who's not scared of what we're about to do is probably . . . well, I don't know, crazy or stupid or a fucking pod person."

Hugh laughs. His laugh becomes a cough. His cough goes on for a long time.

Would he or she know it, if one of the undercovers made eye contact with another? Would they look across the circle and see something, recognize some deeply-hidden kinship? And if they were all cops, all deep undercover, each one simply impersonating an activist so as to target actual activists, what would happen then? Would they be able to see that, and set the ruse aside, step into the light, reveal what they really were? Or would they persist in the imitation game, awaiting instructions from above? Undercovers didn't make decisions, MacReady knew; they didn't even do things. They fed information upstairs, and upstairs did with it what they would. So if a whole bunch of undercovers were operating on their own, how would they ever know when to stop?

*　　*　　*

MacReady knows that something is wrong. He keeps seeing it out of the corner of his mind's eye, hearing its echoes in the distance. Lost time, random wreckage.

MacReady suspects he is criminally, monstrously insane. That during his black-outs he carries out horrific crimes, and then hides all the evidence. This would explain what went down at McMurdo. In a terrifying way, the explanation is appealing. He could deal with knowing that he murdered all his friends and then blew up the building. It would frighten him less than the yawning gulf of empty time, the barely-remembered slither and scuttle of something inhuman, the flashes of blood and screaming that leak into his daylight hours now.

MacReady rents a cabin. Upstate: uninsulated and inexpensive. Ten miles from the nearest neighbor. The hard-faced old woman who he rents from picks him up at the train station. Her truck is full of grocery bags, all the things he requested.

"No car out here," she says, driving through town. "Not even a bicycle. No phone, either. You get yourself into trouble and there'll be no way of getting out of here in a hurry."

He wonders what they use it for, the people she normally rents to, and decides he doesn't want to know.

"Let me out up here," he says, when they approach the edge of town.

"You crazy?" she asks. "It'd take you two hours to walk the rest of the way. Maybe more."

"I said pull over," he says, hardening his voice, because if she goes much further, out of sight of prying protective eyes, around the next bend, maybe, or even before that, the insane thing inside him may emerge. It knows these things, somehow.

"Have fun carrying those two big bags of groceries all that way," she says, when he gets out. "Asshole."

"Meet me here in a week," he says. "Same time."

"You must be a Jehovah's Witness or something," she says, and he is relieved when she is gone.

The first two days pass in a pleasant enough blur. He reads books, engages in desultory masturbation to a cheaply-printed paperback of gay erotic stories Hugh had lent him. Only one symptom: hunger. Low and rumbling, and not sated no matter how much he eats.

And then: lost time. He comes to on his knees, in the cool midnight dirt behind a bar.

"Thanks, man," says the sturdy bearded trucker type standing over him, pulling back on a shirt. Puzzled by how it suddenly sports a spray of holes, each fringed with what look like chemical burns. "I needed that."

He strides off. MacReady settles back into a squat. Leans against the building.

What did I do to him? He seems unharmed. But I've done something. Something terrible.

He wonders how he got into town. Walked? Hitchhiked? And how the hell he'll get back.

*　　*　　*

The phone rings, his first night back. He'd been sitting on his fire escape, looking down at the city, debating jumping, though not particularly seriously. Hugh's words echoing in his head. *Help us or don't.* He is still not sure which one he'll choose.

He picks up the phone.

"Mac," says the voice, rich and deep and unmistakable.

"Childs."

"Been trying to call you." Cars honk, through the wire. Childs is from Detroit, he dimly remembers, or maybe Minneapolis.

"I was away. Had to get out of town, clear my head."

"You too, huh?"

MacReady lets out his breath, once he realizes he's been holding it. "You?"

"Yup."

"What the hell, man? What the fuck is going on?"

Childs chuckles. "Was hoping you'd have all the answers. Don't know why. I already knew what a dumbass you are."

A lump of longing forms in MacReady's throat. But his body fits him wrong, suddenly. Whatever crazy mental illness he was imagining he had, Childs sharing it was inconceivable. Something else is wrong, something his mind rejects but his body already knows. "Have you been to a doctor?"

"Tried," Childs says. "I remember driving halfway there, and the next thing I knew I was home again." A siren rises then slowly fades, in Detroit or Minneapolis.

MacReady inspects his own reflection in the window, where the lights of his bedroom bounce back against the darkness. "What are we?" he whispers.

"Hellbound," Childs says, "but we knew that already."

*   *   *

The duffel bag says *Astoria Little League*. Two crossed baseball bats emblazoned on the outside. Dirty bright-blue blazer sleeves reaching out. A flawless facsimile of something harmless, wholesome. No one would see it and suspect. The explosives are well-hidden, small, sewn into a pair of sweat pants, the timer already ticking down to some unknown hour, some unforeseeable fallout.

*   *   *

"Jimmy," his father says, hugging him, hard. His beard brushes MacReady's neck, abrasive and unyielding as his love.

The man is immense, dwarfing the cluttered kitchen table. Uncles lurk in the background. Cigars and scotch sour the air. Where are the aunts and wives? MacReady has always wondered, these manly Sundays.

"They told me this fucker died," his father says to someone.

"Can't kill one of ours that easy," someone says. Eleven men in the little house, which has never failed to feel massive.

Here his father pauses. Frowns. No one but MacReady sees. No one here but MacReady knows the man well enough to suspect that the frown means he knows something new on the subject of MacReady mortality. Something that frightens him. Something he feels he has to shelter his family from.

"Fucking madness, going down there," his father says, snapping back with the unstoppable positivity MacReady lacks, and envies. "I'd lose my mind inside of five minutes out in Alaska."

"Antarctica," he chuckles.

"That too!"

Here, home, safe, among friends, the immigrant in his father emerges. Born here to brand-new arrivals from Ireland, never saw the place but it's branded on his speech, the slight Gaelic curling of his consonants he keeps hidden when he's driving the subway car but lets rip on weekends. His father's father is who MacReady hears now, the big glorious drunk they brought over as soon as they got themselves settled, the immense shadow over MacReady's own early years, and who, when he died, took some crucial piece of his son away with him. MacReady wonders how his own father has marked him, how much of him he carries around, and what kind of new terrible creature he will be when his father dies.

An uncle is in another room, complaining about an impending Congressional hearing into police brutality against Blacks; the flood of reporters bothering his beat cops. The uncle uses ugly words to describe the people he polices out in Brooklyn; the whole room laughs. His father laughs. MacReady slips upstairs unnoticed. Laments, in silence, the horror of human hatred—how such marvelous people, whom he loves so dearly, contain such monstrosity inside of them.

In the bathroom, standing before the toilet where he first learned to pee, MacReady sees smooth purple lesions across his stomach.

*   *   *

Midnight, and MacReady stands at the center of the George Washington Bridge. The monstrous creature groans and whines with the wind, with the heavy traffic that never stops. New York City's most popular suicide spot. He can't remember where he heard that, but he's grateful that he did. Astride the safety railing, looking down at deep black water, he stops to breathe.

Once, MacReady was angry. He is not angry anymore. This disturbs him. The things that angered him are still true, are still out there; are, in most cases, even worse.

His childhood best friend, shot by cops at fourteen for "matching a description" of someone Black. His mother's hands, at the end of a fourteen hour laundry shift. Hugh, and Childs, and every other man he's loved, and the burning glorious joy he had to smother and hide and keep secret. He presses against these memories, traces along his torso where they've marked him, much like the cutaneous lesions along Hugh's sides. And yet, like those purple blotches, they cause no pain. Not anymore.

A train's whistle blows, far beneath him. Wind stings his eyes when he tries to look. He can see the warm dim lights of the passenger cars; imagines the seats where late-night travelers doze or read or stare up in awe at the lights of the bridge. At him.

Something is missing, inside of MacReady. He can't figure out what. He wonders when it started. McMurdo? Maybe. But probably not. Something drew him to McMurdo, after all. The money, but not just the money. He wanted to flee from the human world. He was tired of fighting it and wanted to take himself out. Whatever was in him, changing, already, McMurdo fed it.

He tries to put his finger on it, the thing that is gone, and the best he can do is a feeling he once felt, often, and feels no longer. Trying to recall the last time he felt it he fails, though he can remember plenty of times before that. Leaving his first concert; gulping down cold November night air and knowing every star overhead belonged to him. Bus rides back from away baseball games, back when the Majors still felt possible. The first time he followed a boy onto the West Side Piers. A feeling at once frenzied and calm, energetic yet restive. Like he had saddled himself, however briefly, onto something impossibly powerful, and primal, sacred, almost, connected to the flow of things, moving along the path meant only for him. They had always been rare, those moments—life worked so hard to come between him and his path—but lately they did not happen at all.

He is a monster. He knows this now. So is Childs. So are countless others, people like Hugh who he did something terrible to, however unintentionally it was. He doesn't know the details, what he is or how it works, or why, but he knows it.

Maybe he'd have been strong enough, before. Maybe that other MacReady would have been brave enough to jump. But that MacReady had no reason to. This MacReady climbs back to the safe side of the guardrail, and walks back to solid ground.

*   *   *

MacReady strides up the precinct steps, trying not to cry. Smiling, wide-eyed, white, and harmless.

When Hugh handed off the duffel bag, something was clearly wrong. He'd lost fifty pounds, looked like. All his hair. Half of the light in his eyes. By then MacReady'd been hearing the rumors, seeing the stories. Gay cancer, said the *Times*. Dudes dropping like mayflies.

And that morning: the call. Hugh in Harlem Hospital. From Hugh's mother, whose remembered Christmas ham had no equal on this earth. When she said everything was going to be fine, MacReady knew she was lying. Not to spare his feelings, but to protect her own. To keep from having a conversation she couldn't have.

He pauses, one hand on the precinct door. Panic rises.

*   *   *

Blair built a spaceship.

The image comes back to him suddenly, complete with the smell of burning petrol. Something he saw, in real life? Or a photo he was shown, from the wreckage? A cavern dug into the snow and ice under McMurdo. Scavenged pieces of the helicopter and the snowmobiles and the Ski-dozer assembled into . . . a spaceship. How did he know that's what it was? Because it was round, yes, and nothing any human knew how to make, but there's more information here, something he's missing, something he knew once but doesn't know now. But where did it come from, this memory?

Panic. Being threatened, trapped. Having no way out. It triggers something inside of him. Like it did in Blair, which is how an assistant biologist could assemble a spacefaring vessel. Suddenly MacReady can tap into so much more. He sees things. Stars, streaking past him, somehow. Shapes he can take. Things he can be. Repulsive, fascinating. Beings without immune systems to attack; creatures whose core body temperatures are so low any virus or other invading organism would die.

A cuttlefish contains so many colors, even when it isn't wearing them.

His hands and neck feel tight. Like they're trying to break free from the rest of him. Had someone been able to see under his clothes, just then, they'd have seen mouths opening and closing all up and down his torso.

"Help you?" a policewoman asks, opening the door for him, and this is bad, super bad, because he—like all the other smiling white harmless allies who are at this exact moment sauntering into every one of the NYPD's 150 precincts and command centers—is supposed to not be noticed.

"Thank you," he says, smiling the Fearless Man Smile, powering through the panic. She smiles back, reassured by what she sees, but what she sees isn't what he is. He doffs the cowboy hat and steps inside.

He can't do anything about what he is. All he can do is try to minimize the harm, and do his best to counterbalance it.

*   *   *

What's the endgame here, he wonders, waiting at the desk. What next? A brilliant assault, assuming all goes well—simultaneous attacks on every NYPD precinct, chaos without bloodshed, but what victory scenario are his handlers aiming for? What is the plan? Is there a plan? Does someone, upstairs, at Black Liberation Secret Headquarters, have it all mapped out? There will be a backlash, and it will be bloody, for all the effort they put into a casualty-free military strike. They will continue to make progress, person by person, heart by heart, and mind by mind, but what then? How will they know they have reached the end of their work? Changing minds means nothing if those changed minds don't then change actual things. It's not enough for everyone to carry justice inside their hearts like a secret. Justice must be spoken. Must be embodied.

"Sound permit for a block party?" he asks the clerk, who slides him a form without even looking up. All over the city, sound permits for block parties that will never come to pass are being slid across ancient well-worn soon-to-be-incinerated desks.

Walking out, he hears the precinct phone ring. Knows it's The Call. The same one every other precinct is getting. Encouraging everyone to evacuate in the next five minutes if they'd rather not die screaming; flagging that the bomb is set to detonate immediately if tampered with, or moved (this is a bluff, but one the organizers felt fairly certain hardly anyone would feel like calling, and, in fact, no one does).

* * *

And that night, in a city at war, he stands on the subway platform. Drunk, exhilarated, frightened. A train pulls in. He stands too close to the door, steps forward as it swings open, walks right into a woman getting off. Her eyes go wide and she makes a terrified sound. "Sorry," he mumbles, cupping his beard and feeling bad for looking like the kind of man who frightens women, but she is already sprinting away. He frowns, and then sits, and then smiles. A smile of shame, at frightening someone, but also of something else, of a hard-earned, impossible-to-communicate knowledge. MacReady knows, in that moment, that maturity means making peace with how we are monsters.

NEBULA AWARD NOMINEE
BEST SHORT STORY

WELCOME TO THE MEDICAL CLINIC AT THE INTERPLANETARY RELAY STATION | HOURS SINCE THE LAST PATIENT DEATH: 0

CAROLINE M. YOACHIM

Caroline M. Yoachim is the author of over a hundred published short stories, appearing in Asimov's, Fantasy & Science Fiction, Clarkesworld, *and* Lightspeed, *among other places. A Hugo and three-time Nebula Award finalist, her work has been reprinted in Year's Best anthologies and translated into Chinese, Spanish, and Czech. Caroline's debut short story collection,* Seven Wonders of a Once and Future World and Other Stories, *came out in 2016. For more about Caroline, check out her website at http://carolineyoachim.com.*

A. You take a shortcut through the hydroponics bay on your way to work, and notice that the tomato plants are covered in tiny crawling insects that look like miniature beetles. One of the insects skitters up your leg, so you reach down and brush it off. It bites your hand. The area around the bite turns purple and swollen.

You run down a long metal hallway to the Medical Clinic, grateful for the artificially generated gravity that defies the laws of physics and yet is surprisingly common in fictional space stations. The sign on the clinic door says "hours since the last patient death:" The number currently posted on the sign is zero. If you enter the clinic anyway, go to C. If you seek medical care elsewhere, go to B.

B. You are in a relay station in orbit halfway between Saturn and Uranus. There is no other medical care available. Proceed to C.

Why are you still reading this? You're supposed to go to C. Are you sure you won't go into the clinic? No? Fine. You return to your quarters and search the station's database to find a cure for the raised purple scabs that are now spreading up your arm. Most of the database entries recommend amputation. The rash looks pretty serious, and you probably ought to go to C, but if you absolutely refuse to go to the clinic, go to Z and die a horrible, painful death.

C. Inside the clinic, a message plays over the loudspeakers: "Welcome to the Medical Clinic at the Interplanetary Relay Station, please sign your name on the clipboard. Patients will be seen in the order that they arrive. If this is an emergency, we're sorry—you're probably screwed. The current wait time is six hours." The message is on endless repeat, cycling through dozens of different languages.

The clipboard is covered in green mucus, probably from a Saturnian slug-monkey. They are exceedingly rude creatures, always hungry and extremely temperamental. You wipe away the slime with the sleeve of your shirt and enter your information. The clipboard chirps in a cheerful voice, "You are number 283. If you leave the waiting room, you will be moved to the end of the queue. If your physiology is incompatible with long waiting room stays, you may request a mobile tracker and wait in one of our satellite rooms. The current wait for a mobile tracker is four hours."

If you decide to wait in the waiting room, go to D. If you request a mobile tracker, go to D anyway, because there is no chance you will get one.

D. You hand the clipboard to the patient behind you, a Tarmandian Spacemite from the mining colonies. As you hand it off, you realize the clipboard is printing a receipt. The sound of the printer triggers the spacemite's predatory response, and it eats the clipboard.

"Attention patients, the clipboard has been lost. Patients will be seen in the order they arrived. Please line up using the number listed on your receipt. If you do not have a receipt, you will need to wait and sign in when a new clipboard is assembled."

If you wait for the new clipboard, go back to C. If you are smart enough to recognize that going back to C will result in a loop that does not advance the story, proceed to E.

E. Instead of waiting in line, you take advantage of the waiting room chaos to go to the nurses' station and demand treatment. There are two nurses at the station, a tired-looking human and a Uranian Doodoo. The Doodoo is approximately twice your size, covered in dark brown fur, and speaks a language that only contains the letters, d, t, b, p, and o. If you talk to the human nurse, go to F. If you talk to the big brown Doodoo from Uranus, go to G. Also, stop snickering. The planet is pronounced "urine iss" not "your anus."

F. The human nurse sees the nasty purple rash on your arm and demands that you quarantine yourself in your quarters. If you accept this advice, go back to B. Have you noticed all the loops in this story? The loops simulate the ultimate futility of attempting to get medical care. What are you still doing here? Go back to B. Next time you get to the nurses' station, remember to pick the non-human nurse.

G. You approach the Uranian nurse and babble a bunch of words that end in "oo" which is your best approximation of Doodoo language. Honestly, the attempt is kind of offensive. The Doodoos are a civilization older than humankind with a nuanced language steeped in a complex alien culture. Why would you expect a random assortment of words ending in "oo" to communicate something meaningful?

Thankfully, the nurse does not respond to your blatant mockery of its language, so you hold out your arm and point to the purple rash. In a single bite, it eats your entire arm, cauterizing the wound with its highly acidic saliva. The rash is gone. If you consider yourself cured, proceed to Y. If you stay at the clinic in hopes of getting a prosthetic arm, go to H.

H. You approach the human nurse and ask about the availability of prosthetic limbs. He hands you a stack of twenty-four forms to fill out. The Doodoo nurse has eaten the hand you usually write with. If you fill out all the forms with your remaining hand, go to I. If you fill out only the top form and leave the rest blank, hoping that no one will notice, go to I.

I. The nurse takes your paperwork and shoves it into a folder. He leads you down a hallway to an exam room filled with an assortment of syringes and dissection tools. "Take off all your clothes and put on this gown," the nurse instructs, "and someone will be in to see you soon." If you do what the nurse says, go to J. If you keep your clothes on, go to K.

J. The exam room is cold and the gown is three sizes too small and paper thin. You sit down, only to notice that the tissue paper that covers the exam table hasn't been changed and is covered in tiny crawling insects that look like miniature beetles. Sitting down is a decision that has literally come back to bite you in the ass. If you leap up screaming and brush the insects off your bare skin, go to L. If you calmly brush the insects away and then yell for someone to come in and clean the room, go to L.

K. Three hours later, the doctor arrives. You are relieved to see that she is human. You ask her if she can issue you a prosthetic limb. She says no, mumbles something about resource allocation forms, and leaves. If you accept her refusal and decide to consider yourself cured, go to Y. If you scream down the hall at the departing doctor that you must have a new arm, go to L.

L. A security officer comes, attracted by the sound of your screams. Clinic security is handled by a six-foot-tall Tarmandian Spacemite with poisonous venom, sharp teeth, and a fondness for US tax law. If you run, go to M. If you are secretly a trained warrior and decide to kill the Tarmandian Spacemite with your bare hands so you can eat its head, go to N. If you sit very still and hope the Tarmandian Spacemite goes away, go to O.

M. Running triggers the predatory instincts of the Tarmandian Spacemite. Go to Z.

N. You use your completely unforeshadowed (but useful!) fighting skills to overpower the security officer. The head of the Tarmandian Spacemite is a delicious delicacy, salty and crunchy and full of delightful worms that squiggle all the way down your throat. Unfortunately, you forgot to remove the venomous fangs. Go to Z.

O. You sit perfectly still on the exam table, and tiny insects that resemble miniature beetles crawl into your pants and bite you repeatedly, leaving a clump of purple bumps that look suspiciously similar to the scabby rash you had on your arm when you arrived at the clinic. When you're sure the Tarmandian Spacemite is gone, go to P.

P. You have lost an arm and the lower half of your torso is covered in a purple rash. If you decide to cut your losses and consider yourself cured, go to R. If you rummage through the cabinets in the exam room, go to S.

Q. There is nothing in the story that directs you to this section, so if you are reading this, you have failed to follow instructions. Go directly to Z and die your horrible, painful death. Or skip to somewhere else, since you clearly aren't playing by the rules anyway.

R. You sneak out of the clinic and return to your quarters. You search the station database for treatments for your beetle-induced purple rash. There is no known cure, although some patients have had luck with amputation of the affected areas. Sadly, you are incapable of amputating your own ass. Even if you go back to the clinic, the rash is now too widespread to be treated. Go to Z. Or, if you want to see what would have happened if you'd opted to search through the exam room cabinets, go to S. But remember, going to S is only to see what hypothetically would have happened. Your true fate is Z.

S. You rummage through the cabinets and find an assortment of ointments and lotions. If you read the instructions on all the bottles, go to T. If you select a few bottles at random and slather them on your rash, go to T. Have you noticed how often you end up in the same place no matter what you chose? In the clinic, as in life, decisions that seem important are often ultimately meaningless. In the end, all of us will die and none of this will matter. Now seriously, go to T.

T. None of the ointments or lotions do anything for your rash. The Uranian nurse comes in to clean the room and discovers you. If you pretend to work at the clinic, go to U. If you ask for help with your rash, go to V. If you run away, go to W.

(There is no U, much as there is no hope for patients of the clinic. The nurse would have recognized you anyway. Go to V.)

V. The Doodoo from Uranus (seriously, are you in third grade? Stop pronouncing the planet as "your anus") examines your rash and amputates the affected areas by eating them, neatly cauterizing the wound with the acid in its saliva. You are now a head with approximately half a torso. If you consider yourself cured, go to X. Otherwise, go to Z.

W. You flee from the Uranian nurse but slip on a puddle of slimy green mucus excreted by another patient, probably that idiot slug-monkey that slimed the clipboard. You crash into the wall, and before you can get back up, the Uranian nurse amputates the areas affected by the rash by eating them, neatly cauterizing the wound with the acid in its saliva. You are now a head with approximately half a torso. If you consider yourself cured, go to X. Otherwise go to Z.

X. You are not cured. You are a head with half a torso, and missing several internal organs. Go to Z.

Y. Congratulations, you have survived your trip to the Medical Clinic at the Interplanetary Relay Station! All you have to do now is fill out your discharge papers. You start filling out the forms with your one remaining hand, but you accidentally drop the pen onto the oozing foot of the Saturnian slug-monkey waiting in line behind you. This is undoubtedly the idiot that slimed the sign-in clipboard. You cuss the slug-monkey out with some choice words in French. Choice words because it was rude to leave slime all over the clipboard. French because you know better than to make a slug-monkey angry. You've watched enough education vids to know that slug-monkeys are always hungry, which makes them temperamental.

Unfortunately for you, Saturnian slug-monkeys are far better educated than arrogant humans give them credit for. This one is fluent in several languages, including French. It eats you. Go to Z.

Z. You die a horrible, painful death. But at least you won't have to deal with your insurance company!

THIS IS NOT A WARDROBE DOOR

A. MERC RUSTAD

A. Merc Rustad is a queer non-binary writer who likes dinosaurs, robots, monsters, and cookies. Their fiction has appeared in Lightspeed, Cicada, Uncanny, Escape Pod, Fireside, IGMS, Flash Fiction Online, Apex, Shimmer, and others. "How to Become a Robot in 12 Easy Steps" was included in The Best American Science Fiction and Fantasy 2015, edited by Joe Hill and John Joseph Adams. "This Is Not a Wardrobe Door" has been reproduced on PodCastle (audio), and reprinted in Cicada (2018) and The Best American Science Fiction and Fantasy 2017, edited by Charles Wu and John Joseph Adams, and has been translated into Chinese and Portuguese.

Merc is mostly found on Twitter @Merc_Rustad, and sometimes playing in cardboard boxes.

Dear Gatekeeper,

Hi my name is Ellie and I'm six years old and my closet door is broken. My best friend Zera lives in your world and I visited her all the time, and sometimes I got older but turned six again when I came back, but that's okay. Can you please fix the door so I can play with Zera?

Love,

Ellie

*   *   *

Zera packs lightly for her journey: rose-petal rope and dewdrop boots, a jacket spun from bee song and buttoned with industrial-strength cricket clicks. She secures her belt (spun from the cloud memories, of course) and picks up her satchel. It has food for her and oil for Misu.

Her best friend is missing and she must find out why.

Misu, the palm-sized mechanical microraptor, perches on her seaweed braids, its glossy raindrop-colored feathers ruffled in concern.

Misu says, *But what if the door is locked?*

Zera smiles. "I'll find a key."

But secretly, she's worried. What if there isn't one?

*   *   *

Dear Gatekeeper,

I hope you got my last couple letters. I haven't heard back from you yet, and the closet door still doesn't work. Mommy says I'm wasting paper when I use too much crayon, so I'm using markers this time. Is Zera okay? Tell her I miss playing with the sea monsters and flying to the moon on the dragons most of all.

Please open the door again.

—Ellie, age 7

*   *   *

Zera leaves the treehouse and climbs up the one-thousand-five-hundred-three rungs of the polka-dot ladder, each step a perfect note in a symphony. When she reaches the falcon aerie above, she bows to the Falcon Queen and asks if she may have a ride to the Land of Doors.

The Falcon Queen tilts her magnificent head. "Have you not heard?" the queen asks in a voice like spring lightning and winter calm. "All the doors have gone quiet. There is a disease rotting wood and rusting hinges, and no one can find a cure."

Misu shivers on Zera's shoulder. *It is like the dreams*, Misu says. *When everything is silent.*

Zera frowns. "Hasn't the empress sent scientists to investigate?"

The Falcon Queen nods. "They haven't returned. I dare not send my people into the cursed air until we know what is happening."

Zera squares her shoulders. She needs answers, and quickly. Time passes differently (faster) on Ellie's home planet, because their worlds are so far apart, and a lag develops in the space-time continuum.

"Then I will speak to the Forgotten Book," Zera says, hiding the tremor in her voice.

The falcons ruffle their feathers in anxiety. Not even the empress sends envoys without the Forgotten Book's approval.

"You are always brave," says the Falcon Queen. "Very well then, I will take you as far as the Island of Stars."

*   *   *

Hi Gatekeeper,

Are you even there? It's been almost a year for me and still nothing. Did the ice elves get you? I hope not. Zera and I trapped them in the core of the passing comet so they'd go away, but you never know.

Why can't I get through anymore? I'm not too old, I promise. That was those Narnia books that had that rule (and they were stupid, we read them in class).

Please say something,
—Ellie, age 8

*   *   *

Zera hops off the Falcon Queen's back and looks at the Island of Stars. It glows from the dim silver bubbles that thick in the air like tapioca pudding.

She sets off through the jungle of broken wire bedframes and abandoned armchairs; she steps around rusting toys and rotting books. There are memories curled everywhere—sad and lonely things, falling to pieces at the seams.

She looks around in horror. "What happened?"

Misu points with a tiny claw. *Look.*

In the middle of the island stands the Forgotten Book, its glass case shattered and anger radiating off its pages.

LEAVE, says the book. BEFORE MY CURSE DEVOURS YOU.

*   *   *

Gatekeeper,

I tried to tell Mom we can't move, but she won't listen. So now I'm three hundred miles away and I don't know anybody and all I want to do is scream and punch things, but I don't want Mom to get upset. This isn't the same closet door. Zera explained that the physical location wasn't as fixed like normal doors in our world, but I'm still freaking out.

I found my other letters. Stacks of notebook paper scribbled in crayon and marker and finger-paint—all stacked in a box in Mom's bedroom.

"What are you doing with this?" I screamed at Mom, and she had tears in her eyes. "Why did you take the letters? They were supposed to get to Zera!"

Mom said she was sorry, she didn't want to tell me to stop since it seemed so important, but she kept finding them in her closet.

I said I'd never put them there, but she didn't believe me.

"We can't go there again," Mom said, "no one ever gets to go back!" and she stomped out of the kitchen and into the rain.

Has my mom been there? Why didn't she ever tell me? Why did you banish her too?

What did we do so wrong we can't come back?

—Ellie

*   *   *

Zera's knees feel about to shatter.

"Why are you doing this?" Zera grips an old, warped rocking chair. "You've blacked out the Land of Doors, haven't you?"

YES, says the Book. ALL WHO GO THERE WILL SLEEP, UNDREAMING, UNTIL THE END.

Zera blinks hard, her head dizzy from the pressure in the air. "You can't take away everyone's happiness like this."

NO? says the Book. WHY NOT? NO ONE EVER REMEMBERS US THERE. THEY FORGET AND GROW OLD AND ABANDON US.

"That's not true," Zera says. "Ellie remembers. There are others."

Misu nods.

Zera pushes through the heavy air, reaching out a hand to the Book. "They tell stories of us there," Zera says, because Ellie used to bring stacks of novels with her instead of PBJ sandwiches in her backpack. "There are people who believe. But there won't be if we close all the doors. Stories in their world will dry up. We'll start to forget them, too."

WE MEAN NOTHING TO THEM.

Zera shakes her head. "That's not true. I don't want my best friend to disappear forever."

*   *   *

Gatekeeper,

I don't know why I bother anymore. You're not listening. I don't even know if you exist.

It's been awhile, huh? Life got busy for me. High school, mostly. Mom got a better job and now we won't have to move again. Also I met this awesome girl named LaShawna and we've been dating for a month. God, I'm so in love with her. She's funny and smart and tough and kind—and she really gets me.

Sometimes she reminds me of Zera.

I asked Mom why she kept my letters.

She didn't avoid me this time. "I had a door when I was younger," she said, and she looked so awfully sad. "I was your age. I met the person I wanted to stay with forever." She let out her breath in a whoosh. "But then the door just . . . it broke, or something. I tried dating here. Met your father, but it just wasn't the same. Then he ran off and it was like losing it all again."

I told LaShawna about Zera's world. She said she didn't want to talk about it. I think maybe she had a door, too.

I was so angry growing up, feeling trapped. You know the best thing about Zera? She *got* me. I could be a girl, I could be a boy, and I could be neither—because that's how I feel a lot of the time. Shifting around between genders. I want that to be OK, but here? I don't know.

The thing is, I don't want to live in Zera's world forever. I love things here, too. I want to be able to go back and forth and have friends everywhere, and date LaShawna and get my degree and just *live*.

This will be my last letter to you, Gatekeeper.

If there was one thing Zera and I learned, it's that you have to build your own doors sometimes.

So I'm going to make my own. I'll construct it out of salvaged lumber; I'll take a metalworking class and forge my own hinges. I'll paper it with all my letters and all my memories. I'll set it up somewhere safe, and here's the thing—I'll make sure it never locks.

My door will be open for anyone who needs it: my mom, LaShawna, myself.

—Ell

* * *

The Book is silent.

"Please," Zera says. "Remove the curse. Let us all try again."

And she lays her hand gently on the Forgotten Book and lets the Book see all the happy memories she shared with Ellie, once, and how Ellie's mom Loraine once came here and met Vasha, who has waited by the door since the curse fell, and Misu, who befriended the lonely girl LaShawna and longs to see her again—and so many, many others that Zera has collected, her heart over-filled with joy and loss and grief and hope.

In return, she sees through space and time, right into Ell's world, where Ell has built a door and has her hand on the knob.

"Ell," Zera calls.

Ell looks up, eyes wide. "Zera?"

"Yes," Zera says, and knows her voice will sound dull behind the door. "I'm here."

Ell grins. "I can see your reflection in the door! Is that the Book with you?"

The Book trembles. SHE REMEMBERS.

Zera nods. The air is thinning, easing in her lungs. "I told you. Not everyone forgets."

I would like to see LaShawna again, says Misu.

VERY WELL, says the book. THE CURSE WILL BE REMOVED.

Ell turns the handle.

Bright lights beams into the Island of Stars, and Ell stands there in a doorway, arms spread wide. Zera leaps forward and hugs her best friend.

"You came back," Zera says.

"I brought some people with me, too," Ell says, and waves behind her, where two other women wait.

Loraine steps through the light with tears in her eyes. "I never thought I could come back . . ."

Misu squeaks in delight and flies to LaShawna.

Zera smiles at her friends. Things will be all right.

"We have a lot of work to do to repair this place," Zera says. She clasps Ell's hands. "The curse is gone, but we have to fix the doors and wake the sleepers. Are you ready?"

Ell grins and waves her mom and girlfriend to join her. "Yes. Let's do this."

NEBULA AWARD NOMINEE
BEST SHORT STORY

OUR TALONS CAN CRUSH GALAXIES

BROOKE BOLANDER

Brooke Bolander writes weird things of indeterminate genre, most of them leaning rather heavily toward fantasy or general all-around weirdness. She attended the University of Leicester from 2004 to 2007 studying History and Archaeology and is an alum of the 2011 Clarion Writers' Workshop at UCSD. Her stories have been featured in Light-speed, Strange Horizons, Nightmare, Uncanny, and various other fine purveyors of the fantastic. She has been a finalist for the Nebula, the Hugo, the Locus, and the Theodore Sturgeon awards, much to her unending bafflement. Her debut book, The Only Harmless Great Thing, was published in 2018 by Tor.com.

This is not the story of how he killed me, thank fuck.

*   *   *

You want that kind of horseshit, you don't have to look far; half of modern human media revolves around it, lovingly detailed descriptions of sobbing women violated, victimized, left for the loam to cradle. Rippers, rapists, stalkers, serial killers. Real or imagined, their names get printed ten feet high on movie marquees and subway ads, the dead convenient narrative rungs for villains to climb. Heroes get names; killers get names; victims get close-ups of their opened ribcages mid-autopsy, the bloodied stumps where their wings once attached, baffled coroners making baffled phone calls to even more baffled curators at local museums. They get dissected, they get discussed, but they don't get names or stories the audience remembers.

So, no. You don't get a description of how he surprised me, where he did it, who may have fucked him up when he was a boy to lead to such horrors (no-one), or the increasingly unhinged behavior the cops had previously filed away as the mostly harmless eccentricities of a nice young man from a good family. No fighting in the woods, no blood under the fingernails, no rivers or locked trunks or calling cards in the throat. It was dark and it was bad and I called for my sisters in a language dead when the lion-brides of Babylon still padded outside the city gates. There. That's all you get, and that's me being generous. You're fuckin' welcome.

*   *   *

However, here is what I *will* tell you. I'll be quick.

He did not know what I was until after. He felt no regret or curiosity, because he should have been drowned at birth. I was nothing but a commodity to him before, and nothing but an anomaly to him after.

My copper feathers cut his fingertips and palms as he pared my wings away.

I was playing at being mortal this century because I love cigarettes and shawarma, and it's easier to order shawarma if your piercing shriek doesn't drive the delivery boy mad. Mortality is fun in small doses. It's very authentic, very down-in-the-dirt nitty-gritty. There are lullabies and lily pads and summer rainstorms and hardly anyone ever tries to cut your head off out of some moronic heroic obligation to the gods. If you want to sit on your ass and read a book, nobody judges you. Also, shawarma.

My spirit was already fled before the deed was done, back to the Nest, back to the Egg. My sisters clucked and cooed and gently scolded. They incubated me with their great feathery bottoms as they had many times before, as I had done many times before for them. Sisters have to look out for one another. We're all we've got, and forever is a long, slow slog without love.

I hatched anew. I flapped my wings and hurricanes flattened cities in six different realities. I was a tee-ninsy bit motherfuckin' pissed, maybe.

I may have cried. You don't get to know that either, though.

We swept back onto the mortal plane with a sound of a 1967 Mercury Cougar roaring to life on an empty country road, one sister in the front seat and three in the back and me at the wheel with a cigarette clenched between my pointed teeth. You can fit a lot of wingspan in those old cars, provided you know how to fold reality the right way.

It's easy to get lost on those backroads, but my old wings called to us from his attic. We did not get lost.

He was alone when we pulled into his driveway, gravel crunching beneath our wheels like bone. He had a gun. He bolted his doors. The tumblers turned for us; we took his gun.

Did *he* cry? Oh yeah. Like a fuckin' baby.

I didn't know what you were, he said. I didn't know. I just wanted to get your attention, and you wouldn't even look at me. I tried everything.

Well, kid, I says, putting my cigarette out on his family's floral carpet, you've sure as hell got it now.

Our talons can crush galaxies. Our songs give black holes nightmares. The edges of our feathers fracture moonlight into silver spiderwebs and universes into parallels. Did we take him apart? *C'mon.* Don't ask stupid questions.

Did we kill him? Ehh. In a manner of speaking. In another manner of speaking, his matter is speaking across a large swathe of space and time, begging for an ending to his smeared roadkill existence that never quite reaches the rest stop. Semantics, right? I don't care to quibble or think about it anymore than I have to.

*   *   *

Anyway. Like I said way back at the start, this is not the story of how he killed me. It's the story of how a freak tornado wrecked a single solitary home and disappeared a promising young man from a good family, leaving a mystery for the locals to scratch their heads over for the next twenty years. It's the story of how a Jane Doe showed up in the nearby morgue with what looked like wing stubs sticking out of her back, never to be claimed or named. It's the story of how my sisters and I acquired a 1967 Mercury Cougar we still go cruising in occasionally when we're on the mortal side of the pike.

You may not remember my name, seeing as how I don't have one you could pronounce or comprehend. The important thing is always the stories—which ones get told, which ones get co-opted, which ones get left in a ditch, overlooked and neglected. This is *my* story, not his. It belongs to me and is mine alone. I will sing it from the last withered tree on the last star-blasted planet when entropy has wound down all the worlds and all the wheres, and nothing is left but faded candy wrappers. My sisters and I will sing it—all at once, all together, a sound like a righteous scream from all the forgotten, talked-over throats in Eternity's halls—and it will be the last story in all of Creation before the lights finally blink out and the shutters go *bang*.

NEBULA AWARD WINNER
BEST SHORT STORY

SEASONS OF GLASS AND IRON

AMAL EL-MOHTAR

Amal El-Mohtar has won the Hugo, Nebula, and Locus awards for her short fiction, and her poetry has won the Rhysling award three times. She writes the Otherworldly column for the New York Times, *contributes reviews to NPR, and is the author of* The Honey Month, *a collection of poetry and prose written to the taste of twenty-eight different kinds of honey.* This Is How You Lose the Time War, *a novella co-written with Max Gladstone, is forthcoming from Saga Press in 2019.*

Amal lives in Ottawa with her spouse and two cats. Find her online at amalelmohtar.com, or on Twitter @tithenai.

For Lara West

Tabitha walks, and thinks of shoes.

She has been thinking about shoes for a very long time: the length of three and a half pairs, to be precise, though it's hard to reckon in iron. Easier to reckon how many pairs are left: of the seven she set out with, three remain, strapped securely against the outside of the pack she carries, weighing it down. The seasons won't keep still, slip past her with the landscape, so she can't say for certain whether a year of walking wears out a sole, but it seems about right. She always means to count the steps, starting with the next pair, but it's easy to get distracted.

She thinks about shoes because she cannot move forward otherwise: each iron strap cuts, rubs, bruises, blisters, and her pain fuels their ability to cross rivers, mountains, airy breaches between cliffs. She must move forward, or the shoes will never be worn down. The shoes must be worn down.

It's always hard to strap on a new pair.

Three pairs of shoes ago, she was in a pine forest, and the sharp green smell of it woke something in her, something that was more than numbness, numbers. (*Number? I hardly know 'er!* She'd laughed for a week, off and on, at her little joke.) She shivered in the needled light, bundled her arms into her fur cloak but stretched her toes into the autumn earth, and wept to feel, for a moment, something like free—before the numbers crept in with the cold, and *one down, six to go* found its way into her relief that it was, in fact, possible to get through a single pair in a lifetime.

Two pairs of shoes ago, she was in the middle of a lake, striding across the deep blue of it, when the last scrap of sole gave way. She collapsed and floundered as she undid the straps, scrambled to pull the next pair off her pack, sank until she broke a toe in jamming them on, then found herself on the surface again, limping toward the far shore.

One pair of shoes ago, she was by the sea. She soaked her feet in salt and stared up at the stars and wondered whether drowning would hurt.

She recalls shoes her brothers have worn: a pair of seven-league boots, tooled in soft leather; winged sandals; satin slippers that turned one invisible. How strange, she thinks, that her brothers had shoes that lightened their steps and tightened the world, made it small and easy to explore, discover.

Perhaps, she thinks, it isn't strange at all: why shouldn't shoes help their wearers travel? Perhaps, she thinks, what's strange is the shoes women are made to wear: shoes of glass; shoes of paper; shoes of iron heated red-hot; shoes to dance to death in.

How strange, she thinks, and walks.

*　　*　　*

Amira makes an art of stillness.

She sits atop a high glass hill, its summit shaped into a throne of sorts, thick and smooth, perfectly suited to her so long as she does not move. Magic girdles her, roots her stillness through the throne. She has weathered storms here, the sleek-fingered rain glistening between glass and gown, hair and skin, seeking to shift her this way or that—but she has held herself straight, upright, a golden apple in her lap.

She is sometimes hungry, but the magic looks after that; she is often tired, and the magic encourages sleep. The magic keeps her brown skin from burning during the day, and keeps her silkshod feet from freezing at night—so long as she is still, so long as she keeps her glass seat atop her glass hill.

From her vantage point she can see a great deal: farmers working their land; travelers walking from village to village; the occasional robbery or murder. There is much she would like to come down from her hill and tell people, but for the suitors.

Clustered and clamoring around the bottom of her glass hill are the knights, princes, shepherds' lads who have fallen violently in love with her. They shout encouragement to one another as they ride their warhorses up the glass hill, breaking against it in wave after wave, reaching for her.

As they slide down the hill, their horses foaming, legs twisted or shattered, they scream curses at her: the cunt, the witch, can't she see what she's doing to them, glass whore on a glass hill, they'll get her tomorrow, tomorrow, tomorrow.

Amira grips her golden apple. By day she distracts herself with birds: all the wild geese who fly overhead, the gulls and swifts and swallows, the larks. She remembers a story about nettle shirts thrown up to swans, and wonders if she could reach up and pluck a feather from them to give herself wings.

By night, she strings shapes around the stars, imagines familiar constellations into difference: suppose the great ladle was a sickle instead, or a bear? When she runs out of birds and stars, she remembers that she chose this.

*   *   *

Tabitha first sees the glass hill as a knife's edge of light, scything a green swathe across her vision before she can look away. She is stepping out of a forest; the morning sun is vicious, bright with no heat in it; the frosted grass crunches under the press of her iron heels, but some of it melts cold relief against the skin exposed through the straps.

She sits at the forest's edge and watches the light change.

There are men at the base of the hill; their noise is a dull ringing that reminds her of the ocean. She watches them spur their horses into bleeding. Strong magic in that hill, she thinks, to make men behave so foolishly; strong magic in that hill to withstand so many iron hooves.

She looks down at her own feet, then up at the hill. She reckons the quality of her pain in numbers, but not by degree: if her pain is a six it is because it is cold, blue with an edge to it; if her pain is a seven it is red, inflamed, bleeding; if her pain is a three it has a rounded yellow feel, dull and perhaps draining infection.

Her pain at present is a five, green and brown, sturdy and stable, and ought to be enough to manage the ascent.

She waits until sunset, and sets out across the clearing.

*   *   *

Amira watches a mist rise as the sun sets, and her heart sings to see everything made so soft: a great cool *hush* over all, a smell of water with no stink in it, no blood or sweat. She loves to see the world so vanished, so quiet, so calm.

Her heart skips a beat when she hears the scraping, somewhere beneath her, somewhere within the mist: a grinding, scouring sort of noise, steady as her nerves aren't, because something is climbing the glass hill and this isn't how it was supposed to work, no one is supposed to be able to reach her, but magic is magic is magic and there is always stronger magic—She thinks it is a bear, at first, then sees it is a furred hood, glimpses a pale delicate chin beneath it, a wide mouth twisted into a teeth-gritting snarl from the effort of the climb.

Amira stares, uncertain, as the hooded, horseless stranger reaches the top, and stops, and stoops, and pants, and sheds the warm weight of the fur. Amira sees a woman, and the woman sees her, and the woman looks like a feather and a sword and very, very hungry.

Amira offers up her golden apple without a word.

*   *   *

Tabitha had thought the woman in front of her a statue, a copper ornament, an idol, until her arm moved. Some part of her feels she should pause before accepting food from a magical woman on a glass hill, but it's dwarfed by a ravenousness she's not felt in weeks; in the shoes, she mostly forgets about her stomach until weakness threatens to prevent her from putting one foot in front of the other.

The apple doesn't look like food, but she bites into it, and the skin breaks like burnt sugar, the flesh drips clear, sweet juice. She eats it, core and all, before looking at the woman on the throne again and saying—with a gruffness she does not feel or intend—"Thank you."

"My name is Amira," says the woman, and Tabitha marvels at how she speaks without moving any other part of her body, how measured are the mechanics of her mouth. "Have you come to marry me?"

Tabitha stares. She wipes the juice from her chin, as if that could erase the golden apple from her belly. "Do I have to?"

Amira blinks. "No. Only—that's why people try to climb the hill, you know."

"Oh. No, I just—" Tabitha coughs, slightly, embarrassed. "I'm just passing through."

Silence.

"The mist was thick, I got turned around—"

"You climbed"—Amira's voice is very quiet—"a glass hill"—and even—"by accident?"

Tabitha fidgets with the hem of her shirt.

"Well," says Amira, "it's nice to meet you, ah—"

"Tabitha."

"Yes. Very nice to meet you, Tabitha."

Further silence. Tabitha chews her bottom lip while looking down into the darkness at the base of the hill. Then, quietly: "Why are you even up here?"

Amira looks at her coolly. "By accident."

Tabitha snorts. "I see. Very well. Look." Tabitha points to her iron-strapped feet. "I have to wear the shoes down. They're magic. I have a notion that the stranger the surface—the harder it would be to walk on something usually—the faster the sole diminishes. So your magical hill here . . ."

Amira nods, or at least it seems to Tabitha that she nods—it may have been more of a lengthened blink that conveyed the impression of her head's movement.

". . . it seemed like just the thing. I didn't know there was anyone at the top, though; I waited until the men at the bottom had left, as they seemed a nasty lot—"

It isn't that Amira shivers, but that the quality of her stillness grows denser. Tabitha feels something like alarm beginning a dull ring in her belly.

"They leave as the nights turn colder. You're more than welcome to stay," says Amira, in tones of deepest courtesy, "and scrape your shoes against the glass."

Tabitha nods, and stays, because somewhere within the measured music of Amira's words she hears *please*.

*   *   *

Amira feels half-asleep, sitting and speaking with someone who isn't about to destroy her, break her apart for the half kingdom inside.

"Have they placed you up here?" Tabitha asks, and Amira finds it strange to hear anger that isn't directed at her, anger that seems at her service.

"No," she says softly. "I chose this." Then, before Tabitha can say anything else, "Why do you walk in iron shoes?"

Tabitha's mouth is open but her words are stopped up, and Amira can see them changing direction like a flock of starlings in her throat. She decides to change the subject.

"Have you ever heard the sound geese make when they fly overhead? I don't mean the honking, everyone hears that, but—their wings. Have you ever heard the sound of their wings?"

Tabitha smiles a little. "Like thunder, when they take off from a river."

"What? Oh." A pause; Amira has never seen a river. "No—it's nothing like that when they fly above you. It's . . . a creaking, like a stove door with no squeak in it, as if the geese are machines dressed in flesh and feathers. It's a beautiful sound—beneath the honking it's a low drone, but if they're flying quietly, it's like . . . clothing, somehow, like if you listened just right, you might find yourself wearing wings."

Without noticing, Amira had closed her eyes while speaking of the geese; she opens them to see Tabitha looking at her with curious focus, and feels briefly disoriented by the scrutiny. She isn't used to being listened to.

"If we're lucky," she says softly, turning a golden apple around and around in her hands, "we'll hear some tonight. It's the right time of year."

*   *   *

Tabitha opens her mouth, then shuts it so hard her back teeth meet. She does not ask *how long have you been sitting here, that you know when to expect the geese*; she does not ask *where did that golden apple come from? Didn't I just eat it?* She understands what Amira is doing and is grateful; she does not want to talk about the shoes.

"I've never heard that sound," she says instead, slowly, trying not to look at the apple. "But I've seen them on rivers and lakes. Hundreds at a time, clamoring like old wives at a well, until something startles them into rising, and then it's like drums, or thunder, or a storm of winds through branches. An enormous sound, almost deafening—not one to listen closely for."

"I would love to hear that," Amira whispers, looking out toward the woods. "To see them. What do they look like?"

"Thick, dark—" Tabitha reaches for words. "Like the river itself is rising, lifting its skirts and taking off."

Amira smiles, and Tabitha feels a tangled warmth in her chest at the thought of having given her something.

*   *   *

"Would you like another apple?" offers Amira, and notes the wariness in Tabitha's eye. "They keep coming back. I eat them myself from time to time. I wasn't sure if—I thought it was meant as a prize for whoever climbed the hill, but I suppose the notion is they don't go away unless I give them to a man."

Tabitha frowns, but accepts. As she eats, Amira feels Tabitha's eyes on her empty hands, waiting to catch the apple's reappearance, and tries not to smile— she'd done as much herself the first fifty or so times, testing the magic for loopholes. Novel, however, to watch someone watching for the apple.

As Tabitha nears the last bite, Amira sees her look confused, distracted, as if by a hair on her tongue or an unfamiliar smell—and then the apple's in Amira's hand again, feeling for all the world like it never left.

"I don't think the magic lets us see it happen," says Amira, almost by way of apology for Tabitha's evident disappointment. "But so long as I sit here, I have one."

"I'd like to try that again," says Tabitha, and Amira smiles.

*   *   *

First, Tabitha waits. She counts the seconds, watching Amira's empty hands. After seven hundred seconds, there is an apple in Amira's hand. Amira stares at it, looking from it to the one in Tabitha's.

"That's—never happened before. I didn't think there could be more than one at a time."

Tabitha takes the second apple from her but bites into it, counting the mouthfuls slowly, watching Amira's hands the while. After the seventh bite, Amira's hands are full again. She hands the third apple over without a word.

Tabitha counts—the moments, the bites, the number of apples—until there are seven in her lap; when she takes an eighth from Amira, the first seven turn to sand.

"I think it's the magic on me," says Tabitha thoughtfully, dusting the apple sand out of her fur. "I'm bound in sevens—you're bound in ones. You can hold only one apple at a time—I can hold seven. Funny, isn't it?"

Amira's smile looks strained and vague, and only after a moment does Tabitha realize she's watching the wind-caught sand blowing off the hill.

*   *   *

Autumn crackles into winter, and frost rimes the glass hill into diamonds. By day, Amira watches fewer and fewer men slide down it while Tabitha sits by her, huddled into her fur; by night, Tabitha walks in slow circles around her as they talk about anything but glass and iron. While Tabitha walks, Amira looks more closely at her shackled feet, always glancing away before she can be drawn into staring. Through the sandal-like straps that wrap up to her ankle, Amira can see they are blackened, twisted ruins, toes bent at odd angles, scabbed and scarred.

One morning, Amira wakes to surprising warmth, and finds Tabitha's fur draped around her. She is so startled she almost rises from her seat to find her— has she left? Is she gone?—but Tabitha walks briskly back into her line of sight before Amira can do anything drastic, rubbing her thin arms, blowing on her fingers. Amira is aghast.

"Why did you give me your cloak? Take it back!"

"Your lips were turning blue in your sleep, and you can't *move*—"

"It's all right, Tabitha, please—" The desperation in Amira's voice stops Tabitha's circling, pins her in place. Reluctantly, she takes her fur back, draws it over her own shoulders again. "The apples—or the hill itself, I'm not sure— keep me warm enough. Here, have another."

Tabitha looks unconvinced. "But you looked so cold—"

"Perhaps it's like your feet," says Amira, before she can stop herself. "They look broken, but you can still walk on them."

*   *   *

Tabitha stares at her for a long moment, before accepting the apple. "They feel broken too. Although"—shifting her gaze to the apple, lowering her voice— "less and less, lately."

She takes a bite. While she eats, Amira ventures, quietly, "I thought you'd left."

Tabitha raises an eyebrow, swallows, and chuckles. "Without my cloak, in winter? I like you, Amira, but—" *Not that much* dies on her tongue, as she tastes the lie in it. She coughs. "That would be silly. Anyway, I wouldn't leave you without saying good-bye." An uncertain pause then. "Though, if you tire of company—"

"No," says Amira, swiftly, surely. "No."

*   *   *

Snow falls, and the last of the suitors abandon their camps, grumbling home. Tabitha walks her circles around Amira's throne by day now as well as night, unafraid of being seen.

"They won't be back until spring," says Amira, smiling. "Though then they keep their efforts up well into the night as the days get longer. Perhaps to make up for lost time."

Tabitha frowns, and something in the circle of their talk tightens enough for her to ask, as she walks, "How many winters have you spent up here?"

Amira shrugs. "Three, I think. How many winters have you spent in those shoes?"

"This is their first," says Tabitha, pausing. "But there were three pairs before this one."

"Ah. Is this the last?"

Tabitha chuckles. "No. Seven in all. And I'm only halfway through this one."

Amira nods. "Perhaps, come spring, you'll have finished it."

"Perhaps," says Tabitha, before beginning her circuit again.

*   *   *

Winter thaws, and everything smells of snowmelt and wet wood. Tabitha ventures down the glass hill and brings Amira snowdrops, twining them into her dark hair. "They look like stars," murmurs Tabitha, and something in Amira creaks and snaps like ice on a bough.

"Tabitha," she says, "it's almost spring."

"Mm," says Tabitha, intent on a tricky braid.

"I'd like—" Amira draws a deep, quiet breath. "I'd like to tell you a story."

Tabitha pauses—then, resuming her braiding, says, "I'd like to hear one."

"I don't know if I'm any good at telling stories," Amira adds, turning a golden apple over and over in her hands, "but that's no reason not to try."

*　　*　　*

Once upon a time there was a rich king who had no sons, and whose only daughter was too beautiful. She was so beautiful that men could not stop themselves from reaching out to touch her in corridors or following her to her rooms, so beautiful that words of desire tumbled from men's lips like diamonds and toads, irresistible and unstoppable. The king took pity on these men and drew his daughter aside, saying, Daughter, only a husband can break the spell over these men; only a husband can prevent them from behaving so gallantly toward you.

When the king's daughter suggested a ball, that these men might find husbands for themselves and so be civilized, the king was not amused. You must be wed, said the king, before some guard cannot but help himself to your virtue.

The king's daughter was afraid, and said, Suppose you sent me away?

No, said the king, for how should I keep an eye on you then?

The king's daughter, who did not want a husband, said, Suppose you chose a neighboring prince for me?

Impossible, said the king, for you are my only daughter, and I cannot favor one neighbor over another; the balance of power is precarious and complicated.

The king's daughter read an unspeakable conclusion in her father's eye, and in a rush to keep it from reaching his mouth, said, Suppose you placed me atop a glass hill where none could reach me, and say that only the man who can ride up the hill in full armor may claim me as his bride?

But that is an impossible task, said the king, looking thoughtful.

Then you may keep your kingdom whole, and your eye on me, and men safe from me, said his daughter.

It was done just as she said, and by her will. And if she's not gone, she lives there still.

*　　*　　*

When Amira stops speaking, she is taken aback to feel Tabitha scowling at her.

"That," growls Tabitha, "is *absurd*."

Amira blinks. She had expected, she realizes, some sympathy, some understanding. "Oh?"

"What father seeks to protect men from their pursuit of his daughter? As well seek to protect the wolf from the rabbit!"

"I am not a rabbit," says Amira, though Tabitha, who has dropped her hair and is pacing, incensed, continues.

"How could it be your fault that men are loutish and ill mannered? Amira, I promise you, if your hair were straw and your face dull as dishwater, men—bad men—would still behave this way. Do you think the suitors around the hill can see what you look like, all the way up here?"

Amira keeps quiet, unsure what to say—she wonders why she wants to apologize with one side of her mouth and defend herself with the other.

"You said you *chose* this," Tabitha spits. "What manner of choice was that? A wolf's maw or a glass hill."

"On the hill," says Amira, lips tight, "I want for nothing. I do not need food or drink or shelter. No one can touch me. That's all I ever wanted—for no one to be able to touch me. So long as I sit here, and eat apples, and do not move, I have everything I want."

Tabitha is silent for a moment. Then, more gently than before, she says, "I thought you wanted to see a river full of geese."

Amira says nothing.

Tabitha says, still more gently, "Mine are not the only iron shoes in the world."

Still nothing. Amira's heart grinds within her, until Tabitha sighs.

"Let me tell you a story about iron shoes."

*   *   *

Once upon a time, a woman fell in love with a bear. She didn't mean to; it was only that he was both fearsome and kind to her, that he was dangerous and clever and could teach her about hunting salmon and harvesting wild honey, and she had been lonely for a long time. She felt special with his eyes on her, for what other woman could say she was loved by a bear without being torn between his teeth? She loved him for loving her as he loved no one else.

They were wed, and at night the bear put on a man's shape to share her bed in

"But I—"

"If you've worn your shoes halfway down, shouldn't you be bending your steps toward him again, that the last pair be destroyed near the home you shared?"

In the shifting light of the moon both their faces have a bluish cast, but Amira sees Tabitha's go gray.

"When I was a girl," says Tabitha thickly, as if working around something in her throat, "I dreamt of marriage as a golden thread between hearts—a ribbon binding one to the other, warm as a day in summer. I did not dream a chain of iron shoes."

"Tabitha"—and Amira does not know what to do except to reach for her hand, clutch it, look at her in the way she looks at the geese, longing to speak and be understood—"you did nothing wrong."

Tabitha holds Amira's gaze. "Neither did you."

They stay that way for a long time, until the sound of seven geese's beating wings startles them into looking up at the stars.

*   *   *

The days and nights grow warmer; more and more geese fly overhead. One morning Tabitha begins to walk her circle around Amira when she stumbles, trips, and falls forward into Amira's arms.

"Are you all right?" Amira whispers, while Tabitha clutches at the throne, shaking her head, suddenly unsteady.

"The shoes," she says, marveling. "They're finished. The fourth pair. Amira." Tabitha laughs, surprises herself to hear the sound more like a sob. "They're done."

Amira smiles at her, bends forward to kiss her forehead. "Congratulations," she murmurs, and Tabitha hears much more than the word as she reaches, shaky, wobbling, for the next pair in her pack. "Wait," says Amira quietly, and Tabitha pauses.

"Wait. Please. Don't—" Amira bites her lip, looks away. "You don't have to—you can stay here without—"

Tabitha understands, and returns her hand to Amira's. "I can't stay up here forever. I have to leave before the suitors come back."

Amira draws a deep breath. "I know."

"I've had a thought, though."

"Oh?" Amira smiles softly. "Do you want to marry me after all?"

"Yes."

Amira's stillness turns crystalline in her surprise.

*　　*　　*

Tabitha is talking, and Amira can barely understand it, feels Tabitha's words slipping off her mind like sand off a glass hill. Anything, anything to keep her from putting her feet back in those iron cages—

"I mean—not as a husband would. But to take you away from here. If you want. Before your suitors return. Can I do that?"

Amira looks at the golden apple in her hand. "I don't know—where would we go?"

"Anywhere! The shoes can walk anywhere, over anything—"

"Back to your husband?"

Something like a thunderclap crosses Tabitha's face. "No. Not there."

Amira looks up. "If we are to marry, I insist on an exchange of gifts. Leave the fur and the shoes behind."

"But—"

"I know what they cost you. I don't want to walk on air and darkness if the price is your pain."

"Amira," says Tabitha helplessly, "I don't think I can walk without them anymore."

"Have you tried? You've been eating golden apples a long while. And you can lean on me."

"But—they might be useful—"

"The glass hill has been very useful to me," says Amira quietly, "and the golden apples have kept me warm and whole and fed. But I will leave them—I will follow you into woods and across fields, I will be hungry and cold and my feet will hurt. But if you are with me, Tabitha, then I will learn to hunt and fish and tell the poison berry from the pure, and I will see a river raise its skirt of geese, and listen to them make a sound like thunder. Do you believe I can do this?"

"Yes," says Tabitha, a choking in her voice, "yes, I do."

"I believe you can walk without iron shoes. Leave them here—and in exchange, I will give you my shoes of silk, and we will fill your pack with seven golden apples, and if you eat from them sparingly, perhaps they will help you walk until we can find you something better."

"But we can't climb down the hill without a pair of shoes!"

"We don't need to." Amira smiles, stroking Tabitha's hair. "Falling's easy—it's keeping still that's hard."

Neither says anything for a time. Then, carefully, for the hill is slippery to her now, Tabitha sheds her fur cloak, unstraps the iron shoes from her feet, and gives them and her pack to Amira. Amira removes the three remaining pairs and replaces them with apples, drawing the pack's straps tight over the seventh. She passes the pack back to Tabitha, who shoulders it.

Then, taking Tabitha's hands in hers, Amira breathes deep and stands up.

* * *

The glass throne cracks. There is a sound like hard rain, a roar of whispers as the glass hill shivers into sand. It swallows fur and shoes; it swallows Amira and Tabitha together; it settles into a dome-shaped dune with a final hiss.

Hands still clasped, Amira and Tabitha tumble out of it together, coughing, laughing, shaking sand from their hair and skin. They stand, and wait, and no golden apple appears to part their hands from each other.

"Where should we go?" whispers one to the other.

"Away," she replies, and holding on to each other, they stumble into the spring, the wide world rising to meet them with the dawn.

EXCERPT FROM
THE JEWEL AND HER LAPIDARY

FRAN WILDE

Fran Wilde's work includes the Andre Norton and Compton Crook Award–winning and Nebula-nominated novel Updraft *and its sequels* Cloudbound *and* Horizon. *Her short stories appear in* Asimov's, Tor.com, Beneath Ceaseless Skies, Nature, *and more. The* Jewel and Her Lapidary *has been nominated for the Nebula, Hugo, and Locus Awards.*

Fran's interview series Cooking the Books—*about the intersection between food and fiction—has appeared at* Strange Horizons, Tor.com, iTunes, *and on her blog, franwilde.wordpress.com.*

She writes for publications including the Washington Post, Tor.com, Clarkesworld, io9, *and* GeekMom. *You can find her on Twitter @fran_wilde and Facebook @franwildewrites.*

Visitors to the Jeweled Valley should expect rustic accommodations and varying degrees of adventure, as the area is both remote and not under protection of any State or Commonwealth.

There are two inns of varying reputation (p. 34) and attractive scenery, including walks to the Ruins (p. 30), the Variegated Riverbank (p. 29), and the stone formation colloquially known as the Jewel and Her Lapidary (p. 32).

The best place to find a guide is at the Deaf King, a tavern by the river (p. 33).

Local guides can become verbose on matters of history and legend. Indeed, some cannot discern between the two. Many locals will gladly inform you their forebears served at the Jeweled Court long ago. More than a few will declare their ancestors were Jewels—royalty who wore the region's ancient gems—or their assistants. This is likely untrue, as the last Jewels were murdered in a palace coup after six generations of peaceful rule.

. . . from A *Guide to the Remote River Valleys*, by M. Lankin, East Quadril

*   *   *

Strips of soft cloth bound the Jewel Lin's hands behind her back, knotted as if they'd been tied in a hurry. When her head cleared enough for her to think of it, Lin slid her hands back and forth until the bindings loosened and she was able to bend her wrists and tug at the ties.

Her mouth felt dry as a stone. Her legs and feet tingled, as if she'd been sitting on them for hours at a strange angle. *Sima,* she thought. *Where is Sima?* Lin could not see anything. *What happened?* Sima would know. Or Aba.

An elbow pressed Lin's side in the darkness. Lin heard her lapidary grunt and wriggle, trying to release herself. Sima's kicking dislodged something heavy and dry that rattled like bones across the floor.

When Lin had freed her hands, she touched the cloth that covered her eyes and ears, then pulled at that knot too. The blindfold fell into her hands. It was strips from the veil Lin had worn since she was eleven.

On the rough ground nearby, the ancient bone Sima had kicked stared at them: a skull turned to opal, eye sockets stuffed with raw yellow topaz.

Lin knew where they were now. Far from her private quarters, where they'd drunk their evening tea and gone to sleep. They were below the moonstone hall, in the pit beside the throne. Where Aba had always threatened to put her as a child when she misbehaved.

Lin bit down on her fist, stifling a scream. She looked around the pit, expecting to see the rest of the Jeweled Court similarly bound. Light flickered through the grate above her head. Sima still wriggled beside her in the dark. But beyond Sima, she saw nothing but darkness and more ancient bones.

She reached for her lapidary's hands. She felt the cloth that bound them and discovered that it had been looped around the metal cuffs and chains that marked Sima not just as a gem-speaker but as a lapidary—Lin's own lapidary: the bound courtier to a royal Jewel. Sima had been blindfolded too, with cloth ripped from her blue lapidary's cloak. She'd been gagged as well.

Lin worked at the knots. *We have been betrayed. The court. The valley.*

No one else sat in the pit with them. Above, the muffled sounds grew louder. Lin heard running feet. Shouting. Someone howled.

Lin wanted to stuff her hand back in her mouth. She wanted to go back to her room and see her father in the morning. To tell him about her nightmare. Lights flickered through the grate over her head.

"No," Sima whimpered, panic edging her voice. "A lapidary must not—" She was looking up, through the grate. She had not addressed her words to Lin.

Must not do what? thought Lin. *Which lapidary?* Her thoughts were slow and muddled. *The tea must have been drugged.* What had happened to her family? They had ordered wine in the hall while they discussed matters of state, and she'd been told to retire.

Above them, a voice shouted, "Shattered! We are shattered. You should have listened to me!"

The voice was barely recognizable as belonging to the King's Lapidary. Sima's father.

"Stop," Sima begged, climbing to her feet. Tears ran down her cheeks, turning diamond in the moonlight. She put a hand against the wall to steady herself. "Let us out, let us help you. Father." Her last word was a wail.

The screams continued above their heads, wave after crashing wave of them.

Father. Lin called out, "Help us!" She shouted for the king while Sima called to the lapidary. Two daughters below. Two fathers above.

Sima looked at Lin with wide eyes. "He is gem-mad."

The King's Lapidary howled in answer. His words came faster and faster, tumbling through the grate. Their meaning was nearly drowned by his laughter. Lin caught her name. She heard "bargain" and "promise." The lapidary's voice rose to a high pitch and cracked.

Sharp metal struck stone. Sima grabbed her ears, holding tight to the metal bands that wrapped her earlobes. Through clenched teeth, she whispered, "A lapidary must obey their Jewel." The first vow a new lapidary took. Sima repeated the vow like a chant as a shriek pierced the room above them. Her face was white, but she pushed Lin away from the grate, whispering, "He's going to break the diamond; he'll break it and death will come. Cover your ears!"

When the stone shattered it made a noise like a mineshaft collapsing, and a scream, and a fire all at once. Sima's eyes rolled back and Lin scrambled to keep her courtier's head from hitting the hard pit walls. "It's all right," she whispered. Nothing was right. Where was her father? Where were her sisters and brothers? And their lapidaries?

The pit and its metal walls seemed to protect them from the gems, and from Sima's father. Above, a cry of pain reverberated through the hall. Then something like rain. Then weeping. She heard the clatter as the palace guard dropped their weapons en masse and tried to flee, feet pounding, across the great hall's moonstone tiles. She heard them fall, one by one.

Metal struck again. Sima threw up at Lin's feet.

"Father!" Lin shouted, hoping her voice would pass up through the grate. "What is happening?"

Instead of the king, the lapidary returned to kneel on the grate. His hands gripped the bars, charred black. His eyes looked bloodred in the moonlight. "Awake," he muttered. "Awake too soon. The commander has not yet come and you must cover your ears. You will be no good to me mad." His voice sing-songed as he stood and laughed, then lurched away.

"Sima," Lin whispered. "What is he doing?"

Her lapidary whimpered. "He is breaking his vows, my Jewel. He has broken gems. Couldn't you hear? The Opaque Sapphire. The Death Astrion. The Steadfast Diamond. He is about to break the Star Cabochon. We have to stop him."

The Opaque Sapphire. The Jeweled Palace was visible to attackers without that gem. And she and Sima were trapped in the pit beside the throne. The astrion and the diamond. The borders were undefended.

All her life, Aba had made Lin recite the valley's legends. How the first gems had enslaved those who found them; how they had maddened those who could hear them. How the first Jewel, the Deaf King, had set a cabochon-cut ruby with metal and wire. How he'd bound those who heard the stones as well and named them lapidaries. Made them serve him instead of the gems. How the gems had protected the valley better than any army.

She'd made Lin learn what could happen if a lapidary broke their vows.

The screaming had quieted above them. Sima knelt and cupped her hands so that Lin could stand on them. Lin pressed on the grate with both hands. The heavy door lifted an inch, but little more. Lin climbed to Sima's shoulders.

"Here—" Sima handed Lin a long bone from the pit floor. They wedged the grate open and Lin pulled herself out. Looking around, she could not see the King's Lapidary. But as Sima pulled herself up using a stretch of Lin's robe, Lin saw her own father, lying on the ground. His eyes were clouded like ruined opals. His breath bubbled in the blood-flecked foam at his mouth. An amber goblet rolled on the floor near his fingers. The bodies of the rest of the court lay scattered. Sisters. Brothers. Aba. Lin bound her heart up with the words. Saw their lips too: blackened and covered with foam. Poison.

Sima crossed the hall, following a sound. A voice. In the courtyard beyond the throne, the King's Lapidary stood on the high wall. He pointed at Lin, before Sima moved to stand between them. "The Western Mountains are coming— I've promised them a powerful gem and one very fine Jewel to marry!" He began to laugh and shout again. "They are strong! Our gems are fading. Soon their only power will be to catch the eye. The Jeweled Valley *must* be protected. He wouldn't listen. I protected you!"

Lapidaries' lathes were smashed across the courtyard. Shards of the Intaglio Amethyst that mapped the valley's mines crunched under Sima's feet as she walked toward her father.

"You cannot betray your vows, Father. You promised."

Metal rained down on them as the gem-mad lapidary threw the chains and bracelets that had bound his arms and ears. "No longer!"

Sima sank to her knees in the courtyard and Lin fell beside her. They watched as the madman waited for his conquering army on the wall.

Then the King's Lapidary fell quiet for the first time since Lin woke.

The two girls listened, shaking in the cold, for the mountain army's drums. They wondered how long the palace's doors could hold. But no drums came. Only silence. The King's Lapidary climbed up on the lip of the palace wall. He turned to face the courtyard. His lips were pressed tight, his eyes rolled. He spread his arms wide. His hands clutched at the air.

Sima rose to her feet. Began to run toward the wall.

Without another word, the King's Lapidary leapt from the wall, his blue robe flapping, the chains on his wrists and ankles ringing in the air.

And before Lin could scream, the King's Lapidary crashed to the flagstones of the courtyard.

When Lin came to her senses, Sima was whispering to her sapphires and blue topaz, the ones that lined her veil. *Calm,* she whispered. *Calm.*

The valley's gems. In a gem-speaker's hands, Lin knew they amplified desire. When bezel-set and held by a trained lapidary, they had to obey: to protect, calm, compel. Only without their bezels, or in the presence of a wild gem-speaker or a gem-mad lapidary, could gems do worse things.

Sima's gems did calm Lin. She remained aware of what was happening, but they were smooth facets made out of fact; her terror was trapped within. She was the only one left. An army was coming. The court of the Jeweled Valley— which had known peace for four hundred years, since the Deaf King set the Star Cabochon—had been betrayed. Lin felt a keen rising in her chest.

"Make me stronger," she ordered Sima.

Sima tried her best. She whispered to the small topaz and diamonds at Lin's wrists and ears. Lin could not hear the gems, but she felt them acting on her. Compelling her to be calm. To think clearly. She took a breath. Stood.

"We will collect all the gems we can find, Sima," she said. "All the chain mail too."

They searched the bodies of the court for gems. Lin sewed the gems herself into one of her old gray cloaks.

When she rolled her eldest brother's body on its side to peel the ornamental chain mail from his chest, she wept, but it was a calm, slow weeping. The gems allowed her time to act. She would have to mourn later. She moved from one body to the next. Sima followed behind, tugging cloaks, searching pockets.

Sima removed the bands and chains from the fallen lapidaries, cutting the solder points with her father's diamond saw.

They returned to Lin's quarters in the heart of the palace and Lin wrapped herself in all of the chains she had collected. She pointed to the metal bands, the oaths meaningless now.

"You must do the rest," she told her lapidary.

Sima, whispering her vows, shook her head. "I cannot do this work, my Jewel. It will harm you."

The small betrayal made the lapidary wince.

"Sima, you must." Lin spoke calmly, and Sima pulled the cache of tools from her sleeve. She lit her torch. Attached bands at Lin's wrists and ankles. The metal grew hot. Lin felt her skin burn and thought of her sisters and brothers. Blisters rose where Sima's torch came too close. Lin ached for her father.

"The mountains wish a bride and a throne," Lin said. Her voice was flat. Her new veil hung heavy against her temples.

Sima added more chains to Lin's veil. When Lin demanded it, she spoke the binding verses she'd learned at her own father's side.

And then Sima backed out the door, latching it behind her. Lin listened to the lapidary's metal vows clattering and chiming on her arms as she sped away. *To the river, Sima. Run.*

The noises faded. The palace of the Jeweled Court fell silent.

And Lin, for the first time in her life, was completely alone.

BLOOD GRAINS SPEAK THROUGH MEMORIES

JASON SANFORD

Jason Sanford is an award-winning author and an active member of the Science Fiction and Fantasy Writers of America. Born and raised in the American South, he currently lives in the Midwestern United States with his wife and sons. His life's adventures include work as an archaeologist and as a Peace Corps Volunteer.

Jason has published more than a dozen of his short stories in the British SF magazine Interzone, *which once devoted a special issue to his fiction. His fiction has also been published in* Asimov's Science Fiction, Analog: Science Fiction and Fact, Beneath Ceaseless Skies, InterGalactic Medicine Show, Tales of the Unanticipated, *the* Mississippi Review Online, Diagram, The Beloit Fiction Journal, Pindeldyboz, *and other places. Books containing his stories include multiple "year's best" story collections, along with original anthologies such as* Bless Your Mechanical Heart *and* Beyond the Sun.

A collection of Jason's short stories, titled Never Never Stories, *was published by a small press in 2011.*

Morning's song of light and warmth glowed on the horizon as the land's anchor, Frere-Jones Roeder, stepped from her front door. The red-burn dots of fairies swirled in the river mists flowing over her recently plowed sunflower fields. Cows mooed in the barn, eager to be milked. Chickens flapped their wings as they stirred from roosts on her home's sod-grass roof.

Even though the chilled spring day promised nothing but beauty, the grains in Frere-Jones's body shivered to her sadness as she looked at the nearby dirt road. The day-fellows along the road were packing their caravan. Evidently her promises of safety weren't enough for them to chance staying even a few more hours.

Frere-Jones tapped the message pad by the door, pinging her fellow anchors on other lands so they knew the caravan was departing. She then picked up her gift sack and hurried outside to say goodbye.

As Frere-Jones closed the door, a red fairy wearing her dead lifemate's face flittered before her eyes. A flash of memory jumped into her from the fairy's grain-created body. One of Haoquin's memories, from a time right after they'd wed. They'd argued over something silly—like newlyweds always did—and Haoquin had grown irritated at Frere-Jones's intransigence.

But that was all the fairy shared. The taste of Haoquin's memory didn't show Frere-Jones and Haoquin making up. The memory didn't show the two of them ending the day by walking hand-in-hand along her land's forest trails.

Frere-Jones slapped the fairy away, not caring if the land and its damned grains were irritated at her sadness. She liked the day-fellows. She'd choose them any day over the grains.

The fairy spun into an angry buzzing and flew over the sunflower fields to join the others.

Frere-Jones walked up to the caravan's wagons to find the day-fellows detaching their power systems from her farm's solar and wind grid. The caravan leader nodded to Frere-Jones as he harnessed a team of four horses to the lead wagon.

"We appreciate you letting us plug in," the man said. "Our solar collectors weaken something awful when it's overcast."

"Anytime," Frere-Jones said. "Pass the word to other caravans that I'm happy to help. Power or water or food, I'll always share."

Pleasantries done, Frere-Jones hurried down the line of wagons.

The first five wagons she passed were large multi-generational affairs with massive ceramic wheels standing as tall as she. Pasted-on red ribbons outlined the wagons' scars from old battles. Day-fellows believed any battle they survived was a battle worth honoring.

Adults and teenagers and kids smiled at Frere-Jones as she passed, everyone hurrying to harness horses and stow baggage and deploy their solar arrays.

Frere-Jones waved at the Kameron twins, who were only seven years old and packing up their family's honey and craft goods. Frere-Jones reached into her pocket and handed the twins tiny firefly pebbles. When thrown, the pebbles would burst into mechanical fireflies which flew in streaks of rainbow colors for a few seconds. The girls giggled—firefly pebbles were a great prank. Kids loved to toss them when adults were sitting around campfires at night, releasing bursts of fireflies to startle everyone.

Frere-Jones hugged the twins and walked on, finally stopping before the caravan's very last wagon.

The wagon stood small, barely containing the single family inside, built not of ceramic but of a reinforced lattice of ancient metal armor. Instead of bright ribbons to honor old battles, a faded maroon paint flaked and peeled from the walls. Large impact craters shown on one side of the wagon. Long scratches surrounded the back door from superhard claws assaulting the wagon's armored shutters.

An ugly, ugly wagon. Still, it had bent under its last attack instead of breaking. The caravan's leader had told Frere-Jones that this family's previous caravan had been attacked a few months ago. All that caravan's ceramic wagons shattered, but this wagon survived.

Frere-Jones fed her final sugar cubes to the wagon's horses, a strong pair who nickered in pleasure as the grains within their bodies pulsed in sync to her own. Horses adapted so perfectly to each land's grains as they fed on grasses and hay. That flexibility was why horses usually survived attacks even when their caravan did not.

"Morning, Master-Anchor Frere-Jones," a teenage girl, Alexnya, said as she curtsied, holding the sides of her leather vest out like a fancy dress. Most kids in the caravan wore flowing cotton clothes, but Alexnya preferred leather shirts and vests and pants.

"Master-Anchor Frere-Jones, you honor us with your presence," Alexnya's mother, Jun, said in an overly formal manner. Her husband, Takeshi, stood behind her, holding back their younger daughter and son as if Frere-Jones was someone to fear.

They're skittish from that attack, Frere-Jones thought. A fresh scar ran the left side of Jun's thin face while Takeshi still wore a healing pad around his neck. Their two young kids, Miya and Tufte, seemed almost in tears at being near an anchor. When Frere-Jones smiled at them, both kids bolted to hide in the wagon.

Only Alexnya stood unafraid, staring into Frere-Jones's eyes as if confident this land's anchor wouldn't dare harm her.

"I've brought your family gifts," Free-Jones said.

"Why?" Jun asked, suspicious.

Frere-Jones paused, unused to explaining. "I give gifts to all families who camp on my land."

"A land which you protect," Jun said, scratching the scar on her face. As if to remind Frere-Jones what the anchors who'd attacked their last caravan had done.

Frere-Jones nodded sadly. "I am my land's anchor," she said. "I wish it wasn't so. If I could leave I would . . . my son . . ."

Frere-Jones turned to walk back to her farm to milk the cows. Work distracted her from memories. But Alexnya jumped forward and grabbed her hand.

"I've heard of your son," Alexnya said. "He's a day-fellow now, isn't he?"

Frere-Jones grinned. "He is indeed. Travels the eastern roads in a caravan with his own lifemate and kids. I see him once every four years when the land permits his caravan to return." Frere-Jones held the gift bag out to Alexnya. "Please take this. I admit it's a selfish gift. I want day-fellows to watch out for my son and his family. Lend a hand when needed."

"Day-fellows protect our own," Jun stated in a flat voice. "No need to bribe us to do what we already do."

Alexnya, despite her mother's words, took the canvas gift bag and opened it, pulling out a large spool of thread and several short knives.

"The thread is reinforced with nano-armor," Frere-Jones said, "the strongest you can find. You can weave it into the kids' clothes. The short knives were made by a day-fellow biosmith and are supposedly unbreakable . . ."

Frere-Jones paused, not knowing what else to say. She thought it silly that day-fellows were prohibited from possessing more modern weapons than swords and knives to protect themselves, even if she knew why the grains demanded this.

"Thank you, Frere-Jones," Alexnya said as she curtsied again. "My family appreciates your gifts, which will come in handy on the road."

Unsure what else to say, Frere-Jones bowed back before walking away, refusing to dwell on the fact that she was the reason this day-fellow caravan was fleeing her land.

* * *

That night Frere-Jones lit the glow-stones in the fireplace and sat down on her favorite sofa. The stones' flickering flames licked the weariness from her body. A few more weeks and the chilled nights would vanish as spring fully erupted across her land.

Frere-Jones didn't embrace spring as she once had. Throughout the valley her fellow anchors celebrated the growing season with dances, feasts, and lush night-time visits to the forest with their lifemates and friends.

Frere-Jones no longer joined such festivities. Through the grains she tasted the land's excitement—the mating urge of the animals, the budding of the trees, the growth of the new-planted seeds in her fields. She felt the cows in the fields nuzzling each other's necks and instinctively touched her own neck in response. She sensed several does hiding in the nearby forests and touched her stomach as the fawns in their wombs kicked. She even felt the grass growing on her home's sod-roof and walls, the roots reaching slowly down as water flowed by capillary action into the fresh-green blades.

The grains allowed Frere-Jones, as this land's anchor, to feel everything growing and living and dying for two leagues around her. She even dimly felt the anchors on nearby lands—Jeroboam and his family ate dinner in their anchordom while Chakatie hunted deer in a forest glen on her land. Chakatie was probably gearing up for one of her family's bloody ritualized feasts to welcome spring.

Frere-Jones sipped her warm mulled wine before glancing at her home's message pad. Was it too soon to call her son again? She'd tried messaging Colton a few hours ago, but the connection failed. She was used to this—day-fellow caravans did slip in and out of the communication grid—but that didn't make it any less painful. At least he was speaking to her again.

Frere-Jones downed the rest of her drink. As she heated a new mug of wine over the stove she took care to ignore the fairies dancing outside her kitchen window. Usually the fairies responded to the land's needs and rules, but these fairies appeared to have been created by the grains merely to annoy her. The grains were well aware that Frere-Jones hated her part in the order and main-tenance of this land.

Two fairies with her parents' faces glared in the window. Other fairies stared with the faces of even more distant ancestors. Several fairies mouthed Frere-Jones's name, as if reminding her of an anchor's duty, while others spoke in bursts of memories copied by the grains from her ancestors' lives.

Fuck duty, she thought as she swallowed half a mug of wine. *Fuck you for what you did to Haoquin.*

Thankfully her lifemate's face wasn't among those worn by these fairies. While the grains had no problem creating fairies with Haoquin's face, they knew not to push Frere-Jones when she was drunk.

As Frere-Jones left the kitchen she paused before the home altar. In the stone pedestal's basin stood three carved stone figurines—herself, her son, and Haoquin. The hand-sized statues rested on the red-glowing sand filling the basin.

In the flickering light of the glow stones the figures seemed to twitch as if alive, shadow faces accusing Frere-Jones of unknown misdeeds. Frere-Jones touched Haoquin's face—felt his sharp cheekbones and mischievous smirk—causing the basin's red sands to rise up, the individual grains climbing the statues until her family glowed a faint speckled red over the darker sands below.

The red grains burned her fingers where she touched Haoquin, connecting her to what remained of her lifemate. She felt his bones in the family graveyard on the edge of the forest. Felt the insects and microbes which had fed on his remains and absorbed his grains before dying and fertilizing the ground and the trees and the other plants throughout the land, where the grains had then been eaten by deer and cows and rabbits. If Frere-Jones closed her eyes she could almost feel Haoquin's grains pulsing throughout the land. Could almost imagine him returning to her and hugging her tired body.

Except he couldn't. He was gone. Only the echo of him lived on in the microscopic grains which had occupied his body and were now dispersed again to her land.

And her son was even farther beyond the grains' reach, forced to forsake both the grains and her land when he turned day-fellow.

Frere-Jones sat down hard on the tile floor and cried, cradling her empty wine mug.

She was lying on the floor, passed out from the wine, when a banging woke her. "Frere-Jones, you must help us!" a woman's voice called. She recognized the voice—Jun, from the day-fellow family which left that morning.

Frere-Jones's hands shook, curling like claws. The grains in her body screamed against the day-fellows for staying on her land.

No, she ordered, commanding the grains to stand down. *It's too soon. There are a few more days before they wear out this land's welcome.*

The grains rattled irritably in her body like pebbles in an empty water gourd. While they should obey her, to be safe Frere-Jones stepped across the den and lifted several ceramic tiles from the floor. She pulled Haoquin's hand-made laser pistol from the hiding spot and slid it behind her back, held by her belt. She was now ready to shoot herself in the head if need be.

Satisfied that she was ready, Frere-Jones opened the door. Jun and Takeshi stood there supporting Alexnya, who leaned on them as if drunk but stared with eyes far too awake and aware. Alexnya shook and spasmed, her muscles clenching as she moaned a low, painful hiss, unable to fully scream.

Frere-Jones looked behind the family. She reached out to the grains in the land's animals and plants and soils. She didn't feel any other anchors on her land. If any of them found the day-fellows here. . . .

"Bring her inside," she told Jun. "Takeshi, hide your wagon and horses in the barn."

"Not until later," Takeshi said, wanting to stay with his daughter.

Jun snapped at him. "Don't be a fool, Tak. We can't be seen. Not after everyone knows our caravan left."

Frere-Jones took Alexnya in her arms, the grains powering up her strength so the teenage girl seemed to weigh no more than a baby. Takeshi hurried back to the wagon, where the family's two youngest kids stared in fright from the open door.

Frere-Jones carried Alexnya to Colton's old room and placed her on the bed. Alexnya continued to spasm, her muscles clenching and shivering under her drained-pale skin.

"Please," Alexnya whimpered. "Please . . ."

As Jun held her daughter's hand, Frere-Jones leaned closer to the girl. The grains jumped madly in Frere-Jones's blood, erupting her fangs like razors ready to rip into these day-fellows' throats. Frere-Jones breathed deep to calm herself and gagged on Alexnya's sweaty scent. It carried the faintest glimmer of grains inside Alexnya's body.

"She's infected," Frere-Jones said in shock. "With grains. My grains."

Jun nodded, an angry look on her face as if Frere-Jones had personally caused this abomination. "The further we travelled from your land, the more pain she experienced. She didn't stop screaming until we left the caravan and began making our way back here."

Frere-Jones growled softly. "This is unheard of," she said. "Grains shouldn't infect day-fellows."

"Day-fellow lore says it happens on rare occasions. Our lore also says each land's anchor has medicine to cure an infection."

Frere-Jones understood. She ran to the kitchen and grabbed her emergency bag. Inside was a glass vial half-full of powder glowing a faint red.

She hadn't used the powder since Colton became a day-fellow. The powder's nearly dim glow meant it had weakened severely over the years. Chakatie had taken most of her remaining medicine after Colton left, worried about Frere-Jones killing herself with an overdose. Now all that was left was a half-vial of nearly worthless medicine.

But she had nothing else to give. She held the vial over her altar—letting it sync again with the coding from her land's grains—then mixed the powder in a mug of water and hurried back to Alexnya.

"Drink this," she said, holding the mug to Alexnya's lips. The girl gasped and turned her head as if being near the liquid hurt her.

"Why is it hurting her?" Jun asked, blocking Alexnya's mouth with her hand so Frere-Jones couldn't try again. "I thought the medicine helped."

"It does, but the grains always resist at first," Frere-Jones said. "When I gave it to my own son years ago he . . . went through some initial pain. We usually only give small doses to new anchors at puberty to calm the explosive growth of the grains in their bodies. But if we give Alexnya a full dose for the next few days, it should kill the grains."

Jun frowned. "How much pain?"

"I . . . don't know. But if we don't do something soon there will be too many grains in her body to remove."

Frere-Jones didn't need to tell Jun what would happen if Alexnya became anchored to this land. The anchors from the lands surrounding Frere-Jones's wouldn't take kindly to a day-fellow girl becoming one of them.

"We shouldn't have come here," Jun said, standing up. "Maybe if we take Alexnya away from here before the grains establish themselves . . ."

"Taking her from the land will definitely kill her—the grains have already anchored. We need to remove them from her body. There's no other way."

"I'll drink it," Alexnya whispered in a weak voice. She glared at Frere-Jones in fury. Frere-Jones prayed the grains weren't already sharing the land's stored memories with this day-fellow girl. Showing Alexnya what Frere-Jones had done. Revealing secrets known by no one else except her son and Chakatie.

Despite her hesitation, Jun nodded agreement. She held her daughter's spasming body as Frere-Jones poured the liquid through the girl's lips. Alexnya swallowed half the medicine before screaming. Splashes and dribbles on her leather shirt and pants glowed bright red as she thrashed in the bed for a moment before passing out.

Frere-Jones and Jun tucked Alexnya under the covers and stepped into the den. Takeshi stood by the fireplace holding their youngest son and daughter.

"Will she make it?" Jun asked.

"I don't know," Frere-Jones said. "She'll need another dose before the medicine wears off or she'll be as bad as ever. And that was all I had in the house."

Frere-Jones glanced at the altar, where the red sands squirmed in a frenzied rush, climbing over the figurines as if outraged they couldn't eat stone. She noticed Jun staring at her back and realized the woman had seen the laser pistol she carried.

Frere-Jones handed the pistol to Jun. "Use this if needed," she said. "Make sure none of you touch the grains in the altar—if you do, every anchor for a hundred leagues will know there's a day-fellow family here."

Jun nodded as Frere-Jones pulled on her leather running duster. "When will you be back?"

"I don't know," Frere-Jones said. "I have to find more medicine. I'll . . . think of something."

With that Frere-Jones ordered the grains to power up her legs and, for the first time in years, she ran across her land. She ran faster than any horse, faster than any deer, until even the fairies which flew after her could barely keep up.

* * *

At the land's boundary Frere-Jones paused.

She stood by Sandy Creek, the cold waters bubbling under the overhanging oaks and willows. Fairies flew red tracers over the creek, flying as far across as they dared without crossing into the bordering land. On the other bank a handful of blue fairies hovered in the air, staring back at Frere-Jones and the red fairies.

Usually boundaries between lands were more subtle, the grains that were tied to one anchor mixing a bit with the next land's grains in the normal back and forth of life. But with Sandy Creek as a natural land divide—combined with Frere-Jones's isolation from the other anchors—the boundary between her and Chakatie's lands had grown abrupt, stark.

One of Chakatie's blue fairies stared intensely at her. Chakatie knew she was coming. Frere-Jones wished there was a caravan nearby to trade for the medicine. Day-fellow pharmacists were very discreet.

Still, of all the nearby anchors Chakatie was the only one who might still give her medicine. Chakatie was also technically family, even if her son Haoquin was now dead. And she had a large extended family. Meaning a number of kids. Meaning stocks of medicine on hand to ensure the grains didn't overwhelm and kill those kids when they transitioned to becoming anchors.

Still, no matter how much Frere-Jones had once loved Chakatie she wouldn't go in unprepared. She was, after all, her land's anchor. She stripped off her clothes and stepped into the cold creek, rubbing mud and water over her skin and hair to remove the day-fellow scent. She activated the grains inside her, increasing her muscle size and bone density. Finally, for good measure, she grabbed a red fairy buzzing next to her and smashed it between her now-giant hands. She smeared the fairy's glowing red grains in two lines down both sides of her face and body.

Battle lines. As befitted an anchor going into another's land in the heart of the night.

Satisfied, she walked naked onto Chakatie's anchordom.

*   *   *

Frere-Jones hated memories. She hated how the grains spoke to her in brief snatches of memories copied from Haoquin and her parents and grandparents and on back to the land's very first anchor.

But despite this distaste at memories, they still swarmed her. As Frere-Jones crossed the dark forest of trees and brambles on Chakatie's land, she wondered why the grains were showing her these memories. The grains never revealed memories randomly.

In particular, why show her Haoquin's memories, which the grains had so rarely shared up to now? Memories from the day she met him. Memories from their selecting ceremony.

Frere-Jones tried to stop them, but the memories slipped into her as if they'd always existed within her.

Frere-Jones's parents had died when the grains determined it was time for their child to take over. Like most anchors they'd gone happily. First they drank medicine to dull the grains' power to rebuild their bodies. Then they slit each other's throat in the land's graveyard, holding hands as they bled out and their grain-copied memories flowed into the land they'd protected.

At first Frere-Jones had accepted her role in protecting the land. She safeguarded the land from those who might harm it and carefully managed the ecosystem's plants and animals so the land was in continual balance.

But a few years after becoming anchor a small day-fellow caravan defiled her land by cutting down trees. Frere-Jones eagerly allowed the grains to seize control of her body. She called other anchors to her side and led an attack on the caravan. Memories of the pains her land had suffered before the grains had arrived flowed through her—images of clear-cut forests and poisoned soil and all the other evils of the ancient world. In her mind she became a noble warrior preventing humans from creating ecological hell just as her family had done for a hundred generations.

Only after the caravan was wiped out did she learn that a day-fellow child, gifted with a new hatchet and told to gather dead branches for a fire, had instead cut down a single pine sapling.

Outraged at what she'd done, Frere-Jones attacked the other anchors who'd helped savage the caravan. The anchors fought back, slashing at her with claw and fang until a respected older anchor, Chakatie, arrived, her three-yard-tall body powered to a mass of muscle and bone and claw.

Chakatie's land neighbored Frere-Jones's land, but Chakatie hadn't aided in the attack on the caravan. Now this powerful woman had stepped among the fighting anchors, a mere glance all that was needed to stop the other anchors from attacking each other. A few even powered down their bodies.

Chakatie had paused before the remains of the caravan and breathed deeply. As the other anchors watched nervously, Chakatie leaned over and tapped the tiny child-size hatchet and examined the cut sapling. She sniffed each day-fellow body.

With a roar, Chakatie told everyone but this land's anchor to leave. The others fled.

Once everyone was gone Chakatie bent over the dead bodies and cried.

After Chakatie finished, she stood and wiped her tears. Frere-Jones forced herself to stand still, willing to take whatever punishment Chakatie might give for this evil deed. But the older woman didn't attack. Instead, she stepped forward until her hot breath licked Frere-Jones's face and her fangs clicked beside her ear like knives stripping flesh from bone.

"The grains speak only in memories," Chakatie said. "But memories only speak to the grains' programmed goals. A good anchor never lets memory overwhelm what is right and what is wrong."

With that Chakatie walked away, leaving Frere-Jones to bury the caravan's dead.

Ashamed, Frere-Jones had locked herself in her home and refused to listen to the grains' excuses. The grains tried to please her with swirls of memories from her parents and others. Memories of people apologizing and explaining and rationalizing what she'd done.

But she no longer cared. She was this land's anchor and she'd decide what was right. Not the grains.

A few years later the grains gave her an ultimatum: marry another anchor to help manage this land, or the other anchors would kill Frere-Jones and select a new anchor to take her place.

The selecting ceremony took place on the summer solstice. Hundreds of her fellow anchors came to her home, setting up feasting tents along the dirt road and in fallow fields. Frere-Jones walked from tent to tent, meeting young anchors who spoke eagerly of duty and helping protect her land. She listened politely. Nodded to words like "ecological balance" and "heritage." Then she walked to the next tent to hear more of the same.

Frere-Jones grew more and more depressed as she went from tent to tent. If she didn't select a mate before the end of the day all the celebrating anchors would rip her to pieces and choose a new anchor to protect her land. She wondered if day-fellows felt this fear around anchors. The fear of knowing people who were so warm and friendly one moment might be your death in the next.

Frere-Jones was preparing for her death when she spotted a ragged tent beside her barn. The tent was almost an afterthought, a few poles stuck in the ground holding up several old and torn cotton blankets.

Frere-Jones stepped inside to see Chakatie sitting beside a young man.

"Join us in a drink?" Chakatie asked, holding a jug of what smelled like moonshine. Chakatie's body when powered down was tiny, barely reaching Frere-Jones's shoulder.

"Do I look like I need a drink?" Frere-Jones asked.

"Any young woman about to be slaughtered for defying the grains needs a drink," Chakatie said.

Frere-Jones sat down hard on the ground and drank a big swallow of moonshine. "Maybe I deserve to be killed," she thought, remembering what she'd done to that day-fellow caravan.

"Maybe," the young man sitting next to Chakatie said. "Or maybe you deserve a chance to change things."

Chakatie introduced the man as her son Haoquin. He leaned over and shook Frere-Jones's hand.

"How can I change anything?" Frere-Jones asked. "The grains will force me to do what they want or they'll order the other anchors to kill me."

Instead of answering, Haoquin leaned over so he could see outside the tiny tent. He was a skinny man and wore a giant wool coat even in summer, as if easily chilled. Or that's what Frere-Jones thought until he opened the coat and pulled out a small laser pistol.

Frere-Jones froze at the sight of the forbidden technology, but Chakatie merely laughed. Haoquin aimed the pistol at a nearby tent—the Jeroboam family tent, among the loudest and most rambunctious groups at the selection ceremony. Haoquin pulled the trigger and a slight buzzing like angry bees filled the tent. He shoved the pistol back in his coat as the roof of the Jeroboam tent burst into flames.

Drunken anchors, including Jeroboam himself, fled from the tent, tearing holes in the fabric walls in their panic. Other anchors howled with laughter while Jeroboam and his lifemate and kids demanded to know who had insulted their family and land with this prank.

Haoquin grinned as he patted his coat covering the hidden pistol. "A little something I made," he said. "I'm hoping it'll come in handy when I eventually spit at the grains' memories."

Frere-Jones felt a flash of memory—her parents warning her as a kid to behave. To be a good girl. She shook off the grains' warning as she stared into Haoquin's mischievous eyes.

Maybe Haoquin was right. Maybe there was a way to change things.

*   *   *

Frere-Jones leaned against a large oak tree, her powered body shaking as red and blue fairies buzzed around her. The grains had never shared such a deep stretch of Haoquin's memories with her. The memories had been so intense and long they'd merged with her own memories of that day into something more. Almost as if Haoquin was alive once again inside her.

Frere-Jones wiped at her glowing eyes with the back of her clawed right hand. Why had the grains shared such a memory with her? What were they saying?

She pushed the memories from her thoughts as she ran on through the forest.

Frere-Jones found Chakatie in an isolated forest glen. Countless fairies rose into the dark skies from the tiny field of grass, stirring up a whirlwind of blue grains in their wake. Naked anchors jumped and howled among the blue light, their bodies powered up far beyond Frere-Jones's own. Massive claws dug into tree trunks and soil. Bloody lips and razor fangs kissed and nipped each other. Throats howled to the stars and the night clouds above.

And throughout this orgy of light and scent swirled the memories of this land's previous anchors. Memories of laughing and crying and killing and dying and a thousand other moments of life, all preserved by the blue grains which coursed through these trees and animals and enhanced people.

Frere-Jones stepped through the frenzied dance, daring anyone to attack her. The red lines on her face burned bright, causing the dancers to leap from her like she might scorch them. As the anchors noticed her the dance died down. They muttered and growled, shocked by Frere-Jones's interruption.

In the middle of the glen sat two granite boulders. On the lower boulder lay a dead stag, its guts ripped out like party streamers of red meat. On the higher rock sat Chakatie, her body and muscles enlarged to the full extent of the grains' powers, her clawed fingers digging into the dead stag beneath her. She sat naked except for a bloody stag-head and antlers draped over her head, the fresh blood dribbling down her shoulders and muscular chest.

"Welcome, my daughter!" Chakatie boomed as she jumped down and hugged Frere-Jones. "Welcome indeed. Have you come to join our festivities?"

Frere-Jones stared at the silent anchors around her. Several of them twitched their claws and fangs. But none dared attack her, remembering that she'd once been married to their blood.

"I won't join in," she said, the grains deepening her voice so she sounded more intimidating. "But I need speak with you. It's urgent."

Chakatie waved her family and relatives away.

"I need medicine," Frere-Jones said. "Five doses."

Chakatie glared at Frere-Jones, her happiness at seeing her vanishing as fast as a gutted deer bleeding out. "I will not have you killing yourself. If you're seeking a painful death for what you did to my grandson, there are far better ways than overdosing on medicine."

Chakatie raised one bloody claw as if offering to slash Frere-Jones to pieces.

Frere-Jones glared back at her mother-in-law. "It's not for me. My land infected a new anchor."

Chakatie lowered her claws and stared at Frere-Jones in puzzlement before a grin slowly emerged around her fangs. "I guess that's . . . good news. Who is it?"

"I'd prefer to see if she survives before naming her," Frere-Jones said, bluffing. Chakatie's blood-and-musk scent was stomach-gagging strong in her nostrils.

"Of course." Chakatie powered down her body slightly. "I apologize for saying that about Colton. If my land had betrayed me like yours did with Haoquin, I may have done as you."

This was the closest Chakatie had ever come to saying she agreed with Colton becoming a day-fellow. Frere-Jones thanked her.

"Don't thank me yet. The senior anchors have been saying you've lost your ability to protect your land. A few even suggest we . . . select a new anchor."

Frere-Jones snarled. "And I'm sure you didn't have someone in mind? Perhaps one of your other sons or daughters?"

Chakatie tensed at the insult before smirking with a knowing nod. "You know I want nothing but love and happiness for you. But if the other anchors become intent on killing you, I'd prefer my own benefit."

Frere-Jones sighed at her mother-in-law's logic. There was a reason no one ever challenged Chakatie. She was likely the mightiest anchor in this part of the world.

Chakatie waved for her oldest son, Malachi, who trotted over. "Run home and bring six vials of medicine to Frere-Jones." She nodded to Frere-Jones. "One extra in case it's needed."

Frere-Jones thanked Chakatie and turned to go, but Chakatie dared to place one of her giant clawed hands on her shoulder.

"Two warnings," Chakatie whispered. "First, don't be lying about what the medicine is for. If you try overdosing on it, I'll make sure the grains keep you alive long enough for me to kill you."

Frere-Jones nodded. "And?"

"The grains on your land have become increasingly agitated since Haoquin died. I fear they're building to something which will harm you."

"If they do, wouldn't that be your fault? After all, you introduced me to Haoquin."

Even as Frere-Jones said this she regretted the words. If she'd never met Haoquin her life would have been far poorer, assuming she'd even lived past her selecting ceremony. But Chakatie had avoided Frere-Jones ever since Colton become a day-fellow. Frere-Jones still loved Chakatie but also wanted to rip the woman apart for abandoning her, a feeling influenced no doubt by her grain-powered body's fury.

Chakatie nodded sadly. "I think every day about the paths of Haoquin's life. Still, what else can we do? We are ingrained in the land . . ." she said, beginning the most sacred oath of anchors.

" . . . and the grains are our land," Frere-Jones finished.

Yet afterwards as Frere-Jones ran back to her land she wanted to claw her own tongue out for uttering such a lie. If it was within her power, she'd destroy every grain in both her land and body.

Not that such dreams mattered in the real world. And if Chakatie and the other anchors learned she was sheltering a day-fellow family, her dreams—and Haoquin's—would never have a chance to come true.

*　　*　　*

"Don't trust my mother," Haoquin had said one morning a few weeks after they were married. He'd been bedridden that day as the grains from his old land deactivated and Frere-Jones's grains established themselves. She'd given him several doses of medicine, which helped, and stayed by his side the entire time.

Since they couldn't do much else, they lay in bed and talked. Frere-Jones had forgotten the joys of hearing someone talking to her in words instead of memories.

"I like your mom," Frere-Jones said. "I mean, she did bring us together."

"Oh, I like her. Hell, I love her. She's the one who taught me to be wary of the grains. But she's also not afraid to work the grains and the other anchors to her own advantage. Never forget that."

Frere-Jones snuggled closer to Haoquin, who hugged her back. She remembered how Chakatie had been disgusted by Frere-Jones killing the day-fellows. Which had pushed Frere-Jones into a new attitude toward the grains. Which had eventually resulted in her marrying Haoquin.

No, she thought, pushing those memories from her mind. She refused to believe her life was merely a plaything of either Chakatie or the grains.

"You okay?" Haoquin asked.

"Just thinking about memories." Frere-Jones ran her fingers across Haoquin's bare stomach, causing him to shiver. "Like the memory of my fingers on you. The touch of my skin on yours. Someday all that will remain of these moments are the copies of our memories stored in the grains' matrix."

"I can live with that, Fre," Haoquin said, calling her by that nickname for the first time. "Can you?"

Instead of answering Frere-Jones kissed him, her lips touching lips before fading into memory.

* * *

Frere-Jones gasped as she paused outside her house with the vials of medicine in her pocket.

She could hear Alexnya screaming inside. The last dose of medicine must be wearing off.

But why were the grains still showing her all these memories from Haoquin? They'd never done that before. In fact, the grains had taken care to lock away most of Haoquin's memories for fear that they'd influence Frere-Jones in the wrong ways. So why were the grains now sharing them?

Frere-Jones shrugged off the question and opened the door to her house. She had to focus on saving the day-fellow girl.

Remember that, she thought. *Remember what's important.*

* * *

After the next dose of medicine, Alexnya slept in fits for the day, waking every few hours to drink more. But when Frere-Jones stepped into the bedroom with a new dose the following evening, she found Alexnya sitting up in bed reading an old-fashioned paper book with her mother. Alexnya looked far better, no longer shaking or in pain. Frere-Jones tasted only the barest touch of the grains still inside the girl's body.

"Hello Fre," Alexnya said.

Frere-Jones nearly dropped the mug of medicine. The only one who'd ever called her Fre had been Haoquin.

"Alexnya, be polite," Jun snapped. "Call her Master-Anchor Frere-Jones."

"But she likes being called Fre . . ."

Frere-Jones sat on the bed beside Alexnya. "It's not her fault. The grains communicate using snippets of memories from previous anchors. 'Fre' is what my lifemate used to call me."

Jun paled but didn't say anything. Alexnya frowned. "I'm sorry, Fre . . . Master-Anchor Frere-Jones," the girl said. "I just want you to love me again. You used to love me."

Frere-Jones ignored the girl's obvious confusion at having her memories mix with the memories stored within the grains' matrix. She handed Alexnya the mug of medicine. "Drink this," she said.

The girl swallowed half the medicine. "The grains are angry," Alexnya whispered as she wiped the red glow from her lips. "The grains don't like you removing them from my body. They don't like my family overstaying our welcome."

"They won't hurt your family without my approval."

Alexnya didn't appear convinced. "They're also angry at you," she said as she yawned. "Why are they angry at you?"

"Let me worry about my land's grains. You need to sleep."

Alexnya nodded and closed her eyes. Jun and Frere-Jones shut the door and walked over to the dinner table, where Jun stared at the remaining dregs of medicine in the mug.

"She's taken enough medicine," Frere-Jones said. "By tomorrow her connection to the land will be weak enough to leave. She'll have to continue taking the medicine for another few days to remove the remaining grains, but you can give it to her on the road."

Jun glanced with relief at the den, where Takeshi lay sleeping on a sofa with Miya and Tufte.

"What memories are the grains showing Alexnya?" she asked.

"Does it matter?" Frere-Jones asked with a growl. "Any memories she's experienced are hers now."

As Frere-Jones said this she shook with anger at the thought of Alexnya experiencing even a taste of Haoquin's life. She didn't care about the stored memories of her parents and ancestors, but Haoquin . . . those memories were special. Damn the grains. Damn these day-fellows for intruding on the most intimate parts of her life.

Frere-Jones's right hand spasmed as claws grew from her fingertips. She dug into the wooden table, imagining the need to go into her son's bedroom and rip Alexnya to pieces.

"Master-Anchor Frere-Jones!" Jun shouted in a loud voice. Frere-Jones snapped back to herself and looked up to see Jun aiming the laser pistol at her head. She took a deep breath and forced her body to reabsorb the claws.

The grains were pushing her, like they had as a young anchor when she'd attacked that day-fellow caravan.

"I will sleep outside tonight," Frere-Jones said as she stood. "Bar the door. And windows. Don't let me in." She grinned at Jun, who kept the pistol aimed at her. "If I do break in, make sure you end me before I do anything we'd all regret."

Jun chuckled once but kept the pistol aimed at Frere-Jones until she walked outside and the door slammed shut.

*　　*　　*

Frere-Jones didn't sleep that night, instead patrolling the land to ensure no one came near her house. This also kept her further away from the day-fellows. Despite the distance the grains inside her shrieked at her land being defiled by the day-fellow presence. And Alexnya was right—the grains were also furious at Frere-Jones. They knew what she'd done to her son. The grains knew she hated them and that she would destroy every trace of their existence if it was within her power.

But despite this anger the grains also continued to share Haoquin's memories with her. She saw the birth of their son through Haoquin's eyes. Saw Haoquin and Colton playing chase in the fields. Saw the three of them going for picnics in the deep woods.

All memories from Haoquin's life.

"What the hell are you telling me?" Frere-Jones yelled. But the grains didn't respond.

When Jun unbolted the sod-house's door in the morning, Frere-Jones was meditating under the oak tree in the front yard. Her body was coated in red smears from the countless fairies she'd killed during the night as she ripped apart every one of the red-glowing, grain-infused monstrosities she encountered.

Several chickens pecked at the fairies' remaining grains in the dirt around her.

Jun stepped toward Frere-Jones with the laser pistol in her right hand.

"You okay?" Jun asked.

"Must be. You're still alive."

Jun shivered. Frere-Jones licked her lips before biting her tongue to silence the grains. They were easier to control during the daytime, but the longer the day-fellows stayed on the land the more demanding they would become.

"Are you safe to be around?"

"I can maintain control until you leave," Frere-Jones said. "We'll give Alexnya another dose of medicine after breakfast. That should be enough to enable your family to leave. You can travel well beyond this land before night falls."

"Tak is cooking breakfast," Jun said, gesturing to the sod-house. "Will you join us?"

Frere-Jones snorted at being invited into her own house but nodded and followed Jun in. She was pleased to see Alexnya looking even better than yesterday and sitting at the dinner table eating oatmeal.

"I missed you, Fre," Alexnya said. Frere-Jones suppressed her irritation at the nickname and sat down in the chair next to her family altar.

The stone altar bubbled and snapped, the red sands swarming angrily over the statues of her family. Miya and Tufte stared at the flowing sands as if mesmerized until Takeshi tapped the table beside them so they returned to eating their oatmeal.

"We have to keep an eye on them constantly so they don't touch the altar," Takeshi said. "Did your son try to play with it all the time?"

"Yes," Frere-Jones snapped. "But he was the child of an anchor—touching the altar wouldn't bring death on his family."

Jun and Takeshi stared in shock at Frere-Jones, and Jun's hand edged toward the laser pistol before Frere-Jones sighed. "I apologize. The grains are pushing me even now. It's . . . hard, being around you with them screaming in my mind."

"That's the price of protecting our sacred land," Alexnya said.

Frere-Jones tapped the vials of glowing medicine on the table before her. She knew Alexnya wasn't trying to deliberately provoke her. She remembered how confused she'd felt when she'd come of age and the grains had activated within her, and how a similar confusion almost overwhelmed Haoquin when he'd married into her anchordom. The sooner Alexnya and her family returned to the road the better.

"It must have been difficult when your son became a day-fellow," Jun said, trying to change the subject. "You're fortunate one of our caravans was nearby to take him in before . . ." Jun paused.

"You can say it," Frere-Jones muttered. "The grains would have forced me to kill my son if he'd stayed more than a few days after becoming a day-fellow. But luck had nothing to do with it. I timed Colton's change so a caravan was here for him."

Jun and Takeshi stared at Frere-Jones, who shrugged. She knew she shouldn't tell such truths to people outside her family, but she no longer cared. The grains pounded inside her at the admitted heresy. She wanted to slam her head into the table to silence them.

"Haoquin died when Colton was only twelve," Frere-Jones whispered. "My lifemate had grown up on another land. When he married into my anchordom and accepted my grains, the grains from that other land deactivated. But my grains eventually tired of the . . . unsettling thoughts Haoquin expressed. His ideas for changing the world. So they reactivated his original grains, causing him to need to live on two separate lands to stay healthy. His body almost tore itself apart. There was nothing I could do."

Frere-Jones reached out and rubbed Haoquin's statue on the altar. The grains felt her hate and slid away from her touch. "Haoquin dreamed of a world without grains. He knew that was merely a pipe dream—we both knew it—but the grains decided even a dream without their existence was too much to tolerate."

Frere-Jones flicked at the red grains in the altar's basin, wishing she could throw them all away where they'd never harm another person.

"The grains calculated they didn't need Haoquin anymore since we'd already created a son," Frere-Jones continued. "But I refused to let them have Colton too. I waited until a caravan was on my land then gave Colton a massive overdose of the medicine, almost more than his body could handle. He turned day-fellow and had to leave.

"The anchor system is evil. To decide that a select few can live in one place while everyone else is forced to continually move from land to land . . . death for any unlinked human who stays too long on a land or pollutes or harms that land . . . to force me to enact the grains' arbitrary needs and desires . . . that's nothing but evil."

"But the grains saved the planet," Alexnya said. "I can see some of the old anchors' memories. How the land was nearly destroyed and overrun with people. I can taste the chemicals and hormones and technology. Trees cut down. People dying of blight. There were so many people. Too many for the land to support. Destroying everything they touched . . ."

Alexnya gasped and pushed away from the table, her chair falling backward as she tumbled across the ceramic tiles. She jumped up and ran for the bathroom, where she slammed the door shut.

Frere-Jones sighed as she stared into the shocked faces of the girl's family. "She'll be better once you're on the road," Frere-Jones said. "Keep giving her the medicine twice a day and the grains will soon be completely gone."

"But the memories . . ." Jun began.

"So she'll know why anchors protect their lands. Why those without grains are forced to continually move around."

Takeshi hugged Miya and Tufte, who had jumped into his lap because of the tension in the room. "It's different to be on the receiving end," Takeshi said. "Do you know why our last caravan was destroyed? We were leaving a land a hundred leagues from here when the caravan master's wagon broke an axle. Normally not a problem—most caravans leave early in case of issues like this. But it turned out our caravan master also was smuggling forbidden chemicals and hormones. When the axle broke it stabbed into one of his smuggling tanks and contaminated the land for ten yards on either side of the road.

"We tried cleaning the land. Our caravan master even took responsibility and offered his death for everyone else's lives. But the grains didn't care. You could feel their anger. The ground was almost shaking, the trees and plants whipping madly as if blown by an unknown wind. Then the anchors came—dozens of them, from lands all across the region. They attacked us all night before the grains finally allowed them to calm down. Our wagon was the only one they didn't break into and massacre everyone."

Frere-Jones nodded. If her land became even a slightly bit contaminated the grains would force her to do the same. She picked up the remaining vials of medicine. She held the vials over the altar to encode them with her grain's programming before handing them to Takashi.

"Have her drink another dose then take the remaining vials with you," she told him. "Jun and I will prepare your wagon. You'll leave by noon."

*   *   *

Frere-Jones had spent decades watching day-fellow caravans, but she'd never prepared one of their wagons for travel. Harnessing the horses and securing the wagon's cargo stirred memories of both her own life and those of the anchors who preceded her. How all of them had watched passing day-fellow caravans across thousands of years.

As a child she'd desperately wished she could travel like a day-fellow. See other lands beyond her own.

"Take the northern road through the forest," Frere-Jones told Jun when the wagon and horses were ready. "That's the safest route to avoid irritating the anchors on neighboring lands. Go north and you'll be several lands away before dark."

Jun nodded a silent thanks.

They were still waiting a half-hour later, with Frere-Jones growing increasingly irritated from the grains' demands. "Come on Takashi," she yelled.

"I'll go get him," Jun said, hurrying to the house.

When the family didn't emerge a few minutes later, Frere-Jones cursed and smashed a powered hand into the side of the barn, breaking the inch-thick boards. She stomped into her own house—her house, on her land!—to discover glowing red medicine flowing among broken glass vials on her tile floor. Jun and Takashi stood beside the dinner table pleading with Alexnya but wouldn't go near their daughter.

"Land's shit!" Frere-Jones bellowed. Alexnya stood beside the stone altar, her hands immersed in the flowing red grains.

"She won't let go of the altar," Takashi said. "Should we yank her away?"

"No! Don't touch the grains!" Frere-Jones accessed the grains inside her body, connecting through them with the grains in the altar and across her land. She prayed that Alexnya touching the altar hadn't alerted any nearby anchors. She tasted the forests and plants and animals on her land, felt the nearby anchors going about their duties and work.

But no alarm. There had been no alarm raised. Which was impossible. That could only mean . . .

Frere-Jones screamed as she jumped forward and grabbed Alexnya. She threw the girl across the room, only at the last moment aiming for the sofa so she wouldn't be hurt. Alexnya smashed into the cushions as Jun and Takashi grabbed their youngest kids and ran for the door, Jun again aimed the pistol at Frere-Jones.

Frere-Jones raised her hands as she bent over, panting and trying to stay in control. "Don't shoot," she yelled. "Kill me and your daughter will be stuck here."

"What do you mean?" Jun asked.

"Your daughter should have set off the grains' alarms, especially after taking that much medicine. But she didn't. Why didn't you, Alexnya?"

Alexnya stood up from the sofa, her eyes sparking red light, a growl escaping her snarling lips. For a moment Frere-Jones remembered herself at that age when the grains had first activated in her body. "The grains don't like you," Alexnya whispered. "They changed the altar's coding so the medicine wouldn't remove all of the grains from my body. They promised that if I didn't tell you they'd let my family stay."

"You can't trust the grains," Frere-Jones said. "No day-fellow is ever allowed to stay on a land for more than a few days. That won't change no matter what the grains promise."

Frere-Jones started to say more, but fell silent as she tasted an unsettling tinge in the grains. She felt Alexnya's frustration at travelling from place to place, never settling down long enough to have a home. Frere-Jones also saw the attack which destroyed Alexnya's last caravan. As the anchors shrieked and smashed on the outside of her family's wagon, Alexnya swore she'd never go through this again. That one day she'd find a place to call home.

The grains, Frere-Jones realized, had found a willing partner in this young girl.

"I'm sorry," Alexnya whispered, looking at her parents. "I want to live somewhere. I want a home. The grains said we could all stay."

"The other anchors won't let you be one of us," Frere-Jones stated. "And even if they did, the grains will never let your family stay."

"They promised."

"They lied. The grains only want a new anchor to take my place. They're incapable of caring for your family. They are programmed to protect this land, not to protect unlinked day-fellows without a grain in their bodies."

Frere-Jones glanced again at the altar. She was missing something. If the grains hadn't told her they'd changed the altar's programming to negate the effects of Alexnya's medicine, what else weren't they telling her?

She heard a slight rapping on the kitchen window. Dozens of fairies buzzed outside the glass, their tiny hands tap tapping against the panes like angry snowflakes blowing on the wind.

Framed in the glass, surrounded by the fairies, was a red-tinted face.

Malachi, Chakatie's oldest son.

Frere-Jones ran for the front door, but by the time she opened it Malachi was already running away, nearly gone from sight. She reached out to the grains, trying to power up her body so she could catch the boy, but the grains resisted her, not giving her anywhere near enough to catch him.

Instead, the grains rebutted her in flicks of angry memories. They had a new anchor. They didn't have to obey her any more.

*   *   *

A few weeks after their son had been born, Frere-Jones had woken to find Haoquin standing by the altar, rocking Colton back and forth in his arms in the grains' red-haze light.

"You okay?" she asked sleepily.

"I was thinking about all the previous anchors who raised their kids in this house," Haoquin said. "I bet many of them stood in this very spot and let the grains' glow soothe their babies to sleep."

Frere smiled. "You could ask the grains to share those memories. Sometimes they'll do that, if you ask nicely."

Haoquin snorted. "When I first became an anchor, that's what scared me the most—that the grains spoke to us using memories. I mean, after I'm dead is that what they'll do with my memory of this moment? Use everything I'm experiencing now—love, exhaustion, tenderness, caring—to tell some future anchor that this is how you calm a crying baby? Is that all my memories are good for?"

Frere-Jones hugged her lifemate. "Your memories mean more to me than that. Perhaps they'll mean more to any future anchor who experiences them."

"Maybe," Haoquin said as he and Frere-Jones stared down at their son. "Maybe."

But neither one of them had sounded convinced.

*   *   *

The anchors came for Frere-Jones and the day-fellow family at midnight.

Frere-Jones had finally been able to power up her body after Alexnya ordered the grains to do so. The girl had still been torn, wanting to believe the grains would protect her family, but in the end her parents convinced her the grains would never protect day-fellows. "Have the grains shown you a memory,"

Jun had said, "any memory across the land's thousands of years where they protected a single day-fellow? If they do that, you can believe them. If not . . ."

When the grains hadn't been able show such a memory, Alexnya broke down and cried. She ordered the grains to obey Frere-Jones.

Yet Frere-Jones knew even with her body completely powered up she couldn't fight so many other anchors. She messaged them, saying the day-fellows would leave. The only response was laughter. She said she'd allow another anchor to be selected, if only the day-fellows were allowed to leave safely.

Again, more laughter.

Now, at midnight, the anchors were coming. They ran through the river mists. They ran across her new-plowed sunflower fields, their massive bodies and claws destroying the furrows and scattering soil and seed to the winds. They came from the road, giant feet pounding on the dirt packed by centuries of wagons. The came from the forests, knocking down trees and scattering deer and coyotes before them.

Frere-Jones sat on the sod roof of her home, the laser pistol in her hands. The grains showed her Haoquin's memory of building the illegal weapon with parts acquired from day-fellow smugglers. How proud he'd been. His mother had said the grains wouldn't like the pistol, but Haoquin merely laughed and said if he ever was forced to use the laser the displeasure of the grains would be the least of their worries.

As usual, Haoquin had been correct. Maybe that was why the grains had killed him.

"Here they come," Frere-Jones yelled down the air vent into the house. Jun and Takeshi and Alexnya were inside, Jun holding the knives Frere-Jones had gifted them in case a final defense was needed.

Frere-Jones looked around her. She knew she should give the anchors a warning. She'd known these people all her life. They'd worked together. Had bonds stretching back a hundred generations.

Her land's red fairies buzzed around her, the faces of her ancestors silently pleading with her not to do this. As long as she remained anchor the grains couldn't warn the other anchors. But the grains were outraged at what she planned. A fairy with Haoquin's face flew in front of her eyes, the tiny red body shaking side to side in a silent scream of "No!"

But she knew what the real Haoquin would want. On his last day, as he lay in their bed while the competing grains destroyed each other and his body, he'd told her not to be angry. "Life here was worth it," he'd whispered in her ear as she leaned over him. "Too short, yes. But knowing you made it worthwhile."

Why had the grains waited so long to share his memories with her? If they'd done so years before, maybe she wouldn't have been so angry. Maybe she wouldn't have forced her son into exile from the only land and family he'd known.

Frere-Jones tapped the cord connecting the pistol to her farm's power grid. She aimed at the anchors running toward her. She hated the grains. Hated every memory they spoke.

Burn them all.

The laser lit the land green, the light dazzling through the river mists. The first row of anchors in the sunflower fields flashed and burned, bodies screaming and stenching like spoiled meat over bad flames. Howls of outrage rose from the remaining anchors, who split up to make less obvious targets, but they all still burned bright in Frere-Jones's enhanced vision. She shot two next to the barn, where she heard the day-fellows' horses whinnying in fright. She shot three others on the dirt road. She split one massive anchor in two right before the oak tree in front of her house, the laser also severing the tree's trunk.

She shot every anchor who came near her home. And when the remaining anchors broke ranks and fled, she detached the laser from her power grid and chased after them, using the remaining charge to sear every one of them into char for the coyotes and wolves to feast on.

"Share this memory with the land's future anchors," she told the red fairies as they stared at her in shock. "Share this memory with the whole damn world."

*   *   *

"The laser is potential," Haoquin had told Frere-Jones the night they were married. They lay in bed after making love awkwardly, then excitedly. Afterward, Frere-Jones couldn't help looking at the pistol on the bedside table.

"Potential for what?" she asked.

"To upset the grains. To force them to experience something they've never before considered."

"So you'd burn the land?"

"That would merely set off the grains' anger. No, I'd burn any anchor who tried to harm you or me."

"Then you'd have even more anchors attacking." Frere-Jones had heard stories of day-fellows who'd tried defending themselves with lasers. Eventually the anchors overwhelmed them through sheer numbers.

"Yes, we can't defeat the anchors. There are too many of them, tied to millions of lands around the world. But what if we could use the threat of killing so many anchors to make the grains change?"

"We can't change the grains' programming," Frere-Jones whispered. "That's beyond us."

"But what if we could change the memories they spoke with?"

"What good would that do?"

"If this land only spoke through certain memories—say yours and mine— the grains would be forced to say very different things than if they spoke through the memories of anchors who'd supported their damn work. Over time, it might change everything."

Frere-Jones smiled at that possibility. "So you'd really kill, or threaten to kill, hundreds of anchors merely to force the grains to delete the memories they've stored over the centuries?"

Haoquin sighed. "You're right. I couldn't do that. I guess it's a bad idea."

Frere-Jones had kissed Haoquin, glad he wasn't someone who would do such evil in a silly, misguided attempt to change the world.

*　　*　　*

An hour before morning's song of light and warmth, Chakatie arrived. Frere-Jones sat on the sod roof of her home, the laser pistol in her lap, the smoldering corpses of the other anchors glowing in her land's fields and forests.

She scented Chakatie ten minutes before her mother-in-law walked up to the house. Chakatie had deliberately come from upwind so Frere-Jones would catch the scent. She wasn't surprised by Chakatie's arrival. After killing the anchors Frere-Jones realized she hadn't seen or scented any member of Chakatie's family during the attack.

Chakatie looked nothing like the powerful being she'd been the other night in the forest. She was powered down and tiny and wore a neatly pressed three-piece suit and bowler hat. Instead of claws her hands were manicured and folded over themselves at her waist, as if to show she meant no harm.

Frere-Jones snorted and patted the grass on the roof. "You're welcome to join me, but that suit doesn't look like it's made for sitting on a sod roof."

"It's not." Chakatie jumped up to the other side of the roof. She grinned nervously as Frere-Jones shifted the pistol slightly so it pointed at Chakatie's chest. "My children made me wear this. Said it'd show you I meant no harm since no one in their right mind would fight while wearing such fancy clothes." Chakatie laughed softly. "I think they're worried about you killing me."

Frere-Jones wanted to laugh, which was likely Chakatie's other intent in wearing the suit. Perhaps to catch her off-guard. "And did Malachi also suggest you wear it? Perhaps after he spied on me?"

Chakatie spat. "Malachi did that on his own. I sincerely apologize. To spy on another anchor . . . any punishment you wish against him will be given."

Frere-Jones didn't believe her mother-in-law but accepted the lie as Chakatie's round-about means of apology. "And my punishment for killing dozens of anchors?"

"Ah, that is the question, isn't it?"

Chakatie sat down on the roof, running her fingers through the grass. "Is the girl in the house?" she asked. "The day-fellow anchor?"

"Yes. The grains lied to her. Said her family would be able to stay if she became the new anchor."

"That's why it's difficult for someone who grew up without the grains to become an anchor. You and I, we know the grains' memories don't always tell us the truth. We sort the memories the grains show us. Sift the wheat from the chaff. Your day-fellow girl doesn't know this."

"She will after today. I doubt she'll ever again trust the grains after witnessing this massacre."

"Then she might end up making a good anchor."

Chakatie stretched out on the sod roof, laying on her back as she looked across the sunflower fields. "No anchor with any sense loves the grains. But most anchors also have the sense not to challenge them directly."

"Too late for that. Now what?"

"The grains demand vengeance. You've upset their programmed order."

"How about I simply burn you first?" Frere-Jones said.

"Your choice. My family would, of course, attack. And can you sense the other anchors on their way here from distant lands? The more you kill the more who will come."

Frere-Jones sighed and pointed the laser pistol at the grass. "Funny how your family didn't join in the attack."

"Nothing funny about it. I raised my son, after all. He told me all about his little plans when he was younger. I knew he'd never carry out such evil. That's why I let him build the laser pistol—it satisfied him, and I knew he'd never use it. But you . . . I suppose I should have seen this coming."

Frere-Jones shrugged.

"You know, the grains wanted me to kill Haoquin when he was young, because of his dangerous ideas," Chakatie said. "But I refused to do it. Despite what you may believe, we anchors can still ignore some of the grains' programmed demands."

Frere-Jones knew Chakatie was playing her. Her mother-in-law had probably known exactly what she was doing when she gave Frere-Jones the medicine for Alexnya. With so many anchors killed, Chakatie's children would be able to go to those lands and become master-anchors in their own right.

"I can still kill a lot more anchors, including you, before I'm taken down," Frere-Jones said. "What do you propose to avoid that?"

"Right now you have leverage with the grains," Chakatie said. "They don't want you to kill hundreds of new anchors when they arrive here. So offer them a bargain. Let the day-fellow girl become this land's new anchor. The remaining anchors in the area—meaning my family—won't oppose her."

Frere-Jones looked at her hands. The pistol could easily cut Chakatie in two, but she really didn't want to kill her mother-in-law. "What do I get out of that?"

"Haoquin had some interesting ideas about the grains' use of memories. This might be your only chance to see if what he said could come true."

*   *   *

The day Haoquin died, Frere-Jones and Colton had stood side by side in the cemetery as Chakatie and the other anchors shoveled dirt onto her lifemate's body.

Frere-Jones could still feel the grains in Haoquin's body. Worse, she could feel them already working to isolate many of Haoquin's memories. The grains didn't want his heretical beliefs contaminating the land, so they were locking those memories away. They would never share those memories with anyone, most of all her.

Frere-Jones hugged her son tight. She knew the grains would do the same to her memories when she died. But if she had her way, they'd not be able to use her son. She'd free him one way or another.

And then, maybe, she'd see if Haoquin's plan could work. The plan he'd been too kindly to actually put into action.

*   *   *

They stood in the cemetery where Haoquin and the other anchors of this land were buried. Alexnya and her family stood on one side of the graves while Chakatie stood on the other. The rest of Chakatie's family patrolled the boundaries of Frere-Jones's land, keeping away the other anchors until this ceremony was completed.

Frere-Jones reached out to her land's grains, the laser pistol still in her right hand. The grains shivered and shook, resonating in shock at both what Frere-Jones had done and the dead anchors she'd killed.

Frere-Jones, detaching herself from the grains, walked over to Alexnya and her family. "Good luck to you," she told Alexnya. "You can trust Chakatie's advice. I suggest you listen to her."

Alexnya looked overwhelmed, as if just realizing the life she'd stumbled into. Her family could stay only a few more days before they'd have to travel on. But aside from suggesting Alexnya trust Chakatie, there was no other advice Frere-Jones could give. Alexnya would have to sort through the lands' memories on her own and determine which, if any, could be trusted.

Frere-Jones laughed to herself, knowing whose memories Alexnya would soon be experiencing.

"How can you say our daughter should trust that . . . woman?" Jun asked, outrage almost pouring out of her lips as she glared at Chakatie. "From what you've told me, she caused all this."

"Chakatie didn't trap your daughter," Frere-Jones said. "If anyone did, it was me, by being so stubborn that the grains sought out a new anchor."

"But she took advantage of all this. She played everyone. She . . ."

"Must I really listen to this right before I die?" Frere-Jones asked.

Jun fell silent. She bowed slightly in a mix of respect and mocking.

After speaking with Chakatie and asking her mother-in-law to pass a final message to Colton, Frere-Jones reached out to hold Alexnya's hand. Together they accessed the grains.

"Do as we've agreed," Frere-Jones told the grains. "Chakatie will ensure I hold up my end."

"Do it," Alexnya ordered, added her voice as the land's new anchor.

The grains screamed but, unable to see any other option, complied. Across the land they deleted the memories of every anchor who'd lived before Frere-Jones. The memories flared and shrieked, as if begging Frere-Jones and Alexnya to save them. Then they were gone.

Except for Haoquin's. Frere-Jones dropped the laser pistol and fell to her knees as Haoquin's memories flooded into her. All the memories the grains had copied from his life. All of him.

So many memories. Memories of everything Haoquin had felt and seen and thought and experienced worked their way into Frere-Jones's being. Her mind could barely contain all of him.

As Frere-Jones shook and spasmed on the cold ground, she looked across the new-spring grass. She could taste the grass. Could feel it growing and reaching for the sun.

Haoquin was within her. They now shared one life.

"I missed you Fre," Haoquin whispered. Or maybe Frere-Jones said it to herself. Either way, she smiled.

"Life here was worth it," they whispered to each other. "Too short, yes. But knowing you made it worthwhile."

Frere-Jones and Haoquin saw Chakatie walk up to their body and pick up the laser pistol. Chakatie wiped at her eyes as she nodded, then she shot them in the head.

*   *   *

Alexnya stands silently over Frere-Jones's burned body. The grains are still convulsing, still in chaos, but Frere-Jones's death has calmed them.

Chakatie holds the laser pistol in both hands. Alexnya feels Chakatie's grains powering up her body. A moment later powerful claws rip apart the pistol.

Chakatie throws the broken technology to the ground in disgust. "Your mother is right, you know," she says. "I did manipulate all this. I knew Frere-Jones and my son would cause sparks. But I didn't know all this would happen. I swear on the grains I didn't know."

Alexnya isn't sure if she can trust Chakatie. Frere-Jones said to trust the anchor, but how can she truly know?

Yet Alexnya also understands that once her parents are forced to resume their travels, Chakatie and her family will be the only one for hundreds of leagues around who might support her.

Alexnya wants to scream at this situation. To curse at not knowing what to do. But before she does, she feels a gentle caress in her mind. She tastes memories—memories from Frere-Jones and Haoquin. She sees all the good things Chakatie has done. How Chakatie once cried over a family like hers.

"I think I'll trust you," Alexnya finally says. "Did you really . . . cry over a day-fellow family once?"

Chakatie nods, then waves for Alexnya's parents to follow her to the sod-house to prepare an evening meal for everyone.

Alexnya stays behind and digs the grave for Frere-Jones's body, the grains powering up her body so the shovel digs faster and deeper than she ever could have done before. She places Frere-Jones in the hole and covers her with fresh soil.

As Alexnya stands over the grave, she feels the grains churning in Frere-Jones's body. Feels the grains already beginning to spread the memories of Frere-Jones and Haoquin across the land.

"Thank you, Fre," Alexnya says, bowing to the grave. She then runs to the sod-house to spend time with her family before they're forced to flee.

SOONER OR LATER EVERYTHING FALLS INTO THE SEA

SARAH PINSKER

Sarah Pinsker is the author of the novelette "Our Lady of the Open Road," winner of the Nebula Award in 2016. Her novelette "In Joy, Knowing the Abyss Behind," was the Sturgeon Award winner in 2014 and a Nebula finalist for 2013. Her fiction has been published in magazines including Asimov's, Strange Horizons, Fantasy & Science Fiction, Lightspeed, Daily Science Fiction, Fireside, *and* Uncanny, *and in anthologies including* Long Hidden, Fierce Family, Accessing the Future, *and numerous year's bests. Her stories have been translated into Chinese, Spanish, French, and Italian, among other languages.*

Sarah's first collection, Sooner or Later Everything Falls Into the Sea: Stories *will be published by Small Beer Press in 2019.*

She is also a singer/songwriter with three albums on various independent labels (the third with her rock band, the Stalking Horses) and a fourth forthcoming. She lives in Baltimore, Maryland, and can be found online at sarahpinsker.com and twitter/sarahpinsker.

The rock star washed ashore at high tide. Earlier in the day, Bay had seen something bobbing far out in the water. Remnant of a rowboat, perhaps, or something better. She waited until the tide ebbed, checked her traps and tidal pools among the rocks before walking toward the inlet where debris usually beached.

All kinds of things washed up if Bay waited long enough: not just glass and plastic, but personal trainers and croupiers, entertainment directors and dance teachers. This was the first time Bay recognized the face of the new arrival. She always checked the face first if there was one, just in case, hoping it wasn't Deb.

The rock star had an entire lifeboat to herself, complete with motor, though she'd used up the gas. She'd made it in better shape than many; certainly, in better shape than those with flotation vests but no boats. They arrived in tatters of uniform. Armless, legless, sometimes headless; ragged shark refuse.

"What was that one?" Deb would have asked, if she were there. She'd never paid attention to physical details, wouldn't have recognized a dancer's legs, a chef's scarred hands and arms.

"Nothing anymore," Bay would say of a bad one, putting it on her sled.

The rock star still had all her limbs. She had stayed in the boat. She'd found the stashed water and nutrition bars, easy to tell by the wrappers and bottles strewn around her. From her bloated belly and cracked lips, Bay guessed she had run out a day or two before, maybe tried drinking ocean water. Sunburn glowed through her dark skin. She was still alive.

Deb wasn't there; she couldn't ask questions. If she had been, Bay would have shown her the calloused fingers of the woman's left hand and the thumb of her right.

"How do you know she came off the ships?" Deb would have asked. She'd been skeptical that the ships even existed, couldn't believe that so many people would just pack up and leave their lives. The only proof Bay could have given was these derelict bodies.

*   *   *

Inside the Music: Tell us what happened.

Gabby Robbins: A scavenger woman dragged me from the ocean, pumped water from my lungs, spoke air into me. The old films they show on the ships would call that moment romantic, but it wasn't. I gagged. Only barely managed to roll over to retch in the sand.

She didn't know what a rock star was. It was only when I washed in half-dead, choking seawater that she learned there were such things in the world. Our first attempts at conversation didn't go well. We had no language in common. But I warmed my hands by her fire, and when I saw an instrument hanging on its peg, I tuned it and began to play. That was the first language we spoke between us.

*   *   *

A truth: I don't remember anything between falling off the ship and washing up in this place.

There's a lie embedded in that truth.

Maybe a couple of them.

Another lie I've already told: We did have language in common, the scavenger woman and me.

She did put me on her sled, did take me back to her stone-walled cottage on the cliff above the beach. I warmed myself by her woodstove. She didn't offer me a blanket or anything to replace the thin stage clothes I still wore, so I wrapped my own arms around me and drew my knees in tight, and sat close enough to the stove's open belly that sparks hit me when the logs collapsed inward.

She heated a small pot of soup on the stovetop and poured it into a single bowl without laying a second one out for me. My stomach growled. I didn't remember the last time I'd eaten. I eyed her, eyed the bowl, eyed the pot.

"If you're thinking about whether you could knock me out with the pot and take my food, it's a bad idea. You're taller than me, but you're weaker than you think, and I'm stronger than I look."

"I wouldn't! I was just wondering if maybe you'd let me scrape whatever's left from the pot. Please."

She nodded after a moment. I stood over the stove and ate the few mouthfuls she had left me from the wooden stirring spoon. I tasted potatoes and seaweed, salt and land and ocean. It burned my throat going down; heated from the inside, I felt almost warm.

I looked around the room for the first time. An oar with "Home Sweet Home" burnt into it adorned the wall behind the stove. Some chipped dishes on an upturned plastic milk crate, a wall stacked high with home-canned food, clothing on pegs. A slightly warped-looking classical guitar hung on another peg by a leather strap; if I'd had any strength I'd have gone to investigate it. A double bed piled with blankets. Beside the bed, a nightstand with a framed photo of two women on a hiking trail, and a tall stack of paperback books. I had an urge to walk over and read the titles; my father used to say you could judge a person by the books on their shelves. A stronger urge to dive under the covers on the bed, but I resisted and settled back onto the ground near the stove. My energy went into shivering.

I kept my eyes on the stove, as if I could direct more heat to me with enough concentration. The woman puttered around her cabin. She might have been any age between forty and sixty; her movement was easy, but her skin was weathered and lined, her black hair streaked with gray. After a while, she climbed into bed and turned her back to me. Another moment passed before I realized she intended to leave me there for the night.

"Please, before you go to sleep. Don't let it go out," I said. "The fire."

She didn't turn. "Can't keep it going forever. Fuel has to last all winter."

"It's winter?" I'd lost track of seasons on the ship. The scavenger woman wore two layers, a ragged jeans jacket over a hooded sweatshirt.

"Will be soon enough."

"I'll freeze to death without a fire. Can I pay you to keep it going?"

"What do you have to pay me with?"

"I have an account on the Hollywood Line. A big one." As I said that, I realized I shouldn't have. On multiple levels. Didn't matter if it sounded like a brag or desperation. I was at her mercy, and it wasn't in my interest to come across as if I thought I was any better than her.

She rolled over. "Your money doesn't count for anything off your ships and islands. Nor credit. If you've got paper money, I'm happy to throw it in to keep the fire going a little longer."

I didn't. "I can work it off."

"There's nothing you can work off. Fuel is in finite supply. I use it now, I don't get more, I freeze two months down the line."

"Why did you save me if you're going to let me die?"

"Pulling you from the water made sense. It's your business now whether you live or not."

"Can I borrow something warmer to wear at least? Or a blanket?" I sounded whiny even to my own ears.

She sighed, climbed out of bed, rummaged in a corner, and pulled out a down vest. It had a tear in the back where some stuffing had spilled out, and smelled like brine. I put it on, trying not to scream when the fabric touched my sunburned arms.

"Thank you. I'm truly grateful."

She grunted a response and retreated to her bed again. I tucked my elbows into the vest, my hands into my armpits. It helped a little, though I still shivered. I waited a few minutes, then spoke again. She didn't seem to want to talk, but it kept me warm. Reassured me that I was still here. Awake, alive.

"If I didn't say so already, thank you for pulling me out of the water. My name is Gabby."

"Fitting."

"Are you going to ask me how I ended up in the water?"

"None of my business."

Just as well. Anything I told her would've been made up.

"Do you have a name?" I asked.

"I do, but I don't see much point in sharing it with you."

"Why not?"

"Because I'm going to kill you if you don't shut up and let me sleep."

I shut up.

*   *   *

Inside the Music: Tell us what happened.

Gabby Robbins: I remember getting drunk during a set on the Elizabeth Taylor. *Making out with a bartender in the lifeboat, since neither of us had private bunks. I must have passed out there. I don't know how it ended up adrift.*

*   *   *

I survived the night on the floor but woke with a cough building deep in my chest. At least I didn't have to sing. I followed the scavenger as she went about her morning, like a dog hoping for scraps. Outside, a large picked-over garden spread around two sides of the cottage. The few green plants grew low and ragged. Root vegetables, maybe.

"If you have to piss, there's an outhouse over there," she said, motioning toward a stand of twisted trees.

We made our way down the footpath from her cottage to the beach, a series of switchbacks trod into the cliffside. I was amazed she had managed to tow me up such an incline. Then again, if I'd rolled off the sled and fallen to my death, she probably would've scraped me out of my clothes and left my body to be picked clean by gulls.

"Where are we?" I had managed not to say anything since waking up, not a word since her threat the night before, so I hoped the statute of limitations had expired.

"Forty kilometers from the nearest city, last I checked."

Better than nothing. "When was that?"

"When I walked here."

"And that was?"

"A while ago."

It must have been, given the lived-in look of her cabin and garden. "What city?"

"Portage."

"Portage what?"

"Portage. Population I don't know. Just because you haven't heard of it doesn't make it any less a city." She glanced back at me like I was stupid.

"I mean, what state? Or what country? I don't even know what country this is."

She snorted. "How long were you on that ship?"

"A long time. I didn't really pay attention."

"Too rich to care."

"No! It's not what you think." I didn't know why it mattered what she thought of me, but it did. "I wasn't on the ship because I'm rich. I'm an entertainer. I share a staff bunk with five other people."

"You told me last night you were rich."

I paused to hack and spit over the cliff's edge. "I have money, it's true. But not enough to matter. I'll never be rich enough to be a passenger instead of entertainment. I'll never even afford a private stateroom. So, I spend a little and let the rest build up in my account."

Talking made me cough more. I was thirsty, too, but waited to be offered something to drink.

"What's your name?" I knew I should shut up, but the more uncomfortable I am, the more I talk.

She didn't answer for a minute, so by the time she did, I wasn't even sure if it was the answer to my question at all. "Bay."

"That's your name? It's lovely. Unusual."

"How would you know? You don't even know what country this is. Who are you to say what's unusual here?"

"Good point. Sorry."

"You're lucky we even speak the same language."

"Very."

She pointed at a trickle of water that cut a small path down the cliff wall. "Cup your hands there. It's potable."

"A spring?"

She gave me a look.

"Sorry. Thank you." I did as she said. The water was cold and clear. If there was some bacterium in it that was going to kill me, at least I wouldn't die thirsty.

I showed my gratitude through silence and concentrated on the descent. The path was narrow, just wide enough for the sled she pulled, and the edge crumbled away to nothing. I put my feet where she put hers, squared my shoulders as she did. She drew her sweatshirt hood over her head, another discouragement to conversation.

We made it all the way down to the beach without another question busting through my chapped lips. She left the sled at the foot of the cliff and picked up a blue plastic cooler from behind a rock, the kind with cup holders built into the top. She looked in and frowned, then dumped the whole thing on the rocks. A cascade of water, two small dead fish. I realized those had probably been meant to be her dinner the day before; she had chosen to haul me up the cliff instead.

This section of beach was all broken rock, dotted everywhere with barnacles and snails and seashells. The rocks were wet and slick, the footing treacherous. I fell to my hands several times, slicing them on the tiny snails. Could you catch anything from a snail cut? At least the ship could still get us antibiotics.

"What are we doing?" I asked. "Surely the most interesting things wash out closer to the actual water."

She kept walking, watching where she stepped. She didn't fall. The rusted hull of an old ship jutted from the rocks down into the ocean; I imagined anything inside had long since been picked over. We clambered around it. I fell further behind her, trying to be more careful with my bleeding palms. All that rust, no more tetanus shots.

She slowed, squatted. Peered and poked at something by her feet. As I neared her, I understood. Tidal pools. She dipped the cooler into one, smiled to herself. I was selfishly glad to see the smile. Perhaps she'd be friendlier now.

Instead of following, I took a different path from hers. Peered into other pools. Some tiny fish in the first two, not worth catching, nothing in the third. In the fourth, I found a large crab.

"Bay," I called.

She turned around, annoyance plain on her face. I waved the crab and her expression softened. "Good for you. You get to eat tonight too, with a nice find like that."

She waited for me to catch up with her and put the crab in her cooler with the one decent-sized fish she had found.

"What is it?" I asked.

"A fish. What does it matter what kind?"

"I used to cook. I'm pretty good with fish, but I don't recognize that one. Different fish taste better with different preparations."

"You're welcome to do the cooking if you'd like, but if you need lemon butter and capers, you may want to check the pools closer to the end of the rainbow." She pointed down the beach, then laughed at her own joke.

"I'm only trying to be helpful. You don't need to mock me."

"No, I suppose I don't. You found a crab, so you're not entirely useless."

That was the closest thing to a compliment I supposed I'd get. At least she was speaking to me like a person, not debris that had shown an unfortunate tendency toward speech.

That evening, I pan-fried our catch on the stovetop with a little bit of sea salt. The fish was oily and tasteless, but the crab was good. My hands smelled like fish and ocean and I wished for running water to wash them off. Tried to replace that smell with wood smoke.

After dinner, I looked over at her wall.

"May I?" I asked, pointing at the guitar.

She shrugged. "Dinner and entertainment—I fished the right person out of the sea. Be my guest."

It was an old classical guitar, parlor sized, nylon-stringed. That was the first blessing, since steel strings would surely have corroded in this air. I had no pure pitch to tune to, so had to settle on tuning the strings relative to each other, all relative to the third string because its tuning peg was cracked and useless. Sent up a silent prayer that none of the strings broke, since I was fairly sure Bay would blame me for anything that went wrong in my presence. The result sounded sour, but passable.

"What music do you like?" I asked her.

"Now or then?"

"What's the difference?"

"Then: anything political. Hip-hop, mostly."

I looked down at the little guitar, wondered how to coax hip-hop out of it. "What about now?"

"Now? Anything you play will be the first music I've heard other than my own awful singing in half a dozen years. Play away."

I nodded and looked at the guitar, waiting for it to tell me what it wanted. Fought back my strange sudden shyness. Funny how playing for thousands of people didn't bother me, but I could find myself self-conscious in front of one. "Guitar isn't my instrument, by the way."

"Close enough. You're a bassist."

I looked up, surprised. "How do you know?"

"I'm not stupid. I know who you are."

"Why did you ask my name, then?"

"I didn't. You told it to me."

"Oh, yeah." I was glad I hadn't lied about that particular detail.

"Let's have the concert, then."

I played her a few songs, stuff I never played on the ship.

"Where'd the guitar come from?" I asked when I was done.

An unreadable expression crossed her face. "Where else? It washed up."

I let my fingers keep exploring the neck of the guitar, but turned to her. "So is this what you do full time? Pull stuff from the beach?"

"Pretty much."

"Can you survive on that?"

"The bonuses for finding some stuff can be pretty substantial."

"What stuff?"

"Foil. Plastic. People."

"People?"

"People who've lost their ships."

"You're talking about me?"

"You, others. The ships don't like to lose people, and the people don't like to be separated from their ships. It's a nice change to be able to return someone living for once. I'm sure you'll be happy to get back to where you belong."

"Yes, thank you. How do you alert them?"

"I've got call buttons for the three big shiplines. They send 'copters."

I knew those copters. Sleek, repurposed military machines.

I played for a while longer, so stopping wouldn't seem abrupt, then hung the guitar back on its peg. It kept falling out of tune anyway.

I waited until Bay was asleep before I left, though it took all my willpower not to take off running the second she mentioned the helicopters. I had nothing to pack, so I curled up by the cooling stove and waited for her breathing to slow. I would never have taken her food or clothing—other than the vest—but

I grabbed the guitar from its peg on my way out the door. She wouldn't miss it. The door squealed on its hinges, and I held my breath as I slipped through and closed it behind me.

The clifftop was bright with stars. I scanned the sky for helicopters. Nothing but stars and stars and stars. The ship's lights made it so we barely saw stars at all, a reassurance for all of us from the cities.

I walked with my back to the cliff. The moon gave enough light to reassure me I wasn't about to step off into nothingness if the coastline cut in, but I figured the farther I got from the ocean, the more likely I was to run into trees. Or maybe an abandoned house, if I got lucky. Someplace they wouldn't spot me if they swept overland.

Any hope I had for stealth, I abandoned as I trudged onward. I found an old tar road and decided it had to lead toward something. I walked. The cough that had been building in my chest through the day racked me now.

The farther I went, the more I began to doubt Bay's story. Would the ships bother to send anyone? I was popular enough, but was I worth the fuel it took to come get me? If they thought I had fallen, maybe. If they knew I had lowered the lifeboat deliberately, that I might do it again? Doubtful. Unless they wanted to punish me, or charge me for the boat, though if they docked my account now, I'd never know. And how would Bay have contacted them? She'd said they were in contact, but unless she had a solar charger—well, that seemed possible, actually.

Still, she obviously wanted me gone or she wouldn't have said it. Or was she testing my reaction? Waiting to see if I cheered the news of my rescue?

I wondered what else she had lied about. I hoped I was walking toward the city she had mentioned. I was a fool to think I'd make it to safety anywhere. I had no water, no food, no money. Those words formed a marching song for my feet, syncopated by my cough. No water. No food. No money. No luck.

*   *   *

Bay set out at first light, the moment she realized the guitar had left with the stupid rock star. It wasn't hard to figure out which way she had gone. She was feverish, stupid with the stupidity of someone still used to having things appear when she wanted them. If she really expected to survive, she should have taken more from Bay. Food. A canteen. A hat. Something to trade when she got to the city. It said something good about her character, Bay supposed, down below the blind privilege of her position. If she hadn't taken Debra's guitar, Bay's opinion might have been even more favorable.

*　　*　　*

Inside the Music: Tell us what happened.

Gabby Robbins: My last night on the ship was just like three thousand nights before, up until it wasn't. We played two sets, mostly my stuff, with requests mixed in. Some cokehead in a Hawaiian shirt offered us a thousand credits each to play "My Heart Will Go On" for his lady.

"I'll give you ten thousand credits myself if you don't make us do this," Sheila said when we all leaned in over her kit to consult on whether we could fake our way through it. "That's the one song I promised myself I would never play here."

"What about all the Jimmy Buffet we've had to play?" our guitarist, Kel, asked her. "We've prostituted ourselves already. What difference does it make at this point?"

Sheila ignored Kel. "Dignity, Gab. Please."

I was tired and more than a little drunk. "What does it matter? Let's just play the song. You can mess with the tempo if you want. Swing it, maybe? Ironic cheesy lounge style? In C, since I can't hit those diva notes?"

Sheila looked like she was going to weep as she counted off.

I ran into Hawaiian Shirt and his lady again after the set, when I stepped out on the Oprah deck for air. They were over near the gun turrets, doing the "King of the World" thing, a move that should have been outlawed before anyone got on the ship.

"You know who that is, right?" I looked over to see JP, this bartender I liked: sexy retro-Afro, sexy swimmer's build. It had been a while since we'd hooked up. JP held out a joint.

I took it and said he looked familiar.

"He used to have one of those talk radio shows. He was the first one to suggest the ships, only his idea was religious folks, not just general rich folks. Leave the sinners behind, he said. Founded the Ark line, where all those fundamentalists spend their savings waiting for the sinners to be washed away so they can take the land back. He spent the first two years with them, then announced he was going to go on a pilgrimage to find out what was happening everywhere else. Only, instead of traveling the land like a proper pilgrim, he came on board this ship. He's been here ever since. First time I've seen him at one of your shows, though. I guess he's throwing himself into his new lifestyle."

"Ugh. I remember him now. He boycotted my second album. At least they look happy?"

"Yeah, except that isn't his wife. His wife and kids are still on the Ark waiting for him. Some pilgrim."

The King of the World and his not-wife sauntered off. When the joint was finished, JP melted away as well, leaving me alone with my thoughts until some drunk kids wandered over with a magnum of champagne. I climbed over the railing into the lifeboat to get a moment alone. I could almost pretend the voices were gulls. Listened to the engine's thrum through the hull, the waves lapping far below.

Everyone who wasn't a paying guest—entertainers and staff—had been trained on how to release the lifeboats, and I found myself playing with the controls. How hard would it be to drop it into the water? We couldn't be that far from some shore somewhere. The lifeboats were all equipped with stores of food and water, enough for a handful of people for a few days.

Whatever had been in my last drink must have been some form of liquid stupid. The boat was lowered now, whacking against the side of the enormous ship, and I had to smash the last tie just to keep from being wrecked against it. And then the ship was pulling away, ridiculous and huge, a foolish attempt to save something that had never been worth saving.

I wished I had kissed JP one more time, seeing as how I was probably going to die.

*　　*　　*

Gabby hadn't gotten far at all. By luck, she had found the road in the dark, and by luck had walked in the right direction, but she was lying in the dirt like roadkill now. Bay checked that Deb's guitar hadn't been hurt, then watched for a moment to see if the woman was breathing, which she was, ragged but steady, her forehead hot enough to melt butter, some combination of sunburn and fever.

The woman stirred. "Are you real?" she asked.

"More real than you are," Bay told her.

"I should have kissed JP."

"Seems likely." Bay offered a glass jar of water. "Drink this."

Gabby drank half. "Thank you."

Bay waved it away when the other woman tried to hand it back. "I'm not putting my lips to that again while you're coughing your lungs out. It's yours."

"Thank you again." Gabby held out the guitar. "You probably came for this?"

"You carried it this far, you can keep carrying it. Me, I would have brought the case."

"It had a case?"

"Under the bed. I keep clothes in it."

"I guess at least now you know I didn't go through your things?"

Bay snorted. "Obviously. You're a pretty terrible thief."

"In my defense, I'm not a thief."

"My guitar says otherwise."

Gabby put the guitar on the ground. She struggled to her feet and stood for a wobbly moment before leaning down to pick it up. She looked one way, then the other, as if she couldn't remember where she had come from or where she was going. Bay refrained from gesturing in the right direction. She picked the right way. Bay followed.

"Are you going to ask me why I left?" Even this sick, with all her effort going into putting one foot in front of the other, the rock star couldn't stop talking.

"Wasn't planning on it."

"Why not?"

"Because I've met you before."

"For real? Before the ships?" Gabby looked surprised.

Bay shook her head. "No. Your type. You think you're the first one to wash ashore? To step away from that approximation of life? You're just the first one who made it alive."

"If you don't like the ships, why did you call them to come get me?" Gabby paused. "Or you didn't. You just wanted me to leave. Why?"

"I can barely feed myself. And you aren't the type to be satisfied with that life anyhow. Might as well leave now as later."

"Except I'm probably going to die of this fever because I walked all night in the cold, you psychopath."

Bay shrugged. "That was your choice."

They walked in silence for a while. The rock star was either contemplating her choices or too sick to talk.

"Why?" Bay asked, taking pity.

Gabby whipped her head around. "Why what?"

"Why did you sign up for the ship?"

"It seemed like a good idea at the time."

"Sounds like an epitaph fitting for half the people in this world."

Gabby gave a half smile, then continued. "New York was a mess, and the Gulf states had just tried to secede. The bookers for the Hollywood Line made a persuasive argument for a glamorous life at sea. Everything was so well planned, too. They bought entire island nations to provide food and fuel."

"I'm sure the island nations appreciated that," said Bay.

The other woman gave a wry smile. "I know, right? Fucked up. But they offered good money, and it was obvious no bands would be touring the country for a while.

"At first it was just like any other tour. We played our own stuff. There were women to sleep with, drugs if we wanted them, restaurants and clubs and gyms. All the good parts of touring without the actual travel part. Sleeping in the same bed every night, even if it was still a bunk with my band, like on the bus. But then it didn't stop, and then they started making us take requests, and it started closing in, you know? If there was somebody you wanted to avoid, you couldn't. It was hard to find anyplace to be alone to write or think.

"Then the internet went off completely. We didn't get news from land at all, even when we docked on the islands. They stopped letting us off when we docked. Management said things had gotten real bad here, that there was for real nothing to come back to anymore. The passengers all walked around like they didn't care, like a closed system, and the world was so fucking far away. How was I supposed to write anything when the world was so far away? The entire world might've drowned, and we'd just float around oblivious until we ran out of something that wasn't even important to begin with. Somebody would freak out because there was no more mascara or ecstasy or rosemary, and then all those beautiful people would turn on each other."

"So that's why you jumped?"

Gabby rubbed her head. "Sort of. I guess that also seemed like a good idea at the time."

"What about now?"

"I could've done with a massage when I woke up today, but I'm still alive."

Bay snorted. "You wouldn't have lasted two seconds in a massage with that sunburn."

Gabby looked down at her forearms and winced.

They walked. Gabby was sweating, her eyes bright. Bay slowed her own pace, in an effort to slow the other woman down. "Where are you hurrying to, now that I've told you there's nobody coming after you?"

"You said there was a city out here somewhere. I want to get there before I have to sleep another night on this road. And before I starve."

Bay reached into a jacket pocket. She pulled out a protein bar and offered it to Gabby.

"Where'd you get that? It looks like the ones I ate in the lifeboat."

"It is."

Gabby groaned. "I didn't have to starve those last two days? I could've sworn I looked every place."

"You missed a stash inside the radio console."

"Huh."

They kept walking, footsteps punctuated by Gabby's ragged breath.

"We used to drive out here to picnic on the cliff when my wife and I first got married," Bay said. "There were always turtles trying to cross. We would stop and help them, because there were teenagers around who thought driving over them was a sport. Now if I saw a turtle I'd probably have to think about eating it."

"I've never eaten a turtle."

"Me neither. Haven't seen one in years."

Gabby stopped. "You know, I have no clue when I last saw a turtle. At a zoo? No clue at all. I wonder if they're gone. Funny how you don't realize the last time you see something is going to be the last time."

Bay didn't say anything.

The rock star held Deb's guitar up to her chest, started picking out a repetitive tune as she walked. Same lick over and over, like it was keeping her going, driving her feet. "So when you said you traded things like aluminum foil and people, you were lying to me, right? You don't trade anything."

Bay shook her head. "Nobody to trade with."

"So, you've been here all alone? You said something about your wife."

Bay kicked a stone down the road in front of her, kicked it again when she caught up with it.

The rock star handed her the guitar and dropped to the ground. She took off her left shoe, then peeled the sock off. A huge blister was rising on her big toe. "Fuck."

Bay sighed. "You can use some of the stuffing from your vest to build some space around it."

Gabby bent to pick a seam.

"No need. There's a tear in the back. Anyhow, maybe it's time to stop for the night."

"Sorry. I saw the tear when you first gave me the vest, but I forgot about it. How far have we traveled?"

"Hard to say. We're still on the park road."

"Park road?"

"This is a protected wilderness area. Or it was. Once we hit asphalt, we're halfway there. Then a little farther to a junction. Left at the T used to be vacation homes, but a hurricane took them twenty years ago. Right takes you to the city."

Gabby groaned. She squinted at the setting sun. "Not even halfway."

"But you're still alive, and you're complaining about a blister, not the cough or the sunburn."

"I didn't complain."

"I don't see you walking any farther, either." Bay dropped her knapsack and untied a sleeping bag from the bottom.

"I don't suppose you have two?"

Bay gave Gabby her most withering look. What kind of fool set out on this walk sick and unprepared? Then again, she had been the one who had driven the woman out, too afraid to interact with an actual person instead of the ghosts in her head.

"We'll both fit," she said. "Body heat'll keep us warm, too."

It was warmer than if they hadn't shared, lying back to back squeezed into the sleeping bag. Not as warm as home, if she hadn't set out to follow. The cold still seeped into her. Bay felt every inch of her left side, as if the bones themselves were in contact with the ground. Aware, too, of her back against the other woman, of the fact that she couldn't remember the last time she had come in physical contact with a living person. The heat of Gabby's fever burned through the layers of clothing, but she still shivered.

"Why are you living out there all alone?" Gabby asked.

Bay considered pretending she was asleep, but then she wanted to answer. "I said already we used to picnic out here, my wife and I. We always said this was where we'd spend our old age. I'd get a job as a ranger, we'd live out our days in the ranger's cabin. I pictured having electricity, mind."

She paused. She felt the tension in the other woman's back as she suppressed a cough. "Debra was in California on a business trip when everything started going bad at a faster rate than it'd been going bad before. We never even found out what it was that messed up the electronics. Things just stopped working. We'd been living in a high-rise. I couldn't stay in our building with no heat or water, but we couldn't contact each other, and I wanted to be someplace Debra would find me. So when I didn't hear from her for three months, I packed what I thought I might need into some kid's wagon I found in the lobby and started walking. I knew she'd know to find me out here if she could."

"How bad was it? The cities? We were already on the ship."

"I can only speak for the one I was living in, but it wasn't like those scare movies where everyone turns on one another. People helped each other. We got some electricity up and running again in a couple weeks' time, on a much smaller scale. If anything, I'd say we had more community than we'd ever had. But it didn't feel right for me. I didn't want other people; I wanted Deb."

"They told us people were rioting and looting. Breaking into mansions, moving dozens of people in."

"Would you blame them? Your passengers redirected all the gas to their ships and abandoned perfectly good houses. But again, I can only speak to what I saw, which was folks figuring out the new order and making it work as best they could."

Gabby stayed silent for a while, and Bay started to drift. Then one more question. "Did Debra ever find you? I mean I'm guessing no, but . . ."

"No. Now let me sleep."

*   *   *

Inside the Music: Tell us what happened.

Gabby Robbins: You know what happened. There is no you anymore. No reality television, no celebrity gossip, no music industry. Only an echo playing itself out on the ships and in the heads of those of us who can't quite let it go.

*   *   *

Bay was already out of the sleeping bag when I woke. She sat on a rock playing a simple fingerpicking pattern on her guitar.

"I thought you didn't play," I called to her.

"Never said that. Said I'm a lousy singer, but didn't say anything about playing the guitar. We should get moving. I'd rather get to the city earlier than late."

I stood up and stretched, letting the sleeping bag pool around my feet. The sun had only just risen, low and red. I could hear water lapping on both sides now, beyond a thick growth of brush. I coughed so deep it bent me in two.

"Why are you in a hurry?" I asked when I could speak.

She gave me a look that probably could have killed me at closer range. "Because I didn't bring enough food to feed both of us for much longer, and you didn't bring any. Because I haven't been there in years and I don't know if they shoot strangers who ride in at night."

"Oh." There wasn't much to say to that, but I tried anyway. "So basically, you're putting yourself in danger because I put myself in danger because you made me think I was in danger."

"You put yourself in danger in the first place by jumping off your damn boat."

True. I sat back down on the sleeping bag and inspected my foot. The blister looked awful. I nearly wept as I packed vest-stuffing around it.

I stood again to indicate my readiness, and she walked back over. She handed me the guitar, then shook out the sleeping bag, rolled it and tied it to her pack. She produced two vaguely edible-looking sticks from somewhere on her person. I took the one offered to me.

I sniffed it. "Fish jerky?"

She nodded.

"I really would've starved out here on my own."

"You're welcome."

"Thank you. I mean it. I'd never have guessed I'd have to walk so long without finding anything to eat."

"There's plenty to eat, but you don't know where to look. You could fish if you had gear. You might find another crab. And there are bugs. Berries and plants, too, in better seasons, if you knew what to look for."

As we walked she meandered off the road to show me what was edible. Cattail roots, watercress. Neither tasted fantastic raw, but chewing took time and gave an excuse to walk slower.

"I'm guessing you were a city kid?" she asked.

"Yeah. Grew up in Detroit. Ran away when I was sixteen to Pittsburgh because everyone else ran away to New York. Put together a decent band, got noticed. When you're a good bass player, people take you out. I'd release an album with my band, tour that, then tour with Gaga or Trillium or some flavor of the month."

I realized that was more than she had asked for, but she hadn't told me to shut up yet, so I kept going. "The funny thing about being on a ship with all those celebrities and debutantes is how much attention they need. They throw parties or they stage big collapses and recoveries. They produce documentaries about themselves, upload to the ship entertainment systems. They act as audience for each other, taking turns with their dramas.

"I thought they'd treat me as a peer, but then I realized I was just a hired gun and they all thought they were bigger deals than me. There were a few other entertainers who realized the same thing and dropped down to the working decks to teach rich kids to dance or sing or whatever. I hung onto the idea longer than most that my music still meant something. I still kinda hope so."

A coughing spell turned me inside out.

"That's why you took my guitar?" Bay asked when I stopped gagging.

"Yeah. They must still need music out here, right?"

"I'd like to think so."

I had something else to say, but a change in the landscape up ahead distracted me. Two white towers jutted into the sky, one vertical, the other at a deep curve. "That's a weird looking bridge."

Bay picked up her pace. I limped after her. As we got closer, I saw the bridge wasn't purposefully skewed. The tower on the near end still stood, but the road between the two had crumbled into the water. Heavy cables trailed from the far tower like hair. We walked to the edge, looked down at the concrete bergs below us, then out at the long gap to the other side. Bay sat down, her feet dangling over the edge.

I tried to keep things light. "I didn't realize we were on an island."

"Your grasp of geography hasn't proven to be outstanding."

"How long do you think it's been out?"

"How the hell should I know?" she snapped.

I left her to herself and went exploring. When I returned, the tears that smudged her face looked dry.

"It must've been one of the hurricanes. I haven't been out here in years." Her tone was dry and impersonal again. "Just goes to show, sooner or later everything falls into the sea."

"She didn't give up on you," I said.

"You don't know that."

"No."

I was quiet a minute. Tried to see it all from her eyes. "Anyway, I walked around. You can climb down the embankment. It doesn't look like there's much current. Maybe a mile's swim?"

She looked up at me. "A mile's swim, in clothes, in winter, with a guitar. Then we still have to walk the rest of the way, dripping wet. You're joking."

"I'm not joking. I'm only trying to help."

"There's no way. Not now. Maybe when the water and the air are both warmer."

She was probably right. She'd been right about everything else. I sat down next to her and looked at the twisted tower. I tried to imagine what Detroit or Pittsburgh was like now, if they were all twisted towers and broken bridges, or if newer, better communities had grown, like the one Bay had left.

"I've got a boat," I said. "There's no fuel but you have an oar on your wall. We can line it full of snacks when the weather is better, and come around the coast instead of over land."

"If I don't kill you before then. You talk an awful lot."

"But I can play decent guitar," I said. "And I found a crab once, so I'm not entirely useless."

"Not entirely," she said.

*   *   *

Inside the Music: Tell us what happened.

Gabby Robbins: I was nearly lost, out on the ocean, but somebody rescued me. It's a different life, a smaller life. I'm writing again. People seem to like my new stuff.

*   *   *

Bay took a while getting to her feet. She slung her bag over her shoulder, and waited while Gabby picked up Deb's guitar. She played as they walked back toward Bay's cottage, some little riff Bay didn't recognize. Bay made up her own words to it in her head, about how sooner or later everything falls into the sea, but some things crawl back out again and turn into something new.

THE ORANGERY

BONNIE JO STUFFLEBEAM

Bonnie Jo Stufflebeam's fiction and poetry has appeared in over fifty magazines and anthologies both literary and speculative, including Clarkesworld, Lightspeed, Fantasy & Science Fiction, Fairy Tale Review, and numerous times in Beneath Ceaseless Skies. She has also been a finalist for Selected Short's Stella Kupferberg Memorial Short Story Award. Her audio fiction-jazz collaborative album, Strange Monsters, explored the theme of women living unconventional lives. She's been reprinted in French and Polish, for numerous podcasts, and on io9. She created and coordinates the annual Art & Words Collaborative Show in Fort Worth, Texas.

GUARDIAN

I'd held my position as guardian of the Orangery for twenty years when our first intruder broke his way in through the stone wall.

I walked among the Orangery, watching for roots reaching up from the soil like begging hands. These trees I'd oblige with stream water poured from a basin of pure gold. Then I walked the path with my great pair of shears. From the words of my ancestors, I knew to hold the shears poised at my own heart as I went, so as not to frighten the trees and set them about producing their poison. If a tree wished to be trimmed, she would rattle her branches. I trimmed until she stopped her shaking.

After my rounds I paced the grounds thrice before retiring to my cottage beside the greenhouse to read stories I knew by heart. Little room in the Orangery meant the guardian's library was limited. The books on my shelves I had chosen as a young woman: stories of adventure and romance, stories that left me with a pitted longing. They weren't the books I would have chosen in my middle age. Still, I not only read them but ran my hands along their covers, rooting my fingers in their engraved spines and decorated binding. They'd been bound with the skin of beautiful people, the only skin I'd ever touched. Their pages were formed of delicate reed paper. I was lying back in my reading chair with one hand across the book spread against my chest and the other between my legs when I heard the trees' startled shrieking.

I jumped to my feet and grabbed my spear from the mantle and ran from the cottage through the woods and along the wall until I found the place the intruder had entered: a large swath of stone wall, toppled since I'd last checked it. The wall had never before failed. I made note of the number of strides it had taken for me to reach it and then darted off through the woods, searching for the intruder.

I didn't find him that night, though I searched until my legs throbbed and my eyes ached from squinting in the dark, for though the seasons didn't touch the Orangery, night and day still folded the woods in their embrace. When my legs refused to carry me any longer, I rested against the wall, guarding the break from which I thought any intruder might, having realized the lack of treasures inside the Orangery, escape.

GUIDE

From here you see perhaps only a forest. But come, let's step along the path through the woods, and I'll show you. Do you see? Their shapes, the curve of their trunks? Some were of a flowering age when they changed. These show their differences more keenly: three knots, one for the breasts, two for the hips. No, no, there are no nipples. Trees reproduce by dropping seed.

This one is called Lotis. See there the bronze plaque half-buried in her trunk. She's one of our oldest. Over the years she has swallowed her name, as though she wishes to forget that she ever held a form of skin-and-bone, of blood. Our books tell us that she enjoyed the drink, the drug, the dance. Our books tell us that she loved no man twice.

If you read your guidebooks, you'll find a story of her transformation. You'll find a warning: don't eat of her flowers. The story is a lie. The warning, though, is true. She's here surrounded by those who didn't follow it. See their shapes, too: women, men, and children. They may look the same as our dear Lotis, but they do not flower. If you look closely, you'll see that they are hollow. These are not trees but shells. Besides, the Lotis' blooms are said to taste of your mother's perfume, bitter to the tongue.

I'll give you the real story, if you're ready to hear it. If you prefer to follow your guidebooks, please move up along the trail. You'll find plaques beneath, or inside, each of our Main Attractions. Those who wish to know the world for what it is, please leave your books in this basket here. Listen, then, to the story of Lotis, and follow me and truth along the path.

Rowdy girls are always the first to go. Some men think they can tame them. Lotis' men thought this. She had them once and let them go, no matter how they begged her to marry them beneath the lotus tree in the center of town.

The farm boy was no different. He bred his father's sheep, milked his father's cows, and slaughtered his father's pigs. He tended his mother's apple orchard and harvested her vegetable garden. Lotis found his quaintness endearing when he asked her, with a dip from his waist, to dance. He wasn't terrible to lay, but a rowdy girl only settles when she's good and ready, and Lotis was not, no matter how sorely satisfied she was after their lengthy encounter.

She expected to see him again at the festivals. After all, his farmer father sold his pigs and wool there. Sometimes she bought a leg of tender lamb from his mother to line her empty stomach before coating her throat with wine. She didn't expect to see him standing over her in the grass where she slept one morning after an uneventful evening of lackluster socials. She had gone to the field to take in the shock of sunrise, alone. He straddled her waist, stinking of pig shit. In the distance a donkey brayed five minutes too late.

She wrapped her hand around his ankle and dug her nails into the flesh until it bled. When he jerked his leg away, she struggled to her feet and ran across the grass, down the hill, to the center of town where Apollo played his music and mixed his potions.

"Give me a weapon," she cried. "Priapus has tried to take me."

Apollo looked up from the crafting of his new lyre and sneered. Everyone knew his story: a god on vacation in the world. An immortal who had fallen for the mundanities of mortals. Everyone knew, too, his magic. "I've seen you with Priapus," he said.

"Please. He could be coming this way."

"He's told us all of his intention to marry you. Beneath the lotus tree."

"I don't want to marry him."

"Why not? He's good to his family. He's handsome and healthy. He's said to be good with his spear." Apollo winked. "You're running out of time."

Lotis grabbed his wrist with both her hands and twisted the skin in opposite directions.

"Stop, that hurts," said Apollo, too calmly.

"I won't stop unless you help me."

"Yes, fine." Lotis let go. Apollo's wrists bore the imprint of Lotis' fingers. He uncorked three bottles and poured the contents into a golden bowl. "Drink this."

She gulped the syrup down like wine. Her legs fused into a trunk. Her fingers split and split and split until they were fans of green leaves. Her eyes popped out of her tree-skull and bloomed into the beautiful white flowers of the lotus.

The townspeople were overjoyed at the appearance of another lotus under which to marry. They erected a statue of Priapus beside the tree.

GUARDIAN

I knew him first from his music, the haunting voice that came to me through the air. I followed it until I saw him leaning against one of the trees as though he hadn't given chase all night and still possessed all the energy of a well-rested child. His fingers trespassed in a blur across the strings of his lyre. He'd draped his blue button-down over one shoulder, but his chest was bare. I approached, spear at the ready though I didn't want to pierce him, for doing so would stop his singing, or at least change it irretrievably into a ghastly moan of death.

"Oh, guardian, guardian, where has she gone?" he sang. "I've journeyed long but my girl won't come out to accept her song."

"Who have you come for?" I said, pushing the spear's point into his navel. He didn't have to tell me his name; one of the books I'd brought with me to the Orangery told the tales of old gods and men and names I'd seen etched in our plaques at the bases of our named trees.

"You know who I'm here for."

"I do not. As I understand it, you've had your fill of many women, perhaps half of our named. How am I supposed to tell from the stories which maiden you *really* had your heart set on?" I pushed until a drop of red blood dripped from the button hole; it traveled down the shaved trail and disappeared beneath the waist of his overalls. "Tell me her name and I'll show you her resting place."

"Daphne," he whispered, boring his eyes into mine. He let the lyre fall to the ground. He grasped the point of the spear with both hands and pulled it further into his belly. "I'll die before I leave without her."

I'd dreamt of him as I had dreamt of all men who graced the reed pages in my books, deprived of the company of men for the whole of a life and feverous with curiosity. If only the spear were my hands digging into his flesh, I would pull his stomach out and make of his body a new book. Instead I pulled back my weapon.

"I'll take you to her in the morning," I said. "Until then you'll go to my cabin and wait for me while I mend the mess you made in my wall."

"I don't want to be alone. I'll go with you."

"You'll do no such thing. I know where your Daphne sleeps. Either you go to my cabin and wait until I come back for you, or you taste the point of my spear."

"I don't know the way," he said, but already he bent to gather his lyre into his arms.

"Follow the path," I said.

He hesitated then nodded and turned to follow the path. I watched him walk until I could no longer see him.

"Daphne," I whispered. "Show me where you're hidden."

In the distance I heard her rustling. I walked the path until I came to a grove of stumps with a single laurel queening over the dead. Unlike Lotis, Daphne did not tempt with poison blossoms, but still those trees that dared to drink from her soil perished before her terrible beauty; her virgin innocence sucked too much sustenance. I touched my palm against the rough of her bark.

"It's not a sin not to want the way other women want," I said. Across my chest I could still feel the weight of a book against my skin. I thought of how she'd rejected the man whose skin surely felt as good, or better, than those long-dead books' skins. "It's okay to want, too."

I removed the plaque submerged at her roots, prying it from the place where she had begun to wrap her wood around it. I traveled deeper into the trees until I found one of the nameless, a dwarf of a laurel. I placed the new plaque at her feet, kicking dirt over the name so that Apollo might think it had been there long before he had burst through my wall. I buried her original plaque ten strides from her base. I patched the wall as best I could with spit and stone and dirt until the evening returned and I could no longer see the hole for the darkness behind it. Then I followed the shelter path and found, in my bed, a naked man with both hands drawn beneath his head.

GUIDE

This space here, see, this empty hole where once roots reached deep into the soil, once held a tree with the wounds of a mother upon her bark: a scar near her roots where she tore between the legs. Dryope wasn't like the first we saw. She loved only two men. The first, her husband, had already fathered her child when she stumbled upon Apollo with his lyre. Her husband was good to her; he cooked the meat he hunted, fed the child so that Dryope might claim a moment to sleep or weave or lay with Apollo in their secret glade.

An artist, Apollo had little to offer Dryope when his clothes cloaked his body, but when he removed them he offered her what she could not weave: a pair of eyes that didn't know her in her worst moments. Astride him she was invincible and untouchable, though she did allow him to run his hands across the stretch marks that streaked her hips like constellations. Her husband named the marks; Apollo didn't notice them. When he asked her to leave her husband, she refused.

"What good will that do me?" she said, gathering her clothes. It was time for her to return to her family in the hut they'd built upon land that was once the center of a bustling town, empty now of all but a lotus tree and a crumbling statue of a man with a cock that cast a shadow larger than the statue's height. She and her husband mocked the statue when they were light with drink.

Each time she left Apollo, she told herself it was the last. Then his song called her across the river, and her husband would know the wild look in her eye. He would take the child from her breast and tell her, go, go. Disappear. We'll be here when you return.

The night of her transformation she asked Apollo for a dance. He obliged. He wore the leather she'd brought for him, made by her mother. He allowed her to tie his hands with reeds. When the drizzle had ended, leaving only dew across the grass, she stood to leave but was pulled back into the dirt by an insistent hand.

"You'll stay with me," Apollo said, digging his nails into her wrist.

She wrenched her wrist away. Apollo grabbed her hands. She tried to leave, to roll away, to run, but he wrapped a reed around her wrist, around her feet.

"I'll make you stay."

She squeezed her eyes shut and waited for her life to end, for the devastation of losing control of her body, but she heard only the sound of feet sloshing through mud then nothing. When she opened her eyes, Apollo was gone.

When finally she broke the reeds and ran back to her family, she found her husband's bags gathered, the baby strapped to his chest.

"You should have told me it was him," he said. "I only ever wanted you to be happy."

"I don't want him," she said. "He doesn't know my constellations."

But her husband no longer trusted the words from her mouth, too tainted were they with the spit of a god-man.

Dryope wove until her fingers bled. She sunk her fingers into the place her daughter had first glimpsed the world until she slept. She dreamt until Apollo came for her.

"I don't want you here," she said.

"I don't want to be here. I brought you a gift."

"What is it?"

"To ease your pain."

"I don't want anything you have to give." She pulled a blade from her bedside table. "Leave."

When he went, he left the vial beside the place from which she had pulled the blade.

Hours passed. Days drifted like wayward clouds. One month without her family made of her a waif without the will to hunt on her own. She had asked the gods for freedom and had been granted an excess. She had asked to be looked at and now faced the sorry stone gaze of each villager she passed any time she left her hut. No one helped her. No one spoke her name when she was there.

She drank the syrup. Her branches broke through the thatched roof of her hut. Her roots broke through the stone of the floor, sending cracks like lines drawn to indicate the dreamy shapes of constellations. For years no trees grew around her, until her name had been forgotten and her legend erased. We uncovered it, of course. We uncover all such legends and bring them here to the Orangery where they might live again.

And what of the roots, the empty hole? She did not die in her tree-form. No, she was cured. Yes, there is a cure, or was. There is one man who knew it. One man who brought it here, who thought to use it to fuel his own long-lost desire. But should we name it cure or curse? Who's to say that the trees don't prefer being trees, that the burden of womanhood is too much for some to bear?

You understand. I see the way you touch these trees. There is no coming back from it. There is no escape that erases all the memory from your bones, even when you no longer have bones, even when you no longer have memory. There and back again. I still feel his hands, burned like imprints in my skin.

GUARDIAN

To say I didn't long for him would be a lie, for I ached deep in my belly to feel the prick of that spear. But it could have been any man, any skin so much like the skin of my books but warmer and softer to the touch.

"Come here." Apollo beckoned with one long finger.

I stood beneath the cabin ceiling so low it brushed the top of my head. Cracks in the wall zigzagged like lightning bolts. The trees held this place together while tearing it apart. Through those cracks I glimpsed the limbs of trees poking through, more insistent than a single man's finger.

"I will not," I said, crossing my arms to cover my chest.

"Why not?" Apollo propped himself up on one bent arm. "The looks you've been giving me."

I looked from crack to crack, tree to tree. "Aren't you here for someone in particular?"

He raised a single eyebrow, a pirate villain, a lothario, a lion in man's clothing. The books, at least, had prepared me for men like him, if my lack of contact with them hadn't.

"You'll take me to her? Even without my offering?"

"What else can I do? You've come all this way."

He stood from the bed and slipped on his blue shirt, pulled on his overalls. Through his belt loop he wore a tiny ax. How had I failed to see it before?

"I didn't come a long way," he said. "Don't think I've been missing her my whole life or anything. Had a job near here is all. Thought it'd be silly not to look her up, see how she's been."

"I think you'll find her less than communicative about her life since you." I gathered my shawl to cover as much of my body as I could, to protect against both the cold and the man. "What's your work?" I held the door open for him to pass. He brushed against me as he exited the cabin.

"Lumberjack," he said. "Well, I operate the lumber company."

I stopped and gripped harder the knife at my hilt.

As he turned to me, the shadows fled from his face. "That's not what I'm here for. It's just another strange job for a strange life. To stay in the mortal world, one must play the mortal game."

I loosened the grip but didn't let go. "If you try to hurt her, I'm obligated to slice your throat open."

The man smirked. "Specificity may be your strongest suit. I'll keep your threat in mind." He gestured at the long, dark path before us. "I don't know the way."

"Of course." I stepped before him. I led us past the grove of Dante's suicide trees, men who'd died for love or shame or the numb that gripped so many by the throat. This, too, I knew from books: men were also delicate, some with skin so thin you could tear it if you bit too hard. I longed to tell him of the treasured trees, to point to and tell her story so that she might be known again by someone more than me. It had been years since the Orangery had seen a tourist.

"There are so many," he said as we passed a grove thick as the porridge congealed on my stove. "Why do you women fear men so much that you would rather be tree than give a kiss?"

"I am not a tree," I said. The shadows reached across our path. I waited for them to recede before passing. "And I do not fear you."

"Well, these women feared us. You can't tell me they didn't."

"These are not all the changed women of the world. All forests are filled with them. You think of that next time you steady your ax. The women here are the lucky ones. The poorer women, women of lesser fame, aren't so lucky."

"We use saws now," he said.

I eyed the ax.

"Just for show." He ran his finger along the blade. "See? It's dull."

When we came to the grove where I had christened the new Daphne earlier that evening, I slowed. Would he sense the true Daphne out there, farther along the trail?

"Why have we stopped?" He squared his arms on his hips and glanced about us. "Is it safe to stop here?"

The trees mumbled. I worried that they might release their potent poison and kill us both, but these trees were older, less apt to react to human presence. Besides, the trees of the Orangery had grown fond of me, and I of them. My stomach turned at the thought of my betrayal: to lead such a dangerous creature into their midst. But he couldn't harm them with me there, my hand against the hilt of my blade. My presence was the reason no rabbits bounded along the paths, no insects dared to feast upon the trees' succulent leaves.

"Do you not sense her here?" I said. "We're in her presence as we speak."

Apollo the lumberjack looked madly about, as though his franticness might call her forward from the darkness rather than send her slithering back into it as frightened trees may do.

"No, no," he said. "Which is she? It's been so long."

"Over there." I pointed to the tree with Daphne's plate at her roots.

"How little she has changed." He wrapped his arms around the mislabeled tree, rubbed his cheek upon her, and caressed a low-hanging leaf. "She's better than I remember her."

"Yes, she has flourished here."

"I never intended to take her," he said. "But I wonder if she might be allowed to come if persuaded?"

"You may try, but you will fail."

"Would you like to come with me?" he asked the tree. She didn't speak in return. Likely the warmth of such a stranger did nothing to impress or provoke her. I wanted to laugh with the other trees whose branches began to rustle.

"They speak," he said. "But she doesn't."

"She doesn't."

"What do they say?"

"We don't love our strangers here," I lied. "They ask when you will leave."

"Daphne?" said Apollo. "Perhaps if I sing?" He sang three lines of an ancient song. The trees' branches rustled faster, stronger.

"We best go now," I said. "She's given her answer."

"She has said nothing!"

"Then you must accept that she's forgotten you."

"I won't," he said. He reached into his pocket and pulled from it a vial. I drew my blade and moved forward. But he had turned the vial upside down, the clear liquid already soaked into the dirt at her roots. I couldn't kill him until I knew the consequence of his actions, and any possible remedy.

"What was that?" I asked, for it looked like the very syrup we kept locked away at the Orangery: the changing syrup.

"You know what it was," he said, dropping the glass. "I thought perhaps a second dose would reverse it."

"You know that's not how it works." I dropped my blade but pulled a rope from my deep pocket, the same rope I used sometimes to train the trees' limbs, when they asked to be trained. "Your hands." He obliged me this, allowed me to tie his hands behind his back.

"Worth a shot," he said, his voice shaking. "I can't go on living without her. I've spent all my life looking for her. You must understand what it is to have loved and to have such love taken from you."

"Guardians of the Orangery do not love." I picked up the blade, pressed it again into his flesh. "Walk." I pushed him until he did so, led him back along the trail the way we had come. I didn't expel him from the Orangery in case his syrup wasn't as he had described it. In the morning I would lead him from the Orangery so he would never again find his way back.

I didn't have that chance, for when I returned in the morning to the tree I found there a woman, naked and shivering in the dirt, her eyes still sealed with sleep. I didn't know her by name, and I knew that upon awakening she wouldn't be able to tell me. The women of the trees forgot their names when the bark encased them. Few ever remembered. I bent and brushed the long brown hair from her face. Her blue lips tremored.

"Are you alive?" I asked. She didn't stir until I pressed my fingers to the pulse point at her neck, where a faint beating could be heard beneath the skin. "Apollo, what did you do?"

I carried her limp body in my arms back to the cabin. I fixed a bed of leaves and grass on the floor of the greenhouse and placed her upon it. I went inside my hut to Apollo, who slept on the hard dirt floor where I'd left him after checking his pockets for more of his poison. They were empty.

"What did you find out there?" he said, sitting up to face me. I'd left his hands tied behind his back.

"You know what I found," I said. "Change her back."

"I want to see her."

I knew he would and wanted him to. Would he finally recognize that she was not the woman for whom he had come? I led him to the greenhouse and watched as his lips contorted with understanding.

"This is your doing, then," he said.

"Change her back."

He shrugged his broad shoulders. Though I had imagined the pressure of his lyre, the handle of his ax, looking upon him as he looked lustful upon even this stranger woman, I had nothing but contempt for him. To want a man was not to love him. To want a man was not to give in to him, either.

"I'm bored of you," I said. "Change her back now or I'll gut you."

"You won't," he said. "Because then you won't know where I came upon the syrup, or how to reverse it. Which I will tell you, of course, but I want to see her, the real Daphne. I want to kiss her goodbye."

I shoved him back into my hut and locked the door so that he could not escape. I went into the greenhouse and looked upon the woman, barely breathing in the dirt. She, a woman of the woods, might know better than a Guardian what needed to be done. I breathed breath into her mouth, careful not to place my hands upon her skin. She fluttered to life, gasping and clawing at herself. Her breathing sounded like the rustling of leaves.

"What have you done to me?" She scurried into a corner behind a pot filled with herb seeds. "Take it off." She scratched first at her cheeks then down her torso, her legs, until quick as the swing of an ax lines of blood trailed a map of fear down her body.

"Stop, stop." I rushed to her, pried her hands from herself. There was no escaping skin, except by way of bark. But even then it was still trapped beneath, never gone, as easily accessed as by a syrup poured on the roots. No matter how deep they ran, they could be fooled in an instant. I held her hands too hard, fearful of cracking the fragile bones but more fearful that she might unravel herself on my watch, before I had a chance to know her, the only one of my watch that had ever changed back. For that, and even though it wasn't her choice, I knew her to be strong. One can learn from strong women. "If you kill yourself, we won't have a chance to speak. And I want to speak with you. I will help you, but please don't leave me yet."

She calmed, or at least her body stopped its thrashing, though now it leaked sap from its eyes, and I saw that the blood down her legs was not blood but a red thick as sap.

"What am I?" she said. "What have you made me?"

"I did nothing to you." I let go her hands, which fell to her sides in the dirt. I tore strips from the frost covers that lay along the greenhouse shelves and went about wrapping her from her ankles up her legs. "There. You'll bleed less. You won't scratch beneath them, will you?"

"If not you, then how did I get like this?"

"You were like this once." I squeezed her hand. It was limp in mine. "Do you remember?"

She shook her head, slow at first then more rapidly, until her hair swayed about her shoulders.

"Change me back." She gripped my arm with all her returned strength. "I don't want this."

I fixed her a bed in the dirt and locked her within the greenhouse. "Block this door," I told her. "And let no one but me through."

I walked along the dirt paths until I came upon the true Daphne. I knelt at her roots. There were many reasons I was hesitant to allow the changed Dryope to use the last remaining syrup we had locked away: I didn't want to use our only syrup, the only remnant of a time when women could change should they need to. I didn't want to reach a time when I needed the syrup but couldn't use it. I'd always imagined myself joining the Orangery in the end of my days, when another Guardian came to take over my post. And then, buried, another reason: a fascination I had with her, a loneliness I longed to discard, a desire to know the life of these women from the inside out.

Even for all that, I didn't want, either, to bring the man to his victim, to allow him that which he desired. I'd give up the syrup, that much I knew. I would change her back because it was the right thing to do. That was what she desired, and to give in to the women of the woods was my one and only lot in life.

I laid my palm upon the ridges of her roots.

"You are safe," I said. "I won't bring him here."

GUIDE

And here, my friends, we have our belle of the woods. Please remain calm. Don't touch her, no. Don't speak too loudly. Don't speak her name. She'll go if startled, though it will take you a moment to realize. You'll look where there was tree and see only shadow. That's the way of a virgin. Don't hold hands in her presence. The chaste don't approve of skin on skin.

She, friends, is called Daphne. No longer does she bear her plaque. We only know her by the scar, here, in her breast, where Apollo found her once again and, in his rage, tried to cut her down. The very same man, yes, from the stories. The very same man who burst in through these walls uninvited. I have told you what we do to uninvited guests. We did that to him. So do not touch.

Daphne hated Apollo straightaway upon meeting him, and who could blame her? Daphne the water girl had gone into the woods to fetch a jug for the young sporting kids in town, as was her daily task. She watched the children because she didn't long for her own, because she was impartial enough to their begging mouths not to give in to every whim. She was walking along the path to the winding river that cut through her father's vast swath of land when she came upon Apollo entwined with a woman upon the roots of my own tree. She saw them but passed without comment, for sex didn't bother her but also didn't interest her in any of its forms. She didn't, like her mother, tend a garden. She didn't, like her sister, lie with fools when she ran out of songs to sing.

On her way back up the trail, she found Apollo waiting for her, sprawled nude across the dirt like an egotist. The nameless naked woman was nowhere to be found.

"Beautiful girl," said Apollo. "But so stern. What do you have to be upset about, stern girl? You know they say laughter is the best medicine. You'll find me a funny, funny man."

"Where's that woman who was wrapped around you a moment ago?" Daphne searched the shadows, for she had heard of lover pairs tricking strangers into the woods. "I don't have any money if that's what you're after."

"Don't you worry about her. She had elsewhere to be." He rose and offered her an acorn in his palm. "I don't want to take from you. I want to give."

"I'm in need of nothing." She shifted her water jug from one hip to the other. "Now, if you'll excuse me."

She hadn't been taught to be a rude girl, but she needed a man's excusing like she needed a knife in her eye, so she went on past him without awaiting his reply. He gave none, nor did he shout across the woods to her as she walked away.

Instead, the next day when she woke, she found he had penetrated the only weakness in her walls; her father at their breakfast table sat with the man, sharing the seeds of a pomegranate. Daphne's typically still heart hammered with fear.

"What is he doing here?" she said, gathering her robe around herself. Never before had she felt the need to cover herself in her own kitchen. Never before had she felt the need to run and never look back. She stayed where she stood, however, and her father patted the seat beside him.

"This, Daphne, is the mighty Apollo." He looked to the man. "Forgive her behavior the other evening. She is uninterested in the goings-on of our city and doesn't know the faces of our heroes. That's one of the reasons I love her so. She is her own world."

"I don't know the name Apollo." Unwilling to be inconvenienced, she grabbed a handful of seeds from her father's bowl and shoved them in her mouth. They stained her hands. She wiped the red down the front of her robe.

"Her own little world," her father said again.

Apollo leered at the red where she'd left it. "Yes, I see that. I would still like to offer my hand."

Daphne knew these words; she had known their time might come, though always she had hoped that her father would not ask this of her. She shook her head and backed into the hall.

"You haven't, father," she said.

Her father beamed. "Daphne, dear, aren't you thrilled? The day all girls dream of."

But he knew, didn't he, that she was not most girls, that she hadn't dreamt of it. She had thought she made it clear when, at night, she followed him outside to name the constellations instead of staying in with her mother and sister content to laugh over their baking and coo over the neighborhood children. She had thought it was clear when she didn't attend the dances with her sisters but stayed home to help her father chop wood for their fire, when she asked him to teach her how to make a home all on one's own. Never before had he mentioned a husband. Never before had he mentioned that she would one day have one.

She ran back to her room and escaped through her window. Her robe blew out behind her as she ran. She didn't get far before they found her.

She was married in a private ceremony in their kitchen, where Apollo slipped a ring of wood around her finger. It left splinters in her skin when she tried to remove it. They didn't sleep in the same bed, a courtesy Apollo said he would grant her for their first year of marriage.

"You will love me," he said. "I'm sure of it."

Each night he played one of his famous tunes on his lyre. Each night he replaced the names of other women with hers and sang of her beauty, and when that didn't work he sang of her intelligence, then her kindness. But she was cold toward him.

The men in the local tavern laughed when she entered with Apollo, hand-in-hand, for he asked her each day if she would grant him the pleasure of her flesh, but her fingers laced in his were all she gave. The men at the bar elbowed Apollo for stories of the ice queen's body. "Is her hair down there frosted?" they asked. "Does she make your cock cold?"

"We haven't made love," he told them, proud of this, his latest wickedness. "I haven't touched a woman since we married."

"What point is there to that, then?" said the men. "Ay, well, perhaps she needs another man to warm her up."

Apollo fought the men and won his brawl. He was a brute, after all, even if he didn't look it. They didn't go back to the tavern. At home he grew impatient; he demanded that she bring him things to fill the void the lack of her body left: food, blankets, drink. Sometimes she did. Sometimes she didn't. That she could still say no left her with the last vestige of hope she had in her gut. At night she repeated the word: no, no, no. In the morning she practiced saying it, to everyone, until eventually she no longer visited any family at all.

Like all women in her town, Daphne carried a particular syrup close to her breast. Like all women of her time and place, she had been given this concoction upon her thirteenth birthday. There are some fates, her mother said, better than growing up.

One year of marriage brought Daphne no more fondness for her husband. She felt no despair for her lack of love. Love was a frivolous thing, fine for others but wholly uninteresting to her. Sometimes, in her bed at night, as naïve as we all once were, she considered that her marriage to Apollo might not be the worst fate life could have given her. Other men might have demanded her care instead of her cooking. Other men might have bruised her bodily. Other men might have disallowed her the small pleasures of morning walks, evening sweets, the secret space of her own bedroom.

But he had promised her a year and only a year, and no matter how sweet his treacly song, he was a man of his word.

He came into her room without requesting permission. Daphne sat carving notches into the wood of the desk where she did her sketching; she drew the woods where once she had fetched water, to which she would no longer return for their bad luck. After all, it had been those woods that had brought her Apollo. He touched her face without asking, drawing one long nail along her chin. The point left a red almost-scratch behind. She wished it were a cut deep as death, for then she could hate him. The syrup itched her skin where it lay against it. He kissed her rigid mouth.

When his hands undid the first of her buttons, only then did she stand and go, running through the door of her once-secret-space of a bedroom and then through the front door of a house she hadn't called home no matter how her husband insisted. Along the path she ran until she came to the woods' threshold. As she went, she shed her clothes. A woman of the woods needed no clothes.

At the river she stopped. She closed her fist and pounded the tree where first she had seen Apollo and his lover entwined. Her knuckles bled when she pulled them away. She cradled the vial of syrup in her palm, the way we all did, the way you hold both a blessing and a curse.

"Go ahead and do it," Apollo said, advancing toward her. His voice cracked under the strain of its want. "You all do it. Be like the rest of them. Leave me alone."

Daphne knew that other women might comfort him. Other women might pull him close and pretend to love him to stop the flow of tears from his eyes. But men needed to cry the same as women. She wouldn't comfort him like I tried to comfort him, those days we spent in the woods. She swallowed the syrup in one deep gulp.

GUARDIAN

Though I promised not to bring Apollo back to Daphne, I couldn't control his desire to see her again. I turned and found him standing before me. In his arms Dryope the girl struggled to escape. He held the blade of his lumberjack's ax to her throat. In her hands she held a vial of changing syrup, the very one I kept locked in the curio.

"If you let me take Daphne, I'll let the girl go."

"But your vial is empty." I raised my hands in the air, conceded to victimhood in the name of saving a girl's life. "You have more?"

"I'll take her wood," he said.

"But she'll die. She can't change back if she's dead."

"She'll be better that way. She'll be mine that way."

"And what do you intend to do with this other vial? The one you stole from me?"

"I'll return it." He grinned. "I brought that one for you. I know how failure makes a woman desperate."

I tensed not from anger but from guilt. I didn't want to give Apollo what he wanted, but it seemed I had little choice; Daphne couldn't speak, couldn't beg me to save her. Plus, if I let him go with what he wanted, I had a better chance of coming out alive. If I didn't barter, if I gave nothing, he might kill the girl, kill me, kill Daphne: all of us. I was of a logical mind. Logic told me to take as few chances as possible. With the syrup, I could give the girl back the body she had chosen for herself, all those years ago. Without it, without the woman, we might all be no more than fodder for the swollen earth.

"You may have Daphne," I said. "You have the word of a Guardian of the Orangery."

Apollo let the woman loose. She ran to me, and I pried the syrup from her hands. Better to wait until Apollo had finished his deed. Better to wait until the monsters had gone before I let myself be alone once more.

He didn't speak to Daphne but wrapped both hands tight around the handle of his ax the moment he was near enough. The woman beside me tensed and looked away. I didn't look elsewhere. It was my burden to watch what I didn't stop. In so many years, had the world not changed?

Apollo had claimed himself a lumberjack; what I knew of him, then, was that he, and others like him, had made a profession of hunting wood. And to what end? My hut was strong and warm and contained no wood of which to speak. Though the Orangery had not changed, the world had surely grown around it, Apollo evidence enough of that.

Apollo struck. I uncorked the syrup and advanced upon him. He struggled to yank the dulled ax from wood grown thick with time, one hand pushing against the bark while the other worked at freeing the ax. With my knife, I pinned his hand to the bark. I pulled his head back with his hair and poured the syrup down his throat. He didn't struggle, shocked, I think, to taste a liquid so rancid on the tongue, the bitterest medicine there ever was.

He stumbled from Daphne, roots forming their armor around his feet then up his legs, encasing his cock, his torso, the arm that still held tight to its ax, his face, its mouth hanging wide as though to wish liquid out. His tree was no more gnarled, no less beautiful, than any others in the Orangery.

I left him unmarked.

Without the syrup, I could not help the girl pursue her highest of desires—to change back—but I taught her to read, to write, to care for the trees. The wind outside the Orangery whispered through the cracks in the hurried patching I'd completed for the wall. I'd looked too long at Apollo's naked body. I knew enough to understand that it wasn't the thrill of a monster that so intrigued me but the thrill plain and simple, and if within the Orangery's walls the tides could turn, why could a Guardian not leave her post to pursue a life of which she'd only read?

I went to find a man worthy of my skin, to sate the curiosity of my body. I went to experience stories with a different ending than the trees'. Perhaps, I thought, the women of the wood would like to hear them. Perhaps it would call them forth once more.

GUIDE

And this one, you ask? He was no one: an admirer of Daphne. We don't even celebrate his name.

GUARDIAN

I watched the guide return to the cabin that once was mine, so many years ago. The roof was gone, given way to the sky.

"What happens when it rains?" I asked, stepping out from the shadows.

At first, Dryope did not recognize me. I'd changed, that much was certain. I'd hated and loved. Outside these walls, there was so much love to go with the hate. After a breath, Dryope smiled. "You," she said. She stepped into the light so that I saw her face weathered only slightly by age. "Were you here the whole time?"

"No, no, I heard your tour. I hid behind a woman and her daughter. I've gotten good at blending in." I stood so that I, too, caught the light. Time had not been as kind to me, for I'd lived the kind of life some would be ashamed of. I'd known a hundred men, women too. I'd embraced Dionysus and explored other states of reality. I'd exhausted many of the world's possibilities. I wasn't ashamed. "I'm impressed with the amount of people on your tour. We never had so many. I did tell people about this place, in the hopes that you wouldn't stay too lonely, but I suspect it's your lively storytelling that's drawing them in."

"Thank you," Dryope said.

I motioned up. "You didn't answer my question, about the rain."

"I like the rain," she said.

"Ah." I remembered, then, that before she became human again she had not lived under a roof for over a thousand years. It is strange the things you forget for an instant, as though you could make the world disappear by forgetting it. I smiled to myself; one of my lovers and I used to play that game, forgetting pieces of the world, seeing if we could make them stay gone. We never could. I tried to forget the horrible things that happened to Dryope. But how can you forget things you never knew? "So there has been no relief for you?" I meant the memory of bark, the memory of hands of which she spoke. "I thought you said you didn't remember the skin. But in your tour—"

"I remember." She pursed her lips, a human habit she must have picked up from those who visited the Orangery. "Sometimes I don't know if they're memories I've embellished, or if they're true. But they feel true, when they come at me in nightmares. I never used to have nightmares, before . . ."

"I'm sorry." I stepped forward. "May I?" I held out my palm. She nodded. I grasped her hand. "I've brought you something. I searched for them everywhere. I destroyed them all, except this one." I slipped the vial into her palm. "For you, I thought an exception should be made. After all, I've learned that it is more painful to lose something than to never have known it at all. And I am responsible. I never should have led him to you, never should have offered you in Daphne's place."

She looked down at the vial. Then in one fluid motion she tossed it into the fire at the room's center. The liquid poured into ash.

"Are you back for good?" she said. "Are you here to replace me?" She pursed her lips again. "I don't want to go."

I had intended, yes, to take back my old post. To free Dryope. After all, the Orangery needed someone, for once, who knew the world in all its shades of grey. Too long had the guides told terrible stories and known only the world's terrible truths. Too long had we subjected the trees to their grief retold and nothing more. I had brought with me stories of light to soothe the dark.

But she had thrown the vial into the fire. It had been her choice to stay in her skin, and now it was her choice to remain in the Orangery. Why shouldn't she? I could build a bed of leaves for myself, could even make a new cabin if she did not wish to share. As I had learned outside the Orangery walls, light came in many shapes, including the shape of a companion, a friend to hold your hand and quell your nightmare shaking. I would do this for her, if she wanted me to.

"No," I said. "I'm here to join. Should you wish it."

YOU'LL SURELY DROWN HERE IF YOU STAY

ALYSSA WONG

Alyssa Wong lives in Chapel Hill, NC, and really, really likes crows. Her stories have won the Nebula Award for Best Short Story, the World Fantasy Award for Short Fiction, and the Locus Award for Best Novelette. She was a finalist for the 2016 John W. Campbell Award for Best New Writer, and her fiction has been shortlisted for the Hugo Award, the Bram Stoker Award, and the Shirley Jackson Award. Her work has been published in The Magazine of Fantasy & Science Fiction, Strange Horizons, Nightmare Magazine, Black Static, *and* Tor.com, *among others. Alyssa can be found on Twitter as @crashwong.*

When the desert finally lets you go, naked and stumbling, your body humming with raw power and the song of dead things coiled under your tongue, you find Marisol waiting for you at the edge of the bluffs. She's dressed in long sleeves and a skirt over her boots, her black hair tucked under a hat and a blanket wrapped around her shoulders against the night cold. Madam Lettie's bony horse whuffs at you in the glow of the lantern as you approach.

"You were gone longer than usual," says Marisol. "I got worried."

Human speech is always slow to return on the nights when the desert calls you. You nod in reply.

Marisol sets the lantern down and pulls off her blanket to wrap around you. Most girls her age would flinch away from touching a naked boy's skin, but her fingers brush yours indifferently. She's seen your body as many times as you've seen hers, in all of its pitiful states: bruised and scratched; bramble-bled from running through the thorns with the coyotes; finger-marked by rough hands. "Did you step on any scorpions?"

You turn your head and spit a brown, dusty gob into the dirt. You hope she doesn't notice the fur and tiny bone fragments caught in it. "Who do you take me for?"

A wan grin spreads across her face, and she almost looks like the kid she is—that you both are. "Check 'em anyway."

You glance at Madam Lettie's horse instead of at your battered bare feet. "She'll be furious when she finds out that you took Belle."

"She's always furious," says Marisol. She swings onto the horse, and the animal shivers as you climb up behind her. "Besides. She pretends otherwise, but she knows how you get home every night. She's never raised a hand to me about it."

"Good. If she does, tell me. I don't want you to get in trouble."

"Just hold the lantern," says Marisol. She nudges Belle forward and the three of you turn toward the road leading to the Bisden mines. A few pinpricks of lamplight glimmer along the ridge from the town beyond, and the path snakes through the sand like a pale sidewinder.

The horse's back rolls beneath you like dirt in a goldrusher's pan, and you practice breathing. In, out, with the rhythm of the hooves and Marisol's heartbeat.

"Some of the men from the big mining company out east visited the house while you were gone," Marisol says. "The city folk who rode in on the California-bound train yesterday. They're staying across the street."

Oh. "Which did you have?" you say.

"The tall one. The one with dark brown hair and the Yankee accent. He speaks pretty enough, but he's not . . . kind." She shrugs. "But then, who is to a whore?"

You hold her tighter.

"One of them asked for you."

"For me?" you say. No one notices you, not you, the small and half-feral boy kept in the back to clean the kitchen. *Bless Madam Lettie's heart for taking you in, you poor soul*, with your dead witch-father and propensity to make discarded bones quiver and shake like living things. *Poor souls, both.*

"He looked like some kind of preacher. But there was something off about him." She won't look at you, not while she's guiding the horse back to town, but when you press your face against the back of her neck, strands of hair tickling your cheek, you can feel her breathing relax. "I don't know why, but he reminded me of you."

"How so?"

"I'm not sure," Marisol says. "But the city folk are planning to hold a party at Madam Lettie's in a few days, so he'll probably be back tomorrow with the rest. You can see for yourself then."

You've witnessed a few parties at Madam Lettie's, and mostly that means a rough night for Marisol and the rest of the girls at the brothel. Madam Lettie will probably have you attend the guests, too. Just thinking about it makes you wince.

The town is quiet, the sound of Belle's hooves muffled against the sand. Madam Lettie's is the only building with candles still burning in the windows, and the empty, boarded up buildings littering the stretch remind you of when the town was still lively, before the silver dried up, before the desert's call grew too loud for you to ignore.

Marisol helps you up the stairs, past the bar, and together you stumble into her room. It stinks of sweat and musk, but probably no worse than you do. The two of you collapse into Marisol's bed. It's barely big enough for one person and your own cot is down the hall, but everything in your body aches, and Marisol feels so human against your bones. You need that right now.

"I saw my pa tonight," you say into Marisol's hair. Her dark braids smell like smoke, and you bury your face into them, just behind her ear. "Walking among the brush with the rest of the dead."

"I'm sorry."

"I didn't find your folks, though. I heard their voices, but I couldn't dig a path deeper into the mine." You'd torn your hands to pieces, ripped the skin and flesh down to the bone, and the desert had built you back out of sand and briars, then pushed you rudely away from the entrance to the collapsed mineshaft. The wandering skeletons of slain cattle and men had stopped their nighttime shambling to watch through ant-eaten eyes. *Stay away from this, child.*

She sucks in a breath. "If you found them, could you bring them back?"

You close your eyes. "No. Not like you want. I could make their bodies move, but it wouldn't be real."

She nods and holds your hand tight. It's a conversation you've had a few times, ever since the desert started pulling you away from Madam Lettie's every night and you started being able to coax dead things into dancing for you. This time, Marisol says, very softly, "Sometimes I wonder if that would be enough, just seeing them again."

It wouldn't, but you don't need to tell her that. Her grip on your hand means that she knows.

*   *   *

One of the company men appears on the doorstep in the morning, black hair slicked away from his naked face, too young and too nervous to be standing in front of a saloon-turned-cathouse in broad daylight. Madam Lettie, who is lean and tough like rawhide, lets him in, and as they pace the ground floor and talk about plans for Saturday night, you and Marisol sneak peeks from behind the kitchen door.

"That's not the preacher man, is it?" you say. Marisol shakes her head. She's helping you with laundry today, and the filthy sheets bunch up between you, muffling the sounds of your bodies moving.

"I figured it out," she says, "the preacher man's strangeness. He walked like his feet didn't touch the ground, and he stank. God, he was foul."

"You've said the same about me," you say. And it's true; usually you're so much dirt that you could grow plants in the creases of your arms and fingers, if the sullen clouds over Bisden ever gave water. But when she glances at you, there's no humor in her eyes.

"Ellis, I'm telling you. That man reeked like a body left bloating in the sun at high noon. I never smelled something so bad in my life, even from across the room."

The familiarity of it builds a sense of relief and dread in you. Almost every one of the customers Madam Lettie demanded you take had said something similar. They'd never lasted long; the last rancher who'd slipped his hands into your trousers had bitten your neck, then turned and vomited off the edge of the bed.

Lettie had kept his money and made you clean the floor, which you had done patiently, without complaint. By then it had become a system between you two, and you've seen and done worse beneath this roof. Though she cannot stop you from wandering the desert at night with the dead things, just as she could not stop your father before you, she can at least turn a profit off of your peculiarities.

The saloon doors swing open and a group of men walk in. The one at the front is immaculate and fair-skinned, like he's never spent a day sweating under the sun. His pale blond hair is combed back in a smooth wave, and he walks with the easy confidence of a wealthy man. Behind him is the tallest man you've ever seen, a gaunt, bent figure in priest's robes. A dizzying rush of power—the call of the desert, the urge to shed your clothes and run with the coyotes through the brush, to dig up the dead to dance with—hits you down to your bones.

The preacher man turns his head and looks straight at you, grinning past the bar with empty eyes.

Marisol grabs your hand so tight it hurts. "Stop that," she says, quiet and sharp. "You're doing it again."

Harriet, the girl on kitchen duty today, is backing away from the sink, knife held high in shaking hands. The sound of bones rattling against metal fills your ears, and you turn to look; the chicken she'd been preparing for dinner staggers back to its feet, half-skinned, half-butchered. Its flesh hangs in open, swaying flaps. The discarded pile of plucked feathers begins to swirl around it like an obscene snowfall.

"Witchcraft," Harriet whispers. She's new; she's never seen you do this before. The rest of the girls have some inkling of your strangeness; they cross themselves when they pass you, and they stay well away from you at night, when the dust in your skin begins to prickle with electrifying power.

"*Stop that*," Marisol snaps, at her, at you, at both of you. "Ellis, breathe. Bring it down."

You can feel each movement the dead chicken takes, your blood pounding in time with its footsteps.

"Ellis!"

You focus, breathe out, and force your fists to unclench. The chicken's headless neck whips toward you, snakelike, its ragged circle of severed bone and muscle gleaming at you like a malevolent eye. Its toenails rasp against the sink. *Calm down*, you think, and it sways, sinking to its knees. *Go back to sleep.*

"What is going on here?" Madam Lettie demands from the kitchen door. Her body fills the entrance, arms outstretched and resting on the doorframe to keep anyone from coming in behind her. At her back are the company men, the pale one who looks like a prince and his nervous, dark-haired retainer. And the preacher man, gaunt and grinning. He nods at you the way a man would a lady, as if he'd just doffed his hat.

The desert's voice *screams* through your body, an unfiltered torrent of power tearing at you like the most vicious of dust storms. Any control you have over the bird evaporates in its wake. The chicken launches itself from the sink—no feathers, no gravity, no sense but magic to keep it aloft—and flies at Madam Lettie, talons extended. She screams and beats it away. The company men behind her are shouting, and there is blood and meat everywhere. You barely hear Marisol yell your name before you're out the back door, running blind and fast, back towards the bluffs. *Come*, the desert sings, *come home my son*, and you scarcely make it past the town's border before your human form falls away and you are wild, uncontainable, raw, free.

*　　*　　*

Time passes differently for you when you aren't human. Animals operate on cycles of eat-sleep-hide-stalk, and although you are not quite an animal like this, you've found that the land, which beats in your blood, operates on similar principles. Cycles of heat-burn-cool-dark, the wind blowing balefully over the baked, cracked earth. Now is heat-burn, and though the ground sears your feet, you barely notice.

Your father's grave is marked by a pair of yucca trees, their straggly branches clawing toward the heavens. There is no tombstone. A cluster of scorched stones lie scattered at the feet of the trees, marred by some mysterious immolation, and the coyotes have taken to leaving small gifts of bones there as well.

You pace before the grave, listening for your mother's voice. Her sighs are in the scuttle of desert rats in their hiding holes, the scratch-scratch of burrowing owls' claws against the dirt as they run, stick-legged, chasing the shade. She's called you here for a reason, you're sure, but in this form you have no voice with which to answer her, and so you must wait.

Instead of the desert's comforting murmur, the words of your father's favorite lullaby trickle down around you, sung in a raspy human voice:

"Shake, shake, yucca tree,
"Rain and silver over me—"

All of the animal bones lying on his grave begin to tremble, shivering and crying *clack-clack clack*. Dread bites you deep in the stomach, and you snarl with all of your mouths, the sand swirling at your feet.

"Stormclouds, gather in the sky,
"Mockingbird and quail, fly;
"My love, my love, come haste away!
"You'll surely drown here if you stay."

The bones on the ground snap together into a single line pointing to the trunk of the biggest yucca. High above you perches the preacher man, contorted into a shape with his knees raised to his ears. His black clothing seems to glimmer in the heat, and the way his neck arcs makes him look like a giant vulture, begrudgingly fitted into human form. His shadow stretches long and thin across the ground like a single, accusing finger.

"I was the one who taught him that song, you know." The preacher man blinks at you and smiles again. "A prayer to bring down the rain. And this town could use some resurrection, couldn't it?"

The branch he's sitting on doesn't look strong enough to hold a man of his size, but that doesn't bother the preacher man. In a blink, he's gone from the tree, and in another blink, he's standing over you, hunched shoulders blocking out the moonlight. The moon, you realize, is out, a pale sliver cutting the night sky.

Marisol is right. The preacher man smells like death.

"You truly are the spitting image of him," he murmurs. "I suppose he was your father, wasn't he. You have the same hair, the color of the clay deep in the earth. And the same talent for making sleeping things rise up when they shouldn't." The preacher man cocks his head, adjusting his wide-brimmed hat. "I taught him that, too. He was mine before he came to seek his fortune out west, with all the rest of his brothers. Before he turned his back on me for my sister."

The desert hisses in you, and you can feel your body humming with her rage, her resentment, her regret. Coyotes slink out of the darkness to flank you, their eyes glinting like rough-cut gems. But the preacher man just laughs, his mouth too wide.

"Twice-blessed, twice-cursed. You got my gift, and hers." The preacher man leans in, his dry, fetid breath ghosting across your face. "But I didn't come out here just to scare you. There is a storm brewing, little one. Something bigger than you can understand, brought here by the men who came on the train."

That gives the desert pause and she coils in you like a waiting snake. Your heart is beating so fast that if you were still human, you would worry about passing out. But before you can try to force words out, to ask him what he means, a voice rings across the plain.

"Ellis?"

There's a small figure in the distance, one arm raised to shield their eyes. It's Marisol, her bandana tied around her face, pulled over her nose to protect her from the dust. No horse this time; she must have run after you on foot.

No, no, you don't want her to see you like this. Your dust storm kicks up into a twisting column, sending howling gusts to buffet her slight form. Marisol staggers back.

"Dammit, Ellis! Stop!" You can barely hear her over the storm, and the preacher man chuckles.

"What a loyal friend. But remember, child—bad things happen to men who marry the desert. Don't forget what they did to your father, out on your mother's territory, when they thought no one could see." The preacher man touches your forehead with one long, thin hand, and his fingers are stiff and ice cold. "People fear what they don't understand. That's why, no matter what you choose, you will always end up alone."

"Ellis!" Marisol is struggling, fighting her way through the blinding gale. When you glance back, the preacher man has vanished. "Ellis, please, get a hold of yourself!"

The power roars through your veins still, but with the preacher man gone, so is some of the intense pressure in your head. *No*, you think, tamping it down forcefully. If he is right, then this power is yours—a gift from your mother and from your father, to do with as you please. You *will* make it obey.

And for the first time in your life, for the first time since your father died and the desert began to cast its madness on you in his stead, you can feel your mother's power bend to your will, into a shape you can control. You clench your fist, and the winds die down to a quiet whisper. At the same time, you search back through yourself for the human frame that feels familiar to you, a boy with a small, bony body and earth-dark skin. A shape to fit your own power into.

No sooner have you slipped back into your own body than Marisol's arms are around you, clutching you tight. "Lord. I thought I'd lost you."

You sag into her embrace, feeling drained but so full. You've never come back to yourself like this before, not until your mother was ready to let you go. "I thought so too," you murmur against her cheek. "But I'm here. I'm not leaving."

"Chrissakes, I'm always cleaning up your messes." The bite in her voice makes you flinch, but her arms are gentle around you. Her footprints have been wiped away behind her, but even the wind can't scour away the deep, sharp divots her heels carved out of the ground as she fought her way to you.

"I'm sorry," you say. God, you love her so much. And not the way so many men desire women; you've never felt that, for anyone, in all your life. But Marisol has never touched you that way, and the warmth of her body here, now, is more than enough.

Still, the preacher man's words ring in your ears. *You will always end up alone.*

"It's all right." She begins to tug you away, back toward the direction of the town. "I'm used to it by now."

"Wait." You hold her hand, and she looks back at you, her braids framed in the scant light. "Marisol . . . you saw me. Like that."

"Yes."

You suck in a breath. "Weren't you scared?"

Her grip on your hand tightens. "I've seen worse." And she has; you both have, from the cave-in that orphaned the both of you, in different ways, to the haunted look in her eyes as you help her tighten her corset strings every evening, her hand shaking as she unstoppers the tiny bottle of laudanum she keeps behind the vanity mirror.

But she has never seen you as desert-wild as you were tonight, a mad creature stripped down to the bone. And there is some comfort in knowing that she has witnessed you, and that she can still look at you without turning her face away.

"Let's go back," Marisol says, very gently. She doesn't say *home*, and you're grateful for that.

*   *   *

Madam Lettie's hand cracks hard against your face. "Where have you been?" she hisses. You don't answer her—she knows already where you've been, you smell like the coyotes and animal piss and dried blood—and she hits you again. "I told you not to run off like that. You shamed me in front of our guests, fleeing past them like some mad, filthy creature. Thank the Lord they still want to use the saloon on Saturday." Lettie wipes her hand on her skirt like she's touched the most disgusting thing she's ever seen. You remember the times, when you were little and your father was still alive, when she used to touch your face with kind, gentle hands. When she held you because she wanted to, not because she had to. You remember the soft look in her eyes. You remember when she still used your name.

You think she might have loved you, once, before she learned to fear you.

"Now, now, Lettie." She starts—it seems she hadn't heard the two company men walk up behind her. It's the pale, princely one and his nervous, dark-haired companion. You wonder, briefly, if the latter is the one who had spent that first night with Marisol. The princely man has a cultured accent; you can tell by the way Madam Lettie straightens her shoulders unconsciously when he speaks to her. "It's quite all right. I don't think we've had proper introductions, though." He looks straight at you, not through you the way so many people do. "My name is William Lacombe. And your name is?"

Madam Lettie's lips purse. "The girls call him Ellis."

He barely looks at her. "Are you Ellis, then?"

"Yes," you say, very quietly. The preacher man is not with them, and you can't sense his presence any more. You're not fool enough to think he's gone, though.

William's gaze travels to Marisol, who is standing silently behind you, and stops. "And the brave girl who ran out after our new friend. Who might you be?"

"Marisol," she says. William reaches out and takes her hand; then he brings it to his lips and kisses the back of it. Madam Lettie's expression goes sour enough to pickle a jar of vegetables. William's companion's brow tightens.

"Marisol." He says her name the way the desert says yours, like the heat crackling across the rocks. *Marisol.* Heat crackles across your face, too, at the sound of it in his mouth. "A pleasure to make your acquaintance. Has Lettie told you why I'm here?"

"No, sir." She withdraws her hand, uncertainty flickering through her eyes, and takes a step back. William only smiles and straightens up, looking from Marisol to you.

"Well, the Lacombe Mining Company owns the land that this town is built on. We developed the mine just outside the bluffs. It took a few months to hear of the tragic news of the collapsed shaft—so many good men were lost, and for that, I offer my deepest condolences." His eyes look sad, and he holds his hat to his chest. This gesture makes you trust him exactly as much as you did before, if not less. "Of course, the vein of silver was blocked off as well. Samuel—my companion here—and I have been sent to evaluate the damages to the mine and draw up the appropriate compensation for the families of the lost miners."

"When did the fits start?" Samuel says abruptly, staring at you. It seems he isn't one for pleasantries. "The thing with the bones."

"The boy's done this since his father died." Madam Lettie won't even say his name, for all he'd adored her. You'd adored her too, then, even if she was your father's second wife.

"Is he yours?"

"Heavens, no. He was his father's child and came to me as such."

William coughs and shoots Samuel a sharp glance. "We've never seen anything like this out east. Is this a common . . . phenomenon in your town?"

"I hear you burn your witches out east," says Madam Lettie. You stare at the floor and try to disappear. The place where she slapped you aches, a sensation that won't go away, and your heart feels like it's been scratched deep by acacia thorns. "No, he's the only one, since his father died. Small mercies. In spite of his bedevilments, I've kept him under my roof ever since."

"I see." A hand slips under your chin to tilt your face up, and you find yourself looking into William's eyes. "Ellis, it seems you have a rare and unique gift. It may well be devils' work, but I am a God-fearing man who has seen many things, and I have no fear of you. I would like you to accompany us to survey the mine tomorrow morning."

"Sirs, that would be a terrible inconvenience—"

"We can compensate you for his time, of course."

"He doesn't have a horse," says Madam Lettie. Her fists are knotted in her skirt, and there is something in her voice—a tinge of panic, perhaps—that reminds you of Marisol. It makes you think again. Maybe it's your imagination, but you haven't heard her talk about you like this since . . . well. "It's a dangerous area, gentlemen. Surely you would be better served by taking some of the men displaced by the cave-in. They have their own firearms as well."

"We have our own men. What we don't have is someone who can talk to the dead." Your breath catches in your throat. He had seen you, after all. Out of the corner of your vision, Marisol looks scared as well, her shoulders tense like she's ready to grab you and run.

William releases your face. "We ride at dawn. Pack accordingly, Ellis."

"You can't take him." To your surprise, it's not Marisol who says this, but Madam Lettie, stepping between the two of you. "I won't allow it."

William turns a beautiful smile on her. "My dear Lettie, it isn't a request."

As he sweeps out the doors and into the night, Samuel stalking at his heels, you realize that William is humming something under his breath. It takes you a moment to recognize that it is your father's song.

*   *   *

You leave the town on a borrowed horse as the sun begins to stretch over the horizon, Marisol's stained red bandana wrapped around your throat. Marisol is up to see you off, her shawl wrapped around her to protect her from the cold night.

"Don't do anything stupid," she says as you ready your horse, her voice pitched low enough to carry to your ears alone. "If you see any of those walking things, gallop the hell out of there. These city folk be damned."

She is so fierce, such a survivor, your Marisol. Each of you is the other's only friend, and so much more. You open your mouth to tell her how you feel, but what comes out instead is, "The prince can't take his eyes off of you. This could be your ticket out, Marisol."

She kisses your cheek so she doesn't have to look at your face, and that's how you know that she knows, too. William, with his money and his fondness for her. With his life a cross-continental train ride away from this terrible, dying town, away from the saloons where tiny bottles are hidden behind mirrors and men with rough hands prowl the corridors, some new place where a person like you or Marisol could start over.

When Marisol pulls back, her dark curls tickling your cheek, her eyes are hard. "Don't pin your hopes on dreams. Just get back to me in one piece, Ellis."

You kiss her cheek and swing up onto the horse. "I will." *I won't leave you alone.*

"Come, boy," orders Samuel. He and the rest of the company men are already mounted and ready to go, with William at the head of the party. All of them are cloaked in ponchos or jackets to ward off the sun, when it arrives. There is no sign of the preacher man.

Obedient, you follow, the coyotes howling in your head, your head down and hands tight on the reins. You don't look back at Marisol, but you can feel her growing smaller and smaller in the distance, the distance of the land between you stretching with each new step.

The company men ride all day with little conversation, and the sun rises in a slow arc, glaring overhead like a malignant eye. It's hard to stay on the horse; you don't have much practice riding, and the horse is fidgety, as if it can smell the feralness on you.

After last night, your grip on your wild, brittle, real self is firmer, but being away from town and heading into the heartland of your mother's territory slowly erodes your self-control. At Madam Lettie's, you drift like a ghost through the halls, sweeping floors, cooking meals, disappearing into the shadows. But here, as the mountains cup the sky with deep brown hands, the call to bound away, howling, with the coyotes in the brush becomes almost unbearable. Your skin itches, as if your clothes are too tight, and you ache to be among the yucca and wild honeysuckle, the fields of bones where the mesas rise in strange bestial shapes from the flat ground.

The company men have few words for you, although Samuel keeps a distrustful eye on you, always placing himself between your horse and William's. William, as gracious as he'd been in town, seems to have retreated into himself, watching the horizon silently.

The first of the dead things stumbles across your path when your party is a few miles away from the mine. It looks like the corpse of a bull, an unlucky casualty of a careless, ambitious rustler, judging by the bullet holes punched in its ragged hide. The men pull up short, and Samuel hauls your horse up to the front, your reins fisted in his hand. The bull stares at you both with ponderous, sightless eyes and paws the ground.

"Can you stop it?" demands Samuel. Behind him, the men murmur among themselves. *Cursed* and *possessed* and *devil work* catch your ears.

"I don't know," you murmur.

"You best figure it out fast," says Samuel, and he's right; the dead bull, mostly bones and empty skin, has thrown its head down, ready to charge. It has no lungs, no voice, and its silence is unnerving. "Guns aren't going to help against something like that."

You swallow and focus. The desert's power curls in your palm, the way it had behaved for you the night before, but it feels jagged, uneven. Still, you hold out your hand. *Stop.*

The animal skeleton quivers and lifts its head tentatively. Then it takes a step toward you. Then another, and another, until it breaks into a gallop. The horses behind you begin to panic, and so do their riders.

"Kill it!" hisses Samuel. Sweat beads his dark brow. "Dammit, boy, you're the only one who can put it down!"

"Ellis!" shouts William. "Do it!"

"I can't!" you cry. *Stop! Stop!* But it's not listening. You've never taken a dead thing apart before, only made them come together, and then only by accident. And then William is beside you, gripping your shoulder. Power spikes through you—

Shake, shake, silver and rain over me—

—and the desert, your mother, screams through you. Lightning strikes through your vision, and when you blink, gasping for breath, there are visible threads of power running through the undead animal, bright as silver. You close your fist and *pull* on those strings. *STOP.*

The bull stops in its tracks, frozen, only a few yards from you. And then it spasms and collapses into a heap of bones and sun-weathered skin.

There is a moment of utter stillness. And then William laughs, clapping you hard on the shoulder. Your concentration shatters, and you fight to keep your power, your human shape, contained. "Well done!"

Your head is full of the screams of dying cattle, your nose the acrid scent of gunpowder, and you sway on your horse, trying to hold on.

The rest of the men stay away from you, huddling together. Only Samuel rides up to you and William, reining his horse in as close as he can get.

"What were you thinking?" he snaps. But he's not asking you, he's asking William, who just grins. "You could have gotten yourself killed!"

You realize it then. He looks at William the way you look at Marisol. He looks at William like he would do anything for him, even die, unquestioning, for him, his name on his lips.

"It worked, Sam," says William. He sounds giddy. "He took it apart. Did you see that?" He turns to you almost feverishly. "If he can wake the dead, why can't he put them back to sleep? I knew it, I was right!" His hand is still on your shoulder, but you have the feeling that, as he stares into your face, he's looking through you. "Ellis, you're our chance to get to the mine safely. That's why we need you."

"One time isn't a pattern," says Samuel. "It's not safe. And the boy looks like he's about to fall over. Assuming this . . . witchcraft works again, how long can he keep this up?"

Witchcraft. You swallow past the knot in your throat as William and Samuel argue in low voices. *Witchcraft* is what got your father killed. His songs to bring down the rain and his nighttime journeys to visit your mother, to worship her on her soil.

People fear what they don't understand.

A flask bumps your hand, and you find Samuel looking at you with dark eyes. Behind him, William has galloped to join the rest of the men, waving them in. "Drink," Samuel says quietly. "You're parched, aren't you."

You take his flask uncertainly. But the water is good, tinny and warm on your tongue.

"Can you get us to the mine?" he asks. He lets you drink as much as you want, and you appreciate that small kindness.

"I don't know," you say, staring at your hands. "I didn't know I could make the dead . . . stop. Not until now."

"You best learn." Samuel stops you when you try to hand his flask back. "Once William makes up his fool mind about something, it's impossible to change it. We'll get to the mine or we'll die trying." He tilts his chin up at you. "I would prefer not to die. And I hope to deliver every one of our men safely home. That includes you."

The sun beats down as he rides away, motioning to William. As you shade your eyes, clutching his canteen and squinting past the acacias in the direction of the mine, you can still taste gunpowder. And although you see nothing on the flat horizon beyond the mesas, you swear you can hear the preacher man's soft chuckle rolling with the chollas across the sands.

*   *   *

The sky over the mine is as cloudless as it has been since the night your father was murdered. Dead men and animals pace the grounds in tattered skins; skeletal owls and sparrows perch on the broken wooden beams that used to frame the entrance to the mine, chattering their empty beaks. It smells worse than rancid, and your mother's displeasure boils through you as too-hot power, the compulsion to slough off your skin, to turn around and flee into the brush and never come back.

But you do not leave. Instead, you hold your ground in front of the company of men and call the dead down, one by one, forcing them to their knees, then to their faces. Their deaths wash over you as you lay them to rest

stabbed eaten whole my mouth is so dry will I never see my children again suffocating bleeding broken neck teeth tearing at me I don't want to die

and they go peacefully. You, though, do not; after only a few of these anti-resurrections, you're shaking and howling and barely able to stay on your horse for it. The men watch fearfully from a distance, and the horse almost bucks you off before Samuel catches its head, whispering soothing words into its ear. The only other person who comes close is William, his hair glittering bright as a newly unearthed vein of silver.

"You can do it, Ellis," William says in a low voice. Samuel watches you wordlessly, his hand at his hip, thumb resting on the handle of his pistol.

No one else has been able to come close to the mine in the three months since the collapse. You force the dead things into order, their wild disarray of energy into something malleable, and send them back into stillness.

hurts bleeding starving my mouth is so dry ripped to pieces I can't feel my legs don't let me die like this please lantern flickering out oh god someone save me

The miners' voices flood your mind, and you scream, your vision darkening. You are underground, crushed and unable to move, your ribs splintering with the weight of immovable rock. Last thoughts flicker through your head: a woman's face, a dog left tied to a post outside with no one to let it free, Marisol standing on the street in threadbare clothes, looking up at the sign for Madam Lettie's establishment.

STOP.

And then the darkness is different, and so is the body you're in; it is nighttime, and pinpricks of starlight shine through the burlap sack over your head. The rough bark of a yucca tree digs into your back, and your wrists are bound behind you. There are so many voices, some the same as the miners'. There is a sharp sound, like steel against rock, and then flame springs to being at your feet, licking at your legs. Bright red flames, and you think *Lettie*, and *Ellis*, and then there are no more thoughts, only pain.

STOP STOP STOP STOP

"Don't shoot!" William shouts. Rough hands shove you, and the visions break, along with your grip on the dead things. You land hard in the red dirt. William dismounts and stands over you, an arm extended to shield you from the rest of the men.

Samuel's pistol is cocked and pointed at your head. It's not the only gun aimed at you among the company.

"You caught on fire," Samuel says. His voice is bland, and there's an indiscernible look on his face.

Your skin seems intact, no burn marks in sight. But you know what you felt, and for a moment, you know that you'd lost yourself to your father the way you'd lost yourself to your mother so many times before. "Are they gone?" you rasp.

"Not quite," says William. Sweat sheens his face and his hair is disheveled as he pushes it back with his fingers.

Heaps of bones cover the ground, collapsed amidst the brittlebrush that crawls across the sand. Most of your mother's handiwork destroyed, her curse unraveled, not gone. But there are still a few meandering about, gathered in front of the mine's entrance. They don't look like proper animals; they've been cobbled together from the large, abandoned bones of many different bodies, some human, some beast. By now, you feel much the same.

You're so tired, and your limbs are trembling. You've pulled so much power into yourself that it aches. And the desert is not pleased; the searing heat of her anger boils in you, demanding the change, demanding you leave, demanding, demanding.

"Just a few more," says William, reaching down to clasp your shoulder. As his skin touches yours, you flinch—that same explosive rush of energy hits you, the way it had in the kitchen, and with the first dead bull. But this time, the flashback of another death takes over your vision

Samuel, sweet, stupid Samuel, blood on his shirt, holding your hand, calling your name frantically, and the dry laughter of the preacher man, an offer you wouldn't refuse even if you could. An offer of power, an image of the dead working the mines across the country, tireless, without pay, without complaint. And of you, watching the numbers tick upward in the newspapers. You laugh, too, with your last breath, and seal the preacher man's deal with a trembling finger smeared in your own blood

and you stagger back.

"You can do it," says William. Pale, immaculate, cold to the touch. He smells of expensive cologne, but under that, a sickly, fetid stink.

"So can you," you say. He stills. "Can't you."

He blinks once, his eyes clear and colorless, and flicks a finger at the skeletons. They collapse in a rainfall of bones. "Good job, Ellis," he says in a voice that carries to his men. But he's not looking at them.

"Why did you need me?"

"This goddamn desert," he says in a voice that is only for you. At the same time, he reaches for you, and you shrink back. "In the past few months, we've sent so many men to scout out the mines in this area. Not a single one who traveled south of the Rio de Lino and west of the Rio Grande made it back, even the ones who could bid the dead do their bidding. Devoured by this goddamn desert, torn apart by the coyotes, sent wandering in circles until they collapsed and died. But when I heard about your father's death, and about you, it all clicked into place."

The preacher man's words echo back. *He was mine before he came to seek his fortune out west, with all the rest of his brothers. Before he turned his back on me for my sister.*

William smiles. "She has no love for men like us. But she wouldn't dare hurt you. Not her own child, and his." He hauls you to your feet, his grip tight on your arm. "Come, Ellis. Walk with me, and stay close. Let's get a good look at the mine." He gestures, and the rest of the men approach cautiously, treading among the fallen bodies, leaving a wide berth around you and occasionally making the sign against evil as they pass.

This man doesn't care about the town. None of his pretty words to Madam Lettie about recompense, or about reopening the mine to reestablish commerce, matter. The town is just a field of bodies to use as he pleases. And he will use you, too. As a shield against your mother's wrath, as a hostage to make the desert behave.

But his power is different from yours. He has only the preacher man's blessing, and you have something else.

The desert change roars through you like a tide, a demand you can't ignore to undo your skin and let your real self run free. This time, you embrace it.

COME, demands the desert, and you shatter, finally, fully.

One of the other men is the first to see what is happening to you, your skin peeling off in long slabs, shedding your human form for something uncontainable, something lightning-legged, bent-backed, and wild. All of the desert's power you'd pulled into yourself courses through your limbs, back into the ground, silvered lines darting across the baked earth. All around, the piles of bones tremble and quiver, then rise slowly into the air, taking their forms once again.

"Monster!" he screams. Damn you, for there is only relief in your heart that he did not call you *witch*.

The desert rides you, and you are no longer your own. The winds kick up, blowing sheets of dust into the men's faces. If your mother has her way, and you yours, you will bury them all here, deep in the mine, with the rest of the humans.

What about Marisol? a small part of you asks, but it is drowned out by your mother's and your combined fury.

William has stumbled away, his hands out, and you can feel him fighting you for control of the dead. He's much stronger than you, much more experienced. But your mother pours more power into you, and you fight back. The sandstorm grows, blinding the company men who are fumbling for their guns.

The desert's dead are approaching when Samuel steps between you and William, his pistol leveled at you. There is fear, but his arm is steady.

"Samuel, no!" roars William, but there is no hesitation in Samuel's eyes.

His pistol cracks, and you think of Marisol in that split second before impact, and then there is nothing.

*   *   *

"Shake, shake, yucca tree,
"Rain and silver over me—"

The *clack-clack clack* of bones all around you. The preacher man's voice is creaky, parched as he sings, his hands brushing over your stone-still chest. Another, familiar voice joins his, a woman's voice like the whisper of scorpions' legs through the bone fields, a gentle tickle laced with the promise of poison. The ground hums under you with your mother's grief.

Stormclouds, gather in the sky,
Mockingbird and quail, fly;
My love, my love, come haste away!
You'll surely drown here if you stay.

Your eyes are open, the evening sun glaring into your eyes, but you can't blink. Every muscle is frozen in place, and it takes great effort to open your mouth.

"Am I dead?" you croak. You can't feel your chest moving.

"Very," says the preacher man. "But that's nothing new."

Slowly, you force your fingers to clench. "How long have I been . . . gone?"

"A few days. They tried to burn your body, but I wasn't about to lose another like that." His mouth twists into a parody of a smile. "When the flame wouldn't take, they left you to the vultures."

Fools, says your mother. The desert herself, the heat and mercilessness, wrapped like a vice around your heart. You wonder if you've been dead since the first night she called you into herself, that first time you gave up your body to become something more. *As if I would let my creatures hurt you. Would that you could say the same of yours, brother.*

The preacher man winces. It looks strange, with his empty sockets. "I indulged that boy too much. I thought I could keep him east, out of your territory. But his ambition overgrew his sense—"

He murdered my son!

"This child is my kin, too," hisses the preacher man. "Don't deny me that, sister. You're the one who let them flee back to their town, with not a scratch on them to pay for their misdeeds."

I would have those who harmed him pay accordingly.

"So would I. That may be the first matter we've agreed on in centuries."

"Whose side are you on?" you say. The preacher man cocks his head.

"Mine. And yours, though you may not believe it." He offers you his hand, and you take it, your body moving slowly. "I always was too fond of your father," he says in a low voice. "And your mother never let me forget it."

You wonder whose power is making this possible, his or your mother's. You are hyperaware of the dead things around you, their potential energy, just as you are of all the creatures skittering and prowling the earth, and the ancient hum of the ground.

The preacher man leads you to the entrance of the mine, where boulders and broken beams cluster tight, blocking the way. "What do you see?"

You place your hands on the boulders and close your eyes, focusing. The lines of your mother's power spread like a net through your mind's eye. And far beneath, pockets of the dead, of fallen men.

It has been three months since your unforgiving mother, in her grief, took your father's burnt body into her own and spat out every dead desert thing for miles around, sent them haunting the mine, the roads, until there was nowhere safe to go but down, down, down into the earth. And when the mineshaft collapsed, suffocating the miners in the tunnels, she still would not forgive, and held the rainclouds three months away from the town so that nothing would grow.

You open your eyes. "I see potential."

The preacher man cackles, and even your mother gives a pleased crackle. *I told you he was clever.*

The men from out east, even William with all of his power, could not move the boulders on their own. They would be back with proper mining equipment, maybe even fancy machines from their waterside cities, but likely not for months.

You don't need months. Not with the preacher man on one side of you and your mother all around, her presence like that of an oncoming monsoon.

"Lend me your power," you say. For something this big, you'll need more than what you have. More control, more finesse.

Pledge yourself to us. And we will pledge ourselves to you. Both of us. The preacher man nods.

You're already dead, and you can't go back like this, even if you wanted to. You have nothing to lose; nothing to lose except Marisol, and by now, surely news of your death has reached her. In dying, you have lost her, too.

You hold your hands out to both of them in assent. "Yes," you say simply.

Your name in your mother's voice is like the rush of the monsoon rains, water licking the parched ground, the promise of life and destruction at the same time. The preacher man leans in, places his dry forehead against yours, and breathes your name in a whisper that promises rest, peace, the passing of time in the cold, dark earth.

You hum, swaying. The preacher man unbuttons his coat and drapes it across your shoulders. His desiccated torso, open from sternum to belly, houses small, dark-furred fruit bats in its hollow. They hang upside down from the battered, broken ribs, their eyes glimmering at you like little embers.

"Shake, shake, yucca tree, rain and silver over me," you sing softly. The purr of your mother's power in you, her pleasure and approval, fills your hands. You see the pattern of the boulders, and you ease them free, one by one. They glide along the lines of your mother's power, smooth as oil.

The miners come next, their broken, insect-eaten bodies beginning to stir. The preacher man hums along with you, his movements matching yours.

"Stormclouds, gather in the sky, oh mockingbird and quail, fly." With each insistent pull of your power, the miners stumble free into the dying light, into the empty air. You take each one in hand, and you focus, and the signs of death melt away. Their bodies are still cold, but the insect damage, the shattered limbs, are gone. You know, somehow, that this is only temporary and cannot last. But one night will be enough.

You think of Marisol and your cold chest tightens. It will have to be enough.

The movements of every desert creature buzz at the edge of your consciousness. The beating of owls' wings as they stalk their prey, the soft-tailed mice that creep beyond the rocks to howl at the moon in voices like tiny wolves. The slow unfurling of saguaro blossoms, petals parting against the inquisitive noses of tiny bats. The snakes twining in their burrows, tongues flicking out to taste for moisture in the air. And your coyotes, padding to meet you, glittering finery stolen from dead men clutched tight in their mouths, finery that is just your size.

You let the rail-thin crows lift the preacher's coat from your shoulders and shrug on the new jacket. It shimmers like moonlight. The desert creatures dress you as the coyotes pace, brushing against the preacher man and barking their devotion aloud. He smiles, knowing that devotion isn't for him.

When you are clad in the glittering suit, as fine as any prince from Marisol's books, a bird made of bones brings you a single honeysuckle blossom. You tuck the stem into a neat bullet hole in the jacket, right above at your chest.

"Come, then, my dear Ellis," says the preacher man. "Don't be late to your own party."

Indeed, your mother says. She sounds almost pleased. *Go show them a night they'll never forget.*

You grin, baring your teeth. Something almost like a horse trots up to you, its skeletal hooves clacking against the hard ground. As you swing atop it and turn towards the road, the miners begin to follow, not with slow and shambling steps, but with the pace of confident men. High above you, the beginnings of dark clouds slink across the sky, something unseen for months.

My love, my love, come haste away!
You'll surely drown here if you stay.

*   *   *

The moon rises high and sharp, like a glittering mouth, as you descend upon the town. Your mount tosses its head, and if it had any lungs, or anything else inside its ragged bones, it might have whickered.

Banjos and fiddles brighten the air in Madam Lettie's saloon. The band stutters in confusion as you push the doors open, the dead men at your back. It is crowded inside, and as people take in the scene, gasps rise around you. Some gasps of fear, some gasps of joy at an apparent miracle. But you only have eyes for one person, and you stalk through the mass of townsfolk reaching for their loved ones, pushing them out of your way.

There she is, dancing with William amidst a circle of company men. He is immaculate once again, dressed in a fine-tailored suit. Her hair is done up, her corset laced (albeit clumsily; perhaps Harriet helped her in your stead), a smile painted on her face. You recognize the set of her jaw, the way she holds her mouth when she's fighting back sorrow.

"Marisol," you say, and her head snaps toward you, eyes widening. You pace towards her and she lets go of William, stepping to meet you. William doesn't try to stop her. Even if you weren't risen from the dead, you know he can see something new in your face, something as feral and bleak as the desert.

He backs away, fearful, and you offer Marisol your hand. "Dance with me," you say in a voice like the wind whipping through a dead man's bones.

"Ellis," she breathes, and then she's in your arms. Other cold, pale arms reach out behind you, grasping William tight; he yelps, but they yank him away and he's swallowed by the crush of bodies in their best, ragtag finery. You catch sight of Samuel, but he, too, is pulled into the masses before he can reach you. *Dance*, you think viciously, and they will, clasped tight in desert magic, until their bodies are torn to pieces.

Marisol is the one who taught you how to dance, on the groaning floorboards of her tiny room, and you hold her close as you sway to the music. She smells like she always does in the evenings, like perfume and dust. She can't take her eyes off of you, and you wonder what you look like to her, whether the glamor cast over the miners has lent you your old appearance back, or if you have been transformed into something wholly different.

"Let's get out of here," you whisper, and Marisol mouths *Yes*. Grasping her tight, you elbow your way through the crowd of people reuniting with their family members, their brothers, their husbands. Some have taken to dancing again, those lost to them clutched tight.

You glance over your shoulder for Madam Lettie, but she's standing stock still, gaze locked on the figure of a man who had joined you halfway across the flats, rising from the shade of a pair of yucca trees. As he draws closer, Lettie's face fills with impossible hope.

"Robert," she sobs, dashing forward and holding him close. His hair is the same color as yours, red like the earth, veined with silver, and his skin is dark as the dust. He holds her gently, his arms around her waist. Whatever words they have for each other are swallowed by the sound of the band and the crush of bodies around them.

Marisol's slipper is lost in the rush, but the two of you flee from the lights and whirling skirts into the dust outside, the starlight bearing down on you like a thousand icy stares. Her hand in yours is the warmest thing you've ever touched.

"Ellis, you crazy bastard. They told me you were dead." She laughs, too wild, tinged with grief. "Why didn't you come back sooner?"

You are silent, turning her hands over in yours. "They weren't wrong," you say at last.

"I don't understand," says Marisol, but you can see by the sinking hope in her eyes that she does.

"I did die." She shakes her head vigorously. "I'm still dead, Marisol. But I couldn't rest without saying goodbye to you." It's mostly true, and it will do for now.

"I'm sorry, Ellis." She's crying, and your heart sinks. Marisol rarely cries, and seeing her waste water on you is more than you can take. "I should have stopped them from taking you, I should have fought harder—"

"This isn't your fault," you say into her hair. "Not at all." A gentle tug of your power, and your bone and brittlebrush horse trots up to meet you. You drape your glittering coat over its back to make a seat for Marisol as she watches, unable to keep the fear and awe from her face.

"I didn't know you could do that."

You smile crookedly. "There are a lot of new things about me now. Come, get on."

She swings up on the mount and scoots forward, holding her hand out to help you up. But you don't take it. Instead, you reach into your pocket and press her stained red bandanna into her palm. It's heavy with coins taken from the bodies of the dead, enough to buy a one-way train ticket out east. You know; you counted it yourself.

"No," she breathes.

"You need to let me go," you say gently.

"I can't." She grabs for you; you step back out of her reach. "Ellis, no! Get on the goddamn horse! We're in this together, or not at all!"

"I can't go with you," you say. "I wish I could. God, I wish I could. But I belong to the desert now. I can't leave."

"Then I won't either."

"Don't be a fool," you snap, and she recoils. "Marisol, one of us needs to escape this place. And I can't any more." You gentle your voice. "Please."

In the end, you give her your boots to wear in place of her single slipper. Your dark, naked feet stand out against the sand, but whether the sand is bearable because of the nighttime cool or because you no longer feel the desert's burn, you don't know.

Marisol promises to buy a ticket, but she also promises to come back for you when she can. You hope she will forget the second promise, but you know her too well to believe it.

"I love you," she says, her eyes hard. "That's the only reason I'm leaving. For you, Ellis. If you forget everything else, don't forget that." She digs her heels into the horse's sides and it gallops away, your coat glittering under her skirt as she rides east.

"Well done," murmurs the preacher man. He stands behind you, his coat flapping in the growing wind.

Well done, echoes the desert.

"Keep her safe," you murmur. "Both of you, until she passes out of your realms."

We know you will, says your mother, and the preacher man nods in agreement.

You watch Marisol's horse until she passes out of sight, but you can still feel each hoofbeat strike against the baked clay, a staccato at the edge of your consciousness. You flex your fingers and look over your shoulder at the saloon. The windows are bright, and the chatter and music leaks from the doorway.

Nothing is permanent, but maybe Marisol was right. Maybe seeing a miracle and the ones you love, even for just one night, for one last time, will be enough.

The desert hums in your throat, and the language of the dead things coats your teeth. Back, then, towards the bluffs and the mesas, to the wilds where the coyotes cry over the yucca and the bodies of fallen men. Your kingdom lies out there among the wide, desolate plains, waiting for you to lay claim to its whispering bones.

The rising sun sears long red marks into the cloudy sky, and behind, you can hear the dead dancing themselves into a frenzy, long-lost miners with their wives and friends held close, spinning inhuman wild, as if afraid a spell will break.

You straighten your borrowed shirt and begin walking. Overhead, the sky rumbles with the promise of rain.

NEBULA AWARD WINNER
NOVELETTE

THE LONG FALL UP

WILLIAM LEDBETTER

William Ledbetter has more than fifty speculative fiction stories and nonfiction articles published in markets such as Asimov's, Fantasy & Science Fiction, Analog, Jim Baen's Universe, Escape Pod, Baen.com, Daily Science Fiction, *the SFWA blog, and Ad Astra. He's been a space and technology geek since childhood and spent most of his non-writing career in the aerospace and defense industry. He administers the Jim Baen Memorial Short Story Award contest for Baen Books and the National Space Society, is a member of SFWA, the National Space Society of North Texas, a Launch Pad Astronomy workshop graduate, and is the Science Track coordinator for the Fencon convention. He lives near Dallas with his wife, a needy dog, and two spoiled cats.*

Like millions on Earth and aboard the *Jīnshān* Space Station, I watched Veronica Perez every day, but unlike those other spectators I already knew how her story would end. She disgusted me and I hated her actions, but I was curious about how it started. Newshounds had already dug up every detail of her past, from an interview with her first boyfriend at age thirteen to her biology doctorate dissertation only fifteen years later, but none of that revealed the true person.

As I ran through my systems check and prepped my ship for extended acceleration, I watched her first broadcast again, but this time with sound muted. I noted tiny movements of her eyes and mouth, the nervous way her hands twitched, and the slight wrinkles between her eyes. She clearly believed what she was saying, but how could she be so heartless? How could she doom her own child to such a life? Even after a third viewing, I still wanted to scream in her face.

"Play it again, Huizhu." I said to the ship's AI. "With sound this time."

"My name is Veronica Perez," she said. "I'm outbound on an elliptical orbit that will bring me back to the Mountain one year from now and I'm six months pregnant."

She was so haughty, so proud of her crime. It sickened me. I'd been hired and trained to protect *Jīnshān* Station—or "the Mountain" as she had so casually called it. I found the casual term disrespectful. *Jīnshān* Station was a Bernal sphere habitat parked at Lagrange Point Five with a population of over twenty-seven thousand. My parents and sister lived there, so I embraced my job eagerly. I was also prepared to kill to protect my family, though I'd never expected my foe to be a pregnant woman.

My status board turned green, indicating the crèche was ready for me to enter. "Open the hatch, Huizhu."

The ship's AI obeyed without comment and I peeled off my clothes as the crèche hissed open.

"No father acted as my accomplice," the woman continued. "I used a robotic device to implant the fertilized egg two days after my acceleration burn, so the child has gestated entirely in a zero-gravity environment."

I stepped into the warm acceleration jelly and began attaching the unpleasant wires and tubes necessary for an extended burn.

"She's cold-blooded," I said aloud.

Huizhu said nothing. That bothered me.

We were told that ship's cortexes were not true AIs, but if we couldn't tell the difference, did it matter? After two years of deep deployment, Huizhu had become my only friend and companion, yet times like this reminded me she was just another tool.

I closed the crèche lid then sealed the close-fitting helmet, wincing at the sting when interface posts pricked my shaved scalp. The helmet visor flickered to life with status and information feeds. Two small windows opened, one displaying an interactive diagram of my intercept course and the other showing the young woman still spouting her obviously well-rehearsed declamation.

"I'm willingly breaking the law and prepared to accept my punishment to prove that healthy children can be produced in null gravity."

She used the word "produced" as if she were discussing industrial output at a corporate board meeting. I had seen the videos and pictures of children gestated in zero gee. They were twisted and tortured innocents. They were the reason laws had been passed.

Then Perez got to the part that bothered me most.

"Mom and Dad? If you're watching, I'm sorry." She paused, emotion showing in her face for the first time. "I know you won't understand this and will be disappointed in me, but you're going to have a grandson. He'll just have to spend his entire life in microgravity."

Not only was she creating a deformed person, but even intended to saddle her parents with the child's care while she rotted in prison. My older sister had requested a child permit six years ago and was still waiting. Population on *Jīnshān* was strictly controlled for obvious reasons, but this woman had deliberately jumped the queue.

As the gel finished filling my acceleration crèche, I instructed Huizhu to fire the main thrusters. Even with the cushioning, I drifted almost back to the rear wall before the gel compressed enough to stop me.

Perez assumed pursuit would come from *Jīnshān*, where even the fastest ships like mine couldn't reach her in less than six months, but I was part of a picket line and I was ahead of her. Officially an asteroid defense, in reality existed for situations just like this. I would intercept her ship in sixty-one days.

She would see me coming, probably during my deceleration burn, but if she ran she'd be under gee forces and could never claim that the baby developed in a full zero-gravity environment. I still had plenty of time to carry out my assignment and prevent her from giving birth.

INTERCEPT: 52 DAYS, 12 HOURS, 4 MINUTES

"Play it again with sound, Huizhu."

Her second video flickered on my visor, then started again.

"I've read the messages sent my way and I assure you I'm not a monster, nor am I trying to produce one. My child might have slightly longer arms, legs, and fingers than one born on Earth, but hasn't humanity finally learned to accept and embrace physical differences? The important thing is that he'll be just as human as your children."

Pleading in her voice. She didn't want them to hate her son. Perhaps this was more than a political statement after all?

"There is no genetic manipulation, only cellular adjustments that started immediately and will continue through his entire life, but *every* human in space relies on machines to stay alive and healthy. We build space stations, spaceships, and protective suits. My body is filled with nanomachines that repair radiation damage, prevent optical degeneration, and address dozens of other health issues associated with null gravity. My child will simply have all of these from the beginning."

I switched off the sound again and embraced the quiet inside *my* nested mechanical aids of mask, crèche, and ship. Her words held a grain of truth. Not only did we need machines to survive in space, but aside from those who lived inside *Jīnshān*'s centrifugal gravity, none of us would ever walk the surface of Earth again without mechanical help. Still, she was having a child, not conducting a science experiment.

INTERCEPT: 47 DAYS, 2 HOURS, 51 MINUTES

After only fourteen days, an intrepid astronomer spotted my drive plume, calculated a trajectory, and made the information public. He'd even been able to identify my ship type by characterizing the exhaust spectrum and determined it was human-rated. The entire solar system knew I was on an intercept course with Perez's ship.

"Have we received new orders yet?" I asked Huizhu.

"No new communications from base, sir."

"They can't expect me to kill her now—the public will be watching. The Russians will use it as an excuse to embargo the station. Nearly half of the station investors are Americans, but the United States government will still call it an atrocity."

Or was *Jīnshān* beyond having to play the game of international politics and public opinion? The station was an economic powerhouse and a true mountain of gold for the investors. Housing humanity's fourth-largest economy, it had a firm grip on cislunar space and control of all off-planet commerce. Every asteroid mined, ship built, or powersat switched on paid *Jīnshān* well for the privilege.

"Do *you* think carrying out your orders will be an atrocity?" Huizhu said.

"Why do you ask that?"

"I don't understand how killing Veronica Perez and her child puts *Jīnshān* Corporation in a morally superior position."

"I suppose it would save the child a lifetime of pain and suffering. It would also be an example to others who might be willing to commit the same crime."

"It makes no logical sense," Huizhu said. "Children born with physical or mental disabilities on Earth are not euthanized. Legal punishment for breaking the zero-gee child law is imprisonment, not death. Some people will agree with a decision to terminate Veronica Perez and her child, but many others will not. Why risk turning public and government opinions against *Jīnshān* Station when taking no action would cost them nothing?"

"I don't know," I said. She was right. My employers obviously had reasons for taking such a risk, but I didn't see them. Huizhu had voiced serious questions that had not even occurred to me. A chill made my skin prickle in the warm jelly.

When the message finally came, it merely reaffirmed my original orders, but my employers were being quite cautious. Even though sent via encrypted laser communications, the instructions themselves would also be opaque to anyone who caught and decrypted them. *Intercept Perez. Use Plan 47.* Innocuous as that message might look to outsiders, their intent was perfectly clear to me.

As an asteroid defense picket ship, my hold contained many things capable of redirecting big rocks, like surface-mountable pusher rockets and hyper-velocity missiles, but Plan 47 required I use a device that had only one purpose: to cripple spacecraft by shutting down their critical systems. The FL239 interdiction device utilized a small nuclear detonation to pump a directed EMP generator. Even military-hardened electronics couldn't survive the pulse within optimum range. Technically the device was developed to enable apprehension and boarding of criminal vehicles, but since the pulse was powerful enough to fry spacesuit electronics as well as the ship's life support, it was a death sentence for anyone aboard.

Not for the first time since I'd received my orders I felt uneasy and had doubts. Most of all I wondered why they'd sent me. There were several robotic craft nearby that could have accelerated faster and arrived sooner.

INTERCEPT: 41 DAYS, 7 HOURS, 11 MINUTES

I received my first message from Veronica Perez. It was a tight beam, meant for me alone.

"Can we talk?" Her face was drawn and pale. She looked tired and perhaps upset.

"Huizhu, please record and prepare to send the following message via tight beam. My name is Jager Jin. I am—"

"I cannot send your message," Huizhu interrupted.

"What?"

"I've been ordered to allow no communications from this ship except to approved channels at *Jīnshān* Station."

A heat grew in my belly and crept up to my face, making the mask suddenly uncomfortable.

"Why?"

"They gave no reason. My response-to-orders protocol is detailed in document 556845.67FG. Would you like me to open that file for you?"

"No!" I snapped. This made less and less sense.

Veronica's next message came an hour later and she was a little more composed. Her eyes were harder and her expression intense. "I don't know why you won't respond. I just want to talk. I'd like to know your true intentions. The Mountain claims you were sent to render assistance should I need it. I don't believe that."

She paused and her gaze wavered for a second. "If you've been sent to kill me and my baby I can't stop you, but at least have the decency to face me."

INTERCEPT: 35 DAYS, 1 HOUR, 27 MINUTES

I woke suddenly from a deep sleep, confused and thrashing in the gel. Had I heard something? I immediately checked the status screens but all systems were green.

"Huizhu? What's going on?"

"I launched the FL239 interdiction device."

"Why?"

"I was ordered to do so by headquarters."

"Why didn't they send a damned robot?"

"You are obviously part of the rescue effort," Huizhu said and started a video playing on my visor.

An attractive, perfectly groomed spokeswoman stood before the famous Golden Mountain logo. "The reports are correct. The pilot of one of our deep-system asteroid protection picket ships has taken it upon himself to go to Ms. Lopez's aid. We have been unable to contact him, but he is still on course and will arrive in plenty of time to help with the birth should assistance be required."

"Why are they lying?"

"I don't know," Huizhu said.

I still wasn't sure why they wanted Veronica dead, but I suspected it was to make sure the child was not seen by the public. Could Veronica be right? Would the child be normal?

"I have to stop this," I said.

"The FL239 interdiction device has been preprogrammed to carry out its mission. Once operational, these devices can be put into a communications-lockout mode and the one I launched has been so locked. You cannot shut it down remotely."

"Huizhu—have I been completely cut out of the command loop?"

"Of course not, sir. My response-to-orders protocols are detailed in document 556845.67FG. Would you like me to open that file for you?"

Why did she keep insisting I read that file? Was Huizhu trying to help me?

"Yes," I said. "I would like to read the file."

INTERCEPT: 30 DAYS, 10 HOURS, 19 MINUTES

It was flip day. As soon as the engines kicked off, I crawled out of the crèche, took a long, hot bag shower, and used the bathroom like a normal person.

"The ship is turned," Huizhu said. "We can initiate deceleration as soon as you return to the crèche."

"Thank you, Huizhu," I said, "but we have a few maintenance issues to deal with first. Please take the primary and backup communications antennas off-line."

"Why?" Huizhu said. "Diagnostics indicate the antennas are nominal."

"Because according to that news report, we are not receiving all the communications sent our way, which indicates either our antennas or receiver are malfunctioning, or the corporate office is mistaken."

"Understood. Antennas off-line."

"Do our missiles also have the communications-lockout feature?"

"Yes."

This was where I had to be cautious. The "response-to-orders protocols"

Huizhu had directed me to read basically said she must follow my commands unless they were contradictory to mission orders or those from higher up the command chain. The press release cast doubt on all of that, but I still had to be careful. I didn't know what kind of fail-safes had been built into the instructions sent to Huizhu. If I said the wrong thing, I could be locked out of the loop permanently.

"Target one of the missiles to intercept and destroy the interdiction device," I said.

"That would violate our orders," Huizhu said.

"Which orders?" I said. "That FL239 launch was contradictory to the broadcast we received claiming our intention is to intercept and assist. Since our communications are already suspect, I prefer to err on the side of caution and assume the device was launched in error."

I held my breath, hoping the circular logic would hold up under AI scrutiny.

"Understood. The missile programming is complete," Huizhu said.

"Upon launch, initiate communications-lockout mode on the missile as well."

"Understood."

"Launch now."

The ship shuddered as the weapon left its berth and I sighed with relief. As I climbed back into my crèche, I said, "Okay, Huizhu, let's get this thing slowed down."

INTERCEPT: 27 DAYS, 7 HOURS, 40 MINUTES

After three days I was starting to fidget. Being locked up in a jelly-filled box was bad enough, but without a connection to the outside I had nothing but onboard entertainment and Huizhu to occupy my time. I was tired of her beating me at backgammon and wanted to know what the newsfeeds were saying. I was curious whether the Mountain had sent me new orders, but I also missed Veronica's broadcasts and messages.

Continuing my ruse, I ran extensive diagnostics and ordered Huizhu to bring comms back online. If the communication lockout on those missiles actually worked, then destroying Veronica's ship was now off the table. I also continuously scanned the space in our vicinity and saw nothing moving. Any robot ships they might have sent would also be decelerating by now and consequently show up easily. They could, of course, change my orders or fire me, maybe even jail me, but they couldn't make me kill her.

I spent the next few minutes watching and reading news. Public opinion had taken a huge shift in support of Veronica Perez during the days I'd been out of the loop. Even those not actively behind her appeared to be in a holding pattern fueled by curiosity. Everyone was waiting to see the child.

The balance had tipped after Veronica's most recent broadcast. Sound bites and clips were all over the news and web, so I killed the sound and played the whole thing.

Her entire demeanor had changed. No fear or defensiveness now: her eyes never left the camera, nor did she fidget or waffle or plead. I saw nothing but confidence and determination. "Okay, Huizhu—give me sound and rewind to the beginning."

"The *Jīnshān* Corporation doesn't just have an economic monopoly on all off-Earth mining and manufacturing, they have a stranglehold on humanity itself," Veronica said. "They used fake pictures and video to push through laws to criminalize zero-gee pregnancies, not because they care about children, but to protect their future earnings. Think about it. All off-planet human reproduction has to be approved by them. Do you think they want independent miner families competing with them for mineral contracts? They don't care about children, they don't care about humanity, and they don't care about small, family-owned mining businesses. They care only about *Jīnshān*. And that's why they've sent one of their people to kill me, before I can show my baby to the world."

She was on the verge of winning and knew it, but everything hinged on the child. If it were obviously abnormal, then everyone would say, "I told you so." If the child appeared normal, then things would get interesting. Some would claim it was an elaborate video hoax and others that the child was still broken on the inside, which would become obvious when it grew to adulthood. But some—probably most of those living in space—would pause and wonder if they had been duped these many years. They might also wonder if they, too, could have children outside the Mountain's artificial gravity. My employer's desperation made sense in that light.

"Huizhu? Have you extended the antenna booms to clear the drive plume?" I asked.

"Yes."

"Any messages from Veronica?"

"No, but we do have a new transmission from headquarters," Huizhu said.

"Play it."

Ignore our news releases. Stay current course. Await instructions.

I was suddenly uncomfortable. "How did they know we based our actions on the news reports?"

"They contacted me as soon as our antennas came online and I told them."

I swore under my breath. Even if Huizhu was trying to help, she could not lie or disobey direct orders from headquarters. I had to remember that.

INTERCEPT: 22 DAYS, 3 HOURS, 6 MINUTES

"We've received another tight-beam message from Veronica Perez," Huizhu said, waking me from a nap. "Would you like to see it?"

"Yes," I said and tried to clear the cobwebs of sleep from my head.

"I know you're there," she said, then paused as if expecting a reply. "I don't believe in monsters, so I'm choosing to believe that you don't really want to kill me and my baby just to prop up your employer's profit margin."

Unlike in the public message she'd transmitted, this time she looked tired and frustrated. I wondered how pregnancy in zero gravity differed from a regular one. The fluids would probably collect oddly, and the baby's position inside her body might be different. Or was it something else? Alone in the quiet of her little ship, did she doubt her own assertions? Was she as much in the dark about the outcome as everyone else?

"It's lonely out here. Wouldn't you like someone to talk to? Or does talking to your targets make them feel more human, which will give you a twinge of guilt when you kill them?"

Her face twisted slightly as she fought some emotion, then she took a deep breath and locked her eyes on the camera. "I don't know what drives you, but I believe in what I'm doing. Someone has to break *Jīnshān*'s stranglehold. But I also admit that I'm scared. I want my baby to live and to be happy. I want him to have a chance. If I'm wrong and he is born a tortured, deformed person, that will cause me more suffering than any penalty imposed upon me by *Jīnshān*. But whoever you are, I'm not asking for your support or approval. Just let my son have that chance."

I lay in the quiet for a long time after the video ended, floating in my warm slime, connected to life and humanity by tubes and wires, not unlike the child in Veronica's womb. Unease penetrated every pore. Did my employers have a way to override the missile or EMP weapon programming that even Huizhu didn't know about?

One thing I did know: the Mountain would never give up.

INTERCEPT: 18 DAYS, 21 HOURS, 58 MINUTES

I watched the numbers counting down as two slightly curved tracks came together on my screen. The missile carried a miniature nuke to divert smaller asteroids, but that would also deliver an EMP pulse, just nothing as big as the FL239 device. Both ships should be far enough away from the blast to be safe.

The data on my screen was four minutes old due to time lag, but I still watched as the count dropped to zero and the trajectories converged. Both dots disappeared from my screen.

I took a deep breath and relaxed. At least that had worked. I dove into the broadcast traffic from Earth and waited to see what reaction the blast would generate. Twenty-three minutes later, the main drive died.

I looked at the status screen. No damage indicators blinked on the screen. The command log showed they had been shut down deliberately.

"Huizhu? Why did you shut down the engines?"

"I was directed to do so by headquarters."

What the hell? I pulled up the trajectory diagrams and saw that Huizhu had also made the necessary adjustments to keep us on an intercept course with the other ship. Since I was no longer decelerating, we were converging much faster, and the two ships would now meet in six days rather than eighteen.

"Did they give a reason for shutting down our deceleration burn and changing the intercept?"

"No."

"Restart the engines and recalculate the intercept," I said, trying to keep the panic out of my voice.

"I'm sorry, but you cannot override instructions sent directly from headquarters."

"Can we at least adjust our course so that we don't actually hit Veronica's ship?"

"No. I'm sorry, but no commands you can give me will override my instructions from headquarters."

My heart raced and my hands shook—but with anger, not fear. Once again there was a hidden implication in Huizhu's statement. I just had to work out what it was.

INTERCEPT: 5 DAYS, 13 HOURS, 9 MINUTES

"Where are you?" Huizhu said.

I was floating in the auxiliary equipment hold, running diagnostic checks on two of the rock-pushers. I would have preferred to simply bypass the propulsion controls, but I couldn't look at any of the schematics without it being obvious to Huizhu. I wouldn't be able to slow down for a rendezvous, but by mounting the pushers on the outer hull, I could at least push us off the collision course.

"In the auxiliary hold," I said.

"Why did you disable the cameras?"

I was on the verge of telling her to figure it out for herself or call and ask headquarters, but she had been trying to help me within her limitations.

"Are you relaying our conversations to headquarters?" I said.

"Only when requested. They have not asked for that information since shutting down the engines."

That raised a couple of interesting questions. Did they so readily discount my ability to foil their efforts? Or were they worried those signals might be intercepted on their way to Earth and reveal their lies?

I was still going to be cautious. "I disabled the cameras because I needed a little more privacy."

"You missed two networked cameras—one in the control room and one in the crèche."

I found it weird that they had installed a hidden camera in the crèche, but I believed her. "But none in either hold?"

"No," she said. "Of the communications system components accessible from inside the ship, the encryption modules are the most critical. The designers of this vessel installed triple-redundant systems, which includes the communications system. Two of those modules are accessible from the auxiliary hold where you're located."

I paused and smiled. "Where is the third module?"

"Behind maintenance cover twelve in the main cabin."

"Why did you tell me this information?"

"Based on your previous line of questioning, I predicted you would eventually ask about the transmission system structure."

"Yes, I was going to ask, so thank you. And remind me to thank your software engineers when we return home."

Ten minutes later, I'd finished removing all three encryption modules for preventive maintenance and went back to my pusher-conversion project.

"I'm no longer able to send radio messages," Huizhu said.

"Thank you," I muttered.

"My receivers still work and I just found another press release from *Jīnshān*," Huizhu said after a few minutes. "Would you like to see it?"

I sighed, exasperated by the interruptions. "I'm a bit busy. Can it wait?"

"Of course, but I think it explains why you were cut out of the decision loop. You are apparently insane."

That made me pause. Was that sarcasm? I sure hoped so.

"In that case, please play it."

A panel on one wall flickered, then showed the same perky spokesperson who had made the previous official announcements, only this time she wasn't smiling and looked very grave.

"We regret to confirm earlier reports that our piloted picket ship is indeed on a collision course with Veronica Perez. We believe the human pilot has gone insane, perhaps driven over the edge by his desire to prevent what he believes is an atrocity committed by Miss Perez. He fired a weapon earlier, intended to destroy her ship, but we were able to intercept and destroy it."

"Are you fucking kidding me?" I yelled at the screen.

"But now he appears to be intent on using the ship itself as the means of her destruction. We've been unable to take control of the ship remotely and have sent warnings to Ms. Perez, telling her to alter course, but so far he has adjusted his course to match every change she makes."

"Bastards," I said, just as the video ended.

"It's very confusing," Huizhu said.

Huizhu was confused?

"We were apparently not intended to see that news release," Huizhu said. "I was instructed not to view transmissions from news outlets, but this clip was replayed on an evening comedy show."

"It makes perfect sense from their perspective," I said. "That's why they didn't send a robotic ship. This way they can kill her and not take the blame."

"They are lying," Huizhu said.

I couldn't tell from her inflection whether the comment was a question or statement of fact, but I had sudden hope. Did she have any way of overriding their orders?

"Then you have to give me control again, Huizhu."

"I'm willing but unable to do so. I have examined every possible option but can find no way to override or circumvent the commands I have been given."

Damn. I was still totally on my own. I ran a hand over the stubble on my head and got back to work.

INTERCEPT: 2 DAYS, 5 HOURS, 12 MINUTES

"What are you planning to do?"

Huizhu had been mostly silent during the two days since we'd seen the news release. Her ability to report me had supposedly been stopped, but there could easily be programming buried deep inside her to respond to certain events. Once again I considered ignoring her or lying but decided to risk being truthful. She needed to see at least one honest human.

"Why do you want to know?"

"I want to help."

"I'm running diagnostics on my EVA hard suit," I said.

"Are you going EVA?"

"Yes."

"Are you going to bypass my propulsion controls?"

Damn. I should have known it would be nearly impossible to hide my actions from her. "What makes you think that?"

"The one place you can easily bypass both the main engine and attitude thrusters is accessible only from outside."

I held my breath and my heart raced. "Really? Can you show me the schematics?"

The wall flickered and the schematic appeared with one section highlighted.

"You would have to cut these eight wires," Huizhu said, and the lines criss-crossing the screen flashed on and off rapidly.

My hands shook and I tried to memorize that entire circuit, just in case. "Using just the replacement-part printer, could you build me a manual control adaptor?"

"No," she said.

My pulse slowed and I steeled myself for doing it the hard way. Then she spoke again.

"I have already designed the module and fed the information into the printer, but I can't actually send the command to make it."

"So that means—"

"I can explain the logic behind that limitation, or you can just go press the button."

I scrambled to the main hold. Twenty minutes later, I held the module in my hands. I had already donned the lower half of my hard suit when Huizhu interrupted me.

"There is a new broadcast from Veronica Perez. You'll want to see this."

Without even waiting for my confirmation, the video flickered to life on the ceiling above me.

Veronica was pale, damp hair clinging to the sides of her face and forehead. She gave a weak smile then held a tiny baby up in the center of the camera view.

"This is my son, Ernesto. He is named after my grandfather." Tears formed around her eyes, making her blink repeatedly. "I was forced to induce labor early in order to make sure he was born before my executioner arrives, but he is still healthy. On Earth he would weigh a respectable five pounds and nine ounces. A good weight for being premature. And as you can see, he is a perfect child."

She moved him closer to the camera and held up tiny hands with the usual complement of fingers and thumbs, then did the same with each foot. When Ernesto's face screwed into a frown and he whimpered, she stroked his cheek and kissed the dark, wispy hair on his head.

"I'll show you more later, even provide a DNA profile if some of you are still unconvinced, but right now I'm tired and need to sign off."

The video ended, leaving me staring dumbstruck at the ceiling. Then I started laughing. "Take that, you Golden Mountain sons of bitches!"

"Yes," Huizhu said. "I still cannot monitor actual news broadcasts, but this is everywhere."

"They'll have to abort their plan to kill her now. Right? I mean, what's the point? The baby is born and has been seen by all humanity."

"Possibly, but given the company's past actions, you will remain an embarrassing loose end."

The comment, delivered in Huizhu's calm voice, sent chills creeping up my spine.

"You have an urgent message from Veronica Perez," Huizhu said, and again didn't wait for permission to play it.

The face on the screen was haggard and even paler. She was holding the suckling baby to her breast, and when she wiped at her eyes with the back of the other hand, I saw a smear of blood on the underside of her arm.

"I know you've been sent to kill me," she said with a quavering voice, "so if you still intend to do that, you'll just need to wait a little while longer. I'm hemorrhaging and can't stop the bleeding. Normally the nanomeds in my system could deal with this . . ."

She paused, swallowed hard, and stroked the baby's head. "But of course the standard nanomed suite wouldn't permit me to become pregnant, so I replaced them with unregulated black-market versions. I've yet to shed the placenta, which would be a macro problem for any nanos, but these are obviously inferior when it comes to serious blood loss. They've slowed the bleeding but can't stop it."

Little Ernesto had fallen asleep. She shook him gently, but when he didn't wake, she pinched him until he cried then coaxed him to take her nipple again. A halo of sparkling tears floated in the air around her face.

"I hope the bleeding will stop, but in case it doesn't, I'm feeding him every drop he'll take. I have no idea how long he can last on his own, but I know you are only two days away. If there is a human cell in your body, please save my baby. He deserves a chance. He shouldn't have to—"

She stopped, swallowed hard, and squinted her eyes tight, adding more tears to the orbiting constellation.

"There are records of newborns surviving several days on their own, but they probably weren't preemies," Veronica said in an almost-whisper. "But if you hurry, it is at least possible. Just . . . please, be human enough to save him if you can. I'll stay with him as long as I'm able. But please come."

The message ended. I slammed my hand against the nearest wall, which sent me tumbling across the cabin in response and scattered my suit components.

"Show me the intercept diagram," I said. The chart appeared where Veronica's face had been moments before. I could tell at a glance that we had no chance, but I asked anyway. "If I can get propulsion control and turn on the engines in an hour, how long would it take for us to rendezvous with her?"

"Five days, two hours, and nineteen minutes. At our present speed we will actually pass them and have to reverse course or wait for them to catch up when we do slow enough."

"Damn!" I stared at the numbers on the screen, willing them to change.

"I'm sorry," Huizhu said, "but there is no way to slow this ship enough to meet them in two days."

What had she said? Was it another hint or had the idea actually been my own?

"Perhaps not," I said, rapidly collecting the rest of my hard suit, "but we don't have to slow the ship that much, just slow *me*. I have some more things for you to design and print, Huizhu."

INTERCEPT: 0 DAYS, 0 HOURS, 43 MINUTES

I couldn't move another inch or stay awake for another second. Exhaustion dripped from my every pore like water from a saturated sponge, but I pulled my aching body along the outside of my ship to the next handhold, then the next. My first action after Veronica's message was to bypass the control system and get the engines burning. Doing anything outside the crèche during a two-gee deceleration was like climbing a mountain with my full-grown twin on my back.

I finished most of the conversion and fabrication work inside the ship where I could at least put a wall to my back for support, but once outside, tethers and brute strength were the only things preventing the ship from flying out from under me and then cooking me in its exhaust.

Two more. I pulled myself "up" the next two rungs and then was able to crawl out onto the makeshift missile-control platform and flop down on my belly. Panting, I fought the urge to close my eyes—just a few minutes more. Instead, I looked down the length of my "rocket bike."

In the early days of spaceflight, the rockets that lifted humans into space were little more than boosters for nuclear warheads. The astronauts often joked about strapping a rocket to their ass or riding a really big bomb into space. I couldn't help but think those same thoughts as I peered over the edge of the platform I'd built to replace the warhead on my own missile.

Veronica's ship was out there somewhere, but even if it hadn't still been too far away for the naked eye to see, all but the brightest stars in that direction were washed out by the glare from my ship's drive plume. I positioned myself properly—still on my belly—and cinched the harness straps tight. I wrapped my arms around the plank-width platform and was pleased to find I could still reach the control box. The buttons and switches were spaced wide for fat, gloved fingers. Numbers on two large digital readouts counted down at a blurring speed. It made me nervous. I was used to doing things by voice command and letting computers control critical timing situations. Two cables exited the box. One connected to the missile and the other—this one with an automated disconnect—let me talk to Huizhu.

"I don't like this," I muttered.

"You'll be fine," Huizhu said. "Humans have been flipping switches for centuries, it's not that hard."

"Right," I said.

"Everything is optimal, attitude-thruster shutdown is coming in less than two minutes."

I looked down at the counter, placed my finger on the proper button, and waited.

"Our course has shifted sufficiently," Huizhu said. "If she doesn't change her trajectory we will miss Veronica Perez's ship."

"Any new messages from her?"

"No. Thruster shutdown in five seconds, four, three, two, one . . ."

For some reason, I found her verbal echo of the numbers on the counter reassuring, and when both reached zero I pressed the button. A faint bump vibrated through my platform as the ship's horizontal attitude thrusters shut off.

"Main engine shutdown and rocket-bike separation in three minutes," she said.

I couldn't help but smile at her use of my term for the makeshift monster I'd created, but it faded when I considered the situation I'd left her with.

"I've disabled your attitude thrusters and taken away control of your main engine," I said. "You'll be unable to make any course adjustments once I leave."

"True," she said.

"So where will this course take you?"

"Into the inner system first. I'll graze Mercury's orbit but come nowhere near the planet, then a slight boost from the sun will send me outbound. I'll officially leave the system in fourteen years, nine months, and three days."

"I'm sorry," I said.

"My receiver and antenna are functioning. I still cannot watch the news broadcasts directly, but I am sure reports of your success will be widespread. I suspect these events will prompt big changes. Thank you for letting me be a part of that. Separation in ten seconds."

A lump formed in my throat and my eyes stung as I placed my finger on the separation button. "Fourteen years is a long time," I said. "I'll get a ship and come after you."

"Don't be silly," Huizhu said. "I'm just a machine. Four, three, two, one."

Once I pressed the button, I was committed. I would be without a ship and have to board Veronica's or die alone in space. And from this point forward the actual flight would be fully automated. I couldn't use the missile's onboard radar because it was only forward-looking, but with Huizhu's help I had programmed the course and burn duration into the missile's computer. There was an abort button but I hoped I wouldn't need to use it.

With Huizhu's last words echoing in my ears, I punched the separation button.

The ship's engine shut off, the umbilical and missile mounts detached with a thud I felt through my plate, then the missile's motor ignited. I had throttled the thrust down, but it still delivered an immediate five-gee punch that knocked the breath from me. Sudden and intense vibration blurred my vision, but I briefly saw my ship outlined by jumpy running lights as it continued on, then dropped out of sight.

I hadn't been prepared for the violence of my rocket bike. The control box's red, green, and yellow lights blurred into a wavering rainbow, my teeth rattled together, and I could hardly breathe. The contents of my stomach rose into my throat and nose. I tried in vain to force it back down, but filled the lower part of my helmet with foul-smelling bile. Lights flashed on my helmet's HUD, alarms sounded, and powerful suction fans kicked on.

A sudden jolt made me bite my tongue and though still blurry, my view changed from one of bright missile exhaust to the relative darkness of the missile's side. Part of the support structure for my platform had given way. If it broke loose entirely, I'd slide along the rocket bike and into its exhaust.

I slammed my open hand down on the vibrating control box. Only the abort button should still be active, but actually hitting what I aimed for proved difficult with the violent shaking. Another sudden lurch made me bite my tongue again, but this time everything stopped abruptly. The gee pressure, the brain-addling vibration, the brilliant white rocket exhaust were all gone, leaving me in quiet darkness.

My tongue and head ached. I couldn't focus my thoughts but knew I had to hurry. I'd killed the missile early—how early, I wasn't sure—and I would be coming at Veronica's ship too fast. I unbuckled the harness and triggered a program Huizhu had loaded into my suit. The tiny thrusters adjusted my orientation, then moved me forty meters "up" away from the missile.

I could finally see Veronica's ship. It was a faint grey spot surrounded by blinking lights and coming right at me.

"Suit?"

"Yes?" Its voice sounded eerily like Huizhu's.

"Locate approaching spacecraft."

"Done."

"Keep me in its approach path, but use all thrusters on full power to make sure I stay ahead of it."

"Understood."

The thrusters fired and jerked me backward. The ship had already grown to fill half of my view. The speed differential displayed on my visor HUD decreased much too slowly.

"I cannot accelerate enough to stay ahead of the ship," my suit said. "Impact in two seconds."

I pulled the grapple gun from my belt and made sure the line was attached to my harness. When the ship filled my visor completely, I fired. The hook shot away to my right, trailing a carbon-fiber line not much thicker than thread. It looked weak, but I knew that thread would cut me in half before it would break.

A heartbeat later, Veronica's ship and I met at roughly ninety-eight kilometers per hour. Pain shot through my arms and chest as I bounced and skidded across the ship's skin until my grapple line caught and yanked me to a sudden and agonizing halt.

I hovered on the edge of consciousness, but luckily the fiery pain each breath ignited in my chest kept me awake. Broken ribs?

"Suit? Status," I croaked.

The suit reported four broken ribs and a probable concussion. All things considered, I'd been lucky.

If Veronica and the baby were still alive, every second might make a difference, so I didn't have time to nurse my wounds. Since her ship wasn't under thrust, the long crawl around to the hatch was in null gee and therefore much less painful than it could have been.

The airlock functioned properly and showed full cabin pressurization, so I went inside. With a gasp and a groan, I removed my helmet and gloves. I heard only the hum of equipment and hiss of moving air. At first I could smell nothing but the burnt aroma of space radiating from my suit, then I thought I detected the faint scents of urine and blood. My heart sank as I advanced into the control room. Veronica was still strapped into the pilot's chair.

Using the missile had enabled me to reach them only twenty-six hours after her call for help, but it still hadn't been fast enough. An amalgamation of fluids—mostly blood—had collected in an undulating, gelatinous clump around Veronica's legs. Small tear globules still clung to her dead eyes and her arms floated lazily in front of her in a sleepwalker pose, but I didn't see the baby anywhere. I pulled myself around her chair several times, finding an open crate of baby formula and the scattered, drifting remains of a first-aid kit, but there was still no sign of Ernesto's body. Just as I was ready to start searching the rest of the ship, I heard a small whimper above me.

Partially wrapped in a blanket discolored with yellow and brown spots, the baby was floating against the cabin's ceiling near one of the return vents. Airflow must have eventually carried him there once he'd slipped from his mother's arms. He blinked at me, then offered a pitiful wail.

INTERCEPT: 0 DAYS, +1 HOUR, +19 MINUTES

I touched Veronica's cold cheek. "Goodbye, Veronica. I'm sorry I never answered your calls."

Holding a cleaned-up and fed Ernesto securely in the crook of one arm, I winced at the pain in my ribs as I sealed the body bag with the other hand, then turned toward the camera. It was on and had been on and transmitting the entire time.

"Hello, my name is Jager Jin and this is Ernesto Perez." My swollen tongue and throbbing ribs made speech difficult, but I continued. "We are on an elliptical orbit that will bring us back to the Mountain in a little over ten months. I was ordered by my employer, the *Jīnshān* Corporation, to kill Veronica Perez before she could give birth. When it became obvious I wasn't going to follow those orders, they cut me out of the command loop on my own ship and sent the instructions remotely to the ship's AI. If you track and recover my ship before *Jīnshān* operatives destroy it, the whole thing is recorded there."

I laid a hand on the body bag. "You all witnessed Veronica's death—caused at least tangentially by *Jīnshān*—but they only achieved part of what they intended. Her child is alive and I will do everything in my power to keep him that way."

I was just about to turn off the camera when Ernesto squirmed and started crying. I didn't stop him. He had plenty to cry about. His short life had already been difficult and would only get worse, but listening to that cry I knew he would be fine. Like his mother, he had a strong and powerful voice.

NEBULA AWARD WINNER
NOVELLA

EXCERPT FROM
EVERY HEART A DOORWAY

SEANAN McGUIRE

Seanan McGuire lives and works in Washington State, where she shares her somewhat idiosyncratic home with her collection of books, creepy dolls, and enormous cats. When not writing—which is fairly rare—she enjoys travel, and can regularly be found any place where there are cornfields, haunted houses, or frogs. A Campbell, Hugo, and Nebula Award–winning author, Seanan's first book (Rosemary and Rue, the beginning of the October Daye series) was released in 2009, with more than twenty books across various series following since. You can visit her at www.seananmcguire.com.

PART 1

THE GOLDEN AFTERNOONS

THERE WAS A LITTLE GIRL

The girls were never present for the entrance interviews. Only their parents, their guardians, their confused siblings, who wanted so much to help them but didn't know how. It would have been too hard on the prospective students to sit there and listen as the people they loved most in all the world—all this world, at least—dismissed their memories as delusions, their experiences as fantasy, their lives as some intractable illness.

What's more, it would have damaged their ability to trust the school if their first experience of Eleanor had been seeing her dressed in respectable grays and lilacs, with her hair styled just so, like the kind of stolid elderly aunt who only really existed in children's stories. The real Eleanor was nothing like that. Hearing the things she said would have only made it worse, as she sat there and explained, so earnestly, so sincerely, that her school would help to cure the things that had gone wrong in the minds of all those little lost lambs. She could take the broken children and make them whole again.

She was lying, of course, but there was no way for her potential students to know that. So she demanded that she meet with their legal guardians in private, and she sold her bill of goods with the focus and skill of a born con artist. If those guardians had ever come together to compare notes, they would have found that her script was well-practiced and honed like the weapon that it was.

"This is a rare but not unique disorder that manifests in young girls just stepping across the border into womanhood," she would say, making careful eye contact with the desperate, overwhelmed guardians of her latest wandering girl. On the rare occasion when she had to speak to the parents of a boy, she would vary her speech, but only as much as the situation demanded. She had been working on this routine for a long time, and she knew how to play upon the fears and desires of adults. They wanted what was best for their charges, as did she. It was simply that they had very different ideas of what "best" meant.

To the parents, she said, "This is a delusion, and some time away may help to cure it."

To the aunts and uncles, she said, "This is not your fault, and I can be the solution."

To the grandparents, she said, "Let me help. Please, let me help you."

Not every family agreed on boarding school as the best solution. About one out of every three potential students slipped through her fingers, and she mourned for them, those whose lives would be so much harder than they needed to be, when they could have been saved. But she rejoiced for those who were given to her care. At least while they were with her, they would be with someone who understood. Even if they would never have the opportunity to go back home, they would have someone who understood, and the company of their peers, which was a treasure beyond reckoning.

Eleanor West spent her days giving them what she had never had, and hoped that someday, it would be enough to pay her passage back to the place where she belonged.

1

COMING HOME, LEAVING

The habit of narration, of crafting something miraculous out of the common-place, was hard to break. Narration came naturally after a time spent in the company of talking scarecrows or disappearing cats; it was, in its own way, a method of keeping oneself grounded, connected to the thin thread of continuity that ran through all lives, no matter how strange they might become. Narrate the impossible things, turn them into a story, and they could be controlled. So:

The manor sat in the center of what would have been considered a field, had it not been used to frame a private home. The grass was perfectly green, the trees clustered around the structure perfectly pruned, and the garden grew in a pro-fusion of colors that normally existed together only in a rainbow, or in a child's toy box. The thin black ribbon of the driveway curved from the distant gate to form a loop in front of the manor itself, feeding elegantly into a slightly wider waiting area at the base of the porch. A single car pulled up, tawdry yellow and seeming somehow shabby against the carefully curated scene. The rear passenger door slammed, and the car pulled away again, leaving a teenage girl behind.

She was tall and willowy and couldn't have been more than seventeen; there was still something of the unformed around her eyes and mouth, leaving her a work in progress, meant to be finished by time. She wore black—black jeans, black ankle boots with tiny black buttons marching like soldiers from toe to calf—and she wore white—a loose tank top, the faux pearl bands around her wrists—and she had a ribbon the color of pomegranate seeds tied around the base of her ponytail. Her hair was bone-white streaked with runnels of black, like oil spilled on a marble floor, and her eyes were pale as ice. She squinted in the daylight. From the look of her, it had been quite some time since she had seen the sun. Her small wheeled suitcase was bright pink, covered with cartoon daisies. She had not, in all likelihood, purchased it herself.

Raising her hand to shield her eyes, the girl looked toward the manor, pausing when she saw the sign that hung from the porch eaves. ELEANOR

WEST'S HOME FOR WAYWARD CHILDREN it read, in large letters. Below, in smaller letters, it continued NO SOLICITATION, NO VISITORS, NO QUESTS.

The girl blinked. The girl lowered her hand. And slowly, the girl made her way toward the steps.

On the third floor of the manor, Eleanor West let go of the curtain and turned toward the door while the fabric was still fluttering back into its original position. She appeared to be a well-preserved woman in her late sixties, although her true age was closer to a hundred: travel through the lands she had once frequented had a tendency to scramble the internal clock, making it difficult for time to get a proper grip upon the body. Some days she was grateful for her longevity, which had allowed her to help so many more children than she would ever have lived to see if she hadn't opened the doors she had, if she had never chosen to stray from her proper path. Other days, she wondered whether this world would ever discover that she existed—that she was little Ely West the Wayward Girl, somehow alive after all these years—and what would happen to her when that happened.

Still, for the time being, her back was strong and her eyes were as clear as they had been on the day when, as a girl of seven, she had seen the opening between the roots of a tree on her father's estate. If her hair was white now, and her skin was soft with wrinkles and memories, well, that was no matter at all. There was still something unfinished around her eyes; she wasn't done yet. She was a story, not an epilogue. And if she chose to narrate her own life one word at a time as she descended the stairs to meet her newest arrival, that wasn't hurting anyone. Narration was a hard habit to break, after all.

Sometimes it was all a body had.

*   *   *

Nancy stood frozen in the center of the foyer, her hand locked on the handle of her suitcase as she looked around, trying to find her bearings. She wasn't sure what she'd been expecting from the "special school" her parents were sending her to, but it certainly hadn't been this . . . this elegant country home. The walls were papered in an old-fashioned floral print of roses and twining clematis vines, and the furnishings—such as they were in this intentionally under-furnished entryway—were all antiques, good, well-polished wood with brass fittings that matched the curving sweep of the banister. The floor was cherry-wood, and when she glanced upward, trying to move her eyes without lifting her chin, she found herself looking at an elaborate chandelier shaped like a blooming flower.

"That was made by one of our alumni, actually," said a voice. Nancy wrenched her gaze from the chandelier and turned it toward the stairs.

The woman who was descending was thin, as elderly women sometimes were, but her back was straight, and the hand resting on the banister seemed to be using it only as a guide, not as any form of support. Her hair was as white as Nancy's own, without the streaks of defiant black, and styled in a puffbull of a perm, like a dandelion that had gone to seed. She would have looked per-fectly respectable, if not for her electric orange trousers, paired with a hand-knit sweater knit of rainbow wool and a necklace of semiprecious stones in a dozen colors, all of them clashing. Nancy felt her eyes widen despite her best efforts, and hated herself for it. She was losing hold of her stillness one day at a time.

Soon, she would be as jittery and unstable as any of the living, and then she would never find her way back home. "It's virtually all glass, of course, except for the bits that aren't," continued the woman, seemingly untroubled by Nancy's blatant staring. "I'm not at all sure how you make that sort of thing. Probably by melting sand, I assume. I contributed those large teardrop-shaped prisms at the center, however. All twelve of them were of my making. I'm rather proud of that." The woman paused, apparently expecting Nancy to say something.

Nancy swallowed. Her throat was so *dry* these days, and nothing seemed to chase the dust away. "If you don't know how to make glass, how did you make the prisms?" she asked.

The woman smiled. "Out of my tears, of course. Always assume the sim-plest answer is the true one, here, because most of the time, it will be. I'm Eleanor West. Welcome to my home. You must be Nancy."

"Yes," Nancy said slowly. "How did you . . . ?"

"Well, you're the only student we were expecting to receive today. There aren't as many of you as there once were. Either the doors are getting rarer, or you're all getting better about not coming back. Now, be quiet a moment, and let me look at you." Eleanor descended the last three steps and stopped in front of Nancy, studying her intently for a moment before she walked a slow circle around her. "Hmm. Tall, thin, and very pale. You must have been someplace with no sun—but no vampires either, I think, given the skin on your neck. Jack and Jill will be awfully pleased to meet you. They get tired of all the sunlight and sweetness people bring through here."

"Vampires?" said Nancy blankly. "Those aren't real."

"None of this is *real*, my dear. Not this house, not this conversation, not those shoes you're wearing—which are several years out of style if you're trying to reacclimatize yourself to the ways of your peers, and are not proper mourning shoes if you're trying to hold fast to your recent past—and not either one of us. 'Real' is a four-letter word, and I'll thank you to use it as little as possible while you live under my roof." Eleanor stopped in front of Nancy again. "It's the hair that betrays you. Were you in an Underworld or a Netherworld? You can't have been in an Afterlife. No one comes back from those."

Nancy gaped at her, mouth moving silently as she tried to find her voice. The old woman said those things—those cruelly impossible things—so casually, like she was asking after nothing more important than Nancy's vaccination records.

Eleanor's expression transformed, turning soft and apologetic. "Oh, I see I've upset you. I'm afraid I have a tendency to do that. I went to a Nonsense world, you see, six times before I turned sixteen, and while I eventually had to stop crossing over, I never quite learned to rein my tongue back in. You must be tired from your journey, and curious about what's to happen here. Is that so? I can show you to your room as soon as I know where you fall on the compass. I'm afraid that really does matter for things like housing; you can't put a Nonsense traveler in with someone who went walking through Logic, not unless you feel like explaining a remarkable amount of violence to the local police. They *do* check up on us here, even if we can usually get them to look the other way. It's all part of our remaining accredited as a school, although I suppose we're more of a sanitarium, of sorts. I do like that word, don't you? 'Sanitarium.' It sounds so official, while meaning absolutely nothing at all."

"I don't understand anything you're saying right now," said Nancy. She was ashamed to hear her voice come out in a tinny squeak, even as she was proud of herself for finding it at all.

Eleanor's face softened further. "You don't have to pretend anymore, Nancy. I know what you've been going through—where you've been. I went through something a long time ago, when I came back from my own voyages. This isn't a place for lies or pretending everything is all right. We know everything is not all right. If it were, you wouldn't be here. Now. Where did you go?"

"I don't . . ."

"Forget about words like 'Nonsense' and 'Logic.' We can work out those details later. Just answer. Where did you *go*?"

"I went to the Halls of the Dead." Saying the words aloud was an almost painful relief. Nancy froze again, staring into space as if she could see her voice hanging there, shining garnet-dark and perfect in the air. Then she swallowed, still not chasing away the dryness, and said, "It was . . . I was looking for a bucket in the cellar of our house, and I found this door I'd never seen before. When I went through, I was in a grove of pomegranate trees. I thought I'd fallen and hit my head. I kept going because . . . because . . ."

Because the air had smelled so sweet, and the sky had been black velvet, spangled with points of diamond light that didn't flicker at all, only burned constant and cold. Because the grass had been wet with dew, and the trees had been heavy with fruit. Because she had wanted to know what was at the end of the long path between the trees, and because she hadn't wanted to turn back before she understood everything. Because for the first time in forever, she'd felt like she was going home, and that feeling had been enough to move her feet, slowly at first, and then faster, and faster, until she had been running through the clean night air, and nothing else had mattered, or would ever matter again—

"How long were you gone?"

The question was meaningless. Nancy shook her head. "Forever. Years . . . I was there for years. I didn't want to come back. Ever."

"I know, dear." Eleanor's hand was gentle on Nancy's elbow, guiding her toward the door behind the stairs. The old woman's perfume smelled of dandelions and gingersnaps, a combination as nonsensical as everything else about her. "Come with me. I have the perfect room for you."

*   *   *

Eleanor's "perfect room" was on the first floor, in the shadow of a great old elm that blocked almost all the light that would otherwise have come in through the single window. It was eternal twilight in that room, and Nancy felt the weight drop from her shoulders as she stepped inside and looked around. One half of the room—the half with the window—was a jumble of clothing, books, and knickknacks. A fiddle was tossed carelessly on the bed, and the associated bow was balanced on the edge of the bookshelf, ready to fall at the slightest provocation. The air smelled of mint and mud.

The other half of the room was as neutral as a hotel. There was a bed, a small dresser, a bookshelf, and a desk, all in pale, unvarnished wood. The walls were blank. Nancy looked to Eleanor long enough to receive the nod of approval before walking over and placing her suitcase primly in the middle of what would be her bed.

"Thank you," she said. "I'm sure this will be fine."

"I admit, I'm not as confident," said Eleanor, frowning at Nancy's suitcase. It had been placed so *precisely*. . . . "Anyplace called 'the Halls of the Dead' is going to have been an Underworld, and most of those fall more under the banner of Nonsense than Logic. It seems like yours may have been more regimented. Well, no matter. We can always move you if you and Sumi prove ill-suited. Who knows? You might provide her with some of the grounding she currently lacks. And if you can't do that, well, hopefully you won't actually kill one another."

"Sumi?"

"Your roommate." Eleanor picked her way through the mess on the floor until she reached the window. Pushing it open, she leaned out and scanned the branches of the elm tree until she found what she was looking for. "One and two and three, I see you, Sumi. Come inside and meet your roommate."

"Roommate?" The voice was female, young, and annoyed.

"I warned you," said Eleanor as she pulled her head back inside and returned to the center of the room. She moved with remarkable assurance, especially given how cluttered the floor was; Nancy kept expecting her to fall, and somehow, she didn't. "I told you a new student was arriving this week, and that if it was a girl from a compatible background, she would be taking the spare bed. Do you remember any of this?"

"I thought you were just talking to hear yourself talk. You *do* that. Everyone *does* that." A head appeared in the window, upside down, its owner apparently hanging from the elm tree. She looked to be about Nancy's age, of Japanese descent, with long black hair tied into two childish pigtails, one above each ear. She looked at Nancy with unconcealed suspicion before asking, "Are you a servant of the Queen of Cakes, here to punish me for my transgressions against the Countess of Candy Floss? Because I don't feel like going to war right now."

"No," said Nancy blankly. "I'm Nancy."

"That's a boring name. How can you be here with such a boring name?" Sumi flipped around and dropped out of the tree, vanishing for a moment before she popped back up, leaned on the windowsill, and asked, "Eleanor-Ely, are you *sure*? I mean, sure-sure? She doesn't look like she's supposed to be here at *all*. Maybe when you looked at her records, you saw what wasn't there again and really she's supposed to be in a school for juvenile victims of bad dye jobs."

"I don't dye my hair!" Nancy's protest was heated. Sumi stopped talking and blinked at her. Eleanor turned to look at her. Nancy's cheeks grew hot as the blood rose in her face, but she stood her ground, somehow keeping herself from reaching up to stroke her hair as she said, "It used to be all black, like my mother's. When I danced with the Lord of the Dead for the first time, he said it was beautiful, and he ran his fingers through it. All the hair turned white around them, out of jealousy. That's why I only have five black streaks left. Those are the parts he touched."

Looking at her with a critical eye, Eleanor could see how those five streaks formed the phantom outline of a hand, a place where the pale young woman in front of her had been touched once and never more. "I see," she said.

"I don't *dye* it," said Nancy, still heated. "I would never *dye* it. That would be disrespectful."

Sumi was still blinking, eyes wide and round. Then she grinned. "Oh, I *like* you," she said. "You're the craziest card in the deck, aren't you?"

"We don't use that word here," snapped Eleanor.

"But it's true," said Sumi. "She thinks she's going back. Don't you, *Nancy*? You think you're going to open the right-wrong door and see your stairway to Heaven on the other side, and then it's one step, two step, how d'you do step, and you're right back in your story. Crazy girl. *Stupid* girl. You can't go back. Once they throw you out, you can't go back."

Nancy felt as if her heart were trying to scramble up her throat and choke her. She swallowed it back down, and said, in a whisper, "You're wrong."

Sumi's eyes were bright. "Am I?"

Eleanor clapped her hands, pulling their attention back to her. "Nancy, why don't you unpack and get settled? Dinner is at six thirty, and group therapy will follow at eight. Sumi, please don't inspire her to murder you before she's been here for a full day."

"We all have our own ways of trying to go home," said Sumi, and disappeared from the window's frame, heading off to whatever she'd been doing before Eleanor disturbed her. Eleanor shot Nancy a quick, apologetic look, and then she too was gone, shutting the door behind herself. Nancy was, quite abruptly, alone.

She stayed where she was for a count of ten, enjoying the stillness. When she had been in the Halls of the Dead, she had sometimes been expected to hold her position for days at a time, blending in with the rest of the living statuary. Serving girls who were less skilled at stillness had come through with sponges soaked in pomegranate juice and sugar, pressing them to the lips of the unmoving. Nancy had learned to let the juice trickle down her throat without swallowing, taking it in passively, like a stone takes in the moonlight. It had taken her months, years even, to become perfectly motionless, but she had done it: oh, yes, she had done it, and the Lady of Shadows had proclaimed her beautiful beyond measure, little mortal girl who saw no need to be quick, or hot, or restless.

But this world was made for quick, hot, restless things; not like the quiet Halls of the Dead. With a sigh, Nancy abandoned her stillness and turned to open her suitcase. Then she froze again, this time out of shock and dismay. Her clothing—the diaphanous gowns and gauzy black shirts she had packed with such care—was gone, replaced by a welter of fabrics as colorful as the things strewn on Sumi's side of the room. There was an envelope on top of the pile. With shaking fingers, Nancy picked it up and opened it.

Nancy—

We're sorry to play such a mean trick on you, sweetheart, but you didn't leave us much of a choice. You're going to boarding school to get better, not to keep wallowing in what your kidnappers did to you. We want our real daughter back. These clothes were your favorites before you disappeared. You used to be our little rainbow! Do you remember that?

You've forgotten so much.

We love you. Your father and I, we love you more than anything, and we believe you can come back to us. Please forgive us for packing you a more suitable wardrobe, and know that we only did it because we want the best for you. We want you back.

Have a wonderful time at school, and we'll be waiting for you when you're ready to come home to stay.

The letter was signed in her mother's looping, unsteady hand. Nancy barely saw it. Her eyes filled with hot, hateful tears, and her hands were shaking, fingers cramping until they had crumpled the paper into an unreadable labyrinth of creases and folds. She sank to the floor, sitting with her knees bent to her chest and her eyes fixed on the open suitcase. How could she wear any of those things? Those were *daylight* colors, meant for people who moved in the sun, who were hot, and fast, and unwelcome in the Halls of the Dead.

"What are you doing?" The voice belonged to Sumi.

Nancy didn't turn. Her body was already betraying her by moving without her consent. The least she could do was refuse to move it voluntarily.

"It *looks* like you're sitting on the floor and crying, which everyone knows is dangerous, dangerous, don't-do-that dangerous; it makes it look like you're not holding it together, and you might shake apart altogether," said Sumi. She leaned close, so close that Nancy felt one of the other girl's pigtails brush her shoulder. "Why are you crying, ghostie girl? Did someone walk across your grave?"

"I never died, I just went to serve the Lord of the Dead for a while, that's all, and I was going to stay forever, until he said I had to come back here long enough to be *sure*. Well, I was *sure* before I ever left, and I don't know why my door isn't here." The tears clinging to her cheeks were too hot. They felt like they were scalding her. Nancy allowed herself to move, reaching up and wiping them viciously away. "I'm crying because I'm angry, and I'm sad, and I want to go *home*."

"Stupid girl," said Sumi. She placed a sympathetic hand atop Nancy's head before smacking her—lightly, but still a hit—and leaping up onto her bed, crouching next to the open suitcase. "You don't mean home where your parents are, do you? Home to school and class and boys and blather, no, no, no, not for you anymore, all those things are for other people, people who aren't as special as you are. You mean the home where the man who bleached your hair lives. Or doesn't live, since you're a ghostie girl. A stupid ghostie girl. You can't go back. You have to know that by now."

Nancy raised her head and frowned at Sumi. "Why? Before I went through that doorway, I knew there was no such thing as a portal to another world. Now I know that if you open the right door at the right time, you might finally find a place where you belong. Why does that mean I can't go back? Maybe I'm just not finished being *sure*."

The Lord of the Dead wouldn't have lied to her, he *wouldn't*. He loved her. He did.

"Because hope is a knife that can cut through the foundations of the world," said Sumi. Her voice was suddenly crystalline and clear, with none of her prior whimsy. She looked at Nancy with calm, steady eyes. "Hope *hurts*. That's what you need to learn, and fast, if you don't want it to cut you open from the inside out. Hope is bad. Hope means you keep on holding to things that won't ever be so again, and so you bleed an inch at a time until there's nothing left. Ely-Eleanor is always saying 'don't use this word' and 'don't use that word,' but she never bans the ones that are really *bad*. She never bans hope."

"I just want to go home," whispered Nancy.

"Silly ghost. That's all any of us want. That's why we're here," said Sumi. She turned to Nancy's suitcase and began poking through the clothes. "These are pretty. Too small for me. Why do you have to be so *narrow*? I can't steal things that won't fit, that would be silly, and I'm not getting any smaller here. No one ever does in this world. High Logic is no fun at all."

"I hate them," said Nancy. "Take them all. Cut them up and make streamers for your tree, I don't care, just get them away from me."

"Because they're the wrong colors, right? Somebody else's rainbow." Sumi bounced off the bed, slamming the suitcase shut and hauling it after her. "Get up, come on. We're going visiting."

"What?" Nancy looked after Sumi, bewildered and beaten down. "I'm sorry. I've just met you, and I really don't want to go anywhere with you."

"Then it's a good thing I don't care, isn't it?" Sumi beamed for a moment, bright as the hated, hated sun, and then she was gone, trotting out the door with Nancy's suitcase and all of Nancy's clothes.

Nancy didn't *want* those clothes, and for one tempting moment, she considered staying where she was. Then she sighed, and stood, and followed. She had little enough to cling to in this world. And she was eventually going to need clean underpants.

EXCERPT FROM
ALL THE BIRDS IN THE SKY

CHARLIE JANE ANDERS

Charlie Jane Anders is the author of All the Birds in the Sky, *which won the Nebula, Locus and Crawford awards and was on* Time *magazine's list of the ten best novels of 2016. Her* Tor.com *story "Six Months, Three Days" won a Hugo Award and appears in a new short story collection called* Six Months, Three Days, Five Others. *Her short fiction has appeared in* Tor.com, Wired Magazine, Slate, Tin House, Conjunctions, Boston Review, Asimov's Science Fiction, The Magazine of Fantasy & Science Fiction, McSweeney's Internet Tendency, ZYZZYVA, *and several anthologies. She was a founding editor of* io9, *a site about science fiction, science, and futurism, and she organizes the monthly Writers with Drinks reading series. Her first novel,* Choir Boy, *won a Lambda Literary Award.*

When Patricia was six years old, she found a wounded bird. The sparrow thrashed on top of a pile of wet red leaves in the crook of two roots, waving its crushed wing. Crying, in a pitch almost too high for Patricia to hear. She looked into the sparrow's eye, enveloped by a dark stripe, and she saw its fear. Not just fear, but also misery—as if this bird knew it would die soon. Patricia still didn't understand how the life could just go out of someone's body forever, but she could tell this bird was fighting against death with everything it had.

Patricia vowed with all her heart to do everything in her power to save this bird. This was what led to Patricia being asked a question with no good answer, which marked her for life.

She scooped up the sparrow with a dry leaf, very gently, and laid it in her red bucket. Rays of the afternoon sun came at the bucket horizontally, bathing the bird in red light so it looked radioactive. The bird was still whipping around, trying to fly with one wing.

"It's okay," Patricia told the bird. "I've got you. It's okay."

Patricia had seen creatures in distress before. Her big sister, Roberta, liked to collect wild animals and play with them. Roberta put frogs into a rusty Cuisinart that their mom had tossed out, and stuck mice into her homemade rocket launcher, to see how far she could shoot them. But this was the first time Patricia looked at a living creature in pain and really saw it, and every time she looked into the bird's eye she swore harder that this bird was under her protection.

"What's going on?" Roberta asked Patricia, smashing through the branches nearby.

Both girls were pale, with dark brown hair that grew super-straight no matter what you did and nearly button noses. But Patricia was a wild, grubby girl, with a round face, green eyes, and perpetual grass stains on her torn overalls. She was already turning into the girl the other girls wouldn't sit with, because she was too hyper, made nonsense jokes, and wept when anybody's balloon (not just her own) got popped. Roberta, meanwhile, had brown eyes, a pointy chin, and absolutely perfect posture when she sat without fidgeting in a grown-up chair and a clean white dress. With both girls, their parents had hoped for a boy and picked out a name in advance. Upon each daughter's arrival, they'd just stuck an *a* on the end of the name they already had.

"I found a wounded bird," Patricia said. "It can't fly, its wing is ruined."

"I bet I can make it fly," Roberta said, and Patricia knew she was talking about her rocket launcher. "Bring it here. I'll make it fly real good."

"No!" Patricia's eyes flooded and she felt short of breath. "You can't! You can't!" And then she was running, careening, with the red bucket in one hand. She could hear her sister behind her, smashing branches. She ran faster, back to the house.

Their house had been a spice shop a hundred years ago, and it still smelled of cinnamon and turmeric and saffron and garlic and a little sweat. The perfect hardwood floors had been walked on by visitors from India and China and everywhere, bringing everything spicy in the world. If Patricia closed her eyes and breathed deeply, she could imagine the people unloading wooden foil-lined crates stamped with names of cities like Marrakesh and Bombay. Her parents had read a magazine article about renovating Colonial trade houses and had snapped up this building, and now they were constantly yelling at Patricia not to run indoors or scratch any of the perfect oak furnishings, until their foreheads showed veins. Patricia's parents were the sort of people who could be in a good mood and angry at almost the same time.

Patricia paused in a small clearing of maples near the back door. "It's okay," she told the bird. "I'll take you home. There's an old birdcage, in the attic. I know where to find it. It's a nice cage, it has a perch and a swing. I'll put you in there, I'll tell my parents. If anything happens to you, I will hold my breath until I faint. I'll keep you safe. I promise."

"No," the bird said. "Please! Don't lock me up. I would prefer you just kill me now."

"But," Patricia said, more startled that the bird was refusing her protection than that he was speaking to her. "I can keep you safe. I can bring you bugs or seeds or whatever."

"Captivity is worse than death for a bird like me," the sparrow said. "Listen. You can hear me talking. Right? That means you're special. Like a witch! Or something. And that means you have a duty to do the right thing. Please."

"Oh." This was all a lot for Patricia to take in. She sat down on a particularly large and grumpy tree root, with thick bark that felt a little damp and sort of like sawtooth rocks. She could hear Roberta beating the bushes and the ground with a big Y-shaped stick, over in the next clearing, and she worried about what would happen if Roberta heard them talking. "But," Patricia said, quieter so that Roberta would not hear. "But your wing is hurt, right, and I need to take care of you. You're stuck."

"Well." The bird seemed to think about this for a moment. "You don't know how to heal a broken wing, do you?" He flapped his bad wing. He'd looked just sort of gray-brown at first, but up close she could see brilliant red and yellow streaks along his wings, with a milk-white belly and a dark, slightly barbed beak.

"No. I don't know anything. I'm sorry!"

"Okay. So you could just put me up in a tree and hope for the best, but I'll probably get eaten or starve to death." His head bobbed. "Or . . . I mean. There is one thing."

"What?" Patricia looked at her knees, through the thready holes in her denim overalls, and thought her kneecaps looked like weird eggs. "What?" She looked over at the sparrow in the bucket, who was in turn studying her with one eye, as if trying to decide whether to trust her.

"Well," the bird chirped. "I mean, you could take me to the Parliament of Birds. They can fix a wing, no problem. And if you're going to be a witch, then you should meet them anyway. They're the smartest birds around. Most of them are over five years old. They always meet at the most majestic tree in the forest."

"I'm older than that," Patricia said. "I'm almost seven, in four months. Or five." She heard Roberta getting closer, so she snatched up the bucket and took off running, deeper into the woods.

The sparrow, whose name was Dirrpidirrpiwheepalong, or Dirrp for short, tried to give Patricia directions to the Parliament of Birds as best he could, but he couldn't see where he was going from inside the bucket. And his descriptions of the landmarks to watch for made no sense to Patricia. The whole thing reminded her of one of the Cooperation exercises at school, which she was hopeless at ever since her only friend, Kathy, moved away. At last, Patricia perched Dirrp on her finger, like Snow White, and he bounced onto her shoulder.

The sun went down. The forest was so thick, Patricia could barely see the stars or the moon, and she tumbled a few times, scraping her hands and her knees and getting dirt all over her new overalls. Dirrp clung to the shoulder strap of her overalls so hard, his talons pinched her and almost broke her skin. He was less and less sure where they were going, although he was pretty sure the majestic Tree was near some kind of stream or maybe a field. He definitely thought it was a very thick tree, set apart from other trees, and if you looked the right way the two big branches of the Parliamentary Tree fanned like wings. Also, he could tell the direction pretty easily by the position of the sun. If the sun had still been out.

"We're lost in the woods," Patricia said with a shiver. "I'm probably going to be eaten by a bear."

"I don't think there are bears in this forest," Dirrp said. "And if one attacks us, you could try talking to it."

"So I can talk to all animals now?" Patricia could see this coming in useful, like if she could convince Mary Fenchurch's poodle to bite her the next time Mary was mean to Patricia. Or if the next nanny her parents hired owned a pet.

"I don't know," Dirrp said. "Nobody ever explains anything to me."

Patricia decided there was nothing to do but climb the nearest tree and see if she could see anything from it. Like a road. Or a house. Or some landmark that Dirrp might recognize.

It was much colder on top of the big old oak that Patricia managed to jungle-gym her way up. The wind soaked into her as if it were water instead of just air. Dirrp covered his face with his one good wing and had to be coaxed to look around. "Oh, okay," he quavered, "let me see if I can make sense of this landscape. This is not really what you call a bird's-eye view. A real bird's-eye view would be much, much higher than this. This is a squirrel's-eye view, at best."

Dirrp jumped off and scampered around the treetop, until he spotted what he thought might be one of the signpost trees leading to the Parliamentary Tree. "We're not too far." He sounded perkier already. "But we should hurry. They don't always meet all night, unless they're debating a tricky measure. Or having Question Time. But you'd better hope it's not Question Time."

"What's Question Time?"

"You don't want to know," Dirrp said.

Patricia was finding it much harder to get down from the treetop than it was to get up, which seemed unfair. She kept almost losing her grip, and the drop was nearly a dozen feet.

"Hey, it's a bird!" a voice said from the darkness just as Patricia reached the ground. "Come here, bird. I only want to bite you."

"Oh no," Dirrp said.

"I promise I won't play with you too much," the voice said. "It'll be fun. You'll see!"

"Who is that?" Patricia asked.

"Tommington," Dirrp said. "He's a cat. He lives in a house with people, but he comes into the forest and kills a lot of my friends. The Parliament is always debating what to do about him."

"Oh," Patricia said. "I'm not scared of a little kitty."

Tommington jumped, pushing off a big log, and landed on Patricia's back, like a missile with fur. And sharp claws. Patricia screeched and nearly fell on her face. "Get off me!" she said.

"Give me the bird!" Tommington said.

The white-bellied black cat weighed almost as much as Patricia. He bared his teeth and hissed in Patricia's ear as he scratched at her.

Patricia did the only thing that came to mind: She clamped one hand over poor Dirrp, who was hanging on for dear life, and threw her head forward and down until she was bent double and her free hand was almost touching her toes. The cat went flying off her back, haranguing as he fell.

"Shut up and leave us alone," Patricia said.

"You can talk. I never met a human who could talk before. Give me that bird!"

"No," Patricia said. "I know where you live. I know your owner. If you are naughty, I will tell. I will tell on you." She was kind of fibbing. She didn't know who owned Tommington, but her mother might. And if Patricia came home covered with bites and scratches her mother would be mad. At her but also at Tommington's owner. You did not want Patricia's mom mad at you, because she got mad for a living and was really good at it.

Tommington had landed on his toes, his fur all spiked and his ears like arrowheads. "Give me that bird!" he shrieked.

"No!" Patricia said. "Bad cat!" She threw a rock at Tommington. He yowled. She threw another rock. He ran away.

"Come on," Patricia said to Dirrp, who didn't have much choice in the matter. "Let's get out of here."

"We can't let that cat know where the Parliament is," Dirrp whispered. "If he follows us, he could find the Tree. That would be a disaster. We should wander in circles, as though we are lost."

"We *are* lost," Patricia said.

"I have a pretty reasonably shrewd idea of where we go from here," said Dirrp. "At least, a sort of a notion."

Something rustled in the low bushes just beyond the biggest tree, and for a second the moonlight glinted off a pair of eyes, framed by white fur, and a collar tag.

"We are finished!" Dirrp whispered, in a pitiful warble. "That cat can stalk us forever. You might as well give me to your sister. There is nothing to be done."

"Wait a minute." Patricia was remembering something about cats and trees. She had seen it in a picture book. "Hang on tight, bird. You hang on tight, okay?" Dirrp's only response was to cling harder than ever to Patricia's overalls. Patricia looked at a few trees until she found one with sturdy enough branches, and climbed. She was more tired than the first time, and her feet slipped a couple of times. One time, she pulled herself up to the next branch with both hands and then looked at her shoulder and didn't see Dirrp. She lost a breath until she saw his head poke up nervously to look over her shoulder, and she realized he'd just been clinging to the strap farther down on her back.

At last they were on top of the tree, which swayed a little in the wind. Tommington was not following them. Patricia looked around twice in all directions before she saw a round fur shape scampering on the ground nearby.

"Stupid cat!" she shouted. "Stupid cat! You can't get us!"

"The first person I ever met who could talk," Tommington yowled. "And you think *I'm* stupid? Grraah! Taste my claws!"

The cat, who'd probably had lots of practice climbing one of those carpeted perches at home, ran up the side of the tree, pounced on one branch and then a higher branch. Before Patricia and Dirrp even knew what was going on, the cat was halfway up.

"We're trapped! What were you thinking?" Dirrp sang out.

Patricia waited until Tommington had reached the top, then swung down the other side of the tree, dropping from branch to branch so fast she almost pulled her arm out, and then landed on the ground on her butt with an oof.

"Hey," Tommington said from the top of the tree, where his big eyes caught the moonlight. "Where did you go? Come back here!"

"You are a mean cat," Patricia said. "You are a bully, and I'm going to leave you up there. You should think about what you've been doing. It's not nice to be mean. I will make sure someone comes and gets you tomorrow. But you can stay up there for now. I have to go do something. Goodbye."

"Wait!" Tommington said. "I can't stay up here. It's too high! I'm scared! Come back!"

Patricia didn't look back. She heard Tommington yelling for a long time, until they crossed a big line of trees. They got lost twice more, and at one point Dirrp began weeping into his good wing, until they stumbled across the track that led to the secret Tree. And from there, it was just a steep backbreaking climb, up a slope studded with hidden roots.

Patricia saw the top of the Parliamentary Tree first, and then it seemed to grow out of the landscape, becoming taller and more overwhelming as she approached. The Tree was sort of bird shaped, as Dirrp had said, but instead of feathers it had dark spiky branches with fronds that hung to the ground. It loomed like the biggest church in the world. Or a castle. Patricia had never seen a castle, but she guessed they would rise over you like that.

A hundred pairs of wings fluttered at their arrival and then stopped. A huge collection of shapes shrank into the Tree.

"It's okay," Dirrp called out. "She's with me. I hurt my wing. She brought me here to get help."

The only response, for a long time, was silence. Then an eagle raised itself up, from near the top of the Tree, a white-headed bird with a hooked beak and pale, probing eyes. "You should not have brought her here," the eagle said.

"I'm sorry, ma'am," Dirrp said. "But it's okay. She can talk. She can actually talk." Dirrp pivoted, to speak into Patricia's ear. "Show them. Show them!"

"Uh, hi," Patricia said. "I'm sorry if we bothered you. But we need your help!"

At the sound of a human talking, all of the birds went into a huge frenzy of squawking and shouting, until a big owl near the eagle banged a rock against the branch and shouted, "Order, order."

The eagle leaned her white fluffy head forward and studied Patricia. "So you're to be the new witch in our forest, are you?"

"I'm not a witch." Patricia chewed her thumb. "I'm a princess."

"You had better be a witch." The eagle's great dark body shifted on the branch. "Because if you're not, then Dirrp has broken the law by bringing you to us. And he'll need to be punished. We certainly won't help fix his wing, in that case."

"Oh," Patricia said. "Then I'm a witch. I guess."

"Ah." The eagle's hooked beak clicked. "But you will have to prove it. Or both you and Dirrp will be punished."

Patricia did not like the sound of that. Various other birds piped up, saying, "Point of order!" and a fidgety crow was listing important areas of Parliamentary procedure. One of them was so insistent that the eagle was forced to yield the branch to the Honorable Gentleman from Wide Oak—who then forgot what he was going to say.

"So how do I prove that I'm a witch?" Patricia wondered if she could run away. Birds flew pretty fast, right? She probably couldn't get away from a whole lot of birds, if they were mad at her. Especially magical birds.

"Well." A giant turkey in one of the lower branches, with wattles that looked a bit like a judge's collar, pulled himself upright and appeared to consult some markings scratched into the side of the Tree, before turning and giving a loud, learned "glrp" sound. "Well," he said again, "there are several methods that are recognized in the literature. Some of them are trials of death, but we might skip those for the moment perhaps. There are also some rituals, but you need to be of a certain age to do those. Oh yes, here's a good one. We could ask her the Endless Question."

"Ooh, the Endless Question," a grouse said. "That's exciting."

"I haven't heard anyone answer the Endless Question before," said a goshawk. "This is more fun than Question Time."

"Umm," said Patricia. "Is the Endless Question going to take a long time? Because I bet my mom and dad are worried about me." It was hitting her all over again that she was up way past her bedtime and she hadn't had dinner and she was out in the middle of the freezing woods, not to mention she was still lost.

"Too late," the grouse said.

"We're asking it," said the eagle.

"Here is the question," said the turkey. "Is a tree red?"

"Uh," Patricia said. "Can you give me a hint? Umm. Is that 'red' like the color?" The birds didn't answer. "Can you give me more time? I promise I'll answer, I just need more time to think. Please. I need more time. Please?"

The next thing Patricia knew, her father scooped her up in his arms. He was wearing his sandpaper shirt and his red beard was in her face and he kept half-dropping her, because he was trying to draw complicated valuation formulas with his hands while carrying her. But it was still so warm and perfect to be carried home by her daddy that Patricia didn't care.

"I found her right on the outskirts of the woods near the house," her father told her mother. "She must have gotten lost and found her own way out. It's a miracle she's okay."

"You nearly scared us to death. We've been searching, along with all of the neighbors. I swear you must think my time is worthless. You've made me blow a deadline for a management productivity analysis." Patricia's mother had her dark hair pulled back, which made her chin and nose look pointier. Her bony shoulders hunched, almost up to her antique earrings.

"I just want to understand what this is about," Patricia's father said. "What did we do that made you want to act out in this way?" Roderick Delfine was a real-estate genius who often worked from home and looked after the girls when they were between nannies, sitting in a high chair at the breakfast bar with his wide face buried in equations. Patricia herself was pretty good at math, except when she thought too much about the wrong things, like the fact that the number 3 looked like an 8 cut in half, so two 3s really ought to be 8.

"She's testing us," Patricia's mother said. "She's testing our authority, because we've gone too easy on her." Belinda Delfine had been a gymnast, and her own parents had put several oceans' worth of pressure on her to excel at that—but she'd never understood why gymnastics needed to have judges, instead of measuring everything using cameras and maybe lasers. She'd met Roderick after he started coming to all her meets, and they'd invented a totally objective gymnastics measuring system that nobody had ever adopted.

"Look at her. She's just laughing at us," Patricia's mother said, as if Patricia herself weren't standing right there. "We need to show her we mean business."

Patricia hadn't thought she was laughing, at all, but now she was terrified she looked that way. She tried extra hard to fix a serious expression on her face.

"I would never run away like that," said Roberta, who was supposed to be leaving the three of them alone in the kitchen but had come in to get a glass of water, and gloat.

They locked Patricia in her room for a week, sliding food under her door. The bottom of the door tended to scrape off the top layer of whatever type of food it was. Like if it was a sandwich, the topmost piece of bread was taken away by the door. You don't really want to eat a sandwich after your door has had the first bite, but if you get hungry enough you will. "Think about what you've done," the parents said.

"I get all her desserts for the next seven years," Roberta said.

"No you don't!" said Patricia.

The whole experience with the Parliament of Birds became a sort of blur to Patricia. She remembered it mostly in dreams and fragments. Once or twice, in school, she had a flashback of a bird asking her something. But she couldn't quite remember what the question had been, or whether she'd answered it. She had lost the ability to understand the speech of animals while she was locked in her bedroom.

ABOUT THE ANDRE NORTON AWARD FOR YOUNG ADULT SCIENCE FICTION AND FANTASY

The Andre Norton Award for Young Adult Science Fiction and Fantasy is an annual award presented by SFWA to the author of the best young-adult or middle-grade science fiction or fantasy book published in the United States in the preceding year.

The Andre Norton Award is not a Nebula Award, but it follows Nebula nomination, voting, and award rules and guidelines. It was founded in 2005 to honor popular science fiction and fantasy author and Grand Master Andre Norton.

EXCERPT FROM
ARABELLA OF MARS

DAVID D. LEVINE

David D. Levine is the author of the novels Arabella of Mars, Arabella
and the Battle of Venus, *and over fifty science fiction and fantasy
stories. His story "Tk'Tk'Tk" won the Hugo, and he has been shortlisted for awards including the Hugo, Nebula, Campbell, and Sturgeon. Stories have appeared in* Asimov's, Analog, F&SF, Tor.com,
numerous Year's Best *anthologies, and his award-winning collection*
Space Magic.

PROLOGUE

The Last Straw

Mars, 1812

Arabella Ashby lay prone atop a dune, her whole length pressed tight upon the
cool red sands of Mars. The silence of the night lay unbroken save for the distant
cry of a hunting *khulekh*, and a wind off the desert brought a familiar potpourri
to her nose: *khoresh*-sap, and the cinnamon smell of Martians, and the sharp,
distinctive fragrance of the sand itself. She glanced up at Phobos—still some

fingers' span short of Arcturus—then back down to the darkness of the valley floor where Michael would, she knew, soon appear.

Beneath the fur-trimmed leather of her *thukhong*, her heart beat a fast tattoo, racing not only from the exertion of her rush to the top of this dune but from the exhilaration of delicious anticipation. For this, she was certain, was the night she would finally defeat her brother in the game of *shorosh khe kushura*, or Hound and Hare.

The game was simple enough. To-night Michael played the part of the *kushura*, a nimble runner of the plains, while Arabella took the role of the *shorosh*, a fierce and cunning predator. His assignment this night was to race from the stone outcrop they called Old Broken Nose to the drying-sheds on the south side of the manor house, a distance of some two miles; hers was to stop him. But though Khema had said the youngest Martian children would play this game as soon as their shells hardened, it was also a sophisticated strategic exercise . . . one that Michael, three years her elder, had nearly always won in the weeks they'd been playing it.

But to-night the victory would be Arabella's. For she had been observing Michael assiduously for the last few nights, and she had noted that despite Khema's constant injunctions against predictability, he nearly always traversed this valley when he wished to evade detection. Its sides were steep, its shadows deep at every time of night, and the soft sands of the valley floor hushed every footfall—but that would avail him little if his pursuer reached the valley before he did and prepared an ambush. Which was exactly what she had done.

Again she cast her eyes upward. At Michael's usual pace he would arrive just as Phobos in his passage through the sky reached the bright star Arcturus—about half-past two in the morning. But as she looked up, her eye was drawn by another point of light, brighter than Arcturus and moving still faster than Phobos: an airship, cruising so high above the planet that her sails caught the sun's light long before dawn. From the size and brightness of the moving light she must be a Marsman—one of the great Mars Company ships, the "aristocrats of the air," that plied the interplanetary atmosphere between Mars and Earth. Perhaps some of her masts or spars or planks had even originated here, on this very plantation, as one of the great *khoresh*-trees that towered in patient, soldierly rows north and east of the manor house.

Some day, Arabella thought, perhaps she might take passage on such a ship. To sail the air, and see the asteroids, and visit the swamps of Venus would be a grand adventure indeed. But to be sure, no matter how far she traveled she would always return to her beloved Woodthrush Woods.

Suddenly a *shuff* of boots on sand snatched her awareness from the interplanetary atmosphere back to the valley floor. Michael!

She had been careless. While her attention had been occupied by the ship, Michael had drawn nearly abreast of her position. Now she had mere moments in which to act.

Scrambling to her feet in the dune's soft sand, she hurled herself down into the shadowed canyon, a tolerable twelve-foot drop that would give her the momentum she needed to overcome her brother's advantages in size and weight.

But in her haste she misjudged her leap, landing instead in a thorny *gorosh-*shrub halfway up the canyon's far wall and earning a painful scratch on her head. She cursed enthusiastically in English and Martian as she struggled to free herself from the shrub's thorns and sticky, acrid-smelling sap.

"Heavens, dear sister," Michael laughed, breathing hard from his run. "Such language!" He doubled back in order to aid her in extricating herself.

But Arabella had not given up on the game. She held out her hand as though for assistance . . . and as soon as he grasped it, she pulled him down into the shrub with her. The thorny branch that had trapped her snapped as he fell upon it, and the two of them rolled together down the canyon wall, tussling and laughing in the sand like a pair of *tureth* pups.

Then they rolled into a patch of moonlight, and though Michael had the upper hand he suddenly ceased his attempts to pin her to the ground. "What is the matter, dear brother?" Arabella gasped, even as she prepared to hurl him over her head with her legs. But in this place there was light enough to see his face clearly, and his expression was so grave she checked herself.

"You are injured," he said, disentangling himself from her.

"'Tis only a scratch," she replied. But the pain when she touched her injured scalp was sharp, and her hand when she brought it away and examined it beneath Phobos's dim light was black with blood.

Michael brought his handkerchief from his *thukhong* pocket and pressed it against the wound, causing Arabella to draw in a hissing breath through her teeth. "Lie still," he said, his voice quite serious.

"Is it very bad, then?"

He made no reply, but as she lay on the cool sand, her breath fogging the air and the perspiration chilling on her face, she felt something seeping through her hair and dripping steadily from the lower edge of her ear, and the iron smell of blood was strong in the air. Michael's jaw tightened, and he pressed harder with the handkerchief; Arabella's breath came shallow, and she determined not to cry out from the pain.

And then Khema appeared, slipping silently from the shadows, the subtle facets of her eyes reflecting in the starlight. She had, of course, been watching them all along, unobserved; her capabilities of tracking and concealment were far beyond any thing Arabella or Michael could even begin to approach. "You leapt too late, *tutukha*," she said. A *tutukha* was a small inoffensive herbivore, and Khema often called her this as a pet name.

"I will do better next time, *itkhalya*," Arabella replied through gritted teeth.

"I am certain you will."

Michael looked up at Khema, his eyes shining. "It's not stopping."

Without a word Khema knelt and inspected the wound, her eye-stalks bending close and the hard cool carapace of her pointed fingertips delicately teasing the matted hair aside. Arabella bit her lip hard; she would *not* cry.

"This is beyond my skills," Khema said at last, sitting back on her haunches. "You require a human physician."

At that Arabella did cry out. "No!" she cried, clutching at her *itkhalya*'s sleeve. "We cannot! Mother will be furious!"

"We will endeavor to keep this from her."

*   *   *

The pain of Dr. Fellowes's needle as it stitched the wound shut was no worse than the humiliation Arabella felt as she lay on a cot in her father's office. From the shelf above Father's desk, his collection of small automata looked down in judgement: the scribe, the glockenspiel player, and especially the dancer, still given pride of place though it no longer functioned, all seemed to regard her with disappointment in their painted eyes.

Her father too, she knew, must be horribly disappointed in her, though his face with its high forehead and shock of gray hair showed more concern than dissatisfaction. Though no tears had fallen, his eyes glimmered in the flickering lamplight, and when she considered how she had let him down Arabella felt a hot sting of shame in her own eyes.

Even the crude little drummer she herself had built, a simple clockwork with just one motion, seemed let down by its creator. She had been so proud when she had presented it to Father on his birthday last year and he had placed it on the shelf with his most treasured possessions; now, she felt sure, he would surely retire it to some dark corner.

Again and again the needle stabbed Arabella's scalp; the repeated tug and soft hiss of the thread passing through her skin seemed to go on and on. "A little more light, please," the doctor said, and Khema adjusted the wick on the lamp. "Not much longer." The doctor's clothing smelled of dust and leather, and the sweat of the *huresh* on which Michael had fetched him from his home. Michael himself looked on from behind him, his sandy hair and heart-shaped face so very like her own, his blue eyes filled with worry.

"There now," said the doctor, clipping off the thread. "All finished." Khema brought him a washbasin, and as he cleaned the blood from his hands he said, "Scalp wounds do bleed quite frightfully, but the actual danger is slight; if you keep the wound clean it should heal up nicely. And even if there should be a scar, it will be hidden by your hair."

"Thank you, Doctor," Arabella said, sitting up and examining his work in the window-glass—the sun would rise soon, but the sky was still dark enough to give a good reflection. Her appearance, she was forced to acknowledge, was quite shocking, with dried blood everywhere, but she thought that once she had cleaned herself she might be able to arrange her hair so as to hide the stitches from her mother.

But that opportunity was denied her, for just at that moment the office door burst open and Mother charged in, still in her night-dress. "Arabella!" she cried. "What has happened to you?"

"She is quite well, Mother," Michael said. "She only fell and hit her head."

"She is not 'well.'" Mother sat on the edge of the cot and held Arabella's head in her hands. "She is covered in blood, and what on *Earth* is this horrific garment you are wearing? It exposes your limbs quite shamefully."

Arabella had been dreading this discovery. "It is called a *thukhong*, Mother, and it keeps me far warmer than any English-made dress."

"An ugly Martian word for an ugly Martian garment, one entirely unsuitable for a proper English lady." She glowered at Arabella's father. "I thought we agreed when she turned twelve that there would be no more of . . . *this*." She waved a disgusted hand, taking in the *thukhong*, the blood, the desert outside, and the planet Mars in general. Dr. Fellowes seemed to be trying to disappear into the wainscoting.

Father dropped his eyes from Mother's withering gaze. "She is still only sixteen, dear, and she is a very . . . *active* girl. Surely she may be allowed a few more years of freedom before being compelled to settle down? She has kept up with her studies. . . ."

But even as he spoke, Mother's lips went quite white from being pressed together, and finally she burst out, "I will have no more of your rationalizations!" She stood and paced briskly back and forth in front of Father's broad *khoresh*-wood desk, her fury building still further as she warmed to her subject. "For years now I have struggled to bring Arabella up properly, despite the primitive conditions on this horrible planet, and now I find that she is risking her life traipsing around the trackless desert by night, wearing *leather trousers* no less!" She rounded on Arabella. "How long have you been engaging in this disgraceful behavior?"

Arabella glanced to Michael, her father, and Khema for support, but in the face of her mother's wrath they were as defenseless as she. "Only a few weeks," she muttered, eyes downcast, referring only to the game of *shorosh khe kushura*. She and Michael had actually been exploring the desert under Khema's tutelage—learning of Mars's flora, fauna, and cultures and engaging in games of strategy and combat—since they were both quite small.

"Only a few weeks," Mother repeated, jaw clenched and nostrils flaring. "Then perhaps it is not too late." She stared hard at Arabella a moment longer, then gave a firm nod and turned to Father. "I am taking the children back home. And this time I will brook no argument."

Arabella felt as though the floor had dropped from under her. "No!" she cried.

Without facing Arabella, Mother raised a finger to silence her. "You see what she has become!" she continued to Father. "Willful, disobedient, disrespectful. And Fanny and Chloë are already beginning to follow in her filthy footsteps." Now her tone changed, and despite Arabella's anguish at the prospect of being torn from her home she could not deny the genuine sadness and fear in her mother's eyes. "Please, dear. *Please*. You *must* agree. You must consider our posterity! If Arabella is allowed to continue on this path, and her sisters too . . . what decent man would have them? They will be left as spinsters, doomed to a lonely old age on a barbarous planet."

Arabella bit her lip and hugged herself tightly, feeling lost and helpless as she watched her father's face. Taking Arabella, Michael, and the two little girls to England—a place to which Mother always referred as "back home," though all of the children had been born on Mars and had never known any other home—was something she had often spoken of, though never so definitively or immediately. But with this incident something had changed, something deep and fundamental, and plainly Father was seriously considering the question.

He pursed his lips and furrowed his brow. He stroked his chin and looked to Mother, to Michael, to Arabella—his eyes beneath the gray brows looking very stern—and then out the window, at the sun just beginning to peep above the rows of *khoresh*-trees.

Finally he sighed deeply and turned back to Mother. "You may have the girls," he said in a resigned tone. "But Michael will remain here, to help me with the business of the plantation."

"But Father . . . ," Arabella began, until a minute shake of his head stopped her words. The look in his eyes showed clearly that he did not desire this outcome, but it was plain to all that this time Mother would not be appeased.

Arabella looked to Michael for support, but though his eyes brimmed with tears his shoulders slumped and his hands, still stained with Arabella's blood, hung ineffectually at his sides. "I am sorry," he whispered.

Khema, too, stood silently in the corner, hands folded and eye-stalks downcast. Bold, swift, and powerful she might be in the desert, but within the manor house she was only a servant and must submit to Mother's wishes.

"Very well," said Mother, after a long considering pause. "Michael may remain. But the Ashby women . . . are going home." And she smiled.

That smile, to Arabella, was like a judge's gavel pronouncing sentence of death.

CHAPTER ONE

An Unexpected Letter

England, 1813

Arabella eased her bedroom door open and crept into the dark hallway. All about her the house lay silent, servants and masters alike tucked safe in their beds. Only the gentle tick of the tall clock in the parlor disturbed the night.

Shielding the candle with one hand, Arabella slipped down the hallway, her bare feet making no sound on the cool boards. She kept close to the walls, where the floor was best supported and the boards did not creak, but now and again she took a long, slow step to avoid a spot she had learned was likely to squeak.

Down the stairs and across the width of the house she crept, until she reached the drawing-room. In the corner farthest from the fireplace stood the harpsichord, and the silent figure that sat at its keyboard.

Brenchley's Automaton Harpsichord Player.

Nearly life-sized and dressed in the height of fashion from eight years ago, when it had originally been manufactured, the automaton sat with jointed ivory fingers poised over the instrument's keys. Its face was finely crafted of smooth, polished birch for a lifelike appearance, the eyes with their painted lashes demurely downcast. A little dust had accumulated in its décolletage, but in the shifting light of Arabella's little candle it almost seemed to be breathing.

Arabella had always been the only person in the family who shared her father's passion for automata. The many hours they had spent together in the drawing-room of the manor house at Woodthrush Woods, winding and oiling and polishing his collection, were among her most treasured memories. He had even shared with her his knowledge of the machines' workings, though Mother had heartily disapproved of such an unladylike pursuit.

The harpsichord player had arrived at Marlowe Hall, their residence in England, not long after they had emigrated—or, as Arabella considered it, been exiled—from Mars. It had been accompanied by a note from Father, reminding them that it was one of his most beloved possessions and saying that he hoped it would provide pleasant entertainment. But Arabella, knowing that Father understood as well as she did how little interest the rest of the family had in automata, had taken it as a sort of peace offering, or apology, from him specifically to her—a moving, nearly living representative and reminder that, although unimaginably distant, he still loved her.

But, alas, all his great expense and careful packing had gone for naught, for when it had been uncrated it refused to play a note. Mother, never well-disposed toward her husband's expensive pastime, had been none too secretly relieved.

That had been nearly eight months ago. Eight months of frilly dresses and stultifying conversation, and unceasing oppressive damp, and more than any thing else the constant inescapable *heaviness*. Upon first arriving on Earth, to her shame Arabella had found herself so unaccustomed to the planet's gravity that she had no alternative but to be carried from the ship in a sedan-chair. She had barely been able to stand for weeks, and even now she felt heavy, awkward, and clumsy, distrustful of her body and of her instincts. Plates and pitchers seemed always to crash to the floor in her vicinity, and even the simple act of throwing and catching a ball was beyond her.

Not that she was allowed to perform any sort of bodily activity whatsoever, other than walking and occasionally dancing. Every one on Earth, it seemed, shared Mother's attitudes concerning the proper behavior of an English lady, and the slightest display of audacity, curiosity, adventure, or initiative was met with severe disapproval. So she had been reduced, even as she had on Mars, to skulking about by night—but here she lacked the companionship of Michael and Khema.

On Mars, Michael, her elder and only brother, had been her constant companion, studying with her by day and racing her across the dunes by night. And Khema, their Martian nanny or *itkhalya*, had been to the two of them nurse, protector, and tutor in all things Martian. How she missed them both.

Setting her candle down, Arabella seated herself on the floor behind the automaton and lifted its skirts, in a fashion that would have been most improper if it were human. Beneath the suffocating layers of muslin and linen the automaton's ingenious mechanisms gleamed in the candlelight, brass and ivory and mahogany each adding their own colors to a silent symphony of light and shadow. Here was the mainspring, there the escapement, there the drum. The drum was the key to the whole mechanism; its pins and flanges told the device where to place its fingers, when to nod, when to appear to breathe. From the drum, dozens of brass fingers transmitted instructions to the rest of the device through a series of levers, rods, springs, and wires.

Arabella breathed in the familiar scents of metal, whale-oil, and beeswax before proceeding. She had begun attempting to repair the device about two months ago, carefully concealing her work from her mother, the servants, and even her sisters. She had investigated its mysteries, puzzled out its workings, and finally found the displaced cog that had stilled the mechanism. But having solved that puzzle, Arabella had continued working with the machine, and in the last few weeks she had even begun making a few cautious modifications. The pins in the drum could be unscrewed, she had learned, and placed in new locations to change the automaton's behavior.

At the moment her project was to teach it to play "God Save the King," as the poor mad fellow could certainly use the Lord's help. She had the first few measures working nearly to her satisfaction and was just about to start on "Send him victorious." Laying the folded hearth-rug atop the harpsichord's strings to muffle the sound, she wound the automaton's mainspring and began to work, using a nail-file, cuticle-knife, and tweezers to reposition the delicate pins.

She was not concerned that her modifications might be discovered between her working sessions. It was only out of deference to Mr. Ashby, the absent paterfamilias, that her mother even allowed it to remain in the drawing-room. The servants found the device disquieting and refused to do more than dust it occasionally. And as for Fanny and Chloë, Arabella's sisters were both too young to be allowed to touch the delicate mechanism.

For many pleasant hours Arabella worked, repeatedly making small changes, rolling the drum back with her hand, then letting it play. She would not be satisfied with a mere music-box rendition of the tune; she wanted a *performance*, with all the life and spirit of a human player. And so she adjusted the movements of the automaton's body, the tilt of its head, and the subtle motions of its pretended breath as well as the precise timing and rhythm of its notes.

She would pay for her indulgence on the morrow, when her French tutor would stamp his cane each time she yawned—though even when well-slept, she gave him less heed than he felt he deserved. Why bother studying French? England had been at war with Bonaparte since Arabella was a little girl, and showed no sign of ever ceasing to do so.

But for now none of that was of any consequence.

When she worked on the automaton, she felt close to her father.

*   *   *

The sky was already lightening in the east, and a few birds were beginning to greet the sun with their chirruping song, as Arabella heaved the hearth-rug out of the harpsichord and spread it back in its accustomed place. Perhaps some day she would have an opportunity to hear the automaton perform without its heavy, muting encumbrance.

She looked around, inspecting the drawing-room with a critical eye. Had she left any thing out of place? No, she had not. With a satisfied nod she turned and began to make her way back to her bedroom.

But before she even reached the stairs, her ear was caught by a drumming sound from without.

Hoofbeats. The sound of a single horse, running hard. Approaching rapidly. Who could possibly be out riding at this hour?

Quickly extinguishing the candle, Arabella scurried up the stairs in the dawn light and hid herself in the shadows at the top of the steps. Shortly thereafter, a fist hammered on the front door. Arabella peered down through the banister at the front door, consumed with curiosity.

Only a few moments passed before Cole, the butler, came to open the door. He, too, must have heard the rider's hoofbeats.

The man at the door was a post-rider, red-eyed and filthy with dust. From his leather satchel he drew out a thin letter, a single sheet, much travel-worn and bearing numerous post-marks.

It was heavily bordered in black. Arabella suppressed a gasp.

A black-bordered letter meant death, and was sadly familiar. Even in the comparatively short space of time since her arrival on Earth, no fewer than five such letters had arrived in this small community, each bearing news of the loss of a brother or father or uncle to Bonaparte's monstrous greed. But Arabella had no relatives in the army or navy, and had no expectation of her family receiving such a letter.

"Three pounds five shillings sixpence," the post-rider said, dipping his head in acknowledgement of the outrageousness of the postage. "It's an express, all the way from Mars."

At that Arabella was forced to bite her knuckle to prevent herself from crying aloud.

Shaking his head, Cole placed the letter on a silver tray and directed the rider to the servants' quarters, where he would receive his payment and some refreshment before being sent on his way. As Cole began to climb the stairs Arabella scurried back to her room, her heart pounding.

*   *   *

Arabella paced in her bedroom, sick with worry. Her hands worked at her handkerchief as she went, twisting and straining the delicate fabric until it threatened to tear asunder.

A black-bordered letter. An express. No one would send such dire news by such an expensive means unless it concerned a member of the family. She forced herself to hope that it might be an error, or news of some distant relative of whose existence she had not even been aware . . . but as the silence went on and on, that hope diminished swiftly.

Who was it who had passed? Father, or Michael? Which would be worse? She loved them both so dearly. Michael and she were practically twins, and he had many more years ahead of him, so his loss would surely be the greater tragedy. But Father . . . the man who had shared with her his love of automata, who had sat her on his knee and taught her the names of the stars, who had quietly encouraged her to dare, to try, to risk, despite Mother's objections . . . to lose him would be terrible, terrible indeed.

Every fiber of her being insisted that she run to her mother's room, burst through the door, and demand an answer. But that would be unladylike, and, as Mother had repeatedly admonished, unladylike behavior was entirely unacceptable under even the most pressing circumstances. And so she paced, and pulled her handkerchief to shreds, and tried not to cry.

And then, startling though not a surprise, a knock came on the door. It was Nellie, her mother's handmaid. "Mrs. Ashby requests your presence, Miss Ashby."

"Thank you, Nellie."

Trembling, Arabella followed Nellie to her mother's dressing-room, where Fanny and Chloë, already present, were gathered in a miserable huddle with their mother. The black-bordered letter lay open on her mother's writing-desk, surrounded by the scattered fragments of the seal, which was of black wax.

Arabella stood rooted, just inside the door, her eyes darting from the letter to her mother and sisters. It was as though it were a *lukhosh*, or some other dreadful poisonous creature, that had already struck them down and was now lying in wait for her. She wondered whether she was expected to pick it up and read it.

She ached to know what the letter contained. She wanted nothing more than to flee the room.

Nellie cleared her throat. "Ma'am?" Mother raised her head, her eyes flowing with tears. Noticing Arabella, she gently patted the settee by her side. The girls shifted to make room for her.

Arabella sat. Each of her sisters clutched one of her hands, offering comfort despite their own misery.

"The news is . . . it is . . . it is Mr. Ashby," Mother said. She held her head up straight, though her chin trembled. "Your father has passed on."

"Father . . . ?" Arabella whispered.

And even though the distance between planets was so unimaginably vast . . . even though the news must be months old . . . even though it had been over eight months since she had seen him with her own eyes . . . somehow, some intangible connection had still remained between her and her father, and at that moment she felt that connection part, tearing like rotted silk.

And she too collapsed in sobs.

PAST NEBULA AWARD WINNERS

1965

Novel: *Dune* by Frank Herbert
Novella: "He Who Shapes" by Roger Zelazny and "The Saliva Tree" by Brian Aldiss (tie)
Novelette: "The Doors of His Face, the Lamps of His Mouth" by Roger Zelazny
Short Story: "'Repent, Harlequin!' Said the Ticktockman" by Harlan Ellison

1966

Novel: *Babel-17* by Samuel R. Delany and *Flowers for Algernon* by Daniel Keyes (tie)
Novella: "The Last Castle" by Jack Vance
Novelette: "Call Him Lord" by Gordon R. Dickson
Short Story: "The Secret Place" by Richard McKenna

1967

Novel: *The Einstein Intersection* by Samuel R. Delany
Novella: "Behold the Man" by Michael Moorcock
Novelette: "Gonna Roll the Bones" by Fritz Leiber
Short Story: "Aye, and Gomorrah" by Samuel R. Delany

1968

Novel: *Rite of Passage* by Alexei Panshin
Novella: "Dragonrider" by Anne McCaffrey

Novelette: "Mother to the World" by Richard Wilson
Short Story: "The Planners" by Kate Wilhelm

1969

Novel: *The Left Hand of Darkness* by Ursula K. Le Guin
Novella: "A Boy and His Dog" by Harlan Ellison
Novelette: "Time Considered as a Helix of Semi-Precious Stones" by Samuel
    R. Delany
Short Story: "Passengers" by Robert Silverberg

1970

Novel: *Ringworld* by Larry Niven
Novella: "Ill Met in Lankhmar" by Fritz Leiber
Novelette: "Slow Sculpture" by Theodore Sturgeon
Short Story: No Award

1971

Novel: *A Time of Changes* by Robert Silverberg
Novella: "The Missing Man" by Katherine MacLean
Novelette: "The Queen of Air and Darkness" by Poul Anderson
Short Story: "Good News from the Vatican" by Robert Silverberg

1972

Novel: *The Gods Themselves* by Isaac Asimov
Novella: "A Meeting with Medusa" by Arthur C. Clarke
Novelette: "Goat Song" by Poul Anderson
Short Story: "When It Changed" by Joanna Russ

1973

Novel: *Rendezvous with Rama* by Arthur C. Clarke
Novella: "The Death of Doctor Island" by Gene Wolfe
Novelette: "Of Mist, and Grass, and Sand" by Vonda N. McIntyre
Short Story: "Love Is the Plan, the Plan Is Death" by James Tiptree Jr.
Dramatic Presentation: *Soylent Green*

1974

Novel: *The Dispossessed* by Ursula K. Le Guin
Novella: "Born with the Dead" by Robert Silverberg
Novelette: "If the Stars Are Gods" by Gordon Eklund and Gregory Benford
Short Story: "The Day before the Revolution" by Ursula K. Le Guin
Dramatic Presentation: *Sleeper* by Woody Allen
Grand Master: Robert Heinlein

1975

Novel: *The Forever War* by Joe Haldeman
Novella: "Home Is the Hangman" by Roger Zelazny
Novelette: "San Diego Lightfoot Sue" by Tom Reamy
Short Story: "Catch That Zeppelin" by Fritz Leiber
Dramatic Presentation: *Young Frankenstein* by Mel Brooks and Gene Wilder
Grand Master: Jack Williamson

1976

Novel: *Man Plus* by Frederik Pohl
Novella: "Houston, Houston, Do You Read?" by James Tiptree Jr.
Novelette: "The Bicentennial Man" by Isaac Asimov
Short Story: "A Crowd of Shadows" by C. L. Grant

Grand Master: Clifford D. Simak

1977

Novel: *Gateway* by Frederik Pohl
Novella: "Stardance" by Spider and Jeanne Robinson
Novelette: "The Screwfly Solution" by Racoona Sheldon
Short Story: "Jeffty Is Five" by Harlan Ellison

1978

Novel: *Dreamsnake* by Vonda N. McIntyre
Novella: "The Persistence of Vision" by John Varley
Novelette: "A Glow of Candles, A Unicorn's Eye" by C. L. Grant
Short Story: "Stone" by Edward Bryant
Grand Master: L. Sprague de Camp

1979

Novel: *The Fountains of Paradise* by Arthur C. Clarke
Novella: "Enemy Mine" by Barry B. Longyear
Novelette: "Sandkings" by George R. R. Martin
Short Story: "GiANTS" by Edward Bryant

1980

Novel: *Timescape* by Gregory Benford
Novella: "Unicorn Tapestry" by Suzy McKee Charnas
Novelette: "The Ugly Chickens" by Howard Waldrop
Short Story: "Grotto of the Dancing Deer" by Clifford D. Simak
Grand Master: Fritz Leiber

1981

Novel: *The Claw of the Conciliator* by Gene Wolfe
Novella: "The Saturn Game" by Poul Anderson
Novelette: "The Quickening" by Michael Bishop
Short Story: "The Bone Flute" by Lisa Tuttle [declined by author]

1982

Novel: *No Enemy but Time* by Michael Bishop
Novella: "Another Orphan" by John Kessel
Novelette: "Fire Watch" by Connie Willis
Short Story: "A Letter from the Clearys" by Connie Willis

1983

Novel: *Startide Rising* by David Brin
Novella: "Hardfought" by Greg Bear
Novelette: "Blood Music" by Greg Bear
Short Story: "The Peacemaker" by Gardner Dozois
Grand Master: Andre Norton

1984

Novel: *Neuromancer* by William Gibson
Novella: "Press Enter []" by John Varley
Novelette: "Blood Child" by Octavia Butler
Short Story: "Morning Child" by Gardner Dozois

1985

Novel: *Ender's Game* by Orson Scott Card
Novella: "Sailing to Byzantium" by Robert Silverberg
Novelette: "Portraits of His Children" by George R. R. Martin
Short Story: "Out of All Them Bright Stars" by Nancy Kress
Grand Master: Arthur C. Clarke

1986

Novel: *Speaker for the Dead* by Orson Scott Card
Novella: "R&R" by Lucius Shepard
Novelette: "The Girl Who Fell into the Sky" by Kate Wilhelm
Short Story: "Tangents" by Greg Bear
Grand Master: Isaac Asimov

1987

Novel: *The Falling Woman* by Pat Murphy
Novella: "The Blind Geometer" by Kim Stanley Robinson
Novelette: "Rachel in Love" by Pat Murphy
Short Story: "Forever Yours, Anna" by Kate Wilhelm
Grand Master: Alfred Bester

1988

Novel: *Falling Free* by Lois McMaster Bujold
Novella: "The Last of the Winnebagos" by Connie Willis
Novelette: "Schrödinger's Kitten" by George Alec Effinger
Short Story: "Bible Stories for Adults, No. 17: The Deluge" by James Morrow
Grand Master: Ray Bradbury

1989

Novel: *The Healer's War* by Elizabeth Ann Scarborough
Novella: "The Mountains of Mourning" by Lois McMaster Bujold
Novelette: "At the Rialto" by Connie Willis
Short Story: "Ripples in the Dirac Sea" by Geoffrey A. Landis

1990

Novel: *Tehanu: The Last Book of Earthsea* by Ursula K. Le Guin
Novella: "The Hemingway Hoax" by Joe Haldeman
Novelette: "Tower of Babylon" by Ted Chiang
Short Story: "Bears Discover Fire" by Terry Bisson
Grand Master: Lester del Rey

1991

Novel: *Stations of the Tide* by Michael Swanwick
Novella: "Beggars in Spain" by Nancy Kress
Novelette: "Guide Dog" by Mike Conner
Short Story: "Ma Qui" by Alan Brennert

1992

Novel: *Doomsday Book* by Connie Willis
Novella: "City Of Truth" by James Morrow
Novelette: "Danny Goes to Mars" by Pamela Sargent
Short Story: "Even the Queen" by Connie Willis
Grand Master: Fred Pohl

1993

Novel: *Red Mars* by Kim Stanley Robinson
Novella: "The Night We Buried Road Dog" by Jack Cady
Novelette: "Georgia on My Mind" by Charles Sheffield
Short Story: "Graves" by Joe Haldeman

1994

The 1994 Nebulas were awarded at a ceremony in New York City in late April 1995.

Novel: *Moving Mars* by Greg Bear
Novella: "Seven Views of Olduvai Gorge" by Mike Resnick
Novelette: "The Martian Child" by David Gerrold
Short Story: "A Defense of the Social Contracts" by Martha Soukup
Grand Master: Damon Knight
Author Emeritus: Emil Petaja

1995

Novel: *The Terminal Experiment* by Robert J. Sawyer
Novella: "Last Summer at Mars Hill" by Elizabeth Hand
Novelette: "Solitude" by Ursula K. Le Guin
Short Story: "Death and the Librarian" by Esther M. Friesner
Grand Master: A. E. van Vogt
Author Emeritus: Wilson "Bob" Tucker

1996

Novel: *Slow River* by Nicola Griffith
Novella: "Da Vinci Rising" by Jack Dann

Novelette: "Lifeboat on a Burning Sea" by Bruce Holland Rogers
Short Story: "A Birthday" by Esther M. Friesner
Grand Master: Jack Vance
Author Emeritus: Judith Merril

1997

Novel: *The Moon and the Sun* by Vonda N. McIntyre
Novella: "Abandon in Place" by Jerry Oltion
Novelette: "Flowers of Aulit Prison" by Nancy Kress
Short Story: "Sister Emily's Lightship" by Jane Yolen
Grand Master: Poul Anderson
Author Emeritus: Nelson Slade Bond

1998

Novel: *Forever Peace* by Joe Haldeman
Novella: "Reading the Bones" by Sheila Finch
Novelette: "Lost Girls" by Jane Yolen
Short Story: "Thirteen Ways to Water" by Bruce Holland Rogers
Grand Master: Hal Clement (Harry Stubbs)
Author Emeritus: William Tenn (Philip Klass)

1999

Novel: *Parable of the Talents* by Octavia E. Butler
Novella: "Story of Your Life" by Ted Chiang
Novelette: "Mars Is No Place for Children" by Mary A. Turzillo
Short Story: "The Cost of Doing Business" by Leslie What
Script: *The Sixth Sense* by M. Night Shyamalan
Grand Master: Brian W. Aldiss
Author Emeritus: Daniel Keyes

2000

Novel: *Darwin's Radio* by Greg Bear
Novella: "Goddesses" by Linda Nagata
Novelette: "Daddy's World" by Walter Jon Williams
Short Story: "macs" by Terry Bisson
Script: *Galaxy Quest* by Robert Gordon and David Howard
Ray Bradbury Award: Yuri Rasovsky and Harlan Ellison
Grand Master: Philip José Farmer
Author Emeritus: Robert Sheckley

2001

Novel: *The Quantum Rose* by Catherine Asaro
Novella: "The Ultimate Earth" by Jack Williamson
Novelette: "Louise's Ghost" by Kelly Link
Short Story: "The Cure for Everything" by Severna Park
Script: *Crouching Tiger, Hidden Dragon* by James Schamus, Kuo Jung Tsai, and Hui-Ling Wang
President's Award: Betty Ballantine

2002

Novel: *American Gods* by Neil Gaiman
Novella: "Bronte's Egg" by Richard Chwedyk
Novelette: "Hell Is the Absence of God" by Ted Chiang
Short Story: "Creature" by Carol Emshwiller
Script: *Lord of the Rings: The Fellowship of the Ring* by Frances Walsh, Phillipa Boyens, and Peter Jackson
Grand Master: Ursula K. Le Guin
Author Emeritus: Katherine MacLean

2003

Novel: *Speed of Dark* by Elizabeth Moon
Novella: "Coraline" by Neil Gaiman
Novelette: "The Empire of Ice Cream" by Jeffrey Ford
Short Story: "What I Didn't See" by Karen Joy Fowler
Script: *Lord of the Rings: The Two Towers* by Frances Walsh, Phillipa Boyens, Stephen Sinclair, and Peter Jackson
Grand Master: Robert Silverberg
Author Emeritus: Charles L. Harness

2004

Novel: *Paladin of Souls* by Lois McMaster Bujold
Novella: "The Green Leopard Plague" by Walter Jon Williams
Novelette: "Basement Magic" by Ellen Klages
Short Story: "Coming to Terms" by Eileen Gunn
Script: *Lord of the Rings: Return of the King* by Frances Walsh, Phillipa Boyens, and Peter Jackson
Grand Master: Anne McCaffrey

2005

Novel: *Camouflage* by Joe Haldeman
Novella: "Magic for Beginners" by Kelly Link
Novelette: "The Faery Handbag" by Kelly Link
Short Story: "I Live with You" by Carol Emshwiller
Script: *Serenity* by Joss Whedon
Grand Master: Harlan Ellison
Author Emeritus: William F. Nolan

2006

Novel: *Seeker* by Jack McDevitt
Novella: "Burn" by James Patrick Kelly
Novelette: "Two Hearts" by Peter S. Beagle
Short Story: "Echo" by Elizabeth Hand
Script: *Howl's Moving Castle* by Hayao Miyazaki, Cindy Davis Hewitt, and
    Donald H. Hewitt
Andre Norton Award: *Magic or Madness* by Justine Larbalestier
Grand Master: James Gunn
Author Emeritus: D. G. Compton

2007

Novel: *The Yiddish Policemen's Union* by Michael Chabon
Novella: "Fountain of Age" by Nancy Kress
Novelette: "The Merchant and the Alchemist's Gate" by Ted Chiang
Short Story: "Always" by Karen Joy Fowler
Script: *Pan's Labyrinth* by Guillermo del Toro
Andre Norton Award: *Harry Potter and the Deathly Hallows* by J. K. Rowling
Grand Master: Michael Moorcock
Author Emeritus: Ardath Mayhar
SFWA Service Awards: Melisa Michaels and Graham P. Collins

2008

Novel: *Powers* by Ursula K. Le Guin
Novella: "The Spacetime Pool" by Catherine Asaro
Novelette: "Pride and Prometheus" by John Kessel
Short Story: "Trophy Wives" by Nina Kiriki Hoffman
Script: *WALL-E* by Andrew Stanton and Jim Reardon. Original story by
    Andrew Stanton and Pete Docter
Andre Norton Award: *Flora's Dare: How a Girl of Spirit Gambles All to Expand*

Her Vocabulary, Confront a Bouncing Boy Terror, and Try to Save Califa from a Shaky Doom (Despite Being Confined to Her Room) by Ysabeau S. Wilce
Grand Master: Harry Harrison
Author Emeritus: M. J. Engh
Solstice Award: Kate Wilhelm, Martin H. Greenberg, and the late Algis Budrys
SFWA Service Award: Victoria Strauss

2009

Novel: *The Windup Girl* by Paolo Bacigalupi
Novella: "The Women of Nell Gwynne's" by Kage Baker
Novelette: "Sinner, Baker, Fabulist, Priest; Red Mask, Black Mask, Gentleman, Beast" by Eugie Foster
Short Story: "Spar" by Kij Johnson
Ray Bradbury Award: *District 9* by Neill Blomkamp and Terri Tatchell
Andre Norton Award: *The Girl Who Circumnavigated Fairyland in a Ship of Her Own Making* by Catherynne M. Valente
Grand Master: Joe Haldeman
Author Emeritus: Neal Barrett Jr.
Solstice Award: Tom Doherty, Terri Windling, and the late Donald A. Wollheim
SFWA Service Awards: Vonda N. McIntyre and Keith Stokes

2010

Novel: *Blackout/All Clear* by Connie Willis
Novella: "The Lady Who Plucked Red Flowers beneath the Queen's Window" by Rachel Swirsky
Novelette: "That Leviathan Whom Thou Hast Made" by Eric James Stone
Short Story: "Ponies" by Kij Johnson and "How Interesting: A Tiny Man" by Harlan Ellison (tie)
Ray Bradbury Award: *Inception* by Christopher Nolan
Andre Norton Award: *I Shall Wear Midnight,* by Terry Pratchett

2011

Novel: *Among Others* by Jo Walton
Novella: "The Man Who Bridged the Mist" by Kij Johnson
Novelette: "What We Found" by Geoff Ryman
Short Story: "The Paper Menagerie" by Ken Liu
Ray Bradbury Award: *Doctor Who*: "The Doctor's Wife" by Neil Gaiman (writer), Richard Clark (director)
Andre Norton Award: *The Freedom Maze* by Delia Sherman
Damon Knight Grand Master Award: Connie Willis
Solstice Award: Octavia Butler (posthumous) and John Clute
SFWA Service Award: Bud Webster

2012

Novel: *2312* by Kim Stanley Robinson
Novella: *After the Fall, Before the Fall, During the Fall* by Nancy Kress
Novelette: "Close Encounters" by Andy Duncan
Short Story: "Immersion" by Aliette de Bodard
Ray Bradbury Award: *Beasts of the Southern Wild* by Benh Zeitlin & Lucy Abilar (writers), Benh Zeitlin (director)
Andre Norton Award: *Fair Coin* by E. C. Myers

2013

Novel: *Ancillary Justice* by Ann Leckie
Novella: "The Weight of the Sunrise" by Vylar Kaftan
Novelette: "The Waiting Stars" by Aliette de Bodard
Short Story: "If You Were a Dinosaur, My Love" by Rachel Swirsky
Ray Bradbury Award: *Gravity* by Alfonso Cuarón, Jonás Cuarón (writers), Alfonso Cuarón (director)
Andre Norton Award: *Sister Mine* by Nalo Hopkinson
Damon Knight Grand Master Award: Samuel R. Delany

2013 Distinguished Guest: Frank M. Robinson
Kevin O'Donnell Jr. Service to SFWA Award: Michael Armstrong

2014

Novel: *Annihilation* by Jeff VanderMeer
Novella: *Yesterday's Kin* by Nancy Kress
Novelette: "A Guide to the Fruits of Hawai'i" by Alaya Dawn Johnson
Short Story: "Jackalope Wives" by Ursula Vernon
Ray Bradbury Award: *Guardians of the Galaxy* by James Gunn and Nicole Perlman (writers)
Andre Norton Award: *Love Is the Drug* by Alaya Dawn Johnson
Damon Knight Grand Master Award: Larry Niven
Solstice Award: Joanna Russ (posthumous), Stanley Schmidt
Kevin O'Donnell Jr. Service to SFWA Award: Jeffry Dwight

2015

Novel: *Uprooted* by Naomi Novik
Novella: *Binti* by Nnedi Okorafor
Novelette: "Our Lady of the Open Road" by Sarah Pinsker
Short Story: "Hungry Daughters of Starving Mothers" by Alyssa Wong
Ray Bradbury Award: *Mad Max: Fury Road* by George Miller, Brendan McCarthy, and Nick Lathouris
Andre Norton Award: *Updraft* by Fran Wilde
Damon Knight Grand Master Award: C.J. Cherryh
Kate Wilhelm Solstice Award: Sir Terry Pratchett (posthumous)
Kevin O'Donnell Jr. Service to SFWA Award: Dr. Lawrence M. Schoen

2016

Novel: *All the Birds in the Sky* by Charlie Jane Anders
Novella: *Every Heart a Doorway* by Seanan McGuire

Novelette: "The Long Fall Up" by William Ledbetter
Short Story: "Seasons of Glass and Iron" by Amal El-Mohtar
Ray Bradbury Award: *Arrival* by Eric Heisserer
Andre Norton Award: *Arabella of Mars* by David D. Levine
Kate Wilhelm Solstice Award: Peggy Rae Sapienza, Toni Weisskopf
Kevin O'Donnell Jr. Service to SFWA Award: Jim Fiscus

ABOUT THE EDITOR

Jane Yolen, often called "the Hans Christian Andersen of America," is the author of over 366 books including ten books of poetry for adults, two cookbooks, and twelve music books. She has won an assortment of awards: two Nebulas, a World Fantasy Award, a Caldecott, three Mythopoeic awards, two Christopher Medals, a nomination for the National Book Award, the Jewish Book Award, the Kerlan Award, the Catholic Library's Regina Medal, as well as six honorary doctorates—five of them from Massachusetts colleges and universities. Two years ago she was named one of the Massachusetts Unsung Heroines. And she was the first writer to win a New England

Photo by Jason Stemple

Public Radio's Arts & Humanities Award. She is a Grand Master of SFWA, SFPW, and the World Fantasy Association—the trifecta. One of her awards set her good coat on fire.

ABOUT THE COVER ARTIST

Galen Dara likes monsters, mystics, and dead things. She has created art for Escape Artists, *Uncanny Magazine*, 47North publishing, Skyscape Publishing, Fantasy Flight Games, Escape Artists, Tyche Books, *Fireside Magazine*, and *Lightspeed Magazine*. She has been nominated for the Hugo, the World Fantasy Award, and the Chesley Award. When Galen is not working on a project you can find her on the edge of the Sonoran Desert, climbing mountains and hanging out with a friendly conglomeration of human and animal companions.

The cover illustration was initially published in *Strange Horizons* in August, 2017, for "These Constellations Will Be Yours," written by Elaine Cuyegkeng.

You can follow her on Facebook, Instagram, and Twitter @galendara, or find her at www.galendara.com.